YIELDING TO LOVE

The Taverstons of Iversley
Book 4

By Carol Coventry

ARE YOU SIGNED UP FOR DRAGONBLADE'S BLOG?

You'll get the latest news and information on exclusive giveaways, exclusive excerpts, coming releases, sales, free books, cover reveals and more.

Check out our complete list of authors, too!

No spam, no junk. That's a promise!

Sign Up Here

www.dragonbladepublishing.com

Dearest Reader;

Thank you for your support of a small press. At Dragonblade Publishing, we strive to bring you the highest quality Historical Romance from some of the best authors in the business. Without your support, there is no 'us', so we sincerely hope you adore these stories and find some new favorite authors along the way.

Happy Reading!

CEO, Dragonblade Publishing

Additional Dragonblade books by Author Carol Coventry

The Taverstons of Iversley Series
Counting on Love (Book 1)
Holding Onto Love (Book 2)
Waiting for Love (Book 3)
Yielding to Love (Book 4)

CHAPTER ONE

June 1814

THERE WERE MANY kinds of filth in the world, and Major Crispin Taverston considered himself intimately acquainted with nearly all. Since most could be tidied away—one way or another—he no longer worried about dirtying his hands. Yet some things would not be easily cleansed.

This room, for example. The grime on the walls was thickly layered and its provenance could only be guessed at. The sheet on the bed felt slimy against his skin, skin which could, admittedly, stand a bath. The blanket was so flea-ridden he'd tossed it on the floor. There was no basin of wash water and no pot to piss in. The room stank of sweat and wet boots and sex.

He reached across the bed and patted the hip of the missy snoring beside him. "Lizzie." He gave her a shake, and her eyelids peeled open.

"Yes, Milord," she murmured sleepily. "What can I—" Her eyes grew huge. "Lawks!" She rolled over and sat up, pushing back lank strands of hair from her face and finger combing them. "It's morning! The mistress will give me a basting!"

"Only daybreak. And I paid the night," Crispin reminded her, peeved, though not with her.

She paused her ineffective grooming to give him a baffled look, as though she'd heard his words, but they made no sense. They probably didn't.

He'd hired her for the full night because, after all, that was why he was here. A more refined inn four miles up the road would have been clean and comfortable, but it lacked the primary amenity he sought. His body had been serving him well recently and deserved its reward. So, he'd bribed the stagecoach driver to make an extra stop. Naturally he'd intended to make better use of the hours than sleeping fitfully and scratching at bedbug bites. But the girl who called herself Lizzie, a common alias in her profession, was clearly exhausted. Every time he'd considered waking her for another go, he'd thought better of it. Let her sleep.

The girl gave him a guilty half smile and sidled closer. "A quick tup? Before I be getting downstairs?"

In the dawn's light, he could see the sallowness of her complexion, and her cow eyes didn't have the same appeal as they'd had in the dingy candlelit dining room. Crispin shook his head. It would take him another five hours to reach London. And that assumed his brother had gotten his letter with directions to have his horse delivered to the stable at the inn where he *should* have stayed. No doubt Mercury had had a more restful night than he did.

"Regretfully, no, lass. I have to be on my way." He was anxious to get home. He had a family wedding to attend. Another family wedding. The last.

She looked alarmed. "Was it…was I…?

"Grand," he assured her, though the experience had been far from memorable. Then he gave her a little gift by saying with feigned embarrassment, "I must've been more tired than I realized, sleeping like the dead."

"Wore us both out, you did," she said, then laughed, her laughter rough and coarse and forced.

Crispin climbed from his side of the bed and plucked his carefully folded clothes from the room's single chair. Lizzie rose also, seeking the shift and gaudy dress she'd discarded. He concentrated on his task rather than watching her and risking arousal he hadn't time to satisfy. Her body had been pleasantly round and strong. That much he did recall.

He knew why he'd chosen Lizzie out of the three serving maids working in the dining room. The prettiest had served him the inedible slop the innkeeper passed off as dinner and he held a grudge, while Lizzie had brought him the cider he had asked for after the pretty one brought him the ale he had not. The third girl he did not even look at twice. She was far too young to be in such a godawful place.

He slipped his shirt over his head, tied his hair back with a bit of broken bootlace, then sat on the chair to pull on his stockings and trousers. Everything he wore smelled bad. The room stank. His body offended his own nostrils. Tonight, he would be at 8 Grosvenor Square, the London townhome of the Earl of Iversley—his brother Jasper. There, he'd slough off the filth. For a while.

Perhaps forever. The war was over. Napoleon had been defeated. It still felt unreal. He wondered for the thousandth time, *what did that mean for Major Crispin Taverston?*

He pulled on his worn boots, then stood and stomped his feet firmly into them. What *would* it mean? What would *peace* mean? He hated war, of course; it was unfortunate that he was so bloody good at it.

There were options, of course. Life was full of options. But never before had he felt suspended amongst them with no ability to choose.

Crispin fished half a crown from his purse, then laid it on the chair. "Thank you."

Lizzie gave him a look like he was soft in the head. "For what?"

Crispin shrugged, tossed his red uniform jacket across his shoulder, grabbed his battered knapsack, and left.

THE ROAD FROM Lizzie's nondescript little village to Maidstone, with its posting station and decent inn, was flat and more or less straight. He walked the four miles, knapsack on his back, in a little over an hour. By the time he reached Maidstone, his morning-after melancholy had dissipated. Mercury was in the stable, just as he should be. For a full minute, Crispin simply stared at the glossy brown hide, wide chest, graceful neck. Then a smile bloomed on his face. *Zooks!* What a capital horse. He possessed the best features of his Arabian ancestors—the handsome delicate muzzle, small, pointed ears, large, intelligent eyes. And if there was a swifter horse, he'd never ridden one.

He gave a low whistle, and the stallion's ears perked. He whistled again, and Mercury's head rose. Seeing Crispin, he let out a whinny before rearing back and kicking at the stall.

"Whoa, whoa, there," Crispin said, laughing. He hurried to fling open the door. Mercury pranced toward him. Fully aware of his own idiocy, he threw his arms around the horse's neck and hugged him. "I'm home, you great beast. Or will be, as fast as you can get me there."

He called for the stable hand to fetch Mercury's tack, then waved him away to do the honors himself. Saddling Mercury. He could not stop smiling. He gestured for the boy to come closer again, and pressed a few shillings into his hand.

"Ach, no, sir. The fee's paid."

Oh? "You keep it then." The boy's eyes lit with disbelief and pleasure.

Of course, Jasper would have taken care of the stabling fee. Or rather, Benjamin would have seen to it. Benjamin Carroll, Jasper's supremely competent steward. *Benjamin their soon-to-be brother-in-law.* Crispin's smile burst forth once more. Benjamin and Olivia! He'd thought there was something in the air back at Christmastime, but he hadn't been home long enough to sniff out what.

Crispin backed Mercury away from the boy and mounted, settling into his seat while letting his horse dance about. The stallion's eagerness to run matched his own.

And good for Olivia! There was no better man than their old friend Benjamin, lowborn though he might be. Crispin snickered. He would have liked to have been there to see how Jasper handled their little sister's unconventional courtship. For the full tale, he'd have to ask Vanessa, Jasper's brave-hearted wife. Or Reg, their younger brother. Or Georgiana, the duke's daughter who'd chosen Reg over the chance to be Jasper's countess. He imagined they'd all been secretly rooting for Benjamin.

He guided Mercury to the road where he kept him to a walk to warm his muscles before nudging him into a trot.

His grin suddenly felt false. It dropped away, and he blew out a sigh. His siblings had all found their life mates. His *baby sister* would be married in two days. His younger brother now had a son of his own. It was wonderful, but…

Homecoming meant something different when the Taverston siblings were dispersed into three different homes. Four—if he leased himself a set of rooms in London, or moved to his cottage in the lake district. If he even meant to stay in England.

The devil. What *would* homecoming mean for Major Crispin Taverston?

MISS CAMELLIA HARRINGTON disliked wearing black. She was convinced it made her look like a crow, despite the fact that an appalling number of well-meaning but tactless individuals had told her she looked very nice in it. One unthinking old woman told her she should always wear black, a particularly cruel statement, since at this point in Camellia's life, it felt as though she always had. Worn black. Mourned. She pushed away the thought: *and always would.*

Of course, she might wear half mourning, gray or lavender or some such. Her father had been gone almost a year, and dear Mama had been gone for three. But Camellia was superstitious enough to fear that if she dared throw off full mourning, Fate would ricochet it right back at her. And although she knew it was improbable that her fashion choices would doom her poor brother Neville…

It didn't matter how she looked. No one would be looking.

Besides, there were more important things to spend her fast-dwindling inheritance on than fashionable modistes and fine dresses. Or London-made bonnets, gloves, shoes, and fans. Or the various Theaters-Royal. Or lectures. Or, Camellia sighed, the Temple of the Muses, Mr. Lackington's legendary bookshop.

She had always dreamed of seeing the sights of the great city. At one point, she'd even dared hope for a debut during the London Season. A fleeting dream. She'd been nineteen years old and naïve. Now she was twenty-five and whatever the opposite of naïve was. She was "on the shelf" and *finally* in London. And nothing in the city was how it should be.

Nothing in life was as it should be.

Stifling a groan of resignation, Camellia buttoned the cuffs of her crepe dress, put on her drab bonnet, and tied the ribbons, then slipped her hands into black knit gloves. She avoided the mirror, picked up her reticule, and stepped from her guest chamber into the quiet, candlelit hallway of the St. James townhouse where she was staying.

The house belonged to Lord Philip Stirling, husband of Lady Marianne Stirling, Camellia's best friend since childhood. If not for their kindness, Camellia didn't know how she could have come to London and remained for so long. Four months and counting, excluding the three very brief trips back home to Tonbridge to check on the improvements to the house. Marianne insisted she must stay as long as needed, but Camellia was beginning to detect a note of impatience in Lord Stirling's daily greetings. For this reason, she was trying to make herself as inconspicuous as she could.

She practically tiptoed down the marble staircase, waved away an approaching footman, and had almost made it to the front door when she heard Marianne's voice.

"Oh, no, you don't!"

Camellia turned. Looking at her friend, who had golden hair and wore a primrose day dress, was like staring at the sun. She had to blink. "Good morning. I—"

"I know what you're about to say. Colonel Harrington is waiting. You have to speak with his doctor. Or…I don't know. What excuse is it today?"

She flexed her fingers nervously. Marianne meant well. But there wasn't time to argue. "All of them. And I must also meet with Mr. Cooper." This excuse was new, though she had mentioned Mr. Cooper before. He was a singularly competent young man who worked at the Royal Chelsea Hospital. Camellia had come to realize that she could not bring her brother back to Tonbridge without a manservant who could handle his care, and she hoped to sway Mr. Cooper to be that man. One would think that seeing to the needs of a single invalided gentleman in a country home would be a more pleasant occupation than tending to a multitude of injured veterans in a hospital, even if it did not pay as much. But his lack of enthusiasm when Camellia had first approached him about it did not bode well.

Marianne turned her frown into a pout. "Surely this Mr. Cooper can wait until you've had a decent breakfast."

"I'm afraid not. He has patients to see to. I'm fortunate he even agreed to give me this much of his time." She regretted her clipped tone, but her words were true. Camellia was torn between annoyance that Mr. Cooper would not allot her an extra quarter hour, and admiration for his dedication to duty. Of course, that dedication was the reason she wanted to hire him. That, and the fact that he and Neville seemed to put up with one another.

"Honestly, Camellia. He's an attendant at Chelsea Hospital, not the Duke of Kent. He should make time for you, not the other way around."

Camellia waved away the complaint. "I am the petitioner. If

he says 'no' I don't know what I'll do."

Marianne's gaze fell and she bit her lip. Whatever she might have wanted to say, she did not. Camellia wouldn't listen anyway. She *was* going to take Neville back home. She'd promised him. Four months ago, impetuously, she'd promised. And now she was even more determined to get him out of that awful hospital. He had ceased to improve. Even his doctors said so. The smashed bones of his hips had knit badly; he would never walk again. There was no point pretending that he would.

Unfortunately, her brother's expectations for a speedy discharge were not realistic. He wanted to go "home" to a place he had rarely even visited since his youth. He'd seemingly blocked from his memory the cobbled drive, the uneven steps leading to the front door, and the fact that the bedchambers were all up a flight of stairs on the second floor. She had understood the difficulties he would face the moment she first saw him again, her poor, beloved, *stranger* of a brother. And so, for the past few months, she had been devoting herself and all her resources to making their house a place where he might live in comfort. Relative comfort. Maybe it was impractical, but she'd done what she needed to do.

But she really did have to hurry. It was an hour-long walk to the hospital.

"Marianne, Neville is probably awake already, staring at the walls."

Her friend sighed. "Go, then. But please say you'll take some time for yourself before you go back to Tonbridge. Promise you'll see *something* in London besides the hospital."

She felt a stab of yearning so strong she feared she might cry. And she didn't even know what she was yearning for. A life, she supposed.

"I promise I'll *try*."

CHAPTER TWO

THE EARL OF Iversley's London townhome was located along a row of grand houses that rimmed Grosvenor Square's acres of gardens. It was not the largest or the most ornate—Taverstons did not believe in ostentation—but, Crispin thought, it would certainly do for a home. There were three expansive levels, not counting the servants' attic or the cellars. The house fronted on the Square and also had its own private garden and stable in the back.

Crispin intended to make use of the rear entrance, as per usual. He had made it a habit, granted, an annoying one, to bookend his visits by sneaking in and slinking out.

He did not mind exuberant "welcome homes." In fact, he enjoyed them. But he never let his family know exactly when to expect him, or usually not even *if* they should expect him, because there was inevitably a delay, and he hated to worry them. Besides, he equally enjoyed their delighted surprise.

As for leave-taking, he avoided it. To say he hated goodbyes was a maudlin cliché. But the tears in his mother's eyes, Olivia's frank bawling, Reg's stoicism, Jasper's sorry attempts at humor—he couldn't have borne it, time after time. The difficulty with going off to war was that loved ones always imagined every goodbye to be the last one. He was not simply sparing himself, he also spared them.

Seven years of this. How in God's name had it been seven years?

He'd gone to join the fight against Bonaparte at the callow age of twenty-two, fully intending to die a hero's death. Illness had stalked him all his life, and he'd thought it preferable to die on the battlefield rather than in a sick bed. Yet somehow, it had never happened. While other men died all around him, he'd never even been wounded.

He dismounted at the stable and left Mercury in the hands of a groom, then sauntered across the rear yard, bone weary. It unsettled him that his mount had also been flagging the last several miles. At ten years old, Mercury should still be in his prime. The stallion needed more exercise. He belonged out in the countryside, not in London with its foul air and rutted streets.

Crispin rapped on the back door as though delivering the day's fish. A plump young kitchen wench opened it. Her face brightened and she squealed, "Major! You're home!"

"Hullo, Bess." He smiled at her, and kept smiling as she continued to bob up and down. Finally, he asked, "May I come in?"

With a start, she jumped out of his way. "Yes, Major. Of course. Excuse me." Then she yelled out, "The major is here!"

Six servants immediately surrounded him, babbling welcomes and congratulations, as if he had won the war all by himself. He nodded greetings, his smile rigidly in place. Thank God Peters, the butler—gray templed, stolid, invaluable—strode up and scattered them.

"Welcome home, Milord," he said solemnly, but Crispin did not miss the sheen in his eyes.

"Thank you, Peters. Is there any chance I might have a bath before the family descends upon me?"

"I will have one drawn at once. Your rooms are ready."

"Then I will sneak up the back stairs."

"I doubt that is necessary." Peters almost smiled. "Everyone is out, except for the earl."

"Out?" He felt a moment's affront, then mocked himself for

it. It was a busy time. They wouldn't be hovering at the door awaiting him.

Peters nodded. "They will be back for tea. They expect you this evening." His mouth tightened almost imperceptibly. Unnecessarily, he added, "Lady Olivia's wedding is the day after tomorrow."

Olivia was Peters's favorite, Crispin knew. And he had just been called to task for cutting his arrival so close. It wasn't as if he could help it. He had not, not yet, resigned his commission. He was on half pay. Wellington still owned him.

"I'd like my bath water extra hot," he said. "And my clothes will need laundering. Boiling, most likely." He had avoided lice for seven years by dint of meticulous attention to personal cleanliness. The small fortunes his fellow officers had spent on gambling or on local wines and spirits, he had spent on laundress-es. He thought it unpleasantly ironic that he'd been itching since he left Lizzie's inn.

"It will be seen to, Milord."

"Major Taverston!" Cook's voice boomed as she steered into the back entryway like a ship into port. "You must be hungry. What might I bring you?"

He was starving. And even out here, he could smell the aromas of the kitchen. The staff must have been working doubly hard for days, preparing for the wedding breakfast. But Cook had learned not to push rich foods upon him. His requirements were strict.

"Apples? Nuts?" he asked. Better to fill his stomach before he surrendered and ate something he should not. He was all the more weak willed having supped twice with Wellington in France—duck, beef in pastry, bread, glass of wine—with no repercussions. But he felt well and wanted to stay well. "And a pot of tea? If you would send any or all of that to my chamber, I will feast in the bath."

She nodded, sour-faced, as though insulted. "Yes, Major."

With that, he threaded past the servants, deciding upon the

main staircase after all. It would allow him to indulge in quiet appreciation for the home—one of the homes—he had grown up in. He could no longer call it *his* home, the way a child would. It was Jasper's now. But the memories were his to keep.

He walked through the hallways, pausing to breathe in the familiar. Jasper had not changed anything, Crispin was grateful to see. The same countryside landscape paintings covered the same pale-yellow walls. But it was early days. Jasper and Vanessa had not been married a full year. No babe yet either. It amused Crispin that Reg, their younger brother, was the first to produce a child. It was still hard to believe that he'd taken his nose out of his books long enough to notice Georgiana, the stunning young lady his brother had been courting, and steal her away. Crispin could not wait to lay eyes on Arthur, his nephew. A brand-new Taverston.

He began his ascent of the sweeping central staircase. He thought he was being quiet, but Jasper appeared at the head of the stairs and came running down. Arms outstretched, blond hair like a halo, he looked like Gabriel the Archangel.

Crispin called up, "If you were truly in a hurry, you would come down the banister." They'd done that as boys, infuriating, or more probably terrifying, their mother. He ducked when Jasper reached him. "Don't hug me, for Christ sake, I stink."

They used to make do with handshakes. He blamed Georgiana for the outbreak of hugging among the Taverston males. It had all seemed to begin with her. But it might rather have started with Father's death.

Jasper ignored his words and embraced him. Then he stepped back, nose wrinkled. "You were not joking. What have you been rolling in?"

"Lizzie." When Jasper *tch'd*, Crispin grinned.

Then Jasper stared at him a long moment, and he merely stared back. He would say that married life suited his brother, but Jasper would look the same—tall, broad shouldered, glowing with health, ungodly handsome, sartorially elegant—if he were to emerge from three years in a French prison.

Jasper swatted his shoulder. "You look well."

That spoke volumes. He answered, "I feel well." Enough said. "How is Vanessa?"

Jasper hesitated. "Fine. She is fine now." He shook his head. "We've a lot to talk about. I just…well, suffice to say, please don't jest about…about Arthur being in line for the earldom. Or my laggardness in that regard."

Crispin squinted a question, then his knapsack slipped from his hand and hit the step. "What happened?"

"A miscarriage. Back in January. I couldn't put word in a letter."

"No. Of course not." He swallowed hard. Vanessa had suffered so much. And bore it all so stoically. "But she is recovered?'

Jasper nodded slowly. "The thing is, I don't know if you knew, but she lost Henry's babe back at Corunna."

Crispin swore under his breath. "I didn't know." He thought back to the army's retreat from Spain. Vanessa had been following the drum. Her husband, a soldier under his command, had died in the fighting, and Crispin had helped Vanessa escape back to England. "She looked like hell in Corunna, but we all did."

"The doctor says it's nothing to be concerned about."

"But, of course, you're concerned."

"No more than you must be."

Crispin's eyebrows rose. "Me?"

Jasper smiled crookedly. "You are still my heir."

His stomach dipped before he recovered enough to smirk. "I have all faith in your procreative abilities." He picked up his knapsack. "Thank you for the warning. I won't say anything insensitive. Not about babies, at any rate."

He started up the stairs again, with Jasper alongside. "So Olivia will be Mrs. Carroll, eh?"

Jasper groaned. "We need to discuss this, too." *The devil.* Crispin prayed Jasper hadn't made things difficult for Benjamin, taking his head-of-the-family role too seriously. He'd probably had twelve peers of the realm lined up to court their sister. Before he could say anything, Jasper touched his arm and said, head bent as if confessing to a priest, "I may have promised Mercury to Olivia."

"What!" He started to laugh, but stopped, seeing his brother's pained expression. He repeated more quietly, "What?"

"I'll compensate you, naturally—"

Then he did laugh. "Shut up, Jasper. You can't buy Mercury." He shook his head. There was a story here, amusing because it had ended well. But even his elastic imagination could not come up with a scenario where Olivia marrying Benjamin would lead to Jasper promising her *his* horse. "Let me go wash and change my clothes. There is time enough to discuss whatever needs to be discussed."

CRISPIN TOOK *TWO* hot baths, during which he examined himself closely for crawling things. He was relieved to find only several bites, nothing living. When the second bath cooled to tepid, he toweled off and sent for Jasper's valet. He needed a decent shave, and to steal a splash of Jasper's cologne.

Tomorrow, he would avail himself of the Bond Street shops and buy his own. Jasper's blend of sandalwood with a few light floral notes was pleasant, but Crispin had no wish to walk around smelling like his brother.

Spending a morning choosing a cologne. There was something absurd about civilian life.

While waiting for the valet, he opened his wardrobe. Tentatively. He kept a few clothes in London but nothing suitable for a ton wedding at St. James's Church. His eye lit upon a dark blue jacket that he'd never seen before. He threw the door open wider. A flash of irritation was followed quickly by resignation.

Then gratitude. *Jasper.*

Not only was there a new jacket, but also a crisp white linen shirt and a pair of superfine buff trousers. A note was pinned to the jacket.

Our tailor still had your measurements, but has agreed to see you tomorrow for any necessary alterations. If you choose. I'm not telling you what to wear to Livvy's wedding. Or suggesting you should not be in uniform. I am simply glad to have you here and wanted to give you something.—J.

Crispin sucked his teeth a moment, then chuckled. It was impossible to be angry with a man so tactful, but of course, Jasper was telling him what he must wear to the wedding. Moreover, he was subtly conveying a message: *Resign your commission. The war is done.*

Maybe. Maybe he would.

He quickly donned the new clothes to check the fit. A warm feeling of well-being spread through his body. The waistband was snug. The shoulders…he tried hunching, straightening, lifting his arms. Both the shirt and jacket were binding about the shoulders. He'd put on weight. He peered more closely at his reflection. Still skinny as a fencepost, but perhaps a more substantial fencepost.

The valet knocked and entered, carrying a basin of steaming water. A shaving kit dangled from one arm, and towels were draped over his shoulder. "Do you require assistance, Major?"

"If you would be so good," Crispin said, dropping his smile. Men should not be caught grinning at their own reflections. He peeled off the jacket and hoisted the shirt over his head. "A shave. Trim my hair. And make me an appointment with the earl's tailor for tomorrow morning."

"Very good, Major." He gestured to a chair. "If I may, welcome home."

VANESSA SUMMONED HIM with a note. *Tea in the parlor at 4:30.* A very countess-like summons. Good for her.

Rather than arriving late to make a grand entrance, Crispin decided to go early. The parlor, with its woodsy décor and well-worn furnishings, was the most informal of the family's gathering places. He could sit calmly in a chair by the hearth as if he'd never been gone. But when he stepped over the threshold at quarter past, he found his family had been more impatient than he was. They leaped from their seats. Olivia, who was closest to the door, launched herself into him with such force he nearly toppled over.

He hugged everyone in turn, willingly, now that he knew he would not be infesting his loved ones. He reached his mother last, and held her the longest. When she stepped back, he saw tears in her eyes and fine lines at the corners that he'd never noticed before. She said, "You survived."

He nodded. God's will, he supposed. His unfathomable will. But, too, his own will to live had somehow always been stronger than his wish to die.

He moved to the center of the room and bowed. "Behold, the victor. Now, tell me everything I've missed." He ignored the rumble of complaints. They wanted to hear his stories, but he didn't want to talk of soldiering. He turned to the first of his sisters-in-law. Beautiful as always, yet he thought she looked a bit peaked. Her red-blonde hair was dulled and her cheeks looked blotchy. "Georgiana, we must start with you. Where is Arthur?"

"Sleeping, thank God. When he wakes, his nurse will bring him to meet you. Be forewarned, he is teething."

Teething? Having no idea what that meant, he merely said, "Good. Next, Vanessa." He spun toward her. Brown-haired, brown-eyed, she was pretty rather than beautiful, though Jasper would challenge him on that. More importantly, he was glad to see she appeared well. "The ton did not toss you out on your ear?" Vanessa was a widowed commoner who had been Jasper's mistress. A lesser woman would have been eaten alive by "polite" society.

She gave him a wry look. "They are more accepting than I expected."

"Accepting?" Jasper protested, the pitch of his voice high with disbelief. "They are welcoming!"

Vanessa ran her hand down Jasper's arm, but her focus remained on Crispin. "I underestimated Jasper's hold on his following. The men commanded their womenfolk not to snub me."

"*You* are winning them over," Jasper insisted.

"Slowly." Then Vanessa smiled. "I think, slowly, they are coming around."

Always clear-eyed and brave, she was the most admirable woman Crispin had ever known.

"And our fellows in Cartmel?" he asked. Their mutual acquaintances were wounded veterans turned bootmakers. Their boot mill had been floundering until Vanessa discovered a leather craftsman who transformed dull men's Hessians into pretty, practical footwear for women. She'd made it her mission to bring those boots to the ladies of London.

He should pay a visit to Cartmel, but there were old army fellows here in London he needed to call upon first.

Vanessa's smile grew. "They are doing very well." She lifted her hem two inches. Olivia, Georgiana, even Mother followed suit. Crispin laughed.

Olivia said, "I want to wear these to the wedding—"

An indignant chorus of "no" dissolved into laughter. Crispin's heart warmed. His ridiculous family. His gaze went to Benjamin, who stood just apart. Crispin realized he had not specifically greeted the man who would soon be his brother-in-law. The man who had once saved his life.

He crossed the room and stuck out his hand. "Benjamin. Welcome to the family."

The concern etched in Benjamin's brow faded. Crispin felt mildly offended that Benjamin could have doubted his approval. He'd never been a prig like Jasper.

At that moment, three maids entered the room with tea and trays of teacakes and sandwiches. Crispin eyed the offerings and exhaled with relief to see the oatmeal biscuits he knew he could safely eat, as well as jam, black butter, and a bowlful of nuts. They all took their seats. Vanessa poured. Jasper distributed the cups, which was amusing to watch.

"Now," Jasper said, when everyone was chewing or sipping. "What are your plans?"

Crispin swallowed. He did not scowl outwardly, though he was doing so inwardly. He didn't want his family to see his pathetic state of indecision. He considered shrugging, but that would be an admission of sorts. *The devil.* He was known for decisiveness, an ability to take swift and total control of difficult situations. Not for dithering. Then he rescued himself by noticing something he should have seen earlier. The family gathering was incomplete.

"Where is Hazard?" Viscount Haslet. Jasper's closest friend. An accessory brother. He was always about somewhere.

It unnerved him to see the way they all exchanged glances.

Reg said, "Jasp, didn't you write to tell him?"

"No, I didn't write," Jasper answered, bristling. "I assumed Haz would have."

"What is wrong?" Crispin asked, his gut tightening. Hazard was the best of fellows, but, considering his...proclivities, any number of things could be wrong.

"Nothing." Jasper shook his head as if to loosen the clench of his jaw. "Nothing. He is on his way back from Cumbria. He and Alice would not miss Olivia's wedding for all the world."

Crispin tried to rearrange Jasper's words into some semblance of sense, but the phrases did not fit together. "And where is Alice?" She, too, should be with them. Alice Fogbotham was Georgiana's cousin, and Olivia had taken to her at once. Crispin liked her a good deal, despite a certain intensity of purpose that made him wary.

No one answered. "What is wrong?" he demanded once more.

"Nothing!" Olivia cried. "It's all wonderful. Alice is with Hazard. They're on their honeymoon."

He stared at her, trying to discern if she was joking. Perhaps they were all pulling his leg, and Hazard and Alice would leap out from behind the draperies.

Jasper said, "It's for the best."

Vanessa harumphed and said, "It *is* the best."

All at once, Crispin understood. Hazard and Alice had solved their own difficulties—Haz's need for an heir, his not-so-well-hidden preference for men, Alice's lack of a dowry, and her bizarre fondness for arguing politics.

"It is perfect." It seemed everyone had sorted themselves out. Except for him.

CHAPTER THREE

CAMELLIA RETURNED TO Marianne's house at dusk. The porter greeted her with, "Lady Stirling would like you to join her in the sitting room." She dragged herself to the doorway of a cozy chamber decorated in muted yellows and Egyptian Brown, with a birdcage housing a sweetly noisy pair of lovebirds. Her friend appeared so serene, dressed in pale-blue muslin, with lamplight spilling across the needlework in her lap, that Camellia hated to bring her troubles across the threshold.

Marianne glanced up, then laid her work on the side table. "Philip is dining at his club tonight, so I thought we might have an early supper in here." She frowned. "You look exhausted."

Camellia entered, removing her bonnet, and stripping off her gloves. "I am." Everything that could have gone wrong, had gone wrong.

"Sit. I'll send for tea. Clara will bring the children down afterward." She sighed theatrically as she rose to pull the bell cord. "Once we've fortified ourselves." Marianne's three little boys were darlings, but rambunctious, and Camellia had noticed she liked to pretend they were a trial. A maid appeared at once. "Tilly, we will have our supper now with tea."

"Yes, Milady."

As the girl hurried off, Camellia sank into a velvet armchair and let her bones melt. She tried to gather her scattered thoughts while regarding the lovebirds chirping merrily. With a groan, she faced her friend. "Tell me how *your* day went. Cheer me, please."

Marianne gave a little laugh. "I went to a breakfast at the Marypoles'. We were supposed to hear a missionary speak about India, but the man was ill, so everyone gossiped about the Taverston wedding instead."

"Whose wedding?" Her forehead knotted. She couldn't keep these London people straight.

Marianne put a hand to her heart and exclaimed with exaggerated disbelief, "You don't know Lady Olivia Taverston is marrying her brother's *steward*? The day after tomorrow? Camellia, it is the talk of the town!"

"Who is Lady Olivia?"

"The Earl of Iversley's sister."

She had heard of the earl. Or perhaps she'd read a snippet of gossip in the *Morning Post.* "Didn't he also wed someone unsuitable?"

"He married a commoner." Marianne leaned forward in her chair and lowered her voice. "The woman had been his mistress for years."

"Oh." Camellia waved a hand dismissively. "Then he did the right thing, marrying her."

Marianne laughed. "That is a delightful way to look at it. Anyway, his sister supposedly had any number of more suitable admirers, including a duke, but if she is in love with the steward, all the better. Love matches are the very best kind." Then her beaming smile faltered, as though she realized whom she addressed: Camellia the spinster.

She hated to be an object of pity. She wanted to remind her friend that she *had* had suitors. Two of them. She didn't regret turning them down, even if marriage would have brought with it certain advantages. Children, of course. And financial stability. But also the things that Marianne hinted at with enthusiasm. Camellia could not deny a certain…curiosity about such things.

Just not with either of those two men.

Her face was becoming a bit heated, and she didn't want Marianne to think she was put off by the subject, so she asked, "Are you going to the wedding?"

"Heavens no. Philip and I are far below the Taverstons' touch. But I'm tempted to stand outside the church and gawk. Just to catch sight of the earl." She grinned like an imp. "But don't tell Philip I said that."

"The earl is handsome?"

"Handsome does not begin to describe him. Oh!" She bounced in her chair. "I just thought of something. We *should* go gawk. The last unmarried Taverston brother is home from the war. He's said to be almost as good looking as the earl. We could maneuver you into his path."

Camellia frowned. Just what everyone wanted to see at a wedding. A crow.

Before she could come up with a response, Tilly reentered the room, bringing a tray with tea, cucumber sandwiches, fresh strawberries, and a separate pitcher of cream. Marianne doused her berries; Camellia left hers plain. Cream upset her digestion.

After devouring three tiny sandwiches and emptying her cup, Camellia was ready to turn the subject from weddings and confide in her friend. "I received bad news today."

Marianne set down her drink, immediately attentive.

"I was unable to speak with Mr. Cooper, but Neville says even if the man accepts the position, he won't be able to go to Tonbridge for a month. Family obligations, you see."

What Neville had said was, "His sister is in trouble. The blackguard agreed to marry her, but Cooper is not leaving London until the deed is done." When she'd asked how long that might be, Neville shrugged, looking past her, dead eyed. "At least a month. They have to have the banns read." She didn't know if Neville would survive another month in that hospital. He was scarcely eating and slept so much. Sometimes she feared he was giving up hope.

"Oh, how unfortunate," Marianne said. She lowered her gaze

to the floor, then raised it. "And there is truly no one else? You mentioned that Mr….*hmmm*, Mr. Diakos? You liked him well enough, didn't you?"

Another attendant. A gentle, knowledgeable man. "Yes, he is wonderful. But he's a foreigner, and Neville doesn't trust him. He mutters at him under his breath."

"Who mutters? Mr. Diakos?"

"No, Neville does." She threw up her hands. "It has to be Mr. Cooper."

This morning, with Mr. Cooper presumably out badgering his sister's seducer, it had been Mr. Frye looking after Neville. The brute hoisted Neville from his bed and practically flung him into a rickety wheelchair. Neville shouted a few words she had no business hearing. The chair shuddered as if he'd plunked a horse into it, even though her brother was just skin and bones. Poor Neville's eyes scrunched tightly, his jaw clenched, and his face went bloodlessly white. After that, Mr. Frye gave Neville *two* doses of laudanum, and he'd slept away the whole morning. She thanked God she was carrying her battered copy of *Lyrical Ballads* in her reticule, or *she* would have spent the hours staring at the walls.

"Well," Marianne said, refilling Camellia's cup, "I am selfishly glad to keep you here longer. Now, do say you'll come with me to Bond Street tomorrow. I'm meeting a few friends at the circulating library to talk about Lord Byron."

"Oh, but I haven't read any of his work yet," she admitted.

Marianne's smile was so devilish she might as well have winked. "That won't matter. We'll be discussing *Byron*. Please come. Neville won't mind you taking a few hours for yourself. I'm sure he *wants* you to!"

She wanted to, too. "I'd better not." It would just make her more envious. The circulating library in Tonbridge had been closed ever since the death of the proprietor. She hadn't read anything new in over a year. And Bond Street was filled with shops that Marianne would insist upon visiting. Camellia knew

Marianne would press her to purchase something for herself. The temptation to do so would be strong. She *needed* new stockings. "I realized today that I must buy Neville his own wheelchair before I can take him home." There were just so many things to arrange. She balled her fists and breathed, counting to ten, trying to slow her racing heart. "I asked the doctor where I might find one, and they have to be *built*." She heaved a sigh. "He gave me a name of a man who might make one, but…" She halted.

"It will be expensive?" Marianne asked, eyes on her teacup.

Camellia nodded, embarrassed. "We'll make do." It was permissible to complain about expenses only if it was done with a laugh and an air of unconcern. But she was concerned. Father's debts had exhausted the sum Neville had received for selling his commission. And she'd spent far too much on changes to the house. Her purse was a sieve.

"Has the colonel begun to receive his pension?" Marianne kept her gaze down.

"No. Neville said it won't start until a year and a day after his injuries were confirmed to be irrecoverable. His physician just submitted his claim." To shift the focus from the crass topic of money, she added, "The problem is, having a special chair made might take weeks."

They sat quietly, eating their sweetly tart strawberries, until the twittering of the lovebirds made Camellia think to ask what other gossip Marianne had heard at the Marypoles'. That was followed by a stream of *on-dits* about people Camellia didn't know and didn't care to know. There was so much snobbery among the elite, they all sounded awful.

Of course, that could be envy speaking.

Camellia was not lowborn; she was descended from landed gentry. But good birth was no guarantee against misfortune. The Harrington property had been whittled down over the years. They no longer had tenants. Nevertheless, Papa had once held a position of consequence in their village—enough, she'd thought, that a London Season was not out of reach. Naturally, it would have been abbreviated and she would not have moved in high circles. Marianne, a mere baroness, was the most exalted person she knew, and if Marianne's mother had not sent her to stay with her grandmother in Tonbridge so often when she was a child, Camellia would not even know her.

"…of course, the biggest event of the Season was last month's wedding between Viscount Haslet and Miss Fogbotham. You remember that."

"*Hmmm?* Oh, yes. Yes, of course." She frowned, trying to remember what Marianne had told her about it. The prince regent had attended? Was that the one?

"Now that I think of it," Marianne mused, "the Taverstons are related by marriage, I think, to Miss Fogbotham. Yes! I remember. The youngest brother's wife is Miss Fogbotham's cousin. Well, I suppose she is not Miss Fogbotham anymore. She is the viscountess."

Camellia nodded and tried to appear interested. How did Marianne keep these things straight. More to the point, *why* did she?

Marianne stopped chattering to give her a narrow look. "You don't care about any of this, do you?"

"I'm sorry. I do, but I'm distracted by what to do about Neville." Camellia bowed her head in case her fear showed in her eyes. She worried Neville would die. He *couldn't* die. She was certain he would fare better in Tonbridge, but she couldn't *get* him there.

"You're doing all you can. I wish I could help. Would you like me to come to the hospital with you tomorrow morning?"

Camellia shook her head. "That isn't necessary, but thank you." Marianne had come with her once, the very first week, and had fainted dead away upon entering Neville's room. The odor of old blood, men's sweat, and dried urine, combined with the sight of limbless men and one who was eyeless, had overwhelmed her. She came around, but then proceeded to blather so nervously she irritated Neville. It was not an experience anyone wanted to repeat.

"Then what about this furniture man? Is he near Bond Street? I could talk to him for you."

"I cannot ask that—"

"Of course you can." Marianne reached over and patted Camellia's knee. "Please let me do something."

She bit her lip. Marianne would demand the very best. "I appreciate the offer, but I have to discuss with him what Neville needs. It's complicated. And his shop isn't near Bond Street." It was on Finsbury Square—almost an hour's walk from Lord Stirling's house, in the opposite direction from the hospital. And she had best go tomorrow rather than putting it off. It would either be feasible or it would not be. And then what? Was she to haul her brother about in a wheelbarrow?

"Then what can I do to help?" Marianne asked.

"You *are* helping." She'd initially told Marianne she would be in London three months. It had turned into four. And now it seemed her stay would be indefinite. "I hate to be such a burden to you and Philip—"

"You are not a burden. You could never be a burden." She swept her hand around the room as if indicating the entire house. "We have all this space, and I love having you here. Philip does, too. You are always welcome."

"Thank you," she murmured. "That's very kind."

Very kind and surely exaggerated. *Always* welcome? Camellia said a silent prayer that she would never have to test the sentiment. If Neville were to die, after all she'd spent on the renovations…any pension would cease…

She couldn't think of that. She shouldn't. Neville was *not* going to die.

Marianne's head cocked to one side. High-pitched voices sounded in the hallway, interspersed with the governess's calm tones. "The children are coming." She smiled a fond, proud, motherly smile. "Can you bear the noise? I could ask Clara to bring them back in an hour…"

"Oh, don't send them away. I can think of nothing I would

enjoy more." Camellia meant it. She loved the innocence and exuberance of children. Of all the things she was resigned to having to forego, it hurt most that she would never have any of her own.

CHAPTER FOUR

THE NEXT MORNING, Crispin took himself to Bond Street to his appointment with Jasper's tailor. He wore old clothes plucked from his wardrobe, which should not have felt strange—they were his clothes, after all—but nevertheless, made him feel like an imposter. Like he was playing at being a civilian. Trying it on. And it chafed.

He carried his new togs wrapped in paper to keep them clean. He expected to be at the tailor's a good while, but the man was waiting, ready to tend to him, and quite efficient. He measured, snipped a few threads, chalked a few seams, then promised to have the altered clothes delivered to Grosvenor Square that very night. Jasper must pay him exceptionally well.

It amused Crispin to think he would be a swell of the first stare at Olivia's wedding. Perhaps that could be his new persona. Rather than cynical soldier/spy, he might be an idle, devil-may-care dandy.

In keeping with that unlikely scenario, he went straight from the tailor to Truefitt's Barbershop on St. James Street to sample colognes. The shop was chock-a-block with adornments for men: neckcloths and pins, cuff links, snuff boxes, soaps, and colognes. He presented to the cologne counter where an unctuous clerk pressed several vials at him, declaiming the advantages of each. All Crispin could smell was sandalwood and citrus.

"Have you nothing different?" he asked. Everything he'd sniffed had the air of the ballroom or gentlemen's club. That was Jasper, not him.

"*Different?*" The clerk's nostrils quivered as though he was appalled. "My lord, they are all different." He held up one of the vials. "Notice the light notes of pepper and orange. And the hint of Lily-of-the-Valley."

"My mother wears Lily-of-the-Valley."

The clerk frowned, then said in a wheedling tone, "Have you a particular scent in mind? I'm sure we can match it."

He had no idea what he wanted. Just something more suited to a soldier. Or ex-soldier. Something more defining. The way Jasper…everything about Jasper was all of a piece. Reg, too. That was what he wanted. Consistency of self. But he wasn't going to find it in a barbershop.

At that moment, another salesman approached. He was older and carried himself with the stiffness of a wealthy cit's butler. He made a flicking motion toward the young clerk and addressed Crispin.

"Perhaps I may suggest a new offering. A musk with woody notes. Hints of spice. You might think of a forest floor."

He'd slept on too many damp forest floors to find that appealing. But he nodded, ready to be done. "That sounds more to my liking."

"Step this way, if you please." They moved to the opposite end of the counter. The man opened one of the cabinets on the wall to remove a small jar. He plucked out the stopper and waved it under Crispin's nose. "This is 'Spanish Leather.'"

It didn't smell like leather, which was too bad. But it had a complex, rich scent of musk, pine, humus, and perhaps vanilla, that *did* put him in mind of a forest. Pleasantly so.

"It will do," he said. "Send it to 8 Grosvenor Square, on the Earl of Iversley's account." That would please Jasper. Crispin truly believed his brother was secretly delighted to be taken advantage of.

He left Truefitt's without being persuaded he needed anything else. A glance at his watch showed it was not yet noon. He'd accomplished too much too quickly for an idle man-about-town—he shouldn't even be awake at this hour. Which proved he was not cut out to be one.

All in all, he was glad to be done with frippery. He had a more important task he'd wanted to accomplish this afternoon while his family engaged in pre-wedding chaos. His old commander, Colonel Harrington, was a patient at the Royal Chelsea Hospital, which was only a short walk away. In the heat of the battle at Vitoria, Old Harry had been fallen upon by his horse. His legs and hips shattered. Had he not been a colonel, the surgeons in the field would have loaded him with rum and laudanum and let him die. But being a man of rank, he'd been carted to various hospitals on the peninsula until—as Crispin had recently learned from some of their fellows—he'd been deemed well enough to survive transport home.

It was surprising that he'd made it, given the extent of his injuries. Nevertheless, the call Crispin meant to pay was not a charitable one. Or not solely a charitable one. Harrington had broken him in back when he was just another green peer's son with no understanding of warfare. Crispin hoped Old Harry might be able to provide some direction now as well.

What was an old soldier to do now that Boney was defeated?

ALTHOUGH HE HAD never been there before, Crispin could not possibly have missed the place. The Royal Chelsea Hospital was a three-story, three-winged, brick structure fronting on the Thames, partially enclosing and surrounded by gardens. A long, tree-lined drive led up to the main, central wing. The building would be majestic if it were not malodorous with the stink of the river and so melancholy in its purpose.

Crispin strolled up the drive, pausing to examine the market stalls encroaching on the property, where sellers of meat pies of dubious origin, bruised fruit, stale bread, and watery ale hawked their wares. Although he was hungry, nothing appealed to him. Here and there, dotting paths leading into the gardens, were more tempting offerings: colorfully dressed women who tried catching his eye, the bolder among them even calling out to him with crude invitations. And this was midday. At night, the place must be crawling with whores. Convenient, but he preferred a bit more privacy.

He went through the main doors and found a clerk with a register. "Major Crispin Taverston to see Colonel Neville Harrington."

The clerk turned a few pages of a large book, then said, "Room 112. West wing." He pointed at a hallway with his quill.

Crispin was not much acquainted with hospitals and hoped never to be. The hallway had a medicinal smell: alcohol, he supposed, but with a smack of urine and vomit. His heels clicked along the floor like a Dutch metronome, setting the tempo for the synchronized moans, coughs, and snores that accompanied his walk down the hall. He caught glimpses inside the first few rooms, then kept his eyes focused straight ahead.

He wasn't squeamish. He'd seen blood, dismemberment, and death on the battlefield. He'd *caused* men to bleed and die. But this was different. This lingering suffering when there was nothing more to accomplish.

Room 112. He paused, drew a breath, and peered inside.

The first thing he noticed was an old woman, swathed in black. His initial impression was of a medieval nun like those in paintings, but it was a mourning veil draped over her bonnet, shrouding the sides of her face, not a wimple. A fringe of white hair peeked out over her forehead. A nurse, then. Military hospitals hired widows to help care for the wounded. She stood beside the farthest bed and fussed over the man lying in it. A sweep of the room revealed six beds, three along each wall. Only three were occupied, but the others had a mussed appearance suggesting recent use. The closest held a man whose head was wrapped in bandages, who might have been sleeping or dead. A one-armed man sat in the middle bed, reading a book in his lap. The man in the far bed, with the morbid-looking woman leaning over him…Crispin blinked and stifled a groan. That was Old Harry.

Colonel Harrington was probably in his mid-forties, but now he looked at least two decades older. His hair was thin and completely gray. And he'd shriveled like a peeled apple left out in the sun.

Crispin adjusted his expectations. Poor Harrington could provide no insight into life after the army. The man was not recuperating, but dying.

He strode into the room. The woman glanced up, then straightened, her movement and posture that of a young woman not an elderly one. Harrington called out in a hoarse, weak voice, "Lieutenant! I'll be damned."

Crispin reached the foot of the bed but could go no closer because a chair fitted out with wheels blocked his path. He saluted. "Colonel."

Harrington's face was lined with pain, but he smiled. "It's good to see you. Let me…" He pushed against his mattress, trying to sit up straighter. The woman tucked her hand into his armpit to help, but he scowled and brushed her away. "Lieutenant, this is my sister, Miss Camellia Harrington. Camellia, this is Lieutenant Taverston."

Miss Harrington. So not a widow. Crispin faced her. She seemed startled, peering questioningly at him as if she were trying to place his name. For his part, he knew Harrington had a sister; Old Harry used to speak of her from time to time. Yet seeing her up close disoriented him completely. Through the gauzy veil, he noted that her bonnet sat atop sheeny, black-as-ebony tresses. Still, he had not mistaken the white fringe of hair at her forehead. That was odd.

And if Harrington was forty-something but looked sixty, this lady looked at least a decade younger than her years—what he assumed her years to be, given she was Harrington's sister. She could rather be Harrington's daughter. Her ivory skin was unlined. She had dark-brown eyes rimmed by long black lashes. And her lips were plump and bow shaped. She was objectively pretty. Very pretty. She could have used a lead comb to darken that white patch, but he respected the fact that she didn't.

He bowed quickly, hoping his studying of her had not been prolonged enough to be impolite. That was an army habit he needed to break—assessing everything and everyone as though scouting the terrain before a battle. "Miss Harrington. It is a pleasure."

She nodded slightly. "Lieutenant."

"Oh. Ah…" He shook his head. This should not be awkward, but it was. "Major. I am Major Taverston."

Harrington snorted. "That was a quick climb. But deserved, I'm sure." He turned to his sister. "You've heard—well, you've *read* about my visitor."

Miss Harrington looked puzzled. More than puzzled, her cheeks had pinkened. "I don't recall the name," she murmured.

"Because I called him Lieutenant Cheatdeath when I wrote to you." He laughed, then coughed. Crispin tried not to grimace as Harrington choked out a compliment. "Bravery verging on recklessness. Led from the front."

"Yes, I recall Cheatdeath," Miss Harrington said, eyes cast down.

"And I recall the sister you boasted of," Crispin said, addressing the colonel, trying to turn the topic away from himself. "A faithful correspondent. And caring for your aged parents if I'm not misremembering."

"Both deceased," Harrington said, drawing a deep breath. "But it was *her* mother and our father she cared for these past few years. And now, she is cursed with me."

"Blessed with you!" Miss Harrington protested.

A second marriage. So the age difference made more sense.

As did the mourning clothes. Their deaths must have been recent. He wondered what her story was. He didn't recall Harrington ever saying anything about her being courted, and she was a "Miss" not a "Mrs." That was unfortunate for her, but it meant Old Harry would be cared for.

"I don't mean to interrupt your visit," he said.

Miss Harrington fluttered her hand. "You are not interrupting. I'm sure Neville is more interested in visiting with you than with me. I'm here all the time." She cast a look around the room, her face falling. "If Mr. Cooper were here, you might go out to the terrace."

"Mr. Cooper?" Crispin asked.

"One of the attendants. Mr. Frye took the others out." She indicated the three empty beds.

But not the colonel? Crispin didn't understand. Was it some hospital rule? Only three men could go out at a time with one attendant? He looked at the wheelchair, sitting empty. "It's a fine day. If the attendants are all busy and you'd like to go outside, I can take you."

Harrington grumbled and Miss Harrington made some inaudible protest, shaking her head.

Having no desire to remain in that depressing room, Crispin tried again. "Why did Mr. Frye take the others out but not you?"

"Mr. Frye is a brute," Miss Harrington said, clearly this time, with a touch of anger. "He tosses Neville around like a sack of dirt. He says it's less painful to do it quickly, but if you saw—"

"Camellia! Enough of that." Harrington went red to his ears, and muttered, "You've already given Frye an earful."

Soldiers did not complain about pain. They endured. But Crispin could put the pieces together. Miss Harrington had refused to let her brother be manhandled by Frye—*good for her!* Except that meant he'd been left behind.

Crispin took hold of the handles on the chair and pulled it into the aisle. Then he stepped to Harrington's side, opposite his sister. "Arms around my neck, Colonel."

Miss Harrington gave a startled chirp. Harrington scowled, but lifted his arms as Crispin bent down and pushed away the sheet. Crispin remembered him as a stocky man, meticulous about his uniform. Now, the colonel wore a grayed white shirt and very baggy navy-blue trousers. Pretending not to notice the wasting, Crispin slid one arm beneath his commander's legs and another around his shoulders. Harrington held his breath. Crispin scooped him up, carried him to the chair, and placed him in it. Harrington let out a sigh. His face relaxed.

Miss Harrington gaped, then composed herself and said, "Thank you, Major." She snatched up a blanket and spread it over her brother's knees.

Crispin grasped the handles again. "Will you show me the way to the terrace, Miss Harrington?"

She nodded, but the colonel said, "I'll direct you. Camellia, there must be something else you'd like to do. The major and I will bore you with our reminiscences."

"Oh! Oh, yes, of course."

Crispin couldn't tell if she was pleased or hurt by the dismissal. Not by her tone. But she'd said she was "here all the time." He wagered that was no exaggeration. Poor girl. He turned the chair toward the door, hiding his grimace from her. The war had ruined too many lives.

CHAPTER FIVE

CAMELLIA WALKED QUICKLY down the hospital's drive, past the vendors and fancy ladies, ignoring them all. She was astounded. She knew what Marianne would say. *There is no such thing as coincidence. This is Fate.*

Earlier, they had been talking about the Taverstons. Marianne said they should maneuver Camellia into the newly returned soldier's path. And suddenly, he had appeared in *her* path. The only part of the Fated encounter that was implausible, if she were to play along with Marianne, was that the Earl of Iversley could be better looking than Major Taverston. *Good Heavens!* He was well over six feet tall with unruly blond hair and the bluest eyes she'd ever seen. He was gaunt, granted, but war did that to a man. And thinness, apparently, did not mean diminished strength.

Of course, Camellia told herself, she was long past the days of fantasizing about suitors. She was thinking only what a boon his visit was for her brother.

It had dizzied her, the way he'd commanded Neville, lifted him from the bed as if he weighed no more than a pin, then set him gently into his chair. He hadn't rushed to get it over with the way Frye did. And he didn't fuss so gingerly over the transfer that it hurt Neville twice as much for twice as long. She had been holding her breath as she watched, waiting for a catastrophe. But instead of a disaster, it was…fine.

Now she had time to go to Finsbury Square to see the furniture maker. She wouldn't have to try to hire a hackney cab, or walk the whole two-hour journey late in the day with the threat of the sun setting before she was done. Meanwhile, Major Taverston would entertain Neville and raise his spirits.

She turned onto Chelsea Road and headed away from the Thames. The stench of rotting fish and manure filled her nose and made her eyes sting, but it was better than the odors inside the hospital. The center of the road was busy with carts and carriages, and a crowd of pedestrians made their way along the periphery. She walked on, still picturing the major in her mind's eye. Wasn't his sister's wedding tomorrow? Yet he'd made time to see his old commander? Her heart thumped. She had been wrong to think that all members of the *haute ton* were awful people. Major Taverston was not awful.

Major Taverston. *Lieutenant Cheatdeath.* Neville tempted Fate assigning him a nickname like that. She caught her foot on an uneven cobble, wrenching her ankle, and had to stop to rub away the ache. Fellow footsloggers parted to stream past her as if she were a rock jutting up from a riverbed. No doubt her mourning clothes saved her from being bumped or shoved. She straightened and resumed at a slower pace, ruminating. *Lieutenant Cheatdeath. Bravery verging on recklessness.* She would have to dig out her brother's old letters when she got back to Tonbridge. She wasn't sure the sobriquet had been complimentary.

But what did it matter? The war was over. Major Taverston was kind to pay a call. She was grateful, and Neville had been pleased.

Things didn't seem quite as hopeless as before.

NOT ENTIRELY HOPELESS, but hope was hard to come by. Mr.

Loffit agreed to make a wheelchair "cheaply" by altering a regular chair in his shop. It would take only a few days, but it would cost fifteen pounds. *Fifteen pounds!* She'd bargained him down from eighteen, but it was still robbery. Yet she had no choice except to say yes. How else could she move Neville from place to place? If she could do nothing but stick him in his bed at home and leave him there, he'd be no better off in Tonbridge than he was at Chelsea Hospital.

She stepped out of Mr. Loffit's shop, onto the street. Her head ached. It must be well past teatime and she'd eaten very little that morning. Of course, it wasn't proper for a solitary lady to enter a teashop. Nor, for that matter, should she be traipsing around London unchaperoned. But she'd found those rules did not apply as stringently to a spinster with no prospects. It had been a liberating realization.

She ran her tongue over her dry lips and decided to walk around Tinsbury Square and see if a teashop beckoned. After a few minutes, she halted and stared at a massive, four-story building spilling down the street before her.

The Temple of the Muses. Mr. Lackington's bookshop. She hadn't known the address, hadn't thought to look for it, but there it was. Coincidence or Fate? She felt like a fish that had swallowed a baited hook. The store reeled her in.

She entered an enormous room with a wide circular counter behind which three clerks busily tended to customers. This was surrounded by wall-to-wall, ceiling-to-floor shelves filled with books. For a long moment, she stood immobile, only breathing. The air was redolent with the powdery smell of paper. *Heaven.* This must be heaven.

She shook herself. She couldn't stay long. She moved to one wall and noted sets of leather-bound histories, something she would not even touch. Marianne had said that the most expensive books were on display on the ground floor, with the prices decreasing as one went up. Camellia didn't intend to buy anything; nevertheless, she made her way to the stairs.

On the next floor, she wandered until she found the gallery holding volumes of poetry. These she browsed for a short time, but unsatisfactorily. It was not possible to appreciate what she was reading while standing up in a shop. There were chairs in the gallery, but they were occupied. So she returned Byron's *Childe Harold's Pilgrimage* to the shelf, promising herself that she would read it properly one day.

Putting aside her disappointment, she moved on to another gallery, one filled with novels. There she found empty seats including a comfortable-looking couch. Although Camellia read novels sparingly, Marianne read them voraciously and could not stop talking about one called *Sense and Sensibility*. Marianne was certain she knew the identity of the anonymous authoress, saying it was the sister-in-law of one of her friends, but she had not yet been able to obtain a copy from her circulating library. Camellia searched the shelves and found it. Twenty-one shillings for the three-volume set. Her heart dipped. She would not be purchasing a gift for her generous hostess.

She took the first volume to the couch, settled down to sample it, and laughed to see that one of the heroines was named Marianne. No wonder *her* Marianne was so eager to read it.

Camellia didn't know how it happened, but she became engrossed in the novel so quickly she lost track of time. Not only time. The store around her faded away and she was in Barton Cottage with the sisters. So divorced was she from the real world, that it didn't register at once that someone was speaking her name. And looming beside the couch. Reluctantly, she pulled her eyes from the page, then snapped to attention. It was Major Taverston.

"Pardon me." He grinned widely, the wrong expression for a person begging pardon. "I shouldn't have disturbed you."

"No. I mean, no that's all right. I—I was reading." Which was a stupid thing to point out.

"May I ask what has you so captivated?"

"Only a novel." She held it up so he could see the title, then closed it and set it on the couch.

"It must be enjoyable."

"It's wonderful." She wished her tone had not sounded so gushing. He'd think she was silly. "But I prefer poetry." *Lud.* She didn't need to justify her reading choice to him.

"Ah. So do I. My sister loves Ann Radcliffe's novels, but I think she has read them all." He frowned. "And a book is not much of a wedding gift." He pursed his mouth then said with a rueful sigh, "My brother is giving her a house and ten acres." She had no idea how to respond, but her expression must have conveyed more sympathy than he wanted, because he laughed. "I might have to give her my horse." He gestured to a chair next to the couch. "May I?"

Her cheeks warmed. She didn't think it was appropriate. But they had been properly introduced. He was not trying to crowd onto the couch beside her. And she was armored in black. "Yes, of course."

He folded himself into the chair with a graceful lack of self-consciousness. He looked as if he was examining her. She prayed he wasn't puzzling over her hair. If he was, she refused to let it bother her.

She said, "I want to thank you—" at the same time he said, "I had a good visit with your brother." Then they both stopped and waited for the other to speak. He broke the silence by raising one eyebrow and asking, "Thank me?"

"For calling on Neville. It was generous of you to make the time. Especially with your sister's wedding tomorrow."

The eyebrow rose improbably higher. "Did I say the wedding is tomorrow?"

Bollocks. He hadn't. Marianne had. Camellia's whole face and neck grew hot. "No. No, I'm sorry. I should not listen to gossip—but nothing censorious was said."

His expression turned grim. Naturally. It must be irksome to have people tittle-tattling about one's family.

She tried pressing on. "I think Neville is bored most of the time. I've run out of ways to entertain him." She heard her own words and winced. "Oh, dear God," she muttered. "I don't mean that I've been gossiping about your family to entertain Neville."

He snickered. *Good.* Amusement was preferable to anger. The whole predicament was so ridiculous she had to bite her lip to keep from laughing as well. "I suppose I should have stopped at 'thank you for calling on Neville.'"

He flicked his hand as if to dispense with her apology and her gratitude. "It was my pleasure. We had a fine conversation out on the terrace, talking of old army friends."

"Gossiping?"

A gleam of appreciation lit his eyes before he answered, straight-faced, "Nothing censorious was said."

She snorted. He had a sense of humor, thank God. He smiled as if thinking the same.

"Your brother said he would be going home soon. That you are taking him to Tonbridge."

She nodded.

"He requires a good deal of care?" He made it sound like a question, but she guessed that it was more of a statement. Did he imagine she was unaware of the support she would need?

"I'm hiring a manservant to help tend to him."

"Ah. Good." He folded his hands in his lap and studied them. "The hospital is no place for him. He is fortunate to have you." Then he looked up to glance about the room. "No one has come to chase me off. Who is here with you?"

Her chest knotted. Her answer would tell him everything. She had no other family. She hadn't funds to hire a companion. She was careless of her reputation. But she would also have him know that she was honest. And unashamed. "I came alone. I had another errand nearby…" She trailed off, seeing his eyes narrow. Then she strengthened her voice and said, "I'm staying with Lord and Lady Stirling." *They* were respectable. "It is not so far to walk."

"*Walk?* No. Where do they reside?"

Since it was none of his business, she gave him a cutting look and remained silent.

He cleared his throat. "Excuse me. I'm used to barking at people, but I imagine you get enough of that from the colonel. I'm concerned because there are footpads about in the evening."

"It isn't evening yet."

His lips thinned. Then he pressed his hands against his thighs and asked archly, "Miss Harrington, how long were you reading?"

She looked down at the novel. She'd been quite far into the story.

Dash it! She picked up the book and stood abruptly, aware of his eyes on her back as she moved to the shelves to put it back. When she turned around again, she saw he was now also standing, and regarding her steadily.

"Thank you, Major Taverston, for alerting me to the time. I must go."

He shook his head. "Please permit me to see you back to the Stirlings'."

"Oh, no. I cannot put you out. I'm sure you have other plans—"

"Miss Harrington," he interrupted, laughing a little. "I must now browbeat you into putting up with my presence a while longer or else allow you to endanger yourself."

This was disastrous. She had unwittingly put him in the position of having to volunteer to escort her home. He must wish he'd never stopped to talk with her.

"Absolutely not. Major, I appreciate your offer, but I cannot accept. I will take a hackney cab." Paying the fare would be penalty for her carelessness.

His face clouded. He appeared ready to argue, but then blinked as if struck by a sudden thought. "If that is what you prefer." He studied her a moment longer. "Will you permit me to summon one for you?"

Camellia nodded. Mortified. "Thank you." What a perfect cake she had made of herself. She hoped their paths would not cross again.

CHAPTER SIX

MAJOR CRISPIN TAVERSTON entered St. James's Church smiling. Intentionally. Everyone else was smiling, so how could he not? No matter if he felt out of sorts.

He filed into the family pew between his two sisters-in-law. Georgiana's light rosewater perfume and Vanessa's spicy musk vied for pride of place with the scent of burning candles and "Spanish Leather." The jumbled scent of refined Society. It was sour of him to wish for a breath of unperfumed air.

The vastness of the church commanded his immediate attention. With its barrel-vaulted nave, Corinthian pillars, and enormous stained glass windows, it was coldly imposing rather than warmly inviting. It had surprised him that the wedding would take place here in London rather than in Iversley Village. But when he'd asked Olivia last evening at supper if she wouldn't rather be out in the countryside at the family's estate, she'd dismissed the question with a wave of her hand.

"Vanessa said it would make more of a statement if we married here. We shouldn't let it appear as though we sneaked off to Chaumbers to wed in secret."

Her answer had irritated him. He *knew* she preferred the little church in their village. "This is your wedding, not some performance for the ton."

She'd merely grinned. "La! It *is* a performance, Crispin. But

the wedding is just one day. We'll be *married* at Chaumbers."
Thus, Olivia proved she possessed the most down-to-earth
commonsense of them all.

He settled into his seat, trying to focus on the moment, the
beauty of each moment, while waiting for the ceremony to begin.

And then, accompanied by a triumphant organ processional,
Olivia glided down the aisle on Reg's arm. She was dressed in a
blue silk gown, not a riding habit and decorative boots as he'd
half expected, and she was beaming her Olivia smile. Crispin
ached with love and regret. He'd missed so much. Olivia's
growing up. Reg's wedding. Arthur's birth. The last years of his
father's good health before his apoplexy. Jasper being Jasper. How
could he have spent seven years apart from them all? How could
he even consider leaving again?

After delivering Olivia, Reg returned to sit with them. Their
bench was full enough that they bumped shoulders. It would
have been even more crowded if Jasper and Alice had needed to
squeeze in. But Jasper, the earl, was standing up with Benjamin.
And Alice, a viscountess, was Olivia's bridesmaid. It *was* a
performance. They were daring the ton to reject them. Crispin
wagered the ton would not dare.

Hazard, who was practically family, sat in their pew, next to
Mother. Benjamin's three-year-old daughter, Hannah, sat on
Mother's other side, quietly entranced. Earlier that morning, she
had danced up to Crispin announcing, "Olly is Mama!" He'd
replied, "And I am Uncle Crispin." But she said, "No. Major."
With a monstrous pout. He didn't argue. One could not win an
argument with a toddler. But then he'd heard her call Reg "uncle"
and, ridiculously, he'd felt a bit hurt.

The only missing Taverston was Arthur, home with his
nursemaid. Crispin had met him, of course. He'd even held him
briefly and awkwardly before handing the slippery eel back to
Reg. It had been easier to lift Colonel Harrington than to hold
onto his squirming, shrieking, *teething* nephew. Georgiana
pointed out the two little white bumps on his gums. Tiny things.

Arthur was making much of nothing.

Aside from the Taverstons, the guest list was small. Benjamin had no family to speak of and only a few close friends attended. Jasper had jokingly said there would have been more, but they could not invite any of Olivia's disappointed suitors.

Enough wool-gathering. Crispin forced his attention to the service. The rector's message was brief and disappointingly dull. Georgiana started crying, which surprised him. She had never struck him as a sentimental weeper. But then his own eyes moistened when the couple exchanged vows. He'd never seen Olivia so happy, which was saying a lot because she was happy by nature.

The rector pronounced them man and wife.

Olivia, *Livvy-pet*, the baby of the family, a full decade younger than he was, was now Mrs. Carroll. That made him feel old.

The organist struck up the recessional, and husband and wife exited the church, arm-in-arm. A perfect pair. As perfect as Jasper and Vanessa. And Reg and Georgiana.

Now he felt old and *alone*.

The wedding breakfast would be next, with its spread of delicious food he dared not eat and more champagne than he cared to drink. He'd have to make a toast, a more appropriate toast than he'd delivered at Jasper's wedding. Something sweet and funny. He had to play his part. He wasn't selfish enough to draw attention to his own inappropriate gloominess on Olivia's day.

After exiting the church, he stood next to Jasper, watching the ladies throw flowers at the newlyweds as they climbed into a carriage to return to the house.

"Can you believe it?" Jasper said. "Our Olivia? Married?"

"I still remember the first time she picked up a billiard cue."

"I still remember the first time she sat on a horse." Jasper stared after the carriage. "Selfish of me, but I'm glad she'll be at the cottage at Chaumbers."

Crispin snorted. "That's not selfish. You helped make Olivia's dream come true."

Jasper clapped him on the shoulder and steered him toward the coach. Crispin continued musing, unable to quiet his mind by force of will. After the breakfast, the newlyweds would depart for their honeymoon. In keeping with a new Taverston tradition, they would head to Crispin's rustic lakeside cottage in Binnings. They were leaving Hannah with her nurse and Reg and Georgiana, so they would not stay longer than a fortnight.

A fortnight. After which the cottage would be empty, except for two elderly caretakers and one redoubtable housekeeper. Crispin would then have to decide whether he should go to Binnings himself to oversee repairs to the rundown retreat, or lease a place in London so he wasn't living in Jasper's pocket, or put in for military duty abroad, or return to Paris and accept Wellington's offer of a position as an attaché to the embassy.

Bloody hell.

He climbed up into the coach, his smile gone, no closer to a decision than he had been.

IT HAD BEEN ten days since the wedding. Crispin was loathe to admit it, but he was already tired of civilian life. He didn't expect his siblings to dance attendance upon him, but he hadn't anticipated being ignored either. Jasper spent a surprising number of hours sitting in Parliament, and then, like as not, he took himself off to White's afterward to continue talking politics. Vanessa spent the days paying calls or receiving callers, wedging herself into Society for Jasper's sake. Reg locked himself away in the library, merrily translating ancient Greek manuscripts. Georgiana generally took Arthur and Hannah to Watershorn, the London home of her parents. Crispin had spent one enjoyable afternoon as the guest of Hazard and Alice. They made a delightful couple, but yesterday they'd left London for Gladnorshire to visit Haz's friend.

They all had lives.

That was not to say there wasn't plenty for him to do. It was the height of the Social Season. The Marriage Mart. He'd gone with Jasper and Vanessa to one ball, the Prince Regent's Carleton House ball celebrating Wellington, foolishly thinking it would be a pleasant night of dancing. But he was twenty-nine years old, the brother and heir of an earl, discreet in his vices, and in uniform. He might as well have worn a target on his back. Dancing was a prelude to courting. Since he had no intention to marry, he felt he was misleading every young lady he led onto the floor.

And then came Miss Sedgewick. He'd asked her to dance the waltz because she was so tall most fellows wouldn't. She nearly swooned from the heat just as he was whirling her past a door to the balcony. When he began to haul her outdoors for air, Vanessa appeared from nowhere to lend him a hand. Miss Sedgewick recovered promptly and scurried away. Vanessa scoured him with her glare. "Do you see anyone else out on that balcony?"

He'd peered out. "It's too dark to—"

"Exactly. And Miss Talbot was complaining to Lady Rosalind that Miss Sedgewick had set her cap for you and bet she could get caught compromised. Rule number one, Crispin: Don't drag young ladies onto dark, lonely balconies." He must have looked aghast because Vanessa patted his arm and teased, "For *any* reason."

He'd been away so long he'd forgotten that the Marriage Mart was a take-no-prisoners battlefield where slyboots posed as innocents. He wouldn't go to another ball.

He stood in his bedchamber, peering out the window. It was unnerving having no place he needed to be. No task demanding his attention. He'd already taken Mercury out to Hyde Park for a lengthy morning ride. He could go see Jasper's tailor and order another few shirts and a jacket or two. Visiting a brothel was a possibility, but he'd prefer to wait until night for that.

He ambled aimlessly away from the window, then stopped at his bedtable and picked up one of the books in the set he'd purchased for Olivia. In all the wedding excitement, he'd forgotten to give it to her. It was the novel Miss Harrington had been reading. He found it strange that she'd been so captivated, yet left it unfinished rather than purchasing it.

If he were to let fly his imagination, the fact that she'd abandoned the novel bolstered a theory that she had been passing time while waiting for someone. A secret lover? That seemed more plausible than that she had lost track of time reading. He wondered if she had been frantically wishing him away. How embarrassing if he had ruined her tryst by intruding.

Hmmph. Now he was curious. He should have followed the hackney cab to see if she circled back to the shop.

He thumbed the pages, then set the volume down. He was being absurd, of course. And unjustly suspicious of an innocent young lady. He should pay another call on Colonel Harrington. If *he* was bored to distraction, Colonel Harrington must be half out of his mind.

FEELING BOTH IMPATIENT and lazy, he rode Bolt, one of Jasper's better mounts, rather than walking to the hospital or disturbing Mercury's rest. He left Bolt in care of an eager urchin in the drive. He was wearing his redcoat, and the clerk at the entrance saluted before waving him on. He was halfway down the hall when a short, heavyset man with light golden-brown skin and dark-brown hair stepped out of one of the rooms, a frown on his very familiar face.

"Adam!" Crispin called.

The man looked up. "Ah. Lieutenant." Crispin drew near and Adam said, "You are well, I can see."

Crispin nodded. "I've been well. And with largely you to thank."

"Your gratitude cannot compare to mine."

That must be true. Nearly two years earlier, in Portugal, Crispin's regiment had come across an abandoned contingent of wounded French soldiers. They were being tended to by one harried civilian, a Greek with some medical training, who had no business being there since he was not a French army surgeon. Harrington had been in a particularly poor mood that day. He decided, without evidence, that Adam Diakos was a spy. The only way Crispin could talk him out of executing Adam was by guaranteeing the prisoner himself. He made a poor jailor, but, thankfully, Adam was a trustworthy sort. He was also curious and driven. Before Crispin knew it, the man had ferreted out the details of his irregular health, diagnosed him as having "an intolerance for many common foods," and set out to cure him. He wasn't cured, but he was vastly improved. As long as he avoided most everything that everyone else ate with abandon.

"How did you end up here?" he asked. The last he had seen of Adam, he'd been released from parole. Crispin had expected him to hightail it back to Greece.

"I needed work." Adam cast a glance down the hallway, both directions, then dropped his voice. "Why are *you* here? You should leave."

"What? Why?"

Adam took a step closer and lowered his voice even more. "There is contagion. A pox of some kind. On the third floor. It's very bad."

Crispin felt the blood rush down to his feet. "Are *you* leaving?"

"I believe I have had it." He pointed to a small pockmark on his cheek. "I told the physicians I would work with the sick, but I should stay on the third floor. They thought otherwise. They think if I survived, I cannot spread it."

"But you think you might?"

Adam shrugged. "It does not matter what I think. And it will spread regardless. You should leave."

The devil. Colonel Harrington might prefer a quick death, but he should not be condemned to it. And there was Miss Harrington to think of. If she was going to take Old Harry back home to Tonbridge, she should do it now, before *she* caught this pox.

"I'm here to see Colonel Harrington. What is the process for discharge?"

"No one will stop him from going. But Miss Harrington cannot remove him by herself. He cannot walk."

"She said she was hiring a manservant." Unfortunately, it was not likely to be Adam. Harrington did not like to admit it when he'd been wrong.

"Mr. Cooper, I think," Adam said, scratching his chin. "But he will not leave London until his sister is married."

"When will that be?"

"I don't know. Not today. Not soon enough."

"Damn." If it were not Adam speaking, Crispin would dismiss the warnings as alarmist. But he had never trusted any physician the way he did this Greek. "I'll speak with Miss Harrington."

"Yes, but not—" He hesitated, frowning. "Privately. You must tell her privately. We do not want panic. Most of these men have nowhere else to go."

Crispin's skin crawled at the thought of all these doubly cursed soldiers. "Yes, all right. I understand."

Adam nodded. "She is on the terrace with Colonel Harrington." He gestured to the next doorway. "I must…"

"Yes. Of course. And thank you for the warning."

"Try to convince Miss Harrington to stay away until the danger is past." With that, Adam stepped into the room to do whatever it was that he did.

Stay away? As if a woman who'd defended her brother against a careless attendant would abandon him to a pox.

So, here was a problem to solve. Crispin felt a familiar and welcome firing of his blood. This Cooper fellow could not be relied upon. *He* would have to rescue Old Harry.

He had to move fast. From recent experience, he knew Miss Harrington was independent-minded and reluctant to accept help. Fortunately, he could be very persuasive. He shouldn't be smiling, but...he was looking forward to the tussle, bored blackguard that he was.

CHAPTER SEVEN

CAMELLIA READ ALOUD from her book of poems, *Lyrical Ballads,* continuing even after Neville fell asleep in his new chair. He'd said he liked the sun on his face. Camellia imagined the warmth would be pleasant, but she still shaded her own face with her bonnet to *preserve her complexion* as she had been taught.

From time to time, she glanced around at the lush, well-tended flowers. There were two other men on the terrace, also dozing in the sun. It was a peaceful spot. Dull and peaceful.

Glancing up once again, she was startled to see Major Taverston coming toward them with a brisk stride and a stern expression. She had thought, after embarrassing herself at the bookshop, that she didn't want to encounter him again; yet she had looked for him each day and had been disappointed when he didn't come calling.

He was in uniform and appeared quite dashing. She watched him take note of the three sleeping veterans, then slow his pace. He didn't call out a greeting and neither did she. Upon reaching her, he murmured with no preliminaries, "Will you step over toward the roses with me? So we can talk without waking anyone?"

"All right." She rose and set down her book. He glanced at it, then gestured for her to come along, but did not offer his arm. So this was not to be a pleasant stroll about the terrace.

As they walked toward the far edge, he nodded back toward the seats and recited, "'I heard a thousand blended notes, while in a grove I sate reclined.'"

She finished the stanza. "'In that sweet mood when pleasant thoughts bring sad thoughts to the mind.'"

A flicker of a smile crossed his face. "Is Wordsworth your favorite poet? Or Coleridge?"

"I don't believe I have a favorite. But I do admire them both." He didn't press for a better answer, so she asked, "Who is yours?"

"Currently?" He cocked his head to one side. "I'd have to say Donne. Old-fashioned, I know, but he's very clever."

"You must mean his religious themes." Donne's love poetry was shocking.

He seemed to freeze for a moment, then slid a sidelong glance at her. Assessing. She made an exaggeratedly prim little moue. His eyes lit. "Those, too."

She laughed softly as they reached the railing, but his countenance abruptly changed from friendly back to stern. "Miss Harrington, I have some disturbing news. Can you keep a confidence?"

What a horrible thing to ask. "Better than you can, evidently."

His lips twitched. "Ah. Touché." Then he frowned again. "There is pox in the hospital. You should remove your brother at once."

"Pox?" Breath left her chest, and she caught the railing for support. "What do you mean? How do you know?"

"You understand it serves no purpose to terrify men who have no means of fleeing. The physicians will do their best to contain the disease, but it is likely to spread."

She pressed her hand to her mouth, holding back a scream or an oath. Through her fingers, she whispered, "I can't move him. Not without Mr. Cooper's help. And he won't leave London. Not just now."

Neville had said Cooper didn't trust the bounder not to run

off. It seemed to Camellia that being forced to wed a man so untrustworthy was as terrible a fate as the alternative.

Of course, she couldn't explain this to Major Taverston. She wasn't supposed to know about such indelicate things *at all*, let alone as much as she now did. She'd told the story to Marianne, who'd gasped, "Good gracious! The silly girl should have taken precautions!" When Camellia had asked what she meant, Marianne gave her a graphic description of how to prevent pregnancy with a vinegar douche. And then, she'd lent her that book…Camellia hadn't even known how a lady got with child, not in precise detail, but now she knew both how to and how not to. At least, in theory. She wasn't sure if she was pleased or saddened she'd never know in actuality. Though if she had a husband now, she and Neville wouldn't be in such a precarious place.

Major Taverston tapped his fingers against the railing, brow furrowed as if deep in thought. "I cannot offer my brother's house. There is a slight chance, you understand, that the colonel has already been exposed. And there are children—"

"Of course you can't take Neville in! We would never ask it." Frustration gripped her. "I cannot ask the Stirlings either."

"So," he went on, "we must take him to Tonbridge. At once."

"We?"

"Miss Harrington, unless you have another solution, I think you should accept mine. I can borrow one of my brother's carriages. If we leave quickly, we can be there before dark."

She stared at him. She could not believe what he was offering. "Why would you do this?"

He didn't answer right away. He frowned and directed his gaze toward the roses before he uttered, "He was my commander."

That hardly seemed reason enough. "I should refuse." She bit her lip. Could she trust him? "Major, it is too generous of you."

"No, it is the very *least* I can do." He gripped the railing so tightly his knuckles whitened. "I must leave all these unfortunate men to their fates, knowing it is kinder not to warn them when I can do nothing for them." His voice shook. "The war is over, yet there is no end to death." He turned to face her, his expression a bit frantic. "Removing the colonel to safety is the one thing I can do. Please don't deny me this."

She stared at him a moment longer. Those white knuckles. The wild eyes. The theatrics.

She sniffed. "You are doing it far too brown."

His head jerked back, and he blinked.

"Major, you can't expect me to believe that escorting us to Tonbridge is a favor *I* am doing for *you*."

"I—"

"Is there even any contagion?"

"I wouldn't lie about that!"

"What *are* you lying about?"

She saw a small twitch at the corner of his eye before he set his jaw. Then he looked past her, clearly thinking. She wondered if he was reexamining his words. She felt sure of it when he said, "Nothing I said was untrue." His eyes met hers. "Only my manner was false. I worried you would resist my help. As you did the other night—"

"Major! The crisis at issue then was that I'd stayed too long at a bookshop. This is contagion! I'm not a ninny."

He glanced over his shoulder at the sleeping men, then back at her. He lowered his voice. "I apologize. Of course, you'll accept my help."

She felt peeved he was getting his way regardless. "I haven't a choice. Though I would like an honest answer why you're so eager to put yourself out."

"I haven't anything better to do. That is the truth. If you like, we can argue more later. But now, I have a horse out front. I can be back with a carriage in less than an hour. Does the colonel have much in his room?"

"A few clothes and his shaving kit. And the chair he's in. It's his." His, but the wheels did not turn smoothly, and it was difficult to maneuver. It was the best she could do for fifteen pounds.

"Good. That will make it easier. We can collect his things, then go to the Stirlings' for yours. Will it take you long to pack?"

"Not very. And I can send for anything I forget."

"Could you send for all of it? We can be on our way quicker if we don't stop at the Stirlings'."

"Good Lord, no! I have to say goodbye to Marianne." A wave of heat rolled up her neck. She'd told her friend about meeting Major Taverston at the hospital, but not about the encounter at the Temple of the Muses. She could imagine Marianne's astonishment, seeing her ride off with him into the night.

Major Taverston nodded. "Very good. I'll fetch a carriage. If you can, wait here on the terrace until I return."

CAMELLIA COULD NOT have said what she expected, but it certainly was not the carriage Major Taverston brought around to the side door of the hospital. She had never ridden in anything so grand. The wood was painted a glossy black. The handles and metal attachments gleamed so, it wouldn't surprise her to learn they were plated with gold. Four matching black Norfolk Trotters were in the traces. And Major Taverston had also borrowed a driver in livery.

The Major lifted Neville into the carriage and climbed up after him to see him settled. Then he vaulted down and handed Camellia up. The inside was well cushioned and upholstered in a rich brocade. She tried not to gawp, but who lived like this?

"There are sandwiches in that basket and tea in the bottle. I'm sorry but the tea won't be hot. And there are blankets under the red cushion if you need them."

"Thank you, Major," Neville said. His teeth were clenched. "Camellia, I need my laudanum." As she fished the bottle and spoon from her reticule, Major Taverston turned away, frowning. She wondered what worried him now.

To her relief, he wasn't going to ride in the carriage with them. He would ride alongside on a gorgeous chestnut Thoroughbred that must have been at least sixteen hands tall. She felt she had stepped straight into a fairy tale. Handsome prince included.

Neville fell asleep in the short time it took to reach the Stirlings'. Major Taverston opened the carriage door and helped her down.

"I'll wait here with the colonel." He cast an anxious look at the sky. "I think we are in for some rain."

"I'll hurry."

Marianne met her at the door. Fluttering. "What on earth? Whose carriage is that?"

"Major Taverston's." She gave the quickest explanation she could, emphasizing the major's determination to help Neville. Her friend merely stared, open-mouthed, until the story was told.

"My word, Camellia, I don't know what to think. Are you sure he isn't abducting you?"

Why on earth would he? "Don't think, Marianne. Just help me pack."

Less than half an hour later, Major Taverston was handing her back into the carriage. Just before closing the door, he startled her by pressing a brown-paper-wrapped parcel into her hands.

"If the colonel is sleeping and you're bored…at least as long as there is light enough."

She peeled open the paper of Major Taverston's gift a little warily. The last book slipped to her had been the one from Marianne, a "secret" novel that Philip had given her as a wedding gift, *The School of Venus: or, The Ladies Delight, reduced into Rules of Practice*. A rather eye-opening instruction manual. She'd read it then gave it right back. Her hands had felt scorched.

But this! *Sense and Sensibility*. Her vision blurred. She'd never met anyone so thoughtful.

Yet as the carriage began moving, her mind shifted to the practical. *No one* was that thoughtful. She didn't believe the major had nothing better to do than to jaunt to Tonbridge. And he had to have bought this book with the intention of gifting it to her. What was he doing? And why?

⟩⟩⟩⟨⟨⟨

CAMELLIA READ UNTIL it was too dark to see the words on the page. Then she drifted off to sleep despite the jolting of the carriage. She woke to a flash of lightning and a deafening boom of thunder. Rain spattered against the roof and windows. She pulled back the curtains but could see nothing but a wet blur. Inside, everything was shadowy. Neville coughed.

"You're awake?" she asked.

He grunted. "I've been awake for a while."

"Major Taverston is out there." She let the curtain fall closed. "Should we signal the driver to stop?"

"Stop? Why?"

"So that the major can come into the carriage."

Neville didn't say anything, but she felt his scrutiny.

"Neville, he is being so generous, and he'll catch his death—"

"He's a soldier. He has ridden in rain before."

His uncaring tone shocked her. "We are not on campaign. He—"

"Camellia, let me tell you two things about Major Taverston. Two things you need to remember."

She couldn't make out the expression on his face, but he sounded so dour, she quieted, fidgeting uncomfortably with the blanket on her lap. "What are they?"

"First, he is married to the army. He's on half-pay now, but he'll go back. Mark my words. He is a soldier to the marrow."

She understood what "married to the army" meant. Before Neville returned to London injured, she had seen her brother just

three times in her life. She knew him only through correspondence. She'd written to him religiously, and he'd responded, but
she could have passed him on the street and not known him.

So Major Taverston was cut from the same cloth. The war
with France was over, but there was still India, Ireland, America,
the West Indies… Neville was trying to protect her.

"What is the second thing?"

"He is a rake." He shot the words like a bullet into her heart.

"A *rake*?"

"If there was a brothel within ten miles of his billet, he would
sniff it out and be first in line."

"Neville!" Her throat closed and she felt hot with shame.
"That's indecent! You shouldn't speak of—"

"You aren't a child, Camellia. And the *world* is indecent. I
don't believe in keeping ladies in ignorance. Ignorance is
dangerous." He grunted. "I am not concerned about Major
Taverston. He will behave as a gentleman toward *you*. But that
does not change the fact that he is a rake at his core."

He didn't fit Camellia's image of a rake. But then, she had
never met one before. She felt a twinge of disquiet. Or curiosity.
She couldn't tell which.

"I need my laudanum again, damn it. Camellia, give me another dose."

CHAPTER EIGHT

DUSK FADED INTO night. The rain had ceased, but clouds dimmed the moon and erased the stars. Crispin was dog-tired and drenched to the bone. With all he had to worry about, it bothered him most that he'd made such a hash of his "persuasive argument." Old Harry's sister had seen right through him. He must be slipping.

Miss Harrington had given the coachman directions, but after they went past the village of Tonbridge, Crispin grew concerned that they might be lost. Until the carriage passed through a rotting wooden gate and down a muddy lane, and finally, toward what looked to be a rundown farm. The fields to either side of the lane were weedy and untended. *Good God.* The colonel was reduced to this? A cluster of trees loomed adjacent to a small dwelling, largely obscuring it. Was that the *house*?

The place was dark, and it appeared no one was about. This had to be the Harringtons' home. There was nothing else, except a barn further down the drive and a shed of sorts.

"Dan," he called to the coachman as he brought Mercury alongside the carriage, "drive up as close as you can to the door. Bring in the bags, and then I'll come with you to settle the horses." Pray God there were stalls and room in the barn. He could also pray that a few servants would emerge to welcome them, but that would likely require a miracle.

The last several yards of the drive were cobbled, and he imagined the rattling of the carriage must be tooth-jarring. Dan halted. Crispin swung himself off Mercury and approached the nearest carriage door, facing away from the house.

"Colonel? Miss Harrington? We've arrived." He pulled open the door.

The colonel was slumped over and snoring. Miss Harrington was…mussed. She had removed her bonnet, and her chignon was coming undone, spilling thick, black tresses onto her shoulders. His eyes slid back to her face and the white locks at her forehead. She was arresting. Uncannily so. But he doubted she appreciated being stared at.

"Miss Harrington?" He offered his arms, steadying her when her knees softened as she reached the ground. Holding her by the elbows, he thought he smelled lilacs. He was almost loathe to let go.

"I'm sorry you had such an unpleasant ride," she murmured. "Had we known it would rain…"

"Rain doesn't bother me." He gestured to the carriage. "Do you think he'll wake soon? Or should I try to carry him sleeping?"

"He had some of his medicine not too long ago. If he wakes, he's not really awake. If you wait a moment, I'll fetch a lantern so we can see better."

"Yes, all right." As she walked around the carriage to her front door, Crispin motioned to Dan. "Can you start untying the bags? And the colonel's chair?" Their baggage was on top of the carriage, covered with oiled cloth. He hoped most was still dry.

"Oh!" Miss Harrington cried out. "Oh, for Heaven's sake, what did they do?"

Crispin hurried around the carriage to see what had upset her. She was standing before a ramp that led up to the door. A useless thing. It looked as though workman had simply laid a board over three or four stairs, and then nailed rough-cut boards to the sides. The angle was absurdly steep.

"This isn't what I asked for," she said, key in hand, scowling fiercely. "How am I supposed to wheel Neville up that?"

He was too tired for this. "A problem for tomorrow," he said, then swooped her up and deposited her at the top of the ramp. "The lantern?"

She ducked her head, embarrassed. But she got the key into the lock and opened the door. Dan came around the carriage, carrying all three valises. The colonel hadn't much, and Crispin made a point of traveling light. It surprised him though, that Miss Harrington traveled with so little. Dan looked at the ramp, then shook his head, bemused.

Crispin clambered up. "Hand me the bags." Dan did. Crispin tucked them just inside the open door. "Go get the chair."

Miss Harrington came up behind him, lantern light spread before her. He hopped down, took the lantern, and held her hand while she descended the ramp with tiny steps.

"This is ludicrous," she muttered.

Dan came back, rolling the chair.

"Leave it here," Crispin directed. He set the lantern atop the chair, then motioned for them both to follow him. He returned to the carriage, climbed inside, maneuvered the sleeping colonel near to the door, then slid out. It had been easier putting him in than retrieving him. Twisting awkwardly, he reached in and hoisted the man. He shifted him until he could carry him safely, glad Harrington was so deeply drugged. At the foot of the ramp, he sighed. "Stairs would have been easier."

"There are stairs at the back of the house," Miss Harrington said.

"Ah. Good." He shifted the colonel once more. Either the man was growing heavier, or he was getting weaker. "Is there room in your barn for the carriage and horses?"

Her head bowed and her shoulders drooped as if the question saddened her. "Yes. It's empty."

He cleared his throat. "Dan, take the carriage to the barn and see to the horses. I'll come down to care for Mercury. Just—"

"Oh!" Miss Harrington said. "Oh, no. I—I'm so sorry." Her

face contorted. Crispin had the horrified impression she was about to cry. Before he could ask what was wrong, she said, "There is nothing in the barn. I mean, nothing for the horses. If there is any hay, it's surely rotted."

A flame of anger kindled in his chest. He would starve, if need be, but he would not misuse a horse. How could she have agreed to this if the house had not the most basic of accommodations? He opened his mouth, then snapped it shut. *God.* Miss Harrington was not an errant infantryman to be dressed down. And none of this was her fault. He'd thrown her into a panic and then dragged her here. Taking swift control. Playing hero. It was frustration he felt, not anger. He closed his eyes to take a calming breath and think. *Tonbridge was not a wilderness.*

He opened his eyes. "There is an inn? In town?"

"Yes."

"Fine." He hoisted the colonel higher and leaned back to distribute the weight across his chest in a way that allowed him to reach for his purse, attached by a chain to the inside of his jacket. He wiggled it out and extended it toward Miss Harrington. "Give Dan a guinea." She stepped closer and took the purse, which was still attached to him. It was almost entangling, and for a moment, he was afraid he would drop the colonel. He nearly laughed at the farce this had become, but if he started laughing, he *would* drop Old Harry. "Dan, take the carriage and Mercury to the stables at the inn. See to it they are cared for. And then take a room and dinner for yourself."

"Yes, Major," Dan said, accepting the coin from Miss Harrington, blatant relief on his face.

"You may return the earl's carriage to London tomorrow. But leave Mercury in the stable. Tell the innkeeper I'll come for him in a day or two, and I'll pay any additional expenses then."

Dan nodded, then went to tie Mercury to the carriage with a lead rope.

He turned his attention to Miss Harrington. "Show me to the back stairs."

She was still holding his purse. He couldn't very well tell her to tuck it back inside his clothing. And the lewd joke his brain wanted him to make was not funny.

"Just drop it," he said. "The chain will hold."

She let go of his purse and took up the lantern. They went around to the back of the house and up the steps, his purse slapping his thigh and the colonel drooling on his shoulder. Miss Harrington unlocked the door, and they entered through the kitchen. A starkly empty kitchen. When they emerged from it, he saw a staircase down a shadowy hall. He swore under his breath, and started toward it.

"No, Major. Not upstairs. Neville's bedchamber is this way."

She led him toward a chamber that should have been a breakfast parlor. He'd thought the Iversley estate, Chaumbers, was an architectural nightmare, but this farmhouse was worse. Who put a bedchamber next to the kitchen? They passed by a receiving room, its furnishings all covered with dustcloths. The house smelled musty. *The deuce.* This was a mistake.

He followed her into the bedchamber. She set down the lantern and swiped a dustcover from the bed. Defying his expectations, the bed was ready, made up with linens, pillows, and a coverlet which she hastily turned down. Crispin deposited the colonel carefully. Then he flexed his fingers and rolled back his shoulders. *Thank God.*

Miss Harrington stepped around the room removing more dustcovers, revealing a large wardrobe for clothes, a bed table, and a chest of drawers. A door in the far wall was ajar and evidently led to a water closet, disturbingly close to the kitchen. She crooked a finger at him, and he followed her out of the room.

"I had changes made," she said, low voiced, as she pulled the door shut and moved away. "I knew Neville could not climb stairs, so I brought his bedchamber and the library down here. There is a separate chamber for a manservant. And now the dining room is upstairs. I didn't think it would see much use." She trailed off. "You must be starving. There are still some sandwiches if you'd like."

He did not eat sandwiches. Every time he tried to prove to himself that no human being was intolerant of *bread*, he proved himself wrong. But sometimes, the proof took a few days to become manifest. And he *was* starving. "Yes, let us eat."

"Oh, dash it!"

"What?" he asked, feeling a punch-drunk smile start to form. What else could possibly go wrong?

"The sandwiches are halfway to the inn. We didn't bring in the basket."

"Ah." He wanted to laugh, but Miss Harrington was clearly upset.

"I am so sorry, Major. I should have warned you the house is hardly habitable. I've been renovating it for my brother's return. I let the servants go, most all of them, after my father died, and dismissed the last two when I went to London to fetch Neville, when I found out it would be months. Mrs. Tabbit and Mrs. Clay agreed to return when I brought Neville home, but I had no opportunity to let them know we were coming. You must think me witless."

"Not at all." If she had managed all this on her own, in three or four months, he was impressed. "You had a plan, and I disrupted it.

"You didn't disrupt it. The pox did." She crossed her arms and scowled. Then she threw up her hands. "There are apples and potatoes in the cellar. But I've no butter to fry them in. Once I get a fire going, I can boil potatoes if you are willing to eat them plain with salt."

"I would give my right arm for boiled potatoes with salt."

She stared at him. Then smiled. It suited her much better than her scowl. "Liar. Major, you are the kindest man I've ever met."

"Ha! Then I don't imagine—" He halted, swallowing his words. He'd been about to say he didn't imagine she'd met many men. Which was too likely to be true. It would explain why she was unmarried. "I'd like to change into dry clothes. My valise is just inside the front door. Where should I…?"

"There is a guest chamber upstairs, to the right, at the end of the hall. I believe there are linens on the bed, but if not, I'll find you some. And there should be wood on the grate and a tinder box on the mantel."

THEY ATE APPLES and boiled potatoes by candlelight in the kitchen. No wine or ale, only water that Miss Harrington had fetched from a well. With dry clothes and his stomach filled, Crispin felt better capable of taking stock of their situation. While not ideal, it was workable. For one night. After that, he wasn't sure. He couldn't abandon them, but he also couldn't stay.

Over supper, Miss Harrington wanted to talk about the war on the peninsula. Crispin did not, until he realized how specifically her questions focused on her brother. Given their age difference and the length of the war, it must be that she barely knew Harrington. And yet, her devotion to him was clear. It was no hardship to recount stories of Colonel Harrington's bravery and strength of command, but a little trickier to steer away from examples of his arrogance and lack of concern for the common soldiers. Crispin was careful not to embellish, suspecting she was quite capable of calling him out if anything rang false.

He asked her about her life here in Tonbridge. He feared her answers would be grim from the little he'd seen. No siblings except the absent colonel. And now two parents dead. But she told a happier tale of a pampered childhood with a beloved governess, doting parents, and close ties to people in the village. He wondered if she was censoring her memories the way he was his.

It was pleasant in that half-dark kitchen. Very pleasant. He found himself growing too aware of the faint scent of lilacs whenever she moved about, rustling her dress. Too aware of the tumbling black hair she had neglected to fix. She had a marvelous full-throated laugh. And he had already noted her prettiness at their first meeting, though that was something he was trying to ignore.

Something he must ignore. She was Harrington's sister. She was a lady. She was an innocent. For these three reasons and more, she was untouchable. She would make a fine sister-in-law if he had any more brothers. That was the box his brain could shove her into. The sister-in-law box. Beautiful women who held no attraction for him at all.

Miss Harrington suddenly stood up, her mouth a surprised *O*.

"What is it?" he asked.

"I believe there is tea. It might be a bit stale." She stepped, smiling, from the table toward a wall cabinet. "And I think I left some sugar the last time I was here. No cream, I'm afraid. But the fire is still going if you would like tea."

"I would love a cup." Tea with sugar, no cream. Perfect. He hadn't had to refuse anything or make off-putting excuses for his odd eating habits.

She filled a kettle and set in on the stove. Then her head tilted, and she frowned.

"What is it?" he asked.

"Neville." She pointed at the wall. He heard it now, too. A creaking bed. A low groan. She removed the kettle from the heat and picked up a plate of supper she'd set aside. "I hope he'll eat something."

He rose and followed her from the kitchen, then into Harrington's bedchamber. The man was wide eyed and red in the face.

"Where the hell am I?"

"Home, Neville. You're home." Her voice was soothing. Hopeful.

"How?"

Miss Harrington explained, succinctly, how they'd brought

him here. She reminded him of the pox outbreak at the hospital. Harrington nodded along. She told him she'd had his bedchamber furnishings moved to the ground floor. And the library.

He looked peeved. Or pained. But he made appropriate noises of appreciation. Until Miss Harrington began pressing him to eat.

"I'm not hungry."

"Neville, you've eaten nothing all day."

"I can't eat. I'm gut sick," he growled. "I need my medicine."

Crispin kept his face neutral. He knew firsthand the laudanum-induced gut-sickness. A cure worse than the injury, worse than the disease. It had been years since he'd had to resort to it, and he was resolved never to touch it again. Still, Miss Harrington's dismayed expression spurred him to speak. "Try half a dose, Colonel. Then try to eat."

She held out the potatoes like an offering to the gods.

"Just give me the damn laudanum!"

"It's in my reticule," Miss Harrington said, dropping the plate to the bed table, then hurrying from the room.

Crispin scowled but didn't scold. Harrington was still his superior, and a major did not talk back to a colonel. If Old Harry wanted to waste away in his bed, drugged, that was his prerogative. But there was no excuse for being so rude to his sister.

"Damn it," Harrington muttered. Crispin heard a hint of remorse. *Good.*

They waited in silence until Miss Harrington returned. She gave him a spoonful of laudanum.

"Just leave the plate, Camellia. I'll eat when I can." He smacked his lips and grimaced. "Now I need a chamber pot."

Miss Harrington's face went white.

"Is there a pot?" Crispin asked.

"In the water closet," she whispered, with a gesture toward the far door. She'd foreseen this necessity, obviously, or she wouldn't have been waiting to return here until she'd hired a manservant. This was his fault. He'd been too quick to rush her out of London.

"Miss Harrington, there were no linens in the guest chamber. Why don't you go see to that and I'll tend to your brother."

She gave him a look that mixed horror with humiliation and gratitude. She opened her mouth to speak, then closed it, nodded, and sped from the room.

Crispin headed to the water closet. *The devil.* Snap decisions were his forté, but he generally based them on better information. He'd thought only "pox, house in the country, escape." He'd assumed, wrongly, that everything would be in place for the colonel's return. Of course it was clever, practical even, to have moved the colonel's living spaces to the ground floor. But no servants at all? How was that possible?

Extricating himself from this muddle was a problem for tomorrow. For now, he was a manservant. He sniffed a laugh. Not what one expected of an earl's brother. And certainly not on his list of options for what to do with the rest of his life.

CHAPTER NINE

C AMELLIA HAD INTENDED to rise early, but by the time she
awoke, the sun was high. She hurried to dress. Poor Neville
must be waiting. And she wouldn't be able to hear him if he
called. Panic made her fingers clumsy—she dropped three
hairpins while stuffing her hair under her bonnet. *Lud.* Before bed
last night, she'd caught sight of herself in the mirror and she'd
appeared slovenly. No wonder Major Taverston had looked at
her so oddly. And now he would think she was slothful as well.

She smoothed the front of her plain black bombazine dress
and stepped from her bedchamber. Across the hall, the door to
the guest room was closed. Maybe he was still asleep. There had
been no sound from the room all night.

She raced down the stairs, bracing herself for Neville's groans
or shouts. She should have slept downstairs. But...she felt a
twinge of dismay, remembering her uselessness when he'd asked
for a chamber pot. She must send a letter to Mr. Cooper at once
and beg him to come.

The ground floor was surprisingly quiet. Were both men
asleep? That would be a blessing. She tiptoed to Neville's room
and found it empty. The bed had been made up. She stared a
moment, disturbed, before turning on her heel and exiting.

Could they be in the library? She headed there, passing the
receiving room, which was as it had been, with everything draped

in white dustcloths. She pushed open the door to the library. The new shelves were in place, but Papa's books had been chaotically stacked upon them by the workmen. Neville was in his chair, pulled up close to the table. She noted that the four legs of the table had been propped up with books so that the arms of the chair would fit under it. Neville was bent over, reading, and a teacup rested near his elbow. The major had been busy.

Neville turned his head at her approach and grunted a greeting. "Morning."

"Good morning, Neville. I'm sorry to be a slugabed. Can I get you anything?"

"I'm fine." He gestured to the book on the table. "Caesar's *Commentaries on the Gallic Wars*. Wellington should write his own commentaries."

She smiled tentatively, then asked, "And where is Major Taverston?"

He looked away. After a moment, he mumbled, "In the village. Fetching his horse."

What did that mean? "Will he come back?" Her voice quavered. She had no claim on his time. And he had done so much for them already. But she wasn't ready to face this alone.

He gave her a sharp look, then set his jaw. "He might. Or might not. I told him to go to the devil."

Camellia gasped. "Why?"

"He was sticking his nose in. Arrogant blackguard thinks he know everything."

"Oh, Neville." She sighed, frustrated. She'd been on the receiving end of Neville's ill-humor. He could be lacerating. She wouldn't blame the major if he'd thrown up his hands and left. "After he's been so kind?"

"I don't want his 'kindness.'"

She understood how diminished her brother must feel. But didn't Neville see how precarious their situation was?

She was too rattled. Too annoyed. She had to step away. "I'm going to make myself a cup of tea. Would you like another?"

"No, I'm fine."

She left the room and tried to think calming thoughts. Perhaps it was not so terrible. The major's horse and that very noticeable carriage were at the Fitzhenrys' inn. It wouldn't be a full day before everyone in the village knew that she'd returned with her brother. Manfred, their neighbor, would certainly call. And Mr. Castor, the rector. She grimaced—they were the two men who had once been her suitors. She'd rather not see them, but Neville might wish to. Mrs. Tabbit and Mrs. Clay would come around looking for work. Perhaps the older women could help with Neville's more intimate care until she found a manservant. She had been too intent upon hiring someone skilled from the hospital, and had assumed any able-bodied man in the village who was not already employed would be undesirable. But beggars could not be choosers.

It was a long walk into the village, but it wasn't as if she had never done it before. And she had made the hour's long walk to the hospital several times a week if not daily, so she was certainly conditioned to a long trek. In fact, the walk on their country lanes would be far more pleasant. And pleasant smelling. They would be fine without the major.

In the kitchen, to her mixed relief and dismay, she found the woodbin filled and two full buckets of well water. *Was there anything he hadn't thought of?* She rekindled the stove and set the kettle upon it. As she stood there, trying to mentally prioritize the day's tasks, she heard the clopping of hooves and rattling wheels. She threw open the back door to see Major Taverston driving a cart into the yard. Her heart made a little leap. He hadn't abandoned them. Moreover, Mrs. Clay sat in the cart's bed, surrounded by crates. Major Taverston's horse was tied behind.

Camellia ran outside. "Major! What is all this?" She quickly added, "Good day, Mrs. Clay."

"Miss Harrington." Mrs. Clay bobbed her gray-haired head and rocked forward. "I'm so glad you're home. For good this time? The major here says your brother is with you?" She didn't wait for an answer. "Mrs. Tabbit has taken another position, but I can cook and keep house too. My rabbit stew is better than hers. I brought some for tonight. I've always said—"

"Miss Harrington," the major said, cutting across her, "I took the liberty of locating your housekeeper and a few supplies. Mrs. Clay was very helpful, telling me what you might need."

The bed of the cart was lined with hay. She supposed the crates contained foodstuff. Had he put it all on her account? It made her uneasy to think so. But they couldn't live on potatoes and apples.

He hopped down from his seat and helped the plump, short-legged Mrs. Clay to descend. "I'll put these crates in the kitchen, then go settle Mercury and Trotty in the barn. Mr. Fitzhenry was kind enough to allow me to hire his rig."

Camellia finally found her voice. "Major, this is too much. We are taking advantage of your good nature."

"Not at all." He gave her a rueful grin. "I was careless, bringing you here with no provisions. If I were a quartermaster, I would be court-martialed for making no advance inquiries."

Arguing with a man who smiled so readily served no purpose. "Well, then, we are grateful. Even if Neville is too pigheaded to say so. I'm sorry he was rude to you."

Major Taverston laughed. "I've been sent to Lucifer so often, he is tired of seeing me." He hoisted a crate from the cart. "Lead the way, ladies."

CAMELLIA HELPED MRS. Clay unpack the crates while listening to the woman's praise for "the fine gentleman." He'd told her to purchase whatever she needed to prepare whatever the Harringtons preferred. They went to several different shops and he "just opened his purse." The woman was clearly awed by such liberality.

Camellia was embarrassed by it.

"I asked the major what *he'd* like, and he said rice and peas. Can you imagine?" Mrs. Clay laughed. "He said he couldn't get decent rice and peas on the peninsula, and he'd be happy to eat nothing else for a week!"

Camellia returned a wan smile. Did that mean he intended to stay a week? While thinking of a response, she heard a *thwacking* sound coming from outside.

"Excuse me, Mrs. Clay."

She went to the front and opened the door. The major was there, hatless, jacketless, shirtsleeves rolled up to expose muscled forearms, swinging an ax at the ramp. She couldn't help admiring the way he moved his body. All raw strength and grace. Her mouth dried as she watched him pause to yank away a loosened board. What had Marianne said about men with strong hands?

He tossed the board aside, then glanced over at her and grinned. "I decided to liberate your steps."

She smiled back, glad he could not read her mind. "I'd hoped to be able to take Neville outside, but that ramp was more hindrance than help."

"A ramp down the back steps would be better. The dirt in the yard is packed firm and it would be easier to roll that chair. Is there any place in particular on the grounds that he'd like to go?"

"I don't honestly know. He has spent so little time here." Her preparations seemed haphazard now. Naïve. "But there is a fishpond. And a flower garden." She'd hired a mason to lay a brick walkway to the garden, but the garden itself was a disappointment. She'd planted it, then had to abandon it. "This all must seem so foolish. He is no better off than he was in London."

"That isn't true. Home does not cease to be home just because one is absent from it."

"But there he at least had Mr. Cooper."

He shook his head and frowned. "I don't know about your Mr. Cooper, but I'd trust Adam Diakos more than anyone else."

"You know Mr. Diakos?"

After a pause, he said, "I've met him, yes. Miss Harrington, if you'll permit me, I'll write to inquire about Mr. Cooper. And if Mr. Cooper is not available, perhaps Mr. Diakos would be interested in the position."

"Neville does not like Mr. Diakos."

"Yes, I know." The major snickered. "But he doesn't like me very much either. I told him he should reduce his reliance on laudanum."

She gaped. Neville's doctor had said to give him what he needed. He said Neville would be the best judge of his own pain. No wonder Neville called the major arrogant. What could he know of laudanum?

"Perhaps you should ask my brother's permission rather than mine."

He regarded her a moment, then said, "I wanted to be certain *you* would not mind."

The words startled her. It had been a long time since anyone had taken her wishes into account. But perhaps his kind manner was meant to obscure the fact that he wanted her to secure a manservant for Neville quickly. She should assure him he need not stay until they did. Instead, she cleared her throat and said, "Of course I don't mind. And I'll make inquiries in the village. The sooner we can find someone for Neville the better."

CAMELLIA REMOVED THE dustcloths in the receiving room and set the table while Mrs. Clay cooked and Major Taverston sat with Neville in the library. The receiving room was another embarrassment. She'd told the laborers working on the house they could store furniture there until she had a better idea of what should go where. It now held a hodgepodge of chairs and tables, as well as the pianoforte that had been in the music room that was now the library. Since the dining room furniture had been moved upstairs, they crowded around a card table to eat.

To Camellia's surprise, Major Taverston *did* eat only rice and peas. He refused fresh-baked bread and Mrs. Clay's rabbit stew. He said no to wine and drank only tea. Like Camellia, he took no milk in his tea, and when Mrs. Clay brought out a tray of cheese to finish the meal, he refused it, but with an oddly wistful expression. That much, she thought she understood.

Camellia took a small piece. "You don't like cheese, Major?"

"No." His face hardened.

"I didn't either. Most of it makes me feel ill. But Mrs. Faraday, whose farm is on the other side of Tonbridge, makes this from goats' milk and it doesn't bother me. And it's quite delicious."

He gave her an unsettlingly dark look. But then he shrugged and took some, an even smaller piece than hers.

Mrs. Clay came back to clear the table. It was early in what threatened to be a long evening. Camellia wished she could escape to her own chamber to read her novel. Instead, she pushed her brother's chair to a spot a few feet away, facing the pianoforte.

"Do you play?" Neville asked.

She nodded. "A little." Their father had hired a teacher for her when she was young. She had no particular talent for it, but she could accompany herself while she sang. Of course, Neville wouldn't know any of this. He didn't know her any better than she knew him. "I sing more competently than I play."

"Sing for us then, if you would." Neville's voice was rough, and he looked tired. Pained. Usually, he was demanding his medicine by now if he hadn't taken it already, and then he would have fallen asleep before supper. Major Taverston was probably right. He took too much.

She went to the pianoforte and lifted the lid. She sat down and played the opening to *Mary Went Walking*, but she heard Major Taverston make a noise, and when she looked over her shoulder, she swore he was wincing. She stopped. "Do I play that badly, Major?"

"What? No. No, your playing is fine, but that instrument is out of tune." He hastened to add, "Not terribly so."

"Is it?" She sighed. So much for that. "It hasn't been tuned since before Papa died." She didn't know when she would be able to have a man come see to it. Probably never. She closed the lid.

"I beg your pardon." He looked abashed. "That was rude of me."

"Yes, it was," she said, then laughed to set him at ease. "Can you hum, Major? Or whistle? On key?"

With a bit of a smirk, he answered, "Both."

"Do you know *Brown-eyed Susan*?"

He whistled the opening bars. Then hummed them.

"Very good. For penance, you must accompany me by humming."

He cleared his throat, a half-smile on his face, then began. She chimed in singing. After humming the first verse, he joined her in singing the second. He could do anything, it seemed, and make it appear effortless. He had a marvelous baritone that complement-ed what her music teacher had called "an unusually deep voice for a woman."

Neville clapped when they finished, but without enthusiasm, and his face was a sickly pale.

Beaming, Major Taverston exclaimed, "Miss Harrington, that was superb. Should we try another?"

She pointed to Neville. "I don't think..."

He groaned. "I cannot do it. This is torture. I need my medi-cine."

Major Taverston jumped up. "Yes, of course." He grasped the handles of Neville's chair, then turned to her. "Miss Harrington, we will bid you goodnight. I hope you don't mind, but I've moved my things down to the spare chamber next to the colonel's."

He could do anything. And he thought of everything. It was going to be difficult to make do without him.

CHAPTER TEN

CRISPIN HAD BEEN two weeks at the Harringtons' and was in no hurry to leave, even though it was halfway through July, and Wellington was expecting an answer about Paris by mid-August. Rationally, he knew he was no less adrift than he had been in London. Perhaps he was more so, seeing as he was postponing decision making by masquerading as a manservant. He told himself he was practicing being a civilian, to see if he was suited for it. However, knowing the ease with which he lied, he obviously could not believe himself.

More likely it was inertia tying him to the Harringtons. His self-assigned duties were not taxing. He got the colonel dressed in the morning and prepared for bed at night. He took him to the water closet when needed. And he spent a couple hours each day keeping the man company so that Miss Harrington could have some time for herself. He'd noticed she would often escape to her flower garden and return with dirt on her hands, smiling. Serene. He admired that. Misfortune had not embittered her.

As he understood it, she had taken care of her mother, then her father, for five years or so. And then, her brother had come home like this. She must know Old Harry's condition would never improve. No wonder she wore nothing but black. Which was unfortunate—she would be stunning in red.

Although he felt he was being useful, Crispin had no desire to be one of those annoying houseguests who was always underfoot, requiring entertaining. He took himself off riding almost every morning, exercising Mercury and exploring the environs. He'd been into the village of Tonbridge on errands and had also wandered into three of the neighboring towns to see what was there. Two days earlier, in Wheatfield, he'd stopped at a tavern for a cup of cider. The red-headed barmaid who'd brought it to him pressed her hip against his shoulder and said, "There's rooms in the back." He considered it. It had been a long while since Lizzie. Nevertheless, he'd told her *next time*. Hopefully, his disinterest was not a harbinger of returning ill-health. He had succumbed, twice, to the temptation of bread rolls at supper before summoning up enough will and fear to resist.

He was now on his way back from Tonbridge village. *Again.* He drove the cart pulled by Trotty, bringing whatever had been on the list Mrs. Clay had given him to take to the grocer. He'd ignored Miss Harrington's crass instruction to put it on her brother's account. If she was trying to hide the fact that she and the colonel were in damned low water, she was failing.

In addition to foodstuff, he'd purchased a bit of lumber to try his hand at building a ramp over the back stairs. He was no carpenter, but he didn't think it would be difficult. And he knew Miss Harrington wanted to be able to take her brother out to her garden.

While in the village, he had also stopped at the post. There was no response yet from either Mr. Cooper or Adam. He did have a letter from Jasper, a reply to his own note thanking him for the use of his carriage and informing him he would be the guest of Colonel Harrington for a while. He gave no details. Jasper was likewise brief. Olivia and Benjamin were back at Chaumbers. Reg and Georgiana had returned to Cambridge and Mother had gone with them. Vanessa suspected Georgiana was with child again. *That was news!* They would likely all reunite at Chaumbers next month when London's heat became unbearable. They wanted Crispin there.

Surely he would have taken charge of his life by then. But it was so much easier taking charge of the colonel's.

⊱※⊰

THE HARRINGTONS HAD a guest. A guest besides Crispin. When he'd entered the house, Mrs. Clay sent him into the receiving room to greet the man.

"Ah, Major Taverston," Harrington said, "this is my neighbor, Sir Manfred Bodwell."

Bodwell rose slowly. He looked elderly the way Harrington did. A man old before his time. He was of medium height, but stooped. His hands had a very noticeable tremor.

"I'm pleased to make your acquaintance, Major. I understand you helped Camellia bring Neville home."

Camellia and Neville? So Sir Bodwell was a *close* friend. And he wanted Crispin to know this.

"Yes, I did." He offered nothing more. Harrington could tell it however he wanted.

Bodwell sat down again. Crispin followed suit.

"We grew up together," Harrington said. "Neighbors. Eton. Oxford."

Bodwell nodded. "But not the army. I haven't seen Neville in years. It's good to have him home. Isn't it, Camellia?"

Crispin watched her nod. Her expression was guarded.

"And good to have you back as well, Camellia." Bodwell cast his glance around, then settled it upon Crispin. "She didn't like London."

Crispin faced her. Why was she letting the man put words in her mouth? "Didn't you?"

"I didn't see much of it beyond the hospital."

He raised an eyebrow. Her eyes widened and she went a bit pale. She would be remembering that he had seen her at the Temple of the Muses. Unchaperoned. Something she must not want them to know. "That is too bad. London has a great deal to offer." Now, she owed him for his silence. Or would if he kept track of such things.

Harrington changed the subject, likely returning to the conversation they'd been having before Crispin arrived. Old friends. Old memories. Crispin was soon bored. From time to time, Bodwell tried drawing Miss Harrington in, talking of more recent events in Tonbridge, memories that they shared that Harrington did not. And that Crispin did not.

Aside from a mild territorialism, and a strange flatness of countenance, Bodwell was perfectly pleasant. Crispin would have been disposed to like him, except that Miss Harrington seemed uncomfortable. Not frightened. The man was not overbearing or aggressive. But she was uncomfortable. He continued watching their interactions until the answer came to him: Bodwell had been a suitor. Clearly an unsuccessful one. Possibly a persistent one.

It amused Crispin to think that Bodwell might be wondering if he should be jealous. Of *him*.

Mrs. Clay finally reappeared to announce that supper was ready. Miss Harrington extended the obligatory invitation to Bodwell, but he excused himself graciously. When he left, Miss Harrington visibly relaxed. Harrington let out a long sigh.

"A good fellow, Manfred." He turned to Crispin. "A widower. No children, unfortunately. His property is entailed." He waved a hand. "You know how that goes. A vulgar cousin will inherit."

"A shame," Crispin said. He didn't let his gaze go to Miss Harrington. The whole plot of this piece was too obvious. Lady needs security, man needs heir. Still, he hoped she would continue to refuse Sir Bodwell. He might be a good fellow, but Miss Harrington deserved a husband, not another sick man to nurse.

They took their accustomed seats at the small table. Mrs. Clay brought out a tray and served them each a plate of whitefish. The colonel's was covered with a cream sauce. Miss Harrington's and Crispin's were plain. He could tell she was watching him and trying to pretend she wasn't. He'd refused a number of dishes over the fortnight, and although no one said anything, he was aware of their curiosity—Miss Harrington and Mrs. Clay's; the colonel did not care. Crispin cut off a piece of fish and ate it. Miss Harrington's expression turned from sly to triumphant, as if she had solved a particularly difficult puzzle. *Not yet, she hadn't.* He was still trying to solve it himself. Normally, scrutiny of his diet annoyed him, but…he took another bite and gave her a wink. It pleased him enormously when she laughed.

CRISPIN SPENT TWO days building the ramp. Measuring the sideboards was trickier than he expected. He wished he'd had Georgiana with him, or Reg, to do the geometrical calculations. They were both mathematically gifted. But with trial and error, it turned out well, sturdy with a gentle slope.

It was a fine afternoon, not too hot, so he and Miss Harrington took Old Harry outside, down a brick path to the garden. Miss Harrington's time spent tending it had been to good purpose. It was beautiful and fragrant. They passed the afternoon in the shade of an elm, enjoying the setting. Miss Harrington read aloud from the book he'd given her. She read expressively—she would make a fine actress. The colonel fell asleep, but when she would have put the book down, Crispin begged her to go on.

"You like novels?" she teased.

"I like this one." He did, but more so, he enjoyed the company. They laughed at the same scenes, and groaned indignantly together at other ones.

When her voice began to grow hoarse, he took the book from her and read one more chapter before the colonel woke, grumbling, breaking the spell. It was nearly suppertime, so they went back inside, with Crispin pushing the chair up the ramp. He made no comment on the poor quality of the wheels. He'd learned his lesson pointing out that the pianoforte needed tuning.

Supper that night looked like a meat pie. He refused his portion, and took only potatoes and beans. Miss Harrington pursed her lips, miffed.

"It is hake, not beef."

He repeated, "No, thank you."

"Oh, for Heaven's sake," she muttered. "Wrong again. No, don't tell me."

It wasn't a game, but it was beginning to feel like one. He found himself grinning. His misfortune diverted her, and here he was, amused as well. He could imagine what his family would make of that. But his justification was that Miss Harrington could use some entertainment, and he was happy to provide it, even at his own expense.

Besides, she might have an inkling of what he went through. He'd noticed that she also shunned any food or drink produced by a cow.

They finished supper, then moved away from the table. Crispin pushed Harrington's chair near to the couch where Miss Harrington preferred to sit. He remained standing, waiting. Harrington's moods dictated how their evenings would go. Sometimes he took the man straight from supper off to bed. However, tonight Old Harry seemed alert and not particularly bothered by pain. Perhaps Miss Harrington could be persuaded to sing again. He'd gladly whistle.

"Camellia," Harrington said, brow creased with curiosity, "do you still write poetry?"

Miss Harrington blushed. She shook her head. "Not seriously."

Ah, a bad poet. A true kindred spirit.

With a chuckle, the colonel turned to Crispin. "She used to send me charming poems. But not in a long while. I kept them until…well, they were lost somewhere after Vitoria."

"A shame," Crispin said. He shot a teasing smile at Miss Harrington. "I would have liked to read them." Then he added, "Perhaps you kept copies?"

"Do you? Write poetry?" she asked, turning the tables. "I know you like to read it."

"Bad poetry. I write bad poetry."

"Good." The sly expression he was learning to recognize appeared on her face as she focused her attention back on her brother. "Our father did, too. Did you know?"

"Oh, yes. I remember."

"Did he ever play 'poetry challenge' with you?"

"No. What is that?"

Now Miss Harrington laughed. "We would each pick a poem to read aloud. And then we had half an hour to write something in the same vein. The same as each other's choice, not our own." Her smile grew wistful. "Papa was very clever."

"I imagine you were also."

"Not as clever as Papa."

Harrington looked pensive. Crispin felt sorry for him. He must have been hospitalized on the peninsula when he got word of his father's death. When his own father had died, Crispin was privileged to be at his bedside, with the family gathered around.

Then Harrington said, "Major, I'd like to hear your 'bad poetry.' I suspect it is actually quite good. Why don't you and Camellia play this challenge? I'll be the judge."

This was the most engaged the man had been since arriving home. And Miss Harrington was smiling brightly, transforming her arrestingly pretty features to arrestingly beautiful. Crispin chewed his lip with exaggerated hesitation, then said, "Very well. I accept the challenge. Miss Harrington?"

She pointed to the wall clock. "We give each other ten minutes to choose a poem. There are a few volumes in the library if you need one."

"Need one!" Crispin gasped as though offended. He put a hand to his heart. "I carry my favorites here."

Miss Harrington laughed. "I'm ready as well. Just a moment."

She moved to a desk that had been pushed against the back wall and opened a drawer, then returned with foolscap and pencils. "Now we are ready. Marianne shared a poem with me. She said her friend copied it from her sister-in-law's letter. The author is very probably the same lady who wrote *Sense and Sensibility*."

"Then it must be delightful."

"It is." She recited, "Happy the lab'rer in his Sunday clothes!—In light-drab coat, smart waistcoat, well-darn'd hose—And hat upon his head, to church he goes—As oft, with conscious pride, he downward throws—A glance upon the ample cabbage rose—That, stuck in button-hole, regales his nose.—He envies not the gayest London beaux.—In church he takes his seat among the rows—Pays to the place the reverence he owes—Likes best the prayers whose meaning least he knows—Lists to the sermon in a softening doze—And rouses joyous at the welcome close."

Crispin burst into laughter. After a startled moment, both Harringtons laughed along. "I've been in that laborer's shoes." He tried clearing his throat. "So the challenge is to compose a poem where all the lines rhyme with rose?"

"Yes. Or you may pick another word. Something easy to rhyme."

He nodded.

"And now you must give me one," she said.

Unfortunately, his boast might be his undoing. Although he knew many poems by heart, his mind had gone blank, except for one filthy limerick he would not recite, and a poem by Donne that he probably should not recite, for all he found it amusing. "Give me a moment."

Harrington said, "Come now, Major. No waffling."

Donne it was then. "Well, all right. Here is it. *A Woman's Constancy.*"

Miss Harrington rolled her eyes.

"You know it?" he asked.

"Yes. Go on."

He took a breath. "Now thou hast loved me one whole

day,—Tomorrow when thou leav'st, what wilt thou say?—Wilt thou then antedate some new made vow?—Or say that now—We are not just those persons which we were?—Or, that oaths made in reverential fear—Of love, and his wrath, any may forswear?—Or, as true deaths, true marriages untie,—So lovers' contracts, images of those,—Bind but till sleep, death's image, them unloose?—Or, your own end to justify,—For having purposed change, and falsehood, you—Can have no way but falsehood to be true?—Vain lunatic, against these 'scapes I could,—Dispute and conquer, if I would,—Which I abstain to do,—For by tomorrow, I may think so too."

Harrington sniffed. "I say, Major, that's rather rude."

"It's John Donne," Miss Harrington said. "His love poetry is generally rude." She handed Crispin a few pieces of paper and a pencil, then pointed at the clock. "Thirty minutes."

"You are out of time," Harrington announced. "What do you have?"

Crispin winced. He'd forgotten how truly bad he was at writing poetry. Jasper used to taunt him about it. He knew this was a game. And he'd warned them he was bad at it. But this was embarrassing.

"Go on, Major Taverston," Miss Harrington urged. "You may go first."

"Fine." He tried not to grit his teeth. *"Happy the poet who dost compose,—With the same ease with which a river flows,—Who never resorts to overblown prose,—But turns out couplets like well-aimed arrows—"*

"Couplets like arrows?" Harrington's head fell back, and he roared. Laughter was good medicine. He looked less like a slowly dying man and more like a man with something to live for.

Miss Harrington pressed her lips tight, appearing desperate not to guffaw.

Crispin circled his hand in the air. "It goes on like that."

Miss Harrington snorted. "Maybe you should have used 'dear.'"

"It wouldn't have been any better." He tried to look sorrowful, but ended up laughing along. "I concede. Just don't make me read the rest."

When he'd caught his breath, Harrington said, "Let us hear yours, Camellia."

She picked up her paper and read, *"Now I have loved you one whole day,—Or at least, vain lunatic, that is what you say,—For love is not love to you unless—It is something spontaneous, which we confess—At a weak moment, never felt until the words are said,—A newborn emotion, in languor bred.—In that respect, it's true, I did just say—I love you, therefore, I've loved you one whole day.—If you were not so dull, I'd try to make it clear—A woman's love does not just appear.—It is not generated in her lover's arms at night—To fade forgotten or denied in the morning light.—If you knew how devotedly I've loved, and how long—You'd see how silly you appear, and how wrong.—All the excuses you've provided for a love well ended—Are your defense, my constancy need not be defended.—No better proof of devotion could there be—Than loving you till you loved me.—Your spontaneous, painless love for me was earned—By my longing love, so long unreturned.—And tomorrow...who can know—Whether your love will waste away, or grow?—My love, full-grown, has nowhere else to go.—Tomorrow, when I leave, and you ask why,—I'll say, having reached its end, my love could not help but die."*

Silence fell. Crispin knew he should say something, but his chest felt knotted and his throat too tight to speak. Was there truth in her poem? Had she loved someone that much? A love that could not be sustained? Why should that make *his* chest hurt?

Harrington coughed. "Well, we have an obvious winner."

Miss Harrington bobbed theatrically clumsy curtsies. An act. As though the poem meant nothing more than a quickly imagined response to Donne's incivility. But Crispin wanted...he wanted to know *more*.

While he was struggling to find the right words to congratulate her, he grew aware of a noise. A knocking. The Harringtons did, too. They watched Mrs. Clay emerge from the kitchen to go to the front door.

A minute later, she came to them, the visitor trailing behind, looking footsore and weary.

Crispin said, "Adam!" at the same time Miss Harrington said, "Mr. Diakos!"

He bowed. "Pardon me for intruding. I've come at Major Taverston's request." He turned to Crispin as if awaiting permission to say more. But before Crispin acknowledged that he had written to him, Adam said, "I regret to inform you Mr. Cooper succumbed to the pox."

Miss Harrington gasped. Crispin merely swallowed hard. More death.

Adam faced the colonel. "If you are still in need of an attendant, I believe Major Taverston will vouch for me." It impressed Crispin that Adam could say that last without irony.

Harrington grunted. Then he rolled his shoulders in either defeat or apology. "I do need someone. Major Taverston has given us too much of his time."

And now, Crispin thought, he was being summarily dismissed.

But that was a good thing. He glanced sidelong at Miss Harrington. *It was.*

CHAPTER ELEVEN

To Camellia's disappointment, Major Taverston took advantage of Mr. Diakos's appearance and fled the following morning. He barely made his goodbyes before he was out the door.

Without question, Mr. Diakos proved to be a better manservant. After all, he *was* a servant. Neville ordered him about as a matter of course. It must have been uncomfortable for her brother to be tended to by a fellow officer, one who was his social superior, and a friend. It must have been difficult for the major as well.

In contrast, Mr. Diakos's care was impersonal and more thorough. In addition to daily necessities, he cut Neville's hair, trimmed his beard, bathed him, and massaged his limbs. He even had Neville doing exercises. Neville swore at him regularly, but Mr. Diakos was uncowed. He was likely accustomed to being sworn at by invalided men.

However, there were disadvantages. Camellia had even less time for herself. Mr. Diakos did not join them for tea or meals. He ate with Mrs. Clay in the kitchen. He did not play cards with Neville or discuss Caesar's commentaries in the afternoons. And he did not sit with them in the evenings. Camellia and her brother were alone. She had wished for so long to know him better, but Neville didn't like to speak of the war, not to her, and recalling his youth here in Tonbridge seemed to sadden him. This meant Camellia was obliged to carry the conversation, and do so in a light-hearted fashion. She could hardly unburden her soul to him. Also, she didn't know what interested Neville, so she often felt she was babbling, and he was not listening.

Moreover, she missed Major Taverston. She missed his thoughtfulness and the way he found humor in so many things. He had a way about him that made her think if she were to fall, he would catch her. *Catch her then set her on her feet and move on.*

He had been gone only a week when Manfred returned. Camellia appreciated that he spent the afternoon with Neville, but was less glad when he accepted an invitation to supper. It appeared to her he claimed a greater friendship with Neville than their long-ago acquaintance warranted. His interest in renewing that friendship made her nervous. Since his wife's passing, Manfred had asked her three times to marry him; the last proposal occurred shortly after Papa's death. When she'd said no, he'd promised not to ask her a fourth time. Still, the question was always there, just beneath the surface. He didn't seem to accept that she had no interest in becoming Lady Bodwell. No desire to jump from taking care of a brother to taking care of an ailing husband.

"Neville tells me your guest has gone to see his family in the country," Manfred said. His hand shook, but that didn't prevent him from picking up his fork and spearing a piece of chicken. "And that he is likely bound for India before long."

"India?" She looked to Neville.

He shook his head. "Conjecture. He is too valuable to go to the West Indies. It is a graveyard for Englishmen. And he would find it distasteful to police Ireland. He's a young man with important connections. India makes the most sense. Come up through the ranks—and he could well be the next Wellington."

"Wellington would not be Wellington without Napoleon," Manfred said.

Neville sniffed, but did not disagree. The men fell into a discussion of the French Emperor, now Emperor of Elba. Camellia let her thoughts drift away. *India?* She would never see Major Taverston again if he went to India. But, of course, she was unlikely to see him again even if he did not. The realization was sobering but she didn't want to dwell on it.

When supper ended, they moved to the other side of the receiving room, which had felt cold and empty ever since the major's departure.

"Will you play for us?" Manfred asked, indicating the pianoforte.

"I'm sorry, I cannot. It needs tuning."

"Does it?" He dipped his head and frowned sympathetically. Then *hmmmed.* Then turned to Neville. "A round of whist?"

They played for a little over an hour before Neville laid down his cards and said he needed to retire. Camellia pulled the bell cord for Mr. Diakos. Slowly, Manfred rose to take his leave.

"Should we make this a regular party?" he asked. "Cards once a week? Saturday evenings?"

"Supper and cards," Neville said, nodding with satisfaction. "I'm sure Camellia would be pleased to see another face besides mine."

Manfred looked to her, waiting.

Resigned, she said, "Supper and cards would be nice." Nice for them.

IT WAS AUGUST the twenty-seventh. Another card party Saturday. It was also Camellia's twenty-sixth birthday. Neville would not remember, and she had no wish to draw attention to the date. She was now, undeniably, a spinster.

As she dressed for dinner, donning her best black silk dress, she noticed the cuffs were beginning to fray. She'd worn all her mourning gowns too many times. She was going to have to replace the sleeves to keep up appearances.

Before going downstairs, she stepped close to the mirror. She couldn't recall the last time she'd taken more than a quick glimpse at herself, because she never liked what she saw. As a child, she'd always thought that if she prayed hard enough, her tuft of white hair would miraculously turn black, and she would no longer be teased by other children and stared at by adults. But her forelock remained stubbornly white. She remembered, very clearly, her twelfth birthday, when she'd dashed her mirror to the floor, shattering it. She remembered, too, her mother's words: "God gave us eyes to look out at the world. Not to gaze upon ourselves." Words to live by. Nevertheless, Mama replaced the mirror. Camellia smiled sadly. Prone to mixed messages, her mother was. She had also told Camellia she was beautiful. And that *inner* beauty was all that mattered.

Camellia wondered, if she *had* had a London debut, would she have resorted to dye? She liked to think she would not have. She studied her reflection for the first time in a long time. Her lips were too plump. Her eyes too narrow. But she had an acceptable nose and firm chin. Her complexion? She leaned closer, examining her skin, looking for crow's feet or lines about her mouth. No, thank goodness, not yet. But her face was irrelevant when people's eyes went automatically to her hair.

She stepped away from the mirror. Enough of this. *Time to gaze out at the world.*

As she descended the stairs, she heard voices. Manfred. With Neville. And a third man. She heard the plink of a pianoforte key. Upon entering the receiving room, she saw a stranger standing near the instrument. A large black case lay open on the floor, filled with unidentifiable tools.

"Ah," Manfred said, smiling a little uncertainly. "I've brought you a present. Mr. White has come from London to tune your pianoforte."

Neville said, "Isn't that fine? I'd forgotten it was your birthday. You are how old? Twenty-three?"

"Twenty-six," she said faintly. She faced Manfred. "This is really too kind." It was inappropriate. Neville should have told him so.

"You used to sing for your father, I recall. Perhaps you will sing for us?"

"Yes, of course." All at once, she thought of Major Taverston's humming. A tuned pianoforte was a poor substitute for his laughter. "I'd be delighted," she lied.

SHE COULD NOT have turned away a pianoforte tuner who had come all the way from London. Nor, she found, could she send Manfred away when he appeared three days later, to ask her if she'd like to go for a carriage ride. Having accepted the gift, she had to grant him her company.

The carriage was small and plain, the wooden body chipped at the corners. It was wrong to ride in a closed carriage alone with a man, but they weren't in London, parading in Hyde Park. No one would know. The driver opened the door and let down steps. Manfred held her hand while she climbed them. Then the driver helped Manfred. After another few moments, they were speeding along. Manfred spoke pleasantly of people they knew in Tonbridge. Gossiping, she thought wryly. Yet it was good to hear news. She hadn't spoken with anyone in the village for quite a while. Papa's funeral had been well attended, and in the following weeks, she'd had several callers, but she had been in such a fog of grief, she didn't remember details. After a while, people had stopped visiting. She'd seen no one but Mrs. Clay and Mrs. Tabbit for months. And Manfred. She winced inwardly. He'd called many times.

Manfred needed an heir. She knew that. He needed a son to keep his property from going to another branch of the family. What she didn't understand was why that mattered so much to him when he'd be dead when it happened.

She had to acknowledge to herself that he was not a bad-looking man. Just old. His features were ordinary. He would not stand out in a crowd. His hair was salted with gray. His skin was a little coarse and sallow, but not marred in any way. Of course, she was comparing him to Major Taverston, which was unfair. The major was near to her own age, blue eyed, strikingly handsome, and in robust good health. Or, looked to be in good health. She could not account for his curious dietary preferences.

As they passed by one of Neville's fields that had not been tended in a long while, Manfred pointed out the window and said, "Neville has said I might send a few of my men to mow the hay."

"You're welcome to it. We have no use for hay." Not anymore. Her father had once bred Yorkshire Trotters, only a foal or two a year—but that was eons ago. He'd sent the last horse to auction just before Mama died.

"I could have my agent sell it for you."

Prickling warmth crept up her neck. She wanted to refuse his interference, but that would be foolish. "That is up to my brother, naturally."

"Camellia." He sighed. "Neville is a soldier, not a gentleman-farmer. Your property is falling to ruin. You must see that."

She kept her expression bland, refusing to acknowledge the truth in what he said. Unfortunately, the property was Neville's, not hers, and there was no creature more impotent than a half-sister under the guardianship of an absent soldier. She'd had no authority to do anything without proof of Neville's approval. After he'd been sent back to London, in order for her to even hire laborers for the house renovations, she'd had to slip the necessary papers under his nose while he was half-asleep and would ask no questions as he signed.

She'd thought he would take more interest in the farm once he saw the state of it. But Manfred was right. Neville was oblivious.

Manfred said, "I have much to offer you. You and Neville. If you would but consider—"

She shook her head. "You promised not to ask again."

"That was before I spent two months in London looking for a wife. None of the ladies appealed to me the way you do."

He was middle-aged and ailing. Did he imagine he appealed to them? To her? She suspected he thought she was now desperate enough, at twenty-six, to say yes. But she refused to marry out of desperation.

"Please stop," she said. "I don't wish to be unkind, but I've told you I don't wish to marry. I have my brother to care for—"

"The Greek is taking care of him. And you would be less than a mile away if he needed you."

"My answer is no, Manfred. Please respect that."

He looked away. "I won't ask again." He said it as though it were a threat, not a promise, and not one he'd made before.

"Thank you." She drew a shaky breath. "Please take me home."

❯❯❯❯❮❮❮❮

SHE COULD NOT fault Manfred. Over the next few days, he behaved very well for a man whose suit had been rejected four times. He still sent men to mow the field and cart off the hay. Then he gave a ham and two chickens to Mrs. Clay, and promised to send a joint of beef in two weeks as payment, which he'd been under no obligation to do. He arrived on Saturday for supper and cards as usual, and although he was stiff and formal toward her, he remained friendly to Neville.

Nothing had changed. Nothing would ever change.

Another of Mama's bits of wisdom was that it served no purpose to mope. Sorrow was unavoidable. It would come and go, and one must bear it. But moping? That was a choice. A wrong choice. Camellia knew that, compared to many women, hers was not a bad life. Only she wished she'd *experienced* more of it. She wanted to go to the theater. She wanted to meet a poet. She wanted to dance at a ball. Marianne was right. She should have made time for herself when in London.

Yet London would not have answered for all. Just once, she wanted to be kissed. She wanted to know how it felt to be held in a man's arms. But not Manfred's. She didn't want to be trapped for the rest of her life with a man she didn't love.

THE HARRINGTONS WERE not as isolated as Camellia had worried they would be. Mrs. Clay and Mr. Diakos made trips into Tonbridge. Deliveries came to the farm from the grocer, butcher, and fishmonger. An advantage to all the coming and going, and whatever tales Mrs. Clay was telling in Tonbridge, was that people in the village and neighboring towns took notice that Neville was home. Acquaintances of Camellia's and old friends of her mother and father came calling. Occasionally someone would bring along a single young lady eager to meet a war hero. These last were so obviously disappointed by Neville it made Camellia's heart hurt.

Still in all, it raised her spirits to have more variety to her day. One afternoon, a woman who had known Neville in his youth, Mrs. Blackwell, came with her granddaughter from nearby Wheatfield. The granddaughter was plain and bit of a sourpuss, fidgeting and even yawning while Neville and Mrs. Blackwell reminisced. But she wore a pink-and-blue dress that was so pretty, Camellia could not take her eyes from it.

Even Neville noticed the dress. When the women left, he turned to Camellia and said, "Camellia, must you always wear black? Our father has been dead for over a year. It's morbid. I feel like you are sitting vigil over me."

"Neville! What a thing to say!"

"You're young. You should wear something with color. If you don't have anything, there must be a dressmaker in the village."

"The expense—"

"We aren't paupers. Buy yourself a decent dress."

Camellia folded her hands in her lap. Not paupers. But closer than Neville realized. "Perhaps I will go into the village the next time Mrs. Clay goes."

She rose and took her brother into the library, retrieved the book he wanted from the shelves, then excused herself. She went up to her bedchamber, opened her trunk, and examined clothes that she had not worn in years.

What if she had thrown off mourning in London? What if Major Taverston had seen her in pretty, bright dresses instead of her crow costumes?

Silly speculation. In London, he would have been surrounded by beautiful debutantes. A spinster in a dated gown would not have turned his head.

But if Neville felt oppressed by her mourning clothes, she should change them.

She pulled out a pink cotton floral with short, puffed sleeves. The print was too girlish. She put it back and took out another. A red-plaid cotton lawn. More formal. The sleeves were elbow-length and less voluminous. The neckline was square. The bodice was gathered. It was pretty but she couldn't recall ever wearing it. Perhaps she'd thought it dowdy when she was twenty.

She held it out in front of her. The hem looked a bit short. She undressed, then put on the gown. It was tight, but the seams were deep and could be let out. She could fix it and tell Neville she'd had a new dress made.

Maybe she would even wear it.

CHAPTER TWELVE

IVERSLEY VILLAGE WAS the earl's seat in Northamptonshire, a seven-hour journey from London. The family estate, Chaumbers, comprised the Taverston ancestral home and several hundred acres of grounds adjacent to the village. As Mercury loped up the long, beech-tree-lined drive, Crispin felt a slow unwinding of tension. Chaumbers might belong solely to Jasper, the earl, but Crispin knew he would never be unwelcome. It might not be home, but it would always be a haven.

Even so, it was no stately country house. All agreed it appeared to have been dreamed up by a madman or a drunkard. In fact, the blame belonged to Crispin's grandfather and an erstwhile artist friend with ambition to be an architect. It was the first residence the man had ever designed, and Grandfather's interference in the planning might have ensured that the poor fellow was never tasked with another. Built to restore an older house after a fire, Chaumbers' four wings were neither symmetrical nor balanced in their proportions. Windows of different sizes appeared haphazardly slapped over the front. Crispin grinned as it came into view.

At least it was unique.

He took Mercury to the stables, where George, the head groom, greeted him—Mercury, not Crispin—as an old friend. A clean, dry stall awaited him. The horse seemed as pleased to be back as Crispin was.

He spoke with George while watching him rub Mercury down, and learned that the earl and countess were in residence, and Mr. and Mrs. Carroll were at the steward's cottage, but Mr. and Mrs. Taverston and the Dowager had not yet arrived. He chuckled to think of Olivia as "Mrs. Carroll" and Georgiana as "Mrs. Taverston." No doubt they were both queens in their own domains.

Someone must have run up to the house to alert Jasper, because he appeared while Crispin was talking to George about horses, primarily wondering at what age thoroughbreds started losing stamina and speed. And if it might not be a good idea to breed Mercury before he did.

"You are here. Good." Jasper stuck out his hand, and Crispin shook it. No demonstrative affection in front of the stable hands.

"Did you think I wouldn't come?"

"I laid no wagers one way or the other. Come on up to the house. Vanessa will be thrilled."

They left the stables and walked the path to the house. The clean scent of grass and wildflowers flushed the stink of London from his nose, and everywhere he looked, he saw lush, thriving greenery.

"How long will you give us this time?" Jasper asked.

A flicker of stress rekindled between Crispin's shoulder blades. He tried shrugging it away. "Not long enough for you to grow tired of me."

Jasper didn't smile. "We thought to have you a while in London. God, Crispin. Whatever compelled you to cart your old commander off like that?"

"The man can't walk. His sister needed help getting him home."

"But then you stayed with them all this time?"

"Not the whole time. Only until they were able to hire an attendant. Ha! Jasp, you won't believe who. Adam. Adam, my old 'valet.' He'd been working at Chelsea Hospital."

Jasper sniffed. "So you had a reunion with the old spy and your old commander."

"A short one." That was defensiveness speaking. He'd stayed with the Harringtons far too long. He took off his hat and pushed back sweaty hair, then donned it again. "He was my first superior officer, Jasp. He taught me a great deal. I owed him."

He wouldn't mention that the sister was young, pretty, and clever. She sang country ditties in an extraordinary contralto. And she wrote poetry. Jasper would laugh and tell him to turn around and go back. Crispin didn't want to make Miss Harrington an object of fun.

He didn't want to say that she was half the reason he'd stayed so long in Tonbridge. And half the reason he'd left.

Jasper said, "All well and good." They mounted the front steps. The porter opened the door before Jasper knocked. "But please don't run off again."

Vanessa rushed into the entrance hall. "Crispin! Oh, how wonderful! We'll send word to the cottage. Olivia will be so pleased."

He hugged his sister-in-law. Then Jasper grasped him by the elbow.

"Come up to my study. While I have you alone."

Crispin knew he could not avoid this forever. Jasper was using his "earl voice." So he snickered and said, "Yes, *my lord*."

The study looked comfortably official, no different than it had in Father's day, except for Jasper's new brown leather chair, a nod to Reg's uncharacteristic burst of sentiment. Reg had not liked seeing Jasper in Father's seat. Crispin dropped onto a couch facing the desk, laced his fingers together, and said, "You may ask, but I have no answers."

"How do you know when I haven't asked?" Irritation slipped into Jasper's tone. He was generally an even keeled man, but Crispin knew how to needle him.

"You want to know what my plans are. I can't tell you because I don't know."

"What are you thinking, then? You must be thinking something. You always are." Jasper moved to a wall cabinet and pulled out a bottle of brandy. He waggled it at Crispen. "Yes? Or no?"

"No." He waited while Jasper poured a drink for himself. He supposed there was no harm in telling Jasper some of it. And thereby spare himself a grilling. "I thought I might stay on half pay and live an idle life in London."

"Would you?" Jasper's lips bunched skeptically, but his eyes looked more hopeful than doubtful. He sat down. "Not be idle. I don't believe that, but to stay in London?"

"I went to Albany on Piccadilly to see about leasing a set, but they had nothing available. So that ruled out London."

"There are other apartments." He spoke very carefully. "Or you could keep your rooms—"

"I won't live in your home, Jasper. Would you live in mine?"

He frowned. "Well, but why does it have to be Albany?"

Crispin feigned a disbelieving huff. "It is the toniest building for bachelor gentlemen in all of London. It is where Lord Byron lives!"

"Which does nothing to recommend it. What about your cottage in Binnings? I thought you'd be heading there."

"I did, too, but I was distracted by my mission of mercy. I will probably go there from here." He drummed his fingers on his knees, a nervous tic he sometimes forgot to suppress.

Jasper narrowed his eyes at Crispin's knees, then raised his gaze to peer into his face. "What is the alternative? If you don't go to Binnings?"

He sighed. He was divulging more than he wished. And yet, he wasn't likely saying anything Jasper could not have guessed for himself. "I could go back on full pay and see where they send me."

Jasper leaned forward, forearms on his desk. "Obviously, I would prefer that you don't."

"Or"—he drew a deep breath—"I could take the position Wellington wishes me to take. Attaché at the embassy in Paris."

There. He'd confided all. He braced for a storm of unwanted advice.

"Which would mean what? Errand boy? Courier? Advisor?" Jasper's brow darkened. "Or spy? I thought you'd be finished with—"

"I was never a spy, Jasper. I was a soldier. Sometimes I gathered information."

"Will you be 'gathering information' in Paris?"

Crispin shrugged. "My French is good. And I am an aristocrat. I'd be well-positioned to circulate in the restored Bourbon court." Jasper looked more and more disturbed. "Jasp, I would just be listening to gossip."

Until the War Office needed something foul to be done.

"France is still volatile. And you'll recall aristocrats in the previous Bourbon court lost their heads."

"I'm an Englishman. I'll be safe enough." He grimaced involuntarily. "From everything but the food." He shook his head. "France is my last choice. In fact, I intended to speak with Wellington to decline, but I couldn't get an interview. He is trotted from one celebration to the next." Crispin stood. Sharing confidences agitated him, but having started, he couldn't stop. He paced a few steps. "I left my calling card, and he sent a letter two days later telling me to be at the embassy in Paris on September fifteenth."

"The deuce." Jasper harrumphed. "I don't suppose you could decline in a letter?"

"Bad form." Crispin grinned ruefully, though he didn't feel like grinning. He still felt thwarted by Wellington's elusiveness. "I almost did write a refusal, but then had second thoughts. It is the most *interesting* option." He wiggled his eyebrows, attempting to lighten the mood. "French women are said to be beautiful and licentious."

The study door flew open, and Olivia came running in. "Crispin! You're here! We had such a wonderful honeymoon in Binnings. Oh, but your cottage is a disaster. Benjamin kept finding things he wanted to fix, but I reminded him how annoyed you were when Jasper had the new stove installed. You have to come see *our* cottage. It's done up beautifully. You brought Mercury back, didn't you? Can I ride him? You do know he should be mine." She paused to catch her breath.

"Livvy, you staid old matron! Marriage has wrought wonders. I almost didn't know it was you."

Her eyes widened. Then she punched his shoulder and laughed. "Vanessa said to come fetch you both for supper. What does 'licentious' mean?"

CRISPIN PICKED AT the supper offerings, finding little he dared eat. It wasn't Vanessa's fault, or Cook's. They hadn't known to expect him. Fortunately, the lively conversation distracted him from his hunger.

Olivia was full of news about the estate's tenants. Vanessa talked about how well the bootmakers were doing. Jasper talked politics. Words swirled around the table, along with a good deal of laughter. Crispin was grateful to Jasper for not bringing up their earlier discussion. Then he realized the whole table was carefully avoiding asking him about his plans. Maybe they were afraid of chasing him away.

After supper, Benjamin and Olivia said they had to return to their cottage. Hannah, their adopted sprite, would not go to sleep without a kiss goodnight. Crispin, Jasper, and Vanessa adjourned to the parlor. The windows were open to let in a breeze. Jasper sat in a green upholstered armchair whose arms were unevenly worn, right more than left, from the way that Father had always leaned. Crispin joined Vanessa on a floral-print couch. It should have been cozy, but the atmosphere felt strained.

"So, when do you expect the rest of the Taverstons?" Crispin asked.

"Next week, I think," Jasper said. He glanced at Vanessa, then away.

Vanessa said, "It probably depends upon whether Georgiana feels up to traveling."

"Ah." Crispin hesitated. Was Vanessa comfortable discussing this? He barreled ahead. "Is she not well?"

"She is with child," Vanessa said. "And I am envious, but not upset, so you needn't tiptoe around me."

Jasper put in, "We are not upset, but we are concerned." His face reddened. "You see…ah…we thought you might have a talk with Reg."

"A talk?" What the devil? The only thing to say to Reg was congratulations.

Vanessa said, "You were not here for this bit of drama, but Georgiana was nursing Arthur herself."

Odd for a duke's daughter, but Crispin didn't see why that would cause drama. Or, God forbid, why he should talk to Reg about it. "And?"

Jasper said, "I thought it was because they are so absurdly frugal. But when they came to London for Livvy's wedding, they had a wet nurse."

"And Georgiana showed every sign of being with child again."

"I'm not following," Crispin said. "This is not in my baili-wick."

Vanessa signed impatiently. "It is a common belief that nurs-ing mothers cannot conceive."

"Is that true?" Crispin asked.

"Obviously not."

"The point is," Jasper said, "Vanessa thinks they were hoping to spread out their children more."

"It would be safer for Georgiana. A baby every year takes a toll."

"All right. I can see that. But what does this have to do with me?"

After a pause, Jasper said in an embarrassed rush, "I don't think Reg knows about French letters. Someone needs to tell him. And I don't think it should be me."

"*What?*" This had grown awkward fast.

"Think, Crispin. It will look like I'm telling him to stop having children until Vanessa and I manage to have one."

He almost said, *no it won't. That's absurd.* But they both were red-faced and looking at the floor.

Bloody hell. He'd thought he was done with solving his brothers' problems for them. He was happy to play the sage when he could. But, to his embarrassment, he didn't know much about French letters. He knew what they *were:* "cock armor." But he had never used one. Whores had their own tricks to prevent babies, a fact for which he was infinitely grateful.

"I don't know…" But their whole supposition was based on shaky evidence. So Reg and Georgiana had hired a wet nurse. Maybe they did so because they *wanted* another child right away. How idiotic it would be to take Reg aside and lecture him if there was no need. Then he felt a whoosh of relief. "If Georgiana is increasing, it's too late. If this is still a concern after Arthur's sibling appears, I'll talk to Reg."

"Unless you're in Paris," Jasper said.

Crispin sighed. "Then *you* will have to talk to him." Dread of that discussion was enough to *send* him to Paris. He stood. "Now, if you'll permit me, Vanessa, I'm going to go raid your kitchen."

MOTHER RETURNED TWO days later. Reg and Georgiana did not. Mother explained that Arthur had a cough, and they did not want to subject him to travel until he was better. Crispin watched Jasper and Vanessa exchange significant glances. He just shook his head.

Yet August rolled on, and still, they did not come. Four

weeks, and Crispin grew restless.

He couldn't explain his dissatisfaction. After all, he'd spent those weeks doing all of his favorite Chaumbers things. He rode Mercury around the property. He raced Olivia, the best horse-woman he knew. She had a splendid new mare, a gift from Jasper, that she'd named Winner. Crispin called her Second Place. Olivia pretended to be furious. It *should* have been more fun than it was.

He spent time lazing about the folly, a simulated medieval abbey. He enjoyed it more when Olivia brought Hannah to play among the ruins. Hannah still called him "Major," but she also called Jasper "Milord" and Mother "Lady," so he didn't feel singled out as a stranger, even though he was one.

He went swimming and rowing at the lake. There was a new boathouse. That shouldn't have made him feel melancholy. He wasn't such an old man that he should grow moody over change. But he *was* moody.

He thought he was hiding his discontent, but Vanessa cornered him one afternoon while he was desultorily practicing billiards, and asked what was wrong. Not *if* something was wrong, but *what* was.

"Nothing."

"You don't know what to do with yourself, do you?"

He shrugged, then bent over the table. "I'm a gentleman who doesn't drink or gamble. What else does a gentleman do?" He sent a ball careening into a corner pocket.

"I'm serious, Crispin. You went from a headlong gallop chasing Napoleon to a full stop when he was caught. That's a difficult adjustment. Jasper is afraid, we're all afraid, that you'll go back to the army just for something to do and be sent God-knows-where."

"Returning to service is only one option."

"And gathering information?"

Good of her not to call him a spy. "Another option." She gave him a wary look, so he said, "I'm not eager to go back. I have a conscience, Vanessa. I ignored it for so long I thought it was gone. But it's still there. And I'd like to listen to it for a while, to see if it has anything worthwhile to say. I think it might be telling me I've... killed more than my quota." He wouldn't admit that to anyone else.

Vanessa put a hand on his arm. She started to say something, but shook her head. Then she said, "Sell your commission."

He said only, "I might."

He wouldn't yet. But he finally sent a letter to Wellington, saying he that he was unable to be in France by September, and therefore, he must regretfully decline the opportunity. For several days he'd wallowed in concern that he'd made the wrong choice, before coming to terms with the fact that what was done was done. In truth, while the position intrigued him, the French food *would* kill him, and that was not how he wanted to die.

So, he played billiards. He played the pianoforte. He played cards. He bothered Jasper and bothered Benjamin.

Only a month, and he was heartily bored. Too often, he found himself wondering what Miss Harrington was doing. The colonel and Miss Harrington. Far too often. Even in the bosom of his beloved family, he needed better distraction.

Therefore, one morning, he packed his valise, went into the breakfast parlor, and announced to Jasper and Vanessa, "I'm going to Binnings."

"Now?" Jasper said, eying the valise. His face wrinkled with annoyance. "Crispin—"

"I've put it off for too long. You've all been telling me the place is a ruin. It's my inheritance. I have to see to it."

"Yes, but you should talk to Benjamin first— "

"Benjamin is not *my* steward. And I am perfectly capable of assessing my own property and hiring my own workers." He hoped he was. He'd never done so before.

Jasper grumbled. "And I imagine our grandfather thought himself capable of hiring his own architect."

Crispin laughed. "Tell everyone I said goodbye."

"For God's sake, say your goodbyes yourself. They'll all be angry at me for letting you go!"

Crispin walked out of the room, waving his hand over his shoulder. He should have sneaked out before dawn.

THE LAKESIDE COTTAGE needed a top-to-bottom cleaning. Crispin thought the structure was sound. He hoped so. A few window-panes were cracked. Some of the woodwork was rotten. The drapery and rugs smelled of mold. Crispin wandered throughout the house and swam through a river of memories.

The family had gathered here for weeks at a time in the summer. Halcyon days. Here, the children had been allowed to run free and misbehave. Crispin and Jasper thrashed one another regularly, just for the fun of it. They didn't fight with Reg. He was too little. It wouldn't have been sporting. Instead, they taunted the hell out of him, until Reg almost drowned them by drilling holes in their fishing boat. Mother was furious. Father laughed himself sick. Both parents thought Reg was too young and innocent to understand what he'd done, but Jasper and Crispin knew he'd been calculating. Thereafter, they'd accorded him the respect he deserved.

There had been berries to gather, picnics to go on, dogs to train, arrows to shoot, tents to set up and sleep in. Olivia toddled after them, frighteningly determined to do everything they did.

Even in their college years, they'd come to the lake house to throw off their cares. They'd brought Benjamin with them after befriending him at Oxford. Seeing it through Benjamin's grateful eyes had made Crispin appreciate what they had all the more.

Everyone seemed to know that he had claimed the cottage as "his." He believed it meant more to him than it did to anyone else. Perhaps because he had never fallen sick there. Never once.

He received the deed to the house on his twenty-first birth-day. Then furiously sold it for less than its worth before his twenty-second. He'd had to buy his own commission after Father refused to do so. Upon his father's death, he'd learned that the house had been repurchased and deeded to him again. He'd felt gratitude, comfort, and an overwhelming sense of loss. His father had understood him in a way he had not even understood himself.

And yet, he'd allowed the place to fall into disrepair.

The caretakers, Badge and Mrs. Badge were ancient. Jasper had hired a local woman, Mrs. Peele, to help out, mainly to take care of the caretakers. As Crispin stood in the doorway of the one decently refurbished bedchamber, Mrs. Peele came up from behind. She was of an indeterminate age, with steel-gray eyes and the bearing of an Amazon. Jasper had chosen well.

"Where would you like to start, Major?"

"Ha! Where would you suggest?

"Throw out everything moldy. Then scrub all the walls, ceilings, and floors. Patch the holes. Replace the skirtings. Then plaster and paint. To start."

"Yes, that sounds reasonable." She'd evidently been giving this some thought. But she'd left out mention of the garden, now overrun with weeds. He wouldn't mind seeing to that himself. Although a garden might be melancholy without a certain black-haired gardener. *Damn it!* This had to stop. He'd never before been chased from place to place by thoughts of a woman. "But I don't know any laborers around here."

"Well, you wouldn't. You've been off fighting Boney." She hesitated a moment, then said. "I do."

"You do what?"

"I know who you should hire to do what." She frowned. "Mr. Carroll, when he was here with Mrs. Carroll, he made a list. But he said you'd have to approve it when you came."

He laughed. Even on his honeymoon, Benjamin was incapable of enjoying his leisure. Crispin could sympathize. "Bring me the list."

He hoped overhauling the cottage would be an all-consuming project. He needed a challenge. Or else he was just treading water until he drowned.

CHAPTER THIRTEEN

THE LEAVES ON the trees had turned brilliant orange and yellow, compensating somewhat for the faded blooms in the garden. It was still a calm and lovely place for Neville to doze. However, Camellia mused, pulling together the dangling threads of her thoughts as she strolled down the rows, deadheading the flowers, nothing made up for Major Taverston's absence. His short visit had cast a long shadow. Even Neville had remarked that their subsequent guests were dull, and he wished the major had not gone.

"Why the devil does Manfred think I care about the yield of his apple orchard," he'd groused after supper and cards last night.

Camellia had agreed that she didn't know, but in truth, she suspected Manfred was trying to be helpful. It was harvest time, yet they had nothing to harvest. Moreover, they hadn't seen tuppence yet from Neville's pension. When spring came, she would have to swallow her pride and ask Manfred for help in hiring men to till and plant. In the meantime, if need be, perhaps she could sell the pianoforte.

Manfred might be dull, but tonight's guests would be worse. Mr. and Mrs. Castor. It was customary for the local rector to dine occasionally with gentlemen farmers, yet Camellia had put off issuing an invitation as long as she could. Mr. Castor had once tried wooing her. His response to her rejection had been worse

than Manfred's. He'd been certain she would be grateful for his attentions, and was stunned to anger when she was not.

But she wouldn't waste the day fretting over things she could not control. It was one of those perfect, sunny, October afternoons, a last gasp return of summer, and she was out in the garden enjoying it. *And* she was wearing a jonquil dress from her trunk that had needed no alteration. Neville had been right about color. She felt far more optimistic in yellow than in black.

While Neville napped, she reread her most recent letter from Marianne. It was full of titillating gossip. Wellington was having a torrid affair with an opera singer in Paris. *La Grassini.* The same woman had once been a paramour of Napoleon. Camellia felt wickedly awed.

She heard a crunching of leaves, signaling someone's approach. It could not be the Castors. It was too early. It was not Mr. Diakos's plodding gait. And whoever it was walked more briskly than Mrs. Clay. Camellia tore her eyes from the letter to look up.

"Major!" she cried. Her heart started to race. He was here. *Why was he here?*

He grinned. "Pardon me. I shouldn't have disturbed you." Did he mean to remind her of their meeting at the Temple of the Muses? She played along.

"That's all right. I was reading."

His grin widened. "But not a novel, I don't think." He came right up beside her bench. Her stomach flipped over. He was handsomer than ever. He was not in uniform, but wore a dark-blue jacket and fawn trousers. His hair was no longer unfashionably shoulder-length, but styled in close-cropped loose curls that peeked out along the edges of his hat. He lowered his voice and gestured to Neville. "Is the colonel well?"

"He is." She had to crane her neck to look up while they talked. "As well as can be. Bringing him home was the right thing to do. We are indebted to you—"

"Oh, *bosh*, as my sister would say. Friends don't tally debts."

He was standing in the sun, making her squint, so she shifted sideways on the bench and patted it, inviting him to sit. She folded her letter and tucked it into her reticule.

"What brings you back to Tonbridge?" she asked, trying to sound calm. He swooped off his hat and laid it over his knees. His cologne was unusual. Earthy. It blended well with the scent of an autumn afternoon.

"I had business in London." He rubbed his hand in his hair, mussing it more than he straightened it. "I have to furnish my house in the lake district."

"And you got very lost along the way?"

"I have my own unique sense of direction. How are the colonel and Adam getting along?"

"Is it true that Neville would have shot Mr. Diakos for a spy if you hadn't spoken for him?"

His eyes widened with surprise. "Adam told you that?"

"No, Neville did. He sounded chastened. So Mr. Diakos must please him well enough."

"Good." Major Taverston averted his gaze to peer about their surroundings, drumming his fingers on his knees. Then he shot a sideways glance at her. "You look very cheerful. Your dress, I mean."

A little warmth stole into her cheeks. "Neville asked me to stop wearing black."

"Ah. Well, cheerful suits you." She thought a little red crept into his cheeks as well.

"Is Mercury with you?"

He nodded. "Yes. No. I left him at the Fitzhenrys' inn. Do you like to ride? I can hire a mount for you if—"

"I don't ride. We had carriage horses. I never learned."

His jaw sank. "Never learned? Miss Harrington, that is criminal."

She laughed, though she thought he might be serious. In his world, all ladies must ride.

"I've taken a room at the inn—"

"Oh, no! You must stay with us. Neville would insist."

Neville echoed, gravel-voiced, "I do insist." She started, embarrassed that he'd been listening, even though they had said nothing private. He said, "It is good to see you, Major. What brings you?"

"Business in London. It's not far, so I thought…"

Neville harumphed. "It isn't close."

"We used to march this far in a day," the major pointed out. "And I have a very fast horse."

Neville shifted in his chair and grunted. "True, true. But you needn't march back into the village tonight. Since you are here, you'll stay for dinner. And we've had the pianoforte tuned, so I imagine you'll want to hear Camellia play."

"Neville, you *do* recall the Castors are coming to dine with us?" She'd already told her brother she was not going to play for them.

Neville scowled. "Damn. They are."

"I don't want to intrude." The major looked a bit panicked.

"You are not," Neville said. "You'll make the evening bearable. Castor is a bore."

Camellia rose from the major's side. "I'll leave it to Neville to persuade you. Although, Neville, telling him his dinner companions will be boring might not be the best strategy." Major Taverston's lips curved into a smile. "If you'll excuse me, I'll go have a word with Mrs. Clay about the menu. And see to the guest room. Mr. Diakos will likely be along soon, but if he is not, Major, would you bring Neville in if he wants?"

"Yes, of course."

She stepped away, hearing Neville behind her speaking in a loud, excited voice.

"What the devil do you think the duke is doing? All I hear is he is squiring *La Grassini* about and antagonizing the French citizenry."

"The French are easily antagonized. And unfortunately, there are both Bonapartists and Bourbonists in the city who don't take kindly to occupation by a conquering army—"

She didn't hear the rest. But how could there still be Bona-partists in France after all the devilment the man had caused? And shouldn't the Bourbons be grateful?

SHE SPOKE WITH Mrs. Clay to ensure there would be rice and peas for the major, and some of Mrs. Faraday's goat cheese. This was the best she could do on short notice, but at least he would know that she tried. Then she took a pitcher of water up to the guest chamber and set it beside the wash basin on the bed table. She opened the windows to air the room. Fluffed the pillows. She couldn't think of anything else to do to make him feel welcome.

She went into her own room, debating whether to change clothes for supper. Her red-plaid gown was finer, but donning it felt too obvious. The major had complimented the yellow. She didn't want to appear to be seeking more praise.

From her chamber, she could not hear what was happening below, so she went down to the receiving room. It was not the jumble of furniture Major Taverston would remember. With Mr. Diakos's help, she had removed a few of the excess chairs and tables. She'd moved two tea tables together into one corner, with the rest of the furniture directed away from it, to carve out a space for a dining area. It was a little thing, but it made her feel better. More settled.

She heard the back door to the kitchen open, and men's laughter. When he was most amused, Major Taverston had a whooping laugh that caused everyone in earshot to laugh along. Even here, in the next room, she found herself snorting and wondering what the joke was.

The men spilled out of the kitchen into the hallway. Camellia went to greet them. She smiled to see the major carrying a valise, which meant, despite his protests, he'd come prepared to spend the night. Mr. Diakos pushed Neville's chair.

"If I may," the major said, "I will go change. I fear I smell of horse."

He didn't, but Camellia thought better of announcing she'd enjoyed his scent.

"I should clean up as well," Neville said.

Mr. Diakos nodded and wheeled him off to his chamber. That left Camellia in the receiving room to await the Castors. They arrived before Neville or the major returned. She welcomed them with false good humor, and they made awkward conversation while the Castors shot disdainful glances around the room.

Mr. Castor wore a somber black jacket and trousers, appropriate to his calling, but had a diamond pin in his cravat. It was known in the parish that he liked to think he cut a fine figure. However, he was nearly bald and had a large wart on his chin, so jewelry didn't help. Mrs. Castor was jowly with small eyes and a mean smile. Camellia wanted to feel sorry for her, married to Mr. Castor, but the woman acted so superior it was impossible.

Just as Mr. Diakos was bringing Neville in, Mr. Castor said, "I don't understand why you mutilated this house."

"Don't you?" Neville asked.

Mr. Castor whirled around, saw him, and flushed. "I only meant to say she could have had an architect in to make more graceful changes."

Major Taverston stepped into the room just behind Mr. Diakos. "Oh, good Lord, no. One should never trust architects." He was in uniform. And he looked formidable.

Neville made introductions. Mr. Diakos stepped away, but Mrs. Clay hurried in with a tray, carrying glasses of wine. Major Taverston confused Camellia by taking one. He'd always refused wine before.

"Major Taverston? Taverston?" Mr. Castor said. "Your brother is the Earl of Iversley? I'm so sorry."

"Sorry?"

"That wife? It must have been difficult—"

"I can't imagine what you mean," the major cut across him, his voice like knives. The look he gave the rector was shriveling. The room remained dead silent until Major Taverston turned to Neville. "This is excellent wine."

"My father kept a cellar. There are still a few bottles."

"Is it French? It must be."

They discussed the advantages of French wine compared to Spanish or Portuguese wine. Eventually Mr. Castor offered his opinions. The dangerous moment passed. Shortly, Mrs. Clay came out to announce supper. Camellia had asked her to move things along as quickly as possible so they would have an early night.

Other dinner guests had been polite when guided from one side of the receiving room to the other, rather than making a formal progression from receiving room to dining hall. Mrs. Castor gave a sharp burst of laughter and turned up her nose.

"How quaint. It is like an indoor picnic, isn't it, Mr. Castor?"

"What a pleasant way to look at it," Camellia said, misunderstanding on purpose.

Major Taverston agreed. "Picnics are always good fun. Well, depending on the company."

Neville was at the head of the table. Camellia sat between him and Mr. Castor, across from Major Taverston. Mrs. Castor was beside him. The rector said a blessing, then Mrs. Clay served the first course, pease soup. Camellia noticed the major's hesitation. She caught his eye, then put a spoonful in her mouth. She hoped he understood what she meant: no cream. He nodded, then dug in. She felt a small thrill at their secret communication.

The conversation suffered a number of false starts and stops. Then, to Camellia's surprise, Mr. Diakos, who was not expected to serve as their butler, brought in the main course while Mrs. Clay removed the soup bowls. They were taking seriously her request to speed things along.

Camellia saw the major heap his plate with rice and peas and only the tiniest portion of beef stew.

As if taking control of the evening, Mr. Castor said loudly, "Colonel, it is good to have you back, even such as you are. I must say, we had all given you up for dead. Your poor father, pillar of the community, suffering such a terrible blow—"

Camellia jumped in. "It *was* a blow, losing Papa. But then, his heart was broken after my mother's death."

"But it was your brother's—"

"Your glass is empty. Will you have more wine?" She looked about frantically. The bottle was not on the table.

Major Taverston said, "Allow me." He rose and left the room, returning a moment later. "Mr. Diakos will bring more wine." He sniffed a laugh. "Do you know, the colonel and I first met Mr. Diakos in a church, a Roman Catholic church, on the peninsula? He was caring for wounded soldiers. He has a gift for it. And he also knows good wine. He's liable to bring up your father's best, Colonel. I hope you don't mind."

Neville waved his hand. He didn't care. Camellia practically held her breath until the conversation turned to Mrs. Castor's pickles, which were apparently leagues above Mrs. Clay's.

Mr. Diakos returned and poured more wine, then left the bottle on the table and retreated.

"You've given up grieving?" Mrs. Castor said, turning the full force of her unpleasantness upon Camellia. "That dress is…bright."

"It has been over a year," Neville said.

"There is no time limit on grief. When my father died, I wore mourning for five years."

"Yes, five years is the time limit on grief," Major Taverston said, then popped one of Mrs. Clay's pickles into his mouth.

Camellia stifled a laugh, which would have been fatal to the evening. Mrs. Castor was already giving them both the evil eye.

Then the major turned to Mr. Castor. "My brother was going to enter the church, but he thought sermonizing every week would be too burdensome. How do you choose your texts?"

Camellia saw the man's chest expand. He treated them to an

hour-long discourse on writing sermons. She feared Neville would nod off. But it carried them through to the end of the meal.

Unfortunately, they could not then simply tell the Castors to go home.

"Shall we?" Neville said, gesturing across the room. "Camellia will play for us."

They all rose, and the major wheeled Neville's chair toward the pianoforte. Camellia's hands felt hot, and the back of her neck itched at the thought of having to play. The Castors would not be an appreciative audience. And the major had a very discerning ear.

"Do *you* play, Major?" she asked, holding back.

"Yes, I do." He didn't try to downplay his ability. He didn't boast of it, either.

"Why don't you play for us," she said. "I will if I must, but it was my music teacher who said that I sing better than I play."

He gave her a sympathetic grin, then stepped around Neville's chair and took a seat on the bench. He touched a few keys, as if to confirm that it had been tuned. She noted he had a pianist's fine long-fingered hands. He played a Beethoven sonata. Beautifully. From memory.

After he finished, while she and Neville clapped enthusiastically and the Castors clapped petulantly, he stood to offer her the bench.

"Oh no," she said. "I certainly cannot play after that."

"Music isn't a competition." He smirked. "Not like poetry."

She laughed and tilted her head slightly to indicate the Castors, watching them. "Would you like to try the challenge again?"

He widened his eyes with mock horror. "Not for the world. Why don't I play, and you sing?"

THAT NIGHT, AFTER the Castors were gone, Camellia lay awake, listening to the silence. She was aware, very aware, of the major's presence just down the hall. Was he listening to the same silence? In her head, she heard echoes of the sonata he'd played. Songs she had sung lingered on the tip of her tongue.

She wanted to hear something of his. A breath. A snore. A rustle of blankets. The drop of a boot on the floor. Anything. A connection. To prove to her he was still there, and that the evening had not been a dream.

CHAPTER FOURTEEN

CRISPIN DID NOT sleep well. *The devil.* He *always* slept well—except when bedbugs like Lizzie's were biting. His conscience bothered him during the day, not at night to keep him up. The only time he tossed and turned was when he was sick, and he was not sick. He was not. He'd had a random cramp; that was all.

He rose and washed. A peek out the window showed drizzle, putting a damper on his desire for a long walk. He donned his drawers, his shirt, then his uniform. In the colonel's presence, he preferred to be a soldier-in-reserve rather an earl's-second-son-with-no-occupation.

He stepped out of the guest chamber and walked quietly past Miss Harrington's door. A capital lady. A poetess. A contralto. He found her as funny as Georgiana and as resilient as Vanessa. He rather wished the women could meet.

It was too early to be up and about, but that gave him liberty to eat breakfast in solitude. Oat porridge if Mrs. Clay would provide it. *God. This was wearying.* This constant fixation on what he might eat. And people's reaction. As if he must either be malingering, mad, or courting attention. Even his beloved family skidded between skepticism, annoyance, and pity. There were times he wanted to stand up and shout, *It's not my fault!*

Miss Harrington and Adam were the only two people who had ever managed to be helpful rather than irritating.

Adam, when they had first met, had been disinterestedly fascinated by the evidence of Crispin's chronic ill health, to wit: his absurd thinness. He asked about it in such a matter-of-fact way that Crispin answered. And Adam had *believed* what Crispin confided about the bewildering array of symptoms he'd suffered at seemingly random intervals throughout his life. Just being believed had helped. Adam wanted to approach the problem systematically. He was convinced the *condition* could be managed if not cured—without leeches, cupping, purges, or laudanum.

Crispin was not cured. He was markedly improved, but not cured. Removing practically everything from his table had been difficult, but worse was adding things back. Especially after Adam had been released from parole and Crispin had been left to muddle through a course of trial and error on his own.

Now he was cursed to wonder things like: was that cramp in his gut from the bite of beef or the wine? Or was he imagining it because he'd dared to taste both?

As for Miss Harrington, she seemed to empathize. Moreover, she must have guessed that he disliked nothing so much as a small dinner party with strangers. Friends and family were used to him. At large events, no one paid attention to his plate. But it was impossible to hide when there were only five at the table. So Miss Harrington had arranged it so he could appear to be eating what everyone else ate.

Even so, dinner was excruciating. The Castors were an unpleasant couple. Maybe that was why he'd slept poorly. Lingering abhorrence.

He descended the stairs and made his way to the kitchen. It was warm from the heat of the stove, but with no lamps lit and the small window, it was dim. There he found Adam, eating what looked to be the remains of last night's stew.

"Good morning, Major," Adam said, standing up, then sitting back down to continue his meal. The man had adopted some British manners but not all. Crispin suspected he picked and chose.

"Good morning. Is Mrs. Clay about?"

"She is. The laundress comes today, and she is gathering what needs to be washed."

Crispin *hmmm'd*. His breakfast could wait.

Adam gave him a long look. Then he said, "Mrs. Clay is a gossip."

That was blunt. Crispin sat down at the table and leaned on his elbows. "Is she?"

"I do not intend to make it a habit to speak about my employers."

"No, I wouldn't think it of you. But is there something necessary for me to know?" It was too bad Adam *wasn't* a spy. He would make a fine one.

"Not 'necessary.'" Adam laid down his knife and fork. "But possibly helpful."

"Go on."

"Mr. Castor tried to woo Miss Harrington."

Bile rose in his throat. "Did he?"

"Mrs. Clay said he put little effort into it. He told the old gentleman, Mr. Harrington, that there was no point in a long courtship. They knew each other well enough from church."

"He wooed her with his sermons, eh?" Crispin's dislike of the man grew exponentially.

"Mrs. Clay overheard the proposal. I suspect she had her ear to the door."

Crispin snorted. Servants knew everything.

Adam's expression turned thoughtful. "She said he became angry. He told Miss Harrington he'd asked her only as a kindness because no one else would have her. And that marriage to him would make her more acceptable to the parish."

A kindness? What the devil was that supposed to mean? "More acceptable?"

"He told her people say that she looks like a witch. They don't like to be near her."

Crispin stared. No reasonable person believed in witches.

"Why? You can't mean because of her *hair?*"

Adam nodded. "I suspect even if they said such things, they said it in fun."

It wasn't funny. "But she's a beautiful woman." The yellow dress had darkened her soulful eyes. And it had revealed, in a way her black ones did not, that she had a shape. A very appealing shape.

Adam cocked his head to one side and regarded him. "She's pretty. Yes."

Crispin's chest felt tight. "How did Miss Harrington fare after this insulting proposal?"

Adam sniffed. "Mrs. Clay said that she laughed. She thanked him for his consideration, but her answer was still no."

She hid her hurt well.

"I should not have said anything," Adam continued, "but I thought it might explain the atmosphere last evening."

"Castor holds a grudge and Mrs. Castor is jealous."

"That was my thought."

Mrs. Clay bustled into the kitchen. "Oh! Major. Good morning. Have you anything to send to the laundress?"

It startled a laugh from him. "I just got here!"

"Well, but who knows where you came from."

Adam pushed away his bowl. "I hear the colonel stirring." He rose. "I'd best go to him. He had a bad night."

Him, too? "A bad night?"

"He suffers nightmares. About Vitoria. Did you not hear him? I think that is why they gave him so much laudanum at the hospital. To keep him quiet."

That was sobering. Crispin remembered Vitoria as a triumph, the victory the British so desperately needed. But Colonel Harrington would remember it differently.

Crispin had his own torturous memories. Things he'd done of which he was not proud. Things to which he could never confess. Things that had needed doing that it had fallen to him to do.

"Oh, it is wrenching," Mrs. Clay said. "He screams so awfully.

You're fortunate the walls are thick, and you can't hear it upstairs."

He was fortunate in more than thick walls. He had to remember that. He was fortunate.

⟫⟫⟩⟨⟨⟪

CRISPIN STAYED. HE wasn't bored. Strangely, he was anything but bored, and they made it clear he was welcome, so he stayed. He endured two supper-and-cards Saturday evenings with Sir Bodwell, and was still there though it was approaching a third. It amused him, in a cruel way, to see how his continuing presence bothered the man. And then it bothered *him* that he could enjoy being cruel. The war had done that. It had taught him to steel himself against softness. But he had overshot the mark and become mean.

He told himself he was staying for the colonel's sake. Harrington seemed stronger in body under Adam's care, but his spirits were often low. He had things he needed to get off his chest—the young deserter whom he'd caught and sentenced to thirty lashes, a lethal punishment for a mere boy; his willingness to execute Adam who'd been guilty of nothing; the confiscation of a stolen chicken from a starving foot soldier, that he then shared with fellow officers who had plenty to eat. Crispin shared no confidences, but he excused his old superior's offenses in the same way he tried justifying his own.

It was war. It was war. It was war.

⟫⟫⟩⟨⟨⟪

"YOU PLANT YOURSELF here," Crispin said, putting his hand on the seat of the sidesaddle. "Then you hook your...your right knee here, over the pommel."

Miss Harrington paled. "I don't know. Perhaps this would be

better attempted on a pony."

"We don't have a pony." They had Mercury. And they had an old sidesaddle that had been Miss Harrington's grandmother's. He'd checked and rechecked that the saddle fit his horse properly so that it wouldn't rub or slide. Crispin was using Mercury as a training horse. Olivia would have a conniption fit and Jasper would faint. But Miss Harrington had confided that she had never ridden. That was a deficit needing correction. "Hold the reins loosely. I'll have the lead rope. He won't bolt, and I promise you won't fall off."

He'd brought Mercury back to the farm early in his stay, after seeing to it that the barn was well-provisioned. He had to serve as his own stable hand, but that was fine, since he trusted no man with Mercury more than himself.

His pupil looked frightened.

"Miss Harrington, don't let me browbeat you into something you'd rather not do."

She tilted her head to look up at him. "This is the second time you've mentioned browbeating. Are you often accused of such?"

He started. *Yes.* Then made himself chuckle. "By my sister. She says Jasper wins arguments with charm, and I win them by bullying."

"And your younger brother?"

"Reg? Reg wins by being right."

"Are you ever right?"

"Seldom."

"Well, this is a dilemma. Since you have said that I won't fall off."

"If you do, I will catch you."

He saw something in her expression. A flash of something undefinable in her eyes before she turned her head and set her jaw. "All right. Help me up."

"Put your left hand on my shoulder. When I lift you, use your right hand for balance, but don't grab, just rest it on the pommel until you can settle yourself."

She put her hand on his shoulder, and he lifted her. She wasn't wearing a riding habit. She didn't have one. Her yellow dress was as soft as silk. He tried not to notice her narrow waist. The flare of her hips. A flash of ankle. He caught the scent of lilacs.

"Oh, no. Oh, no. Oh, no," she murmured. Or groaned. Until she was sitting in the saddle.

"Turn. Just a little. To put your leg over the pommel. That's right."

She was shaking. Mercury flexed his neck to look over his shoulder. Crispin laughed. "My horse is rolling his eyes. Relax, Miss Harrington. We won't move until you are ready."

They stood still until her quaking stopped and her breathing evened out.

"All right. I'm ready," she said in a tiny voice.

"Keep the reins light in your hands. Don't pull. You aren't to do anything but move *with* him."

They walked very slowly, from one end of the yard to the other.

"A little faster?"

"Yes, all right."

He walked more briskly as they returned to the start. She was smiling now.

"Faster?" he asked.

She pressed her lips together, then nodded.

He urged Mercury into a slow trot and jogged alongside him. They reached the end of the yard and stopped. Miss Harrington was glowing with pleasure, warming his heart.

"Would you like to try without me leading?"

"No!" She recoiled, and everything next happened quickly. She must have had the sensation of falling backwards, because she overcompensated, clumsily jerking forward to right herself. Too far forward. She curled her body instinctively, but it was the utterly wrong thing to do. Her leg disengaged from the pommel, and she toppled into his arms. He set her quickly onto her feet.

"You promised I wouldn't fall!" she accused.

"You didn't fall." He tried very hard not to laugh but didn't quite succeed. "You launched yourself out of the seat."

She glared at him. Then the cloud passed, and she snorted. "That was wonderful, actually. But I am finished for today."

"Another time?"

She hesitated, and it seemed she was going to ask him a question. Like: *Another time? How long do you intend to stay?* Perhaps he was wearing out his welcome after all. Which begged the question: Why was he still here? But then she nodded and said, "Another time."

"MAJOR? IT HAS come to my attention that we are five miles from Tunbridge Wells," Adam said, crossing the back yard to speak to him.

"Your point?" Crispin said, with a squint. His temper was short. He was just returning from an early morning walk, and it had done nothing to ease him.

Last evening had been the fourth Saturday spent in company with Sir Bodwell, who had taken every opportunity and then some to call Miss Harrington by her Christian name. Still, Crispin was aware that his pique made no sense. Certainly, if he asked her to call him Crispin, she would. And he would then call her Camellia. But he didn't want to. He thought it better to maintain that distance. He just wished Bodwell would too.

Of course, he was being ridiculous. It was none of his business. He was not her brother, to be chasing off unwanted suitors. That was Harrington's job. But perhaps Bodwell's suit was not entirely unwanted. The colonel must know he would not live forever. It was possible he saw the benefit to seeing his sister wed and settled. Camellia must see it also.

A disturbing thought crept in: Crispin didn't think she could mistake *his* attentions for anything but friendliness, but what if she did? She couldn't be trying to make him jealous of Bodwell, could she?

Obviously, he was too involved with problems that should not concern him. It was past time for him to move on. It was *November*, for pity's sake. He was simply hiding here from the stagnant waste of his own life.

Adam fell into step alongside him. "It would do Colonel Harrington good to take the waters in the mineral spring. His muscles are stiff from disuse, and it pains him."

"Ah." Tunbridge Wells was a miniature Bath. It had once been the height of fashion but had largely fallen out of favor with the ton because it had been overrun with cits. "And how do you suggest this is to be done?"

"You would hire a carriage. Lease rooms for a fortnight. Take a subscription to the baths. It would not be difficult."

"Wouldn't it?" If they stayed a fortnight, he would not be subjected to the next supper-and-cards Saturday. But would Bodwell still pay a call on Miss Harrington if the colonel was gone? "The travel would not be too much for the colonel?"

Adam paused before answering. "If I had thought so, I would not be suggesting it."

Ha! He'd managed to peeve the unflappable Adam.

Crispin had no use for mineral baths, but this sounded like the needed impetus for change. It would break him of the habit of being with Miss Harrington. And break her of the habit of being with him.

"I'll ride over to Tunbridge Wells this afternoon to see about lodgings." He would take Old Harry to Tunbridge Wells for a fortnight, and then depart for London.

CHAPTER FIFTEEN

CAMELLIA WAS GOING to Tunbridge Wells! When she'd learned that Major Taverston was taking Neville and Mr. Diakos, she said he must also bring her and Mrs. Clay. He'd responded impatiently, "Yes, fine." He didn't look pleased, but he didn't say no.

The following morning, he brought a hired carriage around to the back of the house. It was a bit battered, with peeling paint and yellowed curtains, drawn by two horses that looked long in the tooth. He said he'd left Mercury at the Fitzhenrys' stable since he was driving the carriage himself.

He threw their baggage to the top of the vehicle, then climbed up to tie it all down. She liked to watch him work. He was so…competent.

Mr. Diakos brought Neville alongside, lifted him into the carriage, and then hoisted the chair up to the major. He handed Mrs. Clay in next, and reached for Camellia's hand.

"Miss Harrington," the major called down, "you might prefer to ride with me on the box."

"Oh. Oh, all right." She didn't know why he would think that. The box was even higher than Mercury's back. Still, she stood aside. Mr. Diakos entered the carriage and shut the door. Major Taverston climbed down and helped her to the driver's bench, then mounted the box beside her.

"I apologize," he said. "This carriage was the best I could acquire on short notice. It would be cramped inside with four, and it has an odor."

"I see." She clutched the edge of the seat. There was no cushion, and the wood was worn smooth. Slippery smooth.

He grinned. "Is it heights you fear then? Not horses?"

She made a noncommittal noise. "I love horses. *Little* horses." Her palms were sweating in her gloves. "My father used to breed Yorkshire Trotters. I adored the foals."

"Oh?" For a moment, he looked thoughtful. "Well, you needn't worry." His eyes glinted wickedly. "I promise you won't fall off."

"Go *slowly*." Her tone was threatening, not pleading.

He kept to a mercifully slow pace as they left the yard and started down the drive. They rattled over the cobbles until they reached packed dirt. Then he let the horses trot. She loosened her grip. It wasn't terrible as long as she didn't look down.

"I've never been to Tunbridge Wells. Thank you for taking us."

"Never?" He glanced at her quickly, then back at the road. "When it is so close by?"

"My mother's physician did not think it would help. And my father refused to try."

He was quiet for a long moment, then said, "May I ask, how did your parents die?"

She breathed deeply. "My mother had a wasting disease of some kind. We thought consumption, but after she passed, her doctor said it was more likely a growth."

"She was sick a long time?"

"Years. I was nineteen when we first knew she was sick. She died when I was twenty-three."

"You took care of her?"

"Yes. Although we had more servants then, I rarely left her side. My father took it very hard when she passed. He'd lost two wives and loved them both." She paused. "He was not so much ill as he was broken. He could still do for himself. It wasn't like with Neville."

"You said you let servants go?"

"He had acquired a good deal of debt, so we had to." She hurried to say, "Neville sold his commission, of course, so he cleared Papa's debts." More papers she'd shoved under Neville's nose. She wasn't entirely sure he knew that the money was gone.

"And then your father passed also? Mr. Castor implied…"

"We'd heard about Vitoria. Everyone was celebrating. We thought it meant the war's end was near. Papa seemed to come back to life." She cleared her throat. "It took another month before a letter came from the War Office. It said Colonel Neville Harrington had been severely, likely lethally, wounded at Vitoria. My father had a heart seizure. He died the following day."

He winced. "I'm sorry."

"Neville doesn't need to know that. It isn't Neville's fault, but he doesn't need to know."

"Of course not."

They rode in silence for a while. Camellia shook off her melancholy. "Now, since you have played Inquisitor to me, may I ask you a question?" She was sitting close enough to feel the way his whole body tensed.

"One. But I may not answer."

She had a hundred questions, but decided to ask a simple one because he was so nervous, acting as though he had deep secrets he must hide. "Do you, or don't you, drink wine?"

His gaze slid away. His pursed mouth was something between a smile and a scowl.

"I can," he finally said. "That is, I am fairly certain that I can, so long as I don't drink a vat."

"But that isn't what I asked." She was going to press while she had the advantage. "My question was do you. Not can you."

He sniffed a laugh. "I do on occasion. But I don't enjoy the taste. And I don't like…I like to keep my wits about me. The feeling of drunkenness, that false euphoria, does not appeal to me."

"That is admirable."

He sniffed again. A short time later, he came out with, "It is the same with meat. I think I can eat it so long as there is no gravy. No sauce. But I've never liked eating flesh. It is odd, I know, but the thought of it disgusts me."

"Perhaps because you think of it as flesh. Now I feel disgusted too."

He laughed. And his body relaxed. "What would you like to do in Tunbridge Wells, Miss Harrington? Besides taking the waters. I hear there is a theater. An Assembly Room with dancing. Teashops? Bookshops?"

"Everything. I want to do everything."

THE WATER TASTED horrible. Like drinking rust. And it smelled like rotten eggs. She had no desire to soak in it. Major Taverston said he did not either. So while Mr. Diakos accompanied Neville to the baths, Major Taverston squired Camellia and Mrs. Clay about town.

He took them to teashops, public gardens, a marionette show, a curiosity shop, and a reading of poetry. The poems were mediocre, but afterward, the poet came around and kissed all the ladies' hands. There was nothing to rival the Temple of the Muses, but there was a small shop selling old books. While she didn't purchase anything, the major bought a handful, and later, she found a copy of *Childe Harold's Pilgrimage* tucked into her reticule.

He took everyone to a play one evening, *Much Ado About Nothing*. They were able to wheel Neville's chair into the aisle at the theater. And while her brother nodded off during the second act, Camellia was entranced. Claudio was a true idiot, and Hero should have felt herself well shed of him.

And then, somehow, the whole two weeks had flown by. It

was their last evening, and they were going to an Assembly—
Major Taverston had managed to acquire the necessary tickets. It
was not a London ball, but it was as near to it as she had ever
been. Or was ever likely to be.

The Assembly Hall was as large as a city block. There were
steps to enter, but Mr. Diakos carried Neville up them and the
major brought up the chair. The floor was yellow-painted wood.
The walls were papered with a bird-and-floral design. Chandeliers
dotted the ceiling and made the entire room bright. There were
tables and chairs along one wall to encourage the purchase of
refreshments. They claimed a table close to the front so that
Neville could watch the dancing.

Camellia wore her red-plaid gown and one of her black bonnets, decorated with red roses. The major was in his blue jacket
and white pantaloons. His cravat was elaborately tied. He looked
so splendid it almost hurt to look at him.

Having brought her there, of course he had to ask her to
partner him. The first set was a country dance that left her
breathless. He danced as skillfully as she would expect from a
gentleman of his rank, but he also appeared to be enjoying
himself.

She danced the second set with Mr. Diakos. A cotillion. The
steps were more complex, and he was a bit clumsy, but good-
humored about it. When the set ended, they returned to tables
where they found Neville and Major Taverston talking with a
very well-dressed, dark-haired gentleman with a hook nose.

The major said, "Miss Harrington, permit me to introduce
Lord Gilbert, an old schoolmate of mine. He is here escorting his
mother who is taking the waters. Lord Gilbert, Miss Harrington,
the colonel's sister."

She curtsied. He bowed slightly at the waist, then straightened and stared at her hair. He blinked and said, "Would you care
to dance the next set with me, Miss Harrington?"

"Thank you. I would."

He escorted her onto the floor as the music began again.

What did it matter that he had stared? She was dancing with a *lord!* They made polite conversation as they moved across the floor, weaving through the steps with the other dancers. When the music ended, he brought her back to Neville, and thanked her, smiling. It was quite pleasant. When he stepped away, she turned and beamed at the major, who looked startled a moment, then smiled back.

"Miss Harrington, I believe it is my turn again, if you'd like."

"I would. I'm having a great deal of fun. What is the dance?"

"The program says the next is a waltz."

Her spirits fell. "I can't waltz."

The major whooped. "Of course you can. The female despots of Almack's are not here to stop you."

"I mean that I don't know how." She'd learned the steps to most of the popular dances from Marianne. But that was before the waltz became *the* dance to know.

He came forward, nevertheless. He bent his head and said, "It is easier than riding a horse and lower to the ground."

She ignored the jibe. "You can't mean to teach me here."

He glanced about. "Why not?"

"I'll make a fool of myself!"

"No, you won't. No one is watching." When she set her jaw stubbornly, shaking her head, he said, "Then we can go out—" He halted, and cloud passed over his brow. A moment later he turned his attention to Mrs. Clay, seated at the table beside Neville. "Mrs. Clay, will you accompany us out onto the balcony?"

Mrs. Clay jumped to her feet. "Go on with you both. I'll be right behind."

"We won't be able to hear the music," Camellia protested.

"You forget I can whistle," the major said.

She ran out of arguments. And she didn't want to argue. She let him lead her away, then outside where a chilly wind greeted them.

"The dance will warm you," he said, noticing her shiver. "But if you want to go back inside…"

"Not yet. Show me the steps."

He gave her a melting smile. "The waltz is my favorite dance. Here. Put your left hand here on my arm. Not my shoulder but close to it. Now hold my hand. Here." He extended their arms, then slipped his right hand around to her shoulder blade, pulling her shockingly close. He blinked, opening his eyes slowly. "Lilacs," he said. "I never had a favorite flower, but I think I do now. And you should always wear red. You are fiercely beautiful in red."

Her breath caught, but she managed to exhale quietly and flirt in return. "Is flattery part of this dance? Do I have to say something back to you?"

"Not flattery. But compliments are definitely required."

"I see." She couldn't say any of the things she wanted to say. It would be too revealing. "You are very…tall."

He snickered. "We will work on that. Your compliments, I mean, not my height." He whistled a brief tune, then said. "Now look at my feet. We will walk through this three times, slowly, while you look at my feet and follow with yours. Then look up into my eyes and follow without looking down. The steps are quite simple. Just making a square."

He whistled and moved through the steps, and she followed.

"Now look up," he reminded her. "Look into my eyes so you don't get dizzy."

He held her right hand more securely, and pressed a little more firmly on her back. And whistled. They danced. It felt like floating. Without altering the pattern, he moved her around the balcony. The tempo of his whistling increased, and they began whirling.

Time both sped up and stood still. She wanted to keep dancing forever. But too soon, he slowed, then stopped, then ceased whistling. But he was still looking into her eyes.

"You were right," she said, breathing hard.

"Was I? That is good to know. Right about what?"

"I am warm now."

"You are. Quite." He let go of her and stepped back, quickly, his expression going blank. Then he touched her elbow. "But I fear Mrs. Clay is cold. We should go back inside."

"Yes, all right." She walked with him, then stopped. "Thank you. That was really wonderful. Thank you, Major."

"The pleasure was mine."

"I have that compliment for you now."

"What? Ha! Not if I've browbeaten it out of you." He nudged her elbow to keep moving.

"You do everything well, Major Taverston. It's quite a gift."

"No. The trick is that I *only* do the things I *can* do well. It's actually quite limiting."

"La! That is untrue. Name one thing you would like to do that you can't do well."

"Write poetry."

She stopped in her tracks. Then laughter bubbled out of her. "You win, Major. Arguing is one of the many things you excel at."

He grimaced. "Tall and argumentative. Thank you."

They continued on to Mrs. Clay, who was shivering with cold, but who nevertheless smiled at them in a knowing way. They went back inside. When they reached Neville's table, Mr. Diakos said, "You are finished? We should go back to our rooms. I believe Colonel Harrington has been overtaxed."

⊱❈⊰

CAMELLIA PUT ON her nightdress and slipped beneath the coverlet on her bed. Major Taverston had rented the entire floor of a large townhome, with rooms fit for an earl's brother. The linens were crisp. The mattress was soft and devoid of lumps. There were coal-burning braziers in all of the bedchambers.

He lived like this. Certainly, he'd endured privation on the peninsula, but at home, he slipped right back into the pampered life of a wealthy aristocrat. *It must be nice.*

She rolled to her side, curled up, and closed her eyes.

What had she once thought she wanted from life? What experiences had she been missing? Attending the theater. Meeting a poet. Dancing at a ball.

But there was one more. *One more.*

Two facts about Major Taverston. He was wedded to the army. And he was a rake.

He would suit perfectly. But she wasn't brave enough. She was afraid she would fall.

CRISPIN SPLASHED HIS face with cold water, shed his clothes, and dropped into bed. He stared up at the ceiling, furious with himself. He'd been aroused. When he slept, he was likely to dream of Camellia. Camellia. Given the way his thoughts were running, he would not be thinking of her as "Miss Harrington" in his dreams.

He'd meant what he said. She *was* fiercely beautiful. But that didn't mean he should have said it. They'd been in a setting where they were supposed to flirt lightly, but he had never been able to flirt. Instead, he blurted out truths like a clumsy mooncalf.

He'd held her, breathed in lilacs, waltzed with her. She danced with such a light step, it was hard to believe she'd never waltzed before. And he'd become increasingly aware of how much he wanted her. This was not the usual demand his body made at random intervals when it was healthy. The physical need that sent him out seeking lightskirts. He wanted *her*.

Bloody hell.

She had been so lithe and warm in his arms…but what was he afraid he might do? Seduce her? He wouldn't know how. Sex had always been a matter of a few coins, not compliments and coaxing.

Besides, he wasn't some unprincipled rake, seducing innocents. He'd have to marry her if he wanted to get into her bed. And marriage was out of the question. It had always been out of the question. He didn't want to leave a young widow behind or fatherless children.

And, of all people, Miss Harrington? He'd already established that she deserved a husband, not another sick man to nurse.

CHAPTER SIXTEEN

THERE WAS A time, not so long ago—and Crispin *knew* this—that he'd had the ability to evaluate a situation, make a decision, and act. He was known for, and prided himself on, being able to take quick and total control, no matter how chaotic the circumstance. That was how he'd risen so rapidly in rank. How he'd caught Wellington's attention and that of the War Office. How he'd "browbeaten" his brothers into marrying their ideal mates.

He'd always despised men who hemmed and hawed. Now he was one. Despite his resolution to leave the Harringtons after Tunbridge Wells, he was back at the farm, turning over the soil in Miss Harrington's flower garden, when he should be in London purchasing furniture for his cottage.

He sniffed. Purchasing furniture. *Good God.* When had the stakes in his game of life become so low?

And tonight, Sir Bodwell would come prattling about farming, with his "Nevilles" and "Camellias." Crispin had meant to be gone before suffering through that again.

What he *should* do tonight was make a trip to Wheatfield. Visit the tavern and hire a girl. He hadn't had a girl since Lizzie. Since Lizzie! He didn't dare count the months.

No, what he should do was go to Paris and see if Wellington still had use for him.

He dragged the shovel through clods of dirt and tangled roots to break them up. What he would *likely* do would be to ask Miss Harrington's advice about what to put in his garden in Binnings.

There. He laid the shovel against his shoulder like a blunderbuss to return it to storage.

The barn was damp and smelled of rotten grass and neglect. The disquieting thought sneaked up on him—the Harringtons could use Bodwell's intervention. The man knew farms.

He entered the house through the kitchen. Mrs. Clay was not there. He pinched a radish and strode, crunching, into the receiving room, where he found Miss Harrington on one of the worn blue brocade couches. She had a pile of pink cloth in her lap.

"Your garden is tilled." He gestured to her project. "What are you working on?"

"Thank you." She raised the edge of the cloth. "An old dress of my mother's. I thought..." She grabbed it all up in a bundle and laid it beside her. "The style is ridiculous. Panniers. I thought I could alter it, but I haven't the skill for such an undertaking."

He recalled a letter Olivia had sent him when she was preparing for her London Season. She'd been infuriated by the hours she'd had to spend with dressmakers, the ungodly number of gowns she'd been obliged to have made. He'd been amused by her dilemma. He was not amused by Miss Harrington's.

"Neville is still feeling poorly." She sounded out of sorts. "Mr. Diakos says his muscles are not as stiff. The baths helped, but all the excitement did not. He's overtired."

Crispin did not know how to respond, seeing as he'd organized the excitement.

She said, "I thought we should postpone our supper with Manfred. Mrs. Clay has gone to give him word."

Thank God. "That sounds wise."

She tilted her head and looked at him strangely. Her eyes were tight. Hesitant. "Should we have supper in the dining room? Neville has asked for a tray in his chamber."

"If you like." Something must be bothering her. Beyond her brother's weariness.

She sighed. "I put a great deal of effort into renovations. I didn't 'mutilate the house.' I think the dining room looks nice. Though it is shaped a bit oddly where they took down walls. And there is a parlor upstairs, too. But we only ever sit down here." She added hurriedly, "Which is fine. It's where Neville can join us."

Mutilate? Surely she couldn't be brooding over Castor's idiotic comment. The man hadn't even seen the refurbishments beyond the all-purpose receiving room. "I would love to eat in the dining room. We could also have tea in the parlor if the colonel is indisposed."

She smiled wryly. "I suppose I seem silly to you. Worrying about a few unused rooms."

"No. Not silly." *But yes.* Entire wings at Chaumbers went unused, and no one was concerned.

"Well," she said, drawing herself up. "Then let me pose a question."

"Go on."

"What shall I have Mrs. Clay serve for tea? And supper?"

A soft groan escaped his lips. She'd lured him into a trap. He sat heavily on a short-backed chair facing her. "Generally, for tea, I have only tea. People tend to serve cakes or biscuits, which I do not eat."

"If you were to eat something?"

"Fruit. Nuts."

"And for supper?"

"Plain things. No gravy. No bread. Nothing from a cow."

"No flesh?"

"Sometimes flesh." He grimaced. "When I am hungry enough."

"Eggs?"

"Yes."

"Rice? Potatoes? Peas?"

"Yes. Any garden greens or roots, but cooked plain."

They were quiet for a moment, as she was probably concocting a menu in her head. Then she said, "No wine. Or only occasional wine. But what about ale or small beer? You're not likely to get bosky on small beer."

He shook his head. "I prefer it, but I cannot drink it."

She grinned at him. "Gin? Rum? Snuff?"

"No."

Then she laughed. "Have you no vices, Major?"

"My crimes are unspeakable ones." She would think it a joke, but it was true.

Rattling noises came from the direction of the kitchen.

"Mrs. Clay must be back. I'll go tell her we'll be dining upstairs."

⇶✕⇷

THEY HAD TEA and sliced pears in the parlor, a spacious room, but sparsely furnished. The paint and paper on the walls had a very new, untouched appearance and the air smelled stale. They discussed *Childe Harold's Pilgrimage*, which he had bought for her on a whim. Crispin thought it was overwrought, but that was the very reason Miss Harrington loved it. When she learned that he knew Lord Byron—not well, they'd played commerce at the same table at Prinny's ball—she said, "My word! Did you save any of the cards he played?"

"*What?*"

"Never mind." She put a fingertip to his wrist. "I've touched the hand that touched the cards that Lord Byron touched!" She pretended to swoon.

"If you'd been there, you could have joined the dozen other young ladies sprawled on the ground."

"Were there really?" she asked greedily. "I've heard women faint when he walks into a room."

"Yes, it is a true liability for the London hostesses. They've taken to strewing cushions on the floor. Of course, it makes dancing a challenge—"

Her eyes lit. "I know you're lying, but I do so want that to be true."

After they parted, he went to the guest bedchamber to read his letters that Mrs. Clay had brought back with her from Sir Bodwell's—Bodwell had retrieved their mail from the post in Tonbridge, thinking to bring it himself. Which was either thoughtful or overstepping. And didn't that sum up poor Bodwell?

There was a letter from Jasper and one from Hazard. Both were concerned with Wellington's increasing unpopularity in France. There were even threats against his person. Liverpool and his cabinet were searching for a dignified way to withdraw him. He might be sent to America to conclude the war there. Jasper's letter included an aside stating that Crispin's decision not to go to Paris was wise and he should congratulate himself on his foresight. But, of course, the news had the opposite effect. Threats, subterfuge, ferreting out assassination plots—he should be in Paris, not...cultivating his own garden as per Voltaire. Conscience was a luxury a soldier could not afford.

With a groan, he went down to share *some* of the news with the colonel. But since the colonel was sleeping, he went to the barn to curry Mercury. Then he fetched two buckets of well water and bothered Mrs. Clay to let him heat them on the stove. He carried the hot water up to his chamber. There was no washtub to sit in, but he made do. While he was at it, he took out his shaving kit and scraped the stubble from his cheeks and chin. He daubed himself with Spanish Leather, then put on clean clothes. Linen shirt, fawn trousers, Carmelite-Brown jacket, cravat. As he tied his garters around his stockings, it occurred to him he was taking an inordinate amount of care for a country supper.

However, when he walked into the dining room and saw

Miss Harrington, he was glad he had done so, because she had also taken great care. He would have felt he was insulting her had he come in shabbily dressed, smelling of the barn. Her hair was pulled back into a twist, revealing an elegant neck. She wore a ruby-red satin dress. It was modestly styled with sleeves from shoulder to wrist and a hint of decolletage.

"Another dress of my mother's," she said, obviously aware of his regard. "It is out of date—"

"It's stunning. *You* are stunning." She would invade his dreams again.

She blushed. "It is bold of me to wear red when you said I should. It rather forces you to flatter me."

"Compliment, not flatter. And no force is required." He watched her gaze drop and her blush deepen. He hadn't meant to make her uncomfortable. Or *himself* uncomfortable. In his brain, he had always kept women neatly separated behind sturdy fences. In one pen, there were *ladies*—whom he might like and admire, but who did not stir him. And in the other, there were women for hire—who did. Miss Harrington belonged to the first category. But it seemed she had slipped out the gate.

"So this is the mysterious dining room?" he said quickly. "Explain your renovations if you would. What you've done and why. My lake cottage has been sorely neglected and needs work, and I am quite at a loss where to start."

She gave a nervous laugh, not a titter, but close. "All right. My main goal was to put everything Neville would need on the ground floor. And then shift everything else up here. The reason this room is oddly L-shaped is that they knocked down the wrong walls. I meant to combine two bedchambers, and then make the dressing room into a parlor. But they combined the bedchamber, antechamber, and dressing room, and made the parlor out of another bedchamber."

He smirked. "Were these the same laborers who built the ramp over the front steps?"

She nodded, looking chagrined. "I suppose I didn't make my

wishes clear enough."

"I think the moral is to keep an eye on one's laborers. But it came out well, nevertheless." Compared to Chaumbers, that was not a lie.

At that moment, Mrs. Clay and Adam entered, carrying trays. The table, which would have seated twelve comfortably, had been formally set for two. Both settings were at one end so they wouldn't be shouting to one another. But that also emphasized that they would be dining alone, *tête-à-tête*. Which was not *done*. A chill coursed through his blood. He knew better. And so must she. *What were they playing at?*

Mrs. Clay and Adam laid down covered bowls and a pitcher. He should ask Mrs. Clay to stay. But he did not. After all, he and Miss Harrington were often alone together—why should this be different? Why did it *feel* different? When the servants departed, Miss Harrington removed the covers. Turnips. Boiled eggs. Lettuces. Rice flecked with mushrooms. The pitcher held cider. It was a laughably ghastly menu, but it was supper for him. He was touched.

He took some of everything. While they ate, they talked easily of the garden, the colonel, Tunbridge Wells. Then poetry. What was good and what was bad. He ate until he was sated. That was a rare gift.

He settled back in his chair. She set down her cup. "Shall I ring for dessert?"

"There is more?"

She nodded. "I've seen the way you sugar your tea. You have a sweet tooth." She rose and pulled the bell cord. Then sat again. "Did you have letters from home? I hope nothing is wrong."

"Nothing at home. They were political. Problems in France." Since she looked quizzical, he gave her a censured version of the censured version he'd meant to give the colonel. Her brow furrowed with consternation.

"But I don't understand! They were freed from the tyrant. Why aren't they more grateful?"

Crispin snorted. "I think rather they feel robbed of their empire. With Napoleon, the French believed they ruled the world. Now they are squashed back into their boundaries and under our very British thumb."

She *hmphed*. But then looked thoughtful. "At least Napoleon is gone."

Mrs. Clay came back into the room with a tray holding two servings of what at first glance appeared to be syllabub, a dish made with cream, so neither he nor Miss Harrington would eat it.

"Apples baked in sugar," Miss Harrington said.

"Ah." He smiled.

He ate his, and when she pushed hers away because it was too sweet, he ate hers too.

"Miss Harrington, I thank you," he said, licking his spoon and dropping it into the bowl. "I've gained a stone."

She glowed, victorious. "Now I suppose we should go downstairs. Neville might be feeling more himself. I don't want to leave him out."

So they went down. Crispin sat at the pianoforte and played for a few minutes until Adam came out of his chamber to tell them the colonel was sleeping.

Miss Harrington yawned, then quickly covered her mouth. "Excuse me. I think I will retire as well."

Crispin stood as she did. And realized he was disappointed to have to say goodnight.

He fell asleep when his head hit the pillow. He slept deeply until a sense of movement, not his own, penetrated his dreams. A presence in his room. Although his pulse raced, he didn't move a muscle and kept his breathing steady. Peering through slitted eyelids, he could not make out anything in the dark. Then he heard his door click shut and latch. *Assassins. Where was the duke?*

He slipped his hand under his pillow for his pistol, but it wasn't there. And he'd been stripped naked. Had he been drugged?

Damn.

He startled awake. Fully awake. Of course, his pistol was not under his pillow. It was tucked away in his valise. And he was unclothed because he was safe in a farmhouse near Tonbridge.

But he saw a flicker of movement again. And his eyes began to adjust to the dark. A sinuous shifting of black against black. The scent of lilacs. The shape turned and he saw the pallor of a face.

"Camellia?" he whispered. Then kicked himself. One was not supposed to wake a sleepwalker. And she *had to be* walking in her sleep.

She floated closer. Like a black-garbed ghost. Or a succubus.

He pulled the coverlet up over his chest. Then, for good measure, up to his chin.

She stood beside his bed. Her eyes were wide open and frightened. Yet she fearlessly peeled off her black cloak and dropped it to the floor. She was in her chemise. Silent as a tomb. Pale arms. Pale neck. Pale *legs*.

And he was wildly aroused.

"Miss Harrington," he whispered more loudly. There was no option but to wake her. They would both be mortified, but it was better than the alternative, which was—

She sat on the edge of his bed. He swallowed so hard he thought the gulp must be audible in London.

"Miss Harrington, wake up!" He spoke aloud, remembering that Old Harry had screamed in the night, and they hadn't heard him upstairs. Miss Harrington blinked, and gave the merest shake of her head. She was awake.

He shuddered. Then said a quick prayer that *he* was dreaming.

She put her index finger on his cheek. Light as mist. And ran it down his jaw line. Then down his neck to the coverlet. She sighed shakily before repeating the caress on his other side. He clenched his coverlet so tightly his fingers hurt. Yet he didn't say anything. He didn't catch hold of her hand to stop her when she did it again. Rather, he loosened his grip on the coverlet and allowed her to tuck it down as she caressed him to his collarbone. Then slowly across his chest from shoulder to shoulder. His breathing grew ragged. This game of hers was unbearably pleasureful. If a dream, he never wanted to wake.

She leaned over, her face drawing closer to his, as though she meant to kiss him. He turned his head away and heard her sharp intake of breath. Hurt. It was not his intention to hurt her. But he was terrified.

"Camellia, I want this. I do. But we can't."

Rather than answer him in any rational way, she slid down onto the bed beside him. He swore under his breath. But he didn't protest when she pushed the coverlet down to his hips. She stroked his chest. His ribs. She seemed more curious than impassioned. But if she explored any farther, he would not hold himself accountable...

She lifted the edge of the coverlet and slipped in beside him. He felt her warmth through the thin fabric of her chemise. Her fingers trailed over his belly. To his hipbone.

"Don't," he said. Damn. It was too late for *don't*. In another moment, *he* would grab *her*.

They both held still. Not breaking the spell. Then she draped her arm across his chest. And her leg across his. Skin on skin. How far would she dare take this? How far would he? She shimmied against him, so he shifted and put his hands on her hips to slide her onto him. He gathered her chemise, pulling it up until it bunched about her waist. Abruptly, she raised up to sit across his thighs, straddling him. He held his breath. Then she touched his prick, tentatively, as if awaiting permission. "Go on," he whispered. She stroked him. Made him groan. A stuttering groan. He had never wanted a woman so badly. *Her*. He wanted her.

She stopped, then ran her thumbnail lightly from his breastbone to his waist and below.

A tease. She was killing him. He caught her hand and returned it to his prick. "Keep doing *that*."

"Major—"

"Crispin!" he growled. "If you're going to…to do this…call me Crispin."

She whispered, "Crispin."

He groaned again, guttural. "Keep doing that. You needn't be so gentle." She shifted her weight and changed her grip. "Oh, God, that's good."

She smiled. He saw it. A sly little smile. Triumphant. He thought…triumphant. But the smile turned into a studious frown. She wiggled down his legs and bent down. He shut his eyes tight and willed her to do what he thought she intended. Even so, when she licked his tip, he shouted. No words. An animal sound. She bolted upright. Startled.

Something like a laugh slipped from his mouth. He wriggled to sit up, then wrapped his arms around her, and rolled her beneath him.

Harrington's sister. His conscience stabbed him. He was going to tup Harrington's sister.

"Camellia, are you sure you want this?" *Say yes.*

"Yes."

"You know what we are doing. And that it is wrong. You know that, Camellia."

"Yes, Crispin."

"Good." *God.* This wasn't just wrong; it would be the worst thing he'd ever done.

CAMELLIA LAY IN her own bed fuming, eyes stinging and eyelashes wet. Marianne was wrong. The stupid *School of Venus* was wrong. It was hardly "the most sovereign pleasure we poor mortals enjoy." She'd done what the book said to do. Not everything, naturally, or they would have been there all night, but enough that Crispin obviously enjoyed himself. But he didn't "tickle" her the way the book said he would. *Lud.* He hadn't even *kissed* her! Wasn't it strange that there had been no kisses?

After, he was angry. Maybe not at her. Maybe more at himself—which he shouldn't have been since *she* had seduced *him.* But after he'd...done what *The School of Venus* had described, he rolled away, putting his back to her, leaving her to slip out of the room. And she *had* to slip out. She had to clean herself the way Marianne said.

Still. She swiped the back of her hand across her eyes. She regretted nothing. In fact, she was proud that she'd been brave enough to follow through. Now she *knew.* No better chance would ever present itself. According to Neville, the major was experienced in intimate matters. And he was committed to the army. She wouldn't be trapped into a marriage just because she'd given herself. She trusted he wouldn't say anything to anyone, and neither would she.

So there was nothing to regret.

CHAPTER SEVENTEEN

Ow WAS ONE supposed to behave the morning afterward? Camellia had not thought of that—what to say to him when they saw each other again. What could she possibly say?

She dressed in a modest blue gown, nothing red, and went downstairs. Neville was at the table by himself, a light blanket draped across his shoulders. His face was more haggard than ever. Camellia took the seat beside him.

"Are you feeling better?"

He grunted. "Stop fussing." He pushed aside his plate and picked up his cup of coffee.

"And where is the major this morning?" *Good Lord.* Her voice was pitched as high as a nervous schoolgirl's.

"Gone into Tonbridge. He said that horse of his lost a shoe."

"Oh." Was that true? Or an excuse to avoid her? Across the table from Neville lay a plate and an empty teacup. If Mrs. Clay had not cleared them away yet, the major must have just left. And was that—"Did he have *toast?*" Crumbs and a bite of crust remained on the plate. But he didn't eat bread. He'd said he didn't.

Neville shrugged impatiently. "He'd already finished when Diakos brought me out. Then he bolted."

"The major bolted?"

"In a hurry to get the horse seen to. Bring me another cup of coffee, will you? My throat is dry as sand."

C̲RISPIN POINTED M̲ERCURY in the general direction of London and let him run. It was not until the horse was panting and lathered that he cursed himself and turned around. He had to go back. Rogue he might be, but he would nevertheless go back. His fate was sealed.

At first, he'd tried telling himself that it made no sense. That he couldn't believe Camellia had come to him and he had taken her. But that was denial, not disbelief. He'd fallen into an age-old woman's trap. *God!* He'd heeded Vanessa's warning not to swoop young ladies alone out onto dark balconies. Did he really need her to tell him it was a bad idea to take his ex-commander's sister to bed?

How long had Camellia been dangling after him?

It was not that he considered himself such a prize. But the Taverston name meant something. He had property and a comfortable degree of wealth. And he was in line for an earldom, though it was impossible to see himself outliving Jasper. In catching him, she had done well for herself.

Until he fell sick again. Then she would see the devil's bargain she'd made.

Damn it! He'd *liked* her. That was what made him so furious. He'd liked her. He'd *trusted* her. Even confided in her. And then, she turned around and did this!

It was not even cleverly done. He could have appreciated a well-plotted ensnarement. But she'd merely jumped into his bed. He should have demanded that she leave. Why didn't he? Why the blazes didn't he? Why the bloody hell didn't he?

The same thoughts whirled again and again through his brain as he retraced the path of his flight. He approached a village he'd passed by a short time earlier. He had to stop. Mercury needed a rest. And he was in no hurry to reach the farm. No rush to approach the colonel like some honorable mooncalf and ask for the trollop's hand.

Who had taught her how to pleasure a man? He hoped not Manfred. Certainly not Castor. The idea sickened him. No. Some young fellow in town. Or in London. Surely that night at the Temple of the Muses, she *had* been waiting to rendezvous with an inamorato. The poem she'd written—something about being in her lover's arms at night. *Who?*

He dismounted in the village and led Mercury along a dirt street, oblivious to his surroundings.

His chest ached. Or his heart hurt. He didn't want to believe she'd had other lovers, but neither did he want to have been the one to ruin her. He should have checked the bed linens. He'd been too stupefied to even examine the linens for blood. But she wasn't an innocent. She couldn't be. Not with that wanton's touch. She'd *licked* him.

He came across a tavern. A small, suitably filthy place. He entered and tossed a coin to the man who stepped forward. "Water my horse."

"Yes, Milord. Of course. And for you?"

Damn it all. Let her see what she was getting. "A mug of ale."

CAMELLIA'S STATE OF mind veered from nervous, to calm, to panicky as the day wore on and Major Taverston did not return. At one point, she even went upstairs to sneak a look into his room. A faint hint of his cologne hung in the air, but the chamber was immaculate. Except for his valise in the corner, he might never have been there. But surely the valise indicated he meant to come back.

Standing there in the emptiness, she felt a shiver as it occurred to her how little she knew him. Why had he joined the army? When was he going back to it? Had he ever been in love? Did he have a sweetheart? She wasn't about to go sifting through his valise for clues, but she recalled that she had old letters from Neville that referred to "Lieutenant Cheatdeath."

She spun about and went to her own chamber, where the accumulated clutter of twenty-six years welcomed her, chasing away the oppressive nothingness that she'd felt in the guestroom. She opened the right-hand drawer of her writing desk. The drawer was full of letters, tied with ribbons in neat little stacks.

The earliest ones would be from Neville's posting in Ireland. He'd written her short notes with funny pictures because he was writing to a child. Looking at those would likely make her cry, and they would be from before Neville had met the major, so she moved them aside. She pulled out the bundles from the peninsula and took them to her bed. She sat down, untied the ribbons, and spread the letters out before her.

She skimmed several until she found a possible reference.

A new officer has been assigned to me. Another wet-behind-the-ears son of a peer. But this one listens and follows orders without grumbling. I think he's smart, but we'll see.

The next letter came a few months later. This was certainly about the major.

Terrible weather. Usually that keeps the frogs quiet, but we fell into an unexpected skirmish. We nearly lost a company that was badly situated, but this new lieutenant threw his own men into the fray, and they saved the lot. He leads from the front. A reckless act and I shouldn't condone it, but it is hard to discipline a man for success. Frankly, I've never seen anything so stupidly brave. Lieutenant Cheatdeath. He should not have come out of it unscathed.

Nothing more. And nothing in the next few letters. It was nearly a year later before Neville mentioned him again.

There is a young lieutenant under my command whose sang-froid rivals General Wellesley's. Unfortunately, the General has

*taken notice of Cheatdeath and has begun pulling him from my
regiment for special duties.*

Frustratingly he gave no details. But in the next letter, there
was this.

*Cheatdeath is back with the regiment, which strengthens us.
His men are the best disciplined and will do anything he asks of
them, but whether for love or fear is difficult to say. He is a
cold-blooded devil.*

And that was all. Neville's letters were always murky in that
way. They were mostly concerned with the weather, the scenery,
the food, and amusing anecdotes about the long marches and
coping with boredom. He mentioned military engagements only
in the briefest way. And he referred to other officers in vague
terms with the nicknames he'd given them. She hadn't wondered
before what he meant by "coldblooded devil." But she wondered
now.

⊹≫≪⊹

IT WAS NOT until evening that Camellia heard Mrs. Clay greeting
Major Taverston in the kitchen. His tone sounded short. And
when he came into the receiving room and saw her and Neville,
he scowled at them both.

"Horse shod?" Neville asked.

"*Hmm?* Yes. Taken care of."

She was sitting on the pianoforte's bench but had stopped
practicing a while earlier. She knew she should say something,
but her mind buzzed with such confusion she could not even
greet him. She remembered how his skin had felt, how his voice
shook. Heat flooded her neck.

"I had a letter from Captain Leyton. You remember him,"
Neville said. "He said Wellington is in a tight spot."

"I've heard the same." The major glanced at the couch, then at an empty chair near the pianoforte, but rather than sit, he paced. "The duke said once that Napoleon would be a better ruler for France than King Louis, if it were possible to ensure he would keep within France's borders. But Boney can't be trusted."

"Neither can the Bourbons."

Camellia breathed a little easier as they discussed the instability of the French king's hold on France. Until Mrs. Clay stepped into the receiving room and said, "Should I serve?"

"Yes, do," Neville said.

The major pushed Neville's chair to the table. Then he walked back toward Camellia, meeting her halfway. He offered his arm as though to formally escort her. It was absurd since they were only crossing the room. Still, she laid her hand on his arm. He leaned toward her. "I will speak to your brother after supper." His voice was hard as granite.

"Speak to him?" she murmured back, confused.

"Of course."

Oh, dear God! He couldn't mean to ask for her hand. "No, don't. Please, don't."

He gave her a dark look. "We both know the rules."

"And broke them. That's the end of it." She pulled her hand away and hurried to the table to take a seat beside her brother. Major Taverston followed. He didn't sit. He poured himself a glass of wine and drank it standing.

"I ate in the village," he said. He set the glass down. "If you'll excuse me…" He bowed stiffly and headed for the stairs.

DINNER WAS UNCOMFORTABLE. Neville still did not appear well, and Camellia hated that she found his fatigue to be in her favor. He retired immediately after the meal. Major Taverston could not possibly speak with him tonight. Since she saw little point in sitting alone in the receiving room, she decided to go to her chamber. But nearing the top of the stairs, she heard footsteps in the parlor. The major must have been waiting to hear her come up, because he stepped out of the room the moment she reached the landing.

"Miss Harrington." He grasped her elbow. "Come with me." He didn't return to the parlor, but rather pulled her down the hallway toward their bedchambers. When she tried to twist from his grip, he let go and caught her wrist instead. "Would you prefer to have this discussion here? Or behind closed doors?" His voice was flat and devoid of warmth. She'd rather not have the discussion at all.

"I will come. You have no cause to drag me."

He released her wrist at once, then walked ahead of her. She followed, a cold ball of fear rising in her chest. He opened the door to his bedchamber and, with an exaggerated, mocking swoop of his arm, invited her in. She stepped inside. She jumped when he shut the door and latched it.

"Frightened?" He laughed harshly. "How odd. You weren't last night."

"I'm not frightened."

He regarded her a long moment. His gaze was intense, as if he were digging around in her soul. Then his lips twisted into a cruel smile. "Why don't you want me to talk to the colonel? Afraid he'll refuse? Would you prefer to elope? It makes no difference to me. A run to Gretna Green or—"

"No!"

"There is no choice. Although your chastity is doubtful, you are Colonel Harrington's sister, a gentlewoman, and I've lain with you."

He doubted her chastity? She blinked away a sudden welling of tears. He had good reason to doubt. "I have the right to say no. I don't want to marry you."

"And yet you climbed into my bed."

"Major—"

"Camellia," he wagged his finger at her, "I believe we established that you are to call me Crispin."

"Stop." It was hard to explain herself when his whole bearing was one of mocking disdain. "It was not my intention to compel you to ask for me. I didn't think you would." She couldn't tell him she'd been relying on his *dishonor*. "I won't marry you. I don't intend to marry at all."

"Just a tup then?" He sneered. "You wanted me to oblige you in bed? And you thought I would not mind doing so?"

It was as awful as he made it sound. But she nodded.

"We have to marry." He nearly spat the words. "You may not care a fig for me, but you could be carrying my child."

She shook her head. "I'm not. I—I took care of that."

"You took—?" His eyes flared, then narrowed. "Whores' tricks?" His voice cracked. "You even know whores' tricks?"

She gasped, then retorted, "Harlots have to use 'tricks' for the convenience of men like you!"

"I didn't *ask* for this!" Voice thinned to a whisper, he demanded, "Do I owe you a shilling?"

"Why are you being so hateful?" He was not only insulting her, but also Marianne. "Precautions are used by perfectly respectable wives."

"Which *you* are not. You're nothing but a pleasure-seeking—"

"*Pleasure?* No woman could possibly find pleasure in"—she threw her hand out toward the bed—"in that!" Her voice caught. "Don't judge my pleasure by yours. It was awful! You couldn't even be bothered to kiss me!"

His head drew back. For a fraction of a moment, a shadow passed over his face. Then he dropped his hands to his sides and clenched his fists. "Get out."

"It wasn't a trap," she murmured. She couldn't bear his misconceptions. "I was only—"

"Your motives don't interest me."

"Please don't say anything to Neville."

"We've both been very clear we don't want to be shackled to each other. Now, get out."

CRISPIN QUIT THE Harringtons early the next morning. He said polite goodbyes with the excuse he was overdue at his brother's. He felt like scum as he shook Old Harry's hand, pretending he had not betrayed his former commander in the vilest way. He bowed to Miss Harrington, but could not bring himself to look her in the eye. Not after the heinous things he'd said to her. As Mercury bore him off toward London, Crispin marveled that the animal could still carry him, freighted as he was by self-loathing.

There *had been* blood on the linens. He'd found the stain when he got into bed, proof he'd taken Miss Harrington's maidenhead. She'd been an innocent.

A *guilty* innocent. She'd used him. She robbed him of his honor, or at least, the last bit of honor that he'd believed remained to him. It was selfish of her after he'd been selfless with them.

She'd said it was awful. And complained that he hadn't kissed her. Hadn't bothered to kiss her.

The trick is that I only do the things I can do well.

Damn. What a liar he was.

CHAPTER EIGHTEEN

A MAN MIGHT lose himself in the entertainments London had to offer. Crispin had been back in the city for a month, and he'd tried. Tried but did not succeed. And now, Jasper had summoned him to Chaumbers for the upcoming Christmas festivities. All the comforts and joys of the holidays in the bosom of his family. He wasn't going to go.

He had a new personal failing to dwell upon. Early on in his adult life, he'd learned that lightskirts did not like to be kissed on the mouth. Easy enough, he didn't need to kiss them. And he didn't need a girl to flatter him with a performance of her pleasure. He knew the best way to truly please a trull was to finish his business quickly and pay her more than she'd asked. Camellia was no trull, but he'd treated her like one because he hadn't known how to do anything else.

He regretted ever going to Tonbridge. He couldn't fathom why he had gone *back*.

He turned up the collar of his greatcoat and trudged into the wind. Darkness was falling although it was only teatime. He needed that cup of tea; he felt faint. Weak. He should have taken a hackney cab. Tinsbury Square was farther than he'd thought.

He continued down Picadilly to his lodgings. He'd managed to lease a set at Albany, one left fully furnished by a dead man— he hoped that wasn't a precedent. Four rooms, an entryway, and the all-important privy. He couldn't have remained any longer at 8 Grosvenor Square. He was sick and trying to hide it, and Peters and Cook watched him too closely.

It was his own fault. He'd been courting illness since he'd left Tonbridge. Pains in his gut had begun weeks ago, but he'd pushed on, continuing down the easy path to ruin.

Now he was constantly fatigued. He routinely vomited his breakfast. If he ate anything during the day, he felt bloated like a dead fish in the sun, and didn't dare venture far from his apartment. His clothes were loose; he'd lost at least two stone.

Albany was set back from the road by a small private courtyard. As he crossed it, Crispin saw a man standing outside the gate. *Was it anyone he cared to see?* Tall and slim, wrapped in a fashionable dark-blue greatcoat, top hat, walking stick—it was Hazard. He approached his old friend, resigning himself to being scrutinized.

"I've run you to ground," Hazard said, by way of greeting as they entered the gated area. "Alice is peeved."

"Peeved?" Crispin fished his key from his coat. "So you're hiding?"

"Not peeved with me, you idiot. You refused three invitations to supper, then disappeared. You are a hard man to track down."

"Not hard enough." He opened his door and gestured for Hazard to go in.

Hazard stepped inside and unbuttoned his coat. "You keep it warm."

"I like my luxuries."

Hazard sniffed. "I'll get to the point. Are you unwell?"

"No," he lied.

"Take off your coat. Let me judge."

"Do you think you'll find me covered in boils?"

"Are you?"

Crispin glowered at him, but the man stood firm. He removed his coat, taking the paper-wrapped parcel that had been tucked inside and laying it on a shelf by the umbrella stand.

"You are too thin," Hazard said.

"I am always too thin."

"And you are pale. When did you last eat?"

What was he to say? Three days ago? He'd had nothing but tea and sugar for three days because he'd wanted to go to the Temple of the Muses, and didn't want to shame himself by becoming publicly sick. And if he was going to be housebound, or, God forbid, bedridden, he wanted something to read.

"Breakfast. And I am starving." He looked away. "Would you like a cup of tea? I'll have to make it. I haven't hired a valet yet. The poor sod will have to be valet, housekeeper, butler, and cook."

"I'll send James over."

"James?"

"My underbutler. Superb fellow."

"To spy on me?"

Hazard chuckled. "Face the fact that your loved ones worry. And yes, I will ask James to report back to me. It's either that or I'll come visit you daily. I don't trust your word."

"Fine." He needed a manservant and hadn't the energy to go through the process of hiring one. "There are rooms in the attic for valets. What do you pay him?"

"I'll pay him. He is my spy. And don't imagine you can bribe him. He is irreproachably honest."

Crispin tried to scowl and protest, but a wave of dizziness swept over him. Evidently, the quaking of his legs was obvious, because Hazard said, "Sit down. I'll get the tea."

He didn't argue. He sat. Hazard took off his own coat, laid it on a chair, then disappeared into the next room. He reappeared several minutes later with a cup of lukewarm, weak tea.

"That is the best you could do?"

Hazard shrugged. "I have not cultivated the skill."

"You can't boil water?"

Hazard stepped to the grate and stirred the coals. Then turned. "How sick are you? You look like hell. Should you have been out walking?"

"Why are you still in London? Aren't you going to spend Christmas in Gladnorshire with your...friend?" He loaded the word with innuendo.

Hazard replied evenly, "That was my initial intent. Until Alice said I should go, and she would go to Chaumbers. As it is our first Christmas as man and wife, I thought it better to spend it together."

"I suppose you cannot get a child on her if you are half the breadth of England apart. Are you disappointed she would not go with you to Lord Chesterfield's?" He snorted. "Tell me, how is that supposed to work? It's hard to picture."

Hazard gave him a dark look. "Recall, if you will, that you are speaking about Alice."

Crispin's gaze fell first. He'd meant only to turn the conversation away from himself. "You're right. And I apologize."

Hazard flicked his hand. "You've always been a bit of a turd."

Crispin laughed. Then he drank up his tea and set the cup down.

"Do you want another?" Hazard asked. When Crispin shook his head, Hazard walked away from the grate to the umbrella stand. "This is what you ventured out for?" He reached for the books. Crispin grimaced as Hazard lifted the bundle and untied it, then unwrapped the first book.

"*Devotions upon Emergent Occasions?*" Hazard glanced up. "Donne's treatise on death?"

"I would say rather his treatise on eternal salvation."

Hazard opened the book and skimmed the first page. "'We die, and cannot enjoy death, because we die in this torment of sickness.'"

"It suits my mood."

Hazard set it down and picked up the other. Crispin started to protest, but realized it was better to make little of it. Hazard peeled off the paper.

"Aretino's *The Genuine and Remarkable Amours?*" The book

was a detailed chronicle of the author's sexual adventures. Hazard threw back his head and laughed. "Only you would link these two books together. Or perhaps you and Donne."

He had thought they both might be instructive. "I am building my library. I have great hopes for its variety."

"You are off to a fine start." Hazard pulled out his watch. "And I am late. I'm supposed to escort Alice to a lecture. Will you come to supper tomorrow night?"

"No. I will be reading."

"I'll send James over tonight." He retrieved his greatcoat and donned it. "With blood pudding and boiled beef. Eat something, will you?"

"I am eating."

"Then get better. Don't make me send for Jasper."

⇢⟫⟪⇠

CAMELLIA INVITED MARIANNE and Lord Stirling to Tonbridge for Christmas. She wanted better company than her brother and Manfred, who never talked of poetry and novels, or teased her about her fear of high places, or whistled or played the pianoforte while she sang.

Seducing Major Taverston had been the worst mistake of her life.

And now, she *needed* to talk to Marianne. She had a question that she couldn't put in a letter.

She felt well. Physically well. Her mood was steady. She was not overly tired. She ate what she pleased and never felt sick in the mornings. The only strange thing was her courses were late. She tried not to dwell on it. She'd missed courses before, and it meant nothing.

More concerning was the fact that Neville had never quite recovered from the trip to Tunbridge Wells. He had developed a cough that kept him up nights. He told her she should go to

London and visit her friend if Marianne could not come to see her, but she wasn't about to leave him, ill, over Christmas. Besides, if she were to go to London, Marianne would insist upon taking her around to all the sights and parties. What if she were to cross paths with the major?

Did he ever think of her? Did he ever think of her without contempt?

The week before Christmas, Manfred came for supper and cards at his usual time. As per his habit, he brought with him their mail from Tonbridge.

"A letter for you, Camellia," Neville said, passing it over the table.

"A reply from Marianne!" She took it and walked a few steps away, breaking the seal. It was a no. Marianne and Philip could not come. Camellia skimmed through the regrets. Then stopped.

You see, I'm increasing again, and Philip does not think I should travel. Not even the short distance to Tonbridge. It was a surprise to us both, as you might imagine. But la! Maybe this one will be a girl!

The words swam before Camellia's eyes, and she sat down swiftly.

"Bad news?" Manfred asked.

"Only,"—she cleared her throat—"only that Lord and Lady Stirling can't visit at Christmastime."

"I'm sorry," Manfred said. Neville made a pitying noise.

"It doesn't matter." And it didn't. Because her question had been answered. Sometimes, "whores' tricks" did not work.

You asked about your friend, Major Taverston. He did come to London after leaving Tonbridge. He was quite a man-about-town for a while. Philip pointed him out to me one evening at the theater. You can't say you never noticed how good-looking he is! But now Philip says he's turned recluse. I believe he's still in London. Rumor has it he's at the Albany. But I don't know if anyone knows for sure.

"Neville, I think I will go visit Marianne, after all. After Christmas."

"Good. We will be fine here. You should go."

Camellia folded the letter and set it aside. Major Taverston had better be in London. It appeared they were going to be shackled to one another after all.

CHAPTER NINETEEN

CRISPIN PREVENTED HAZARD from sending for Jasper, and thereby ruining the family's holidays, by permitting him to summon a doctor. He knew Hazard would have done so regardless. James, a burly young man who appeared better suited for boxing than buttling, stood by the bedchamber door while a wizened fellow with yellow eyes looked in Crispin's mouth, pressed on his abdomen, and then examined the contents of his chamber pot.

"And when did you say you last ate?" the doctor asked.

"This morning."

"If I may, Major," James said, "you had one bite of an apple."

Crispin hadn't the strength to scowl. "You tried to feed me sops, when I told you I would eat neither bread nor milk."

The doctor tut-tutted. "You are suffering from a type of bloody flux. It is not food making you ill, but the lack of it will prevent your recovery."

Crispin laid his head back onto his pillow, gritting his teeth, trying not to groan. He felt like a child again, with his mother's hand on his brow, and yet another doctor telling her she must force him to eat. This while his insides turned themselves inside-out.

"It is true, though, that when he eats, he either vomits or he is seized with pains." James gestured to the chamber pot.

"Laudanum will cure that."

"I won't take laudanum."

"Come now," the doctor scolded. "It is a ready cure."

Hazard yelled from the hallway, "Do as the fellow says."

Crispin swallowed back a bitter retort. He had been forced to take laudanum four times in his life. Each time it had been after weeks of worsening ill health when nothing else worked. The first time, he was just twelve years old. It cured him by making him stuporous and stupid. And yet worse than the drug was giving it up. The lack was wrenching. It was always wrenching. He'd told himself he would rather die than go through that again.

And the doctor was a fool. It *was* food making him sick. All his life, he'd accustomed himself to gut cramps and bouts of nausea that came and went. It was *normal* to always feel vaguely ill. This was interspersed with weeks of more profound illness— which left him wrung out like a rag, yet grateful to emerge, still alive. But with Adam's guidance, he had, eventually, felt *well*. It astounded him to think that others lived that way all the time. Feeling well. And yet, he'd squandered that good fortune. Why? To spite Camellia?

No. To punish himself. He should not have lain with her. He was doing penance. Why wear a hairshirt when a cup of ale and a cheese sandwich would serve just as well?

The doctor fished around in his bag and pulled out a bottle. "A spoonful three times a day. Morning, midday, and night. More often if your symptoms warrant. And eat healthful foods. Beef tea. Sops. Blood pudding. Marrow. A glass of brandy for sleep. It is no wonder your bones hurt. You are skeletal."

Crispin wondered if that was supposed to be a joke.

"Leave it there," he said, nodding to his bedtable. "James will see you out."

While James escorted the doctor out, Hazard came in. The hair at his temples was now noticeably gray, and he had wrinkles about his eyes. The man had enough worries of his own, without designating himself Crispin's keeper.

"I've seen your leech. Will you leave me be now?"

"Will you take the medicine?"

He considered lying. *Yes.* He considered saying what he wished to. *No.* He told the truth. "Maybe. I don't know." This was why he'd bought his commission and gone to fight Boney. To die without the torment of sickness. He hated to be weak. He had always hated to be weak.

"Crispin—"

"I know what will work."

"James says you are determined to starve yourself."

"Not to death."

Hazard laughed without humor. "You cannot starve yourself to health."

Perhaps not. But he was determined to try.

A WEEK PASSED with no improvement. Rather Crispin's health declined even further. He was too fatigued even to remain long in his chair. He had to take to his bed.

Hazard did not repeat his threat to send for Jasper. Instead, he and Alice hied off precipitously to Chaumbers. Vanessa had miscarried again. Crispin used to believe Taverstons were blessed. That Jasper was particularly blessed. He didn't believe that anymore.

HE WAS NO longer sure what day it was. He slept more hours than he was awake. He'd given in, at last, to James's entreaties to take the medicine. It didn't matter. Drugged or not drugged—he could no longer rise from his bed.

He woke to the sound of pounding. Or was it the blood in his head? His head ached. Ached so badly he felt nauseated. He didn't deserve this. Not for tupping a tart who had thrown herself between his legs.

"James?" he called. He needed a wet cloth to put over his eyes. "James!" There was no answer. He groaned and gulped air.

James stepped into the room. "Major, there is a caller. I told her you were not receiving, but she insists—"

He cast up his breakfast. Or perhaps it was his supper. Onto the floor, thank God, not in his bed. James grabbed a towel and basin from the chair just inside the door. He dabbed and sponged. "Major—"

"I'm not seeing anyone!" *Good God! Like this?* Was he supposed to receive callers like this? Who would come? Who even knew he was there? Vanessa? No, it would not be Vanessa. Olivia? Mother? Had Hazard spread tales? "Who—"

"She said her name was Miss Harrington."

Camellia? The blazes. He was having a nightmare. Hallucinations. Pursued by the Furies. "Send her away."

"I tried, Major, she said she won't leave until you see her."

"Then she may rot on the stoop for all I care. Go. Leave that." The sick could wait. He was likely to add to it. "Get rid of her. Don't tell her I'm ill. Just say I'm not at home."

James handed him the basin and dropped the towel on the floor. Crispin reached to the table for the laudanum. He pulled out the stopper and took a swig, then threw the bottle against the wall.

He lay curled up and shivering. Sweating and shivering. After several minutes, his brain floated somewhere above his body. The shivering stopped. James finally returned.

"Is she gone?" Crispin thought his voice sounded disembodied. It could not have come from his mouth.

James nodded. He held out a folded piece of paper. "She said to give you this."

Crispin's gut cramped. "Did you read it?"

"Of course not, Major. But I gave her my word—"

"Put it in the fire."

James grimaced. "She said it was important."

"And *I* said, put it in the fire."

CAMELLIA WALKED ACROSS the field between her home and Manfred's. After two weeks of pacing her bedchamber, crying her eyes dry, this was the only possible solution she could see. She'd been certain Major Taverston would do the honorable thing. She'd been wrong. He wouldn't even see her, though she had begged, *begged* his butler to let her in. She could understand that he was too angry to speak with her. But to not respond to her letter? After a fortnight? She could not believe he could be so cold-blooded. Would he abandon his own child to the disgrace of illegitimacy? Did he think she was lying? Did he despise her that much?

Manfred's butler, a staid, elderly fellow, admitted her with a lifted chin and downward stare of haughty disapproval. A lady did not come alone to call upon a gentleman. Camellia knew that. Yet she was making a habit of it, and it was far from the worst thing she had done. He brought her to the receiving room and asked her to wait while he went to see if Sir Bodwell was at home.

She waited, rocking nervously on her feet. The room was overfull of mismatched furniture and the drapes were drawn. It smelled of dust. It had been years, she realized since she had been here. Manfred always came to them. She would not have believed he might be visiting Neville for cheer and comfort for *himself*, but if this was where he spent the rest of his days…

"Camellia?" Manfred walked into the room, then closed the double doors. His movements were slow and stiff, not as though in pain, but as if taking great care. "What is it? Is it Neville?"

She shook her head. He came forward, stooped and shuffling. His hair was almost completely gray now. His expression remained masked.

"Sit down, Camellia. You look faint."

He directed her to the couch. The upholstery was worn smooth. The carpet, too, appeared shabby. A woman's touch was missing. How many years had it been, she wondered since his wife had died? Six? Seven? Camellia had never known the woman, a shadowy presence at rare local events. Had he loved her? Manfred was a mystery she had never bothered to probe.

"Would you like tea?" he asked. His eyes were worried. "Or a bit of sherry?"

"No." She cleared her throat. "No, thank you."

It was quiet for a moment. Then he sat beside her and took her hand. "What is wrong?"

She drew a deep breath. And another. Then she blurted, "Do you still wish to marry me?"

He stared. "You have forbidden me to ask. What is this about?"

"I seem…I seem to find myself in need of a husband." He dropped her hand. His eyes darkened. She hurried to speak. "Manfred, I have to be honest. I know this is a terrible thing to ask of you—"

"Who was it?" he growled. "Taverston or some blackguard in London?"

"I don't wish to say."

"Taverston. I should call him out. He forced himself upon you?"

She started. Then shook her head. "No. No it wasn't like that."

"He seduced you. Camellia, I should have warned you. Neville should have warned you. Men like that, scoundrels like that—damn him to hell!"

She couldn't tell him the truth. "Neville doesn't know. Please. I don't want him to know." Her brother was retreating more and more into gloom. He was more demanding. Nothing pleased him. She couldn't possibly let Neville know.

"No, of course not. It would kill him. He trusted the rogue."

"I don't"—her voice caught—"I have nowhere else to turn."

"Have you told *him*?"

She nodded.

"And still, the devil abandoned you. Have you told anyone else?"

She shook her head. She hadn't even confided in Marianne. She was far too ashamed.

"Ah, don't fret. I'll marry you, Camellia. I would be honored to marry you."

"I don't have a dowry. You should know that, too. I spent it all on the house."

"You don't need a dowry. I don't care about that."

She burst into tears. How good he was, and what a selfish, wanton *fool* she was.

"I'm so sorry," she managed to say. "I should have said yes to you before. You are so good."

"It isn't from goodness."

"I know you want an heir. Not a..." She couldn't say the word. "Not another man's baby. I hope this is a girl, Manfred. And I *will* give you a son. I-I'll be a good wife to you."

"*This* child must be mine. I will swear it is mine," Manfred said, pulling a handkerchief from his jacket and pressing it into her hands. "Dry your eyes. Listen to me. My cousin is a black-hearted devil. A worse man, I daresay, even than the major. I won't list his crimes, but believe me, I'd rather any man's bastard inherit this estate than my cousin. You must promise me, swear to me, that you will tell no one else."

"I won't tell another soul."

He settled against the back of the couch, expressionless. Surprisingly calm. "This is all very strange. It changes everything."

She nodded.

"Camellia, the major left when? Was it two months? Roughly two months?"

"Yes."

"Then I think we had better have the banns read. And marry as soon as possible."

CHAPTER TWENTY

J AMES HELPED CRISPIN move from his bed to a chair by the fire in the sitting room. His bones still ached, his gut still hurt, and he still was weak, but he no longer believed he would die. The laudanum was finally doing what it was supposed to do. Perhaps he must accept that he was doomed to a life of mild stupefaction.

He picked up Donne's *Devotions*. He had read them all but this last.

Though you have by physic and diet raked up the embers of your disease, still there is a fear of a relapse; and the greater danger is in that.

Grand. Just grand. He set down the book and sifted through a pile of broadsheets James had been bringing him, though he had done no more than skim them until now.

He'd gathered this much: Wellington was no longer in Paris. No longer in danger of assassination. He'd been sent to Vienna to replace Castlereagh as Britain's representative at the post-war conference. The Coalition's task was now to reconfigure the boundaries of kingdoms after Napoleon's disruptions.

Tens of thousands of men dead, just to return the world to stasis.

Crispin stared blankly at the window, and summoned the will to push aside the tide of images that would, if he let them, overwhelm him.

At the top of the pile was the day's *Morning Post*. The date was February 15, 1815. *February.* He'd left Tonbridge in late November. Nearly three months of his life, lost to him. And Olivia's wedding? Late June. Eight months. What had he done in eight months? Except turn thirty? Perhaps that was accomplishment enough, considering how doubtful had been the chance of success.

He tried to read, at least the gossipy bits, but could not concentrate. This was what laudanum did to him. He could sleep, eat, fidget, but he could not *think*. Instead, his mind drifted to places it should not go. Tonbridge. The scent of lilacs. Miss Harrington singing. Miss Harrington's bed. Making it up to her for the lack of kisses—in his fevered imagination, he could.

She'd come to see him, and he'd turned her away. Or was that another of his drug-induced fancies? Had there been a letter? Could he have been deadened enough to burn a letter? He had not been able to make himself ask James.

Someone was knocking. Was someone knocking?

"James!" he bellowed. Tried to bellow. He had never been a bellower. "James!"

He heard his front door open. James's voice. Hazard's. *Jasper's?*

A moment later, his brother stormed into the room. "Crispin!" He halted. Appalled. Then his face crumpled. "Crispin."

"Believe it or not, this is recovering."

"Why didn't you tell us? Why don't you *ever* tell us?"

"It is my cross to bear. And you...you had enough to worry over. How is Vanessa?"

"Holding up." He looked away. A muscle ticked in his jaw. "Your condolence letter. I should have known something was wrong. It was incoherent."

He didn't recall writing a letter.

"I thought you were foxed when you wrote it," Jasper said, shaking his head. "I should have known. You are never foxed. But when we last saw you, you were so well, so *confidently* well. And Haz said nothing until two days ago, when Vanessa—the doctor said bedrest—but after a month of that, Vanessa had done with it—and Haz finally told us—"

Hazard walked into the room, and plodding alongside was the Greek.

"Adam?" *How in the blazes?* "What are you doing here?"

Jasper said, "You'd said he'd been hired by the Harringtons. I went and found him."

"The colonel needs—"

"The colonel is being tended to." Adam made a slight bow. "Major, I do not forget I owe my life to you. This"—he swept a hand at Crispin and frowned—"this should not have happened."

"You need his help more than Colonel Harrington does," Jasper said.

"James has—"

"Has been invaluable," Hazard said. "But I am taking him back. Alice is going to Cambridge, and I am not sending my viscountess to Reg's hovel without a footman." He pretended to shudder.

"Cambridge?" Crispin asked.

"Georgiana wants her," Jasper said, stone-faced. "Arthur's sibling will be here any day."

Ah, right. Potent Reg and fecund Georgiana. So much pain. Love and pain. "Vanessa will be next." Crispin heard the words come out of his mouth and cringed. That was the drug. He had no discretion.

"No, it will be Olivia." Jasper let out a long sigh.

"Olivia?"

"They haven't said anything. No one says anything anymore. We've become a family that keeps secrets from one another. But she has that look about her. And she isn't riding."

Crispin didn't know what response to make. So he turned to Adam. "I can only assume Jasper offered you significantly better pay."

Adam frowned. "Am I a mercenary? Then considering I received no pay from the Harringtons, I was under no obligation to stay."

"No pay?"

"It is in arrears. Lady Bodwell assures me—"

"Lady Bodwell?"

Adam's frown deepened. "The colonel has gone to live with the Bodwells. One of the staff will be assigned to his care."

What the devil? "And what about Miss Harrington?"

Adam cocked his head. His frown disappeared. "Miss Harrington *is* Lady Bodwell."

Crispin felt kicked in the gut. Or stabbed in the heart. The pain even penetrated the laudanum's shield. He could do nothing but stare. He must have misheard. Misunderstood.

"She wed Sir Bodwell last week," Adam said.

"She wed Sir Bodwell," he echoed. She had said she wouldn't marry. She wouldn't marry *him*. And she would not marry *at all*. The sly she-devil. She lied. But he could not piece together her motive. Bodwell? God damn it! He wished he could *think*!

Jasper said, "I want to bring you back to Chaumbers."

"What? No. I'm not going to Chaumbers." If he were to go anywhere, it would be to Tonbridge to sort this out. Adam must be wrong.

"You should come home. It would do you good."

"I'm fine here."

"We want you near."

"I don't need a nursemaid."

Jasper's jaw set. "I am not comfortable bringing Vanessa to London. But if you insist *you* won't travel, she will have to."

"Oh, for God's sake." He could not help a twitch of a smile. "Excellent use of filial manipulation, Jasp. I could not have done it better myself."

"Not beef. I cannot eat beef. Not like this." Crispin pushed away the plate with its repulsive slab of flesh. Ignoring Adam's consternation, he turned his focus to the wall. His bedchamber. At Chaumbers. His walls, familiar since childhood, were covered with old light-brown paper with faded yellow fleur-de-lys. The symbol of French royalty. Whoever thought *that* was a good idea?

"Major." Adam rapped his knuckles on the tea table. The table was a new fixture in the room where Crispin took his meals to avoid his family's worried scrutiny. "You've determined it is not meat that makes you ill. If you wish to regain muscle, you must eat muscle."

His throat tightened. He shook his head.

"Why? What is the difficulty?" Adam had a way of posing questions as simple interest. He didn't twist arms. And yet, Crispin found it impossible to refuse to answer Adam's straight-forward *why?*

"I have flayed men." He choked. "Do you understand? I never ordered a flogging unless I was prepared to carry out the punishment myself. Flogging tears a man open. It separates muscle from bone. I look at that plate…"

Adam was quiet a moment. Then he said, "Will you eat fish?"

Crispin nodded.

"You should speak up sooner. We cannot work at cross purposes."

"Yes," he groaned, hating himself, his vulnerability. "I know."

"Then you also know you must stop taking laudanum. You forget half of what we say from one day to the next. You are befogged."

"I don't want to relapse."

"I will give you cat's-claw. An herb from South America. It is better for your particular complaint. I believe your intolerance has progressed to an inflammation of the bowels. I can't agree with using laudanum for—"

"It works. It has always worked. Why should I put myself through—"

"Major, laudanum is for men like the colonel. He suffers from pain that can never be healed. He will not live very much longer. That is not your case."

Crispin slumped. Every word Adam said was true. He murmured a confession. "I don't know if I have the strength."

"You do."

ADAM SAID SOME men required a slow reduction in dosage, but that for others, the best course was to stop all at once. So Crispin did. Adam said he had two great advantages. One, that in spite of everything, his body was sound. *Sound? His body?* And two, he did not enjoy the effects of the drug on his brain. That, of course, was a matter open to debate. But it was true that he preferred being clear-headed to artificial bliss.

He spent a week in the depths of hell. Another week in a lesser hell. And finally, although physically he was still limping along, his head felt clear.

Adam told him to go out in the fresh air. Enjoy the springtime. Stop acting like a sick man. So Crispin was riding Mercury about the property, counting his blessings.

Now that logic had returned to him, it mattered not one jot that Miss Harrington had married that dull stick Sir Manfred Bodwell. He'd foreseen it. Lady needs security; man needs heir. They were lifelong neighbors. Of course, they had eventually wed. If only they had done so sooner.

He was now considering a journey to Cambridge. While he had been in hell, word had come that Arthur now had a baby brother. Randolph. Crispin had missed the celebration with Mother, Jasper, Vanessa, Olivia, and Benjamin. Had it been awkward? Or sincerely joyous?

He should go visiting. He would like to see Reg. Georgiana and Reg. To experience their unadulterated, simple goodness. He wanted to get to know his nephews. The one unalterable fact of his life was that his family meant everything to him. That, and that he had been granted another chance at living.

He was thirty years old. He didn't need any more adventure. He didn't need to witness any more death. He didn't need to kill any more men.

And so, he had decided, finally, to be quit of soldering. He would sell his commission the next time he returned to London. He would keep his set at Albany. Join White's gentlemen's club and do what he could, short of standing for the Commons, to support Jasper's political career. And he would finish refurbishing the cottage so that it would once again be a Taverston retreat. He hoped to be inundated with nieces and nephews.

He returned Mercury to the stable and found, to his delighted surprise, that Hazard's coach was being placed in the carriage house. He'd been in Gladnorshire while Alice was in Cambridge. Were they both here now?

Crispin hurried to the house. Stepping inside, he pulled off his gloves and hat and handed them to Peters. "Viscount Haslet has come?"

Peters nodded. "They are in the parlor. I believe they are waiting for you."

"Very good." He trotted to the stairs. No doubt Hazard was afraid he'd find Crispin a shriveled wreck sitting on the terrace with a blanket tucked around him. He owed Haz a debt of gratitude. A very large debt.

The parlor door was open. He could hear a hum of conversation, but he was in too much of a hurry to try picking out words. He sauntered into the room and the talk ceased. Alice was there too, sitting on the couch beside Olivia—who was definitely increasing. She had sent back a refusal to his written challenge that morning to race Mercury and Second Place. He grinned at her, but as she looked up at him, his grin fell away. She was white-faced. He looked around. They were all white-faced.

"What is it?" His heart dropped into his feet. "Did something happen to Georgiana?"

"No," Alice said. "Everyone is well." Her gaze went to Hazard. So Crispin's did too.

"Haz? What is it?"

He looked grim. Impossibly grim. "I…It was probably absurd of me, of us, to race here. You'll see it in the newspapers tomorrow, I'm sure."

Jasper said, "Crispin, why don't you sit down?"

"I am well enough to stand."

"Yes, well, Hazard told us all to sit down. You should too."

His blood was turning to ice. He crossed the floor to his what was once his father's favorite armchair. One high and deep enough to accommodate his Taverston height. He sank into the cushion. "So?"

"Dispatches have come from France. And from Vienna. Verified dispatches." Hazard's voice was hoarse. "Napoleon escaped."

"My God," Crispin whispered. It was unbelievable, and yet, all too believable. The man was extraordinary. A snake. A curse. But extraordinary. "Where? Where did he go? America? Not Italy. Please don't say Italy."

"Worse," Jasper said. "He's gone back to France."

CAMELLIA HAD BEEN Lady Bodwell for a little over a month and was still adjusting to her strange new circumstance. She was carrying a child. A much-wanted child. But it was not her husband's, and she must pretend that it was. Moreover, marriage was not at all what she had once dreamed it might be. She felt less a wife than a companion to two elderly, infirm men.

She had been so concerned with Neville's physical limitations, that she'd paid no attention to Manfred's. What she had mistaken for steadiness was rather a lack of expressiveness. He could be quite angry—as when Mr. Castor had sneered at them while performing the wedding service, and Manfred gave him quite a set down—but his face did not reflect his fury. It made her wonder, at times, what he might really be thinking when his countenance was so calm.

She'd known, of course, that his hands trembled when he was quiet and that his posture was stooped and rigid, as if he were a far older man. He had a strange way of walking—in short, shuffling steps. But there was a difference between seeing glimpses of this and witnessing these things daily. And more. He could go up and down stairs, but so slowly it was painful to watch. His balance was poor. He dropped things and would not pick them up. And he slept badly or not at all.

That last was something he had told her on their wedding night, when he escorted her to her bedchamber, then kissed her at the door. The kiss startled her. She wasn't prepared for it—a quick peck on the lips that was over before she realized it was happening. She was even less prepared for his retreat.

"You must not take this as judgment, my dear, but I won't lie with you while you are with child. And since I sleep very poorly, it will suit us both better to keep to our separate bedchambers."

She'd been relieved. If lying together had been disappointing with Major Taverston, she couldn't imagine how much worse it would be with Manfred. But she felt guilty for her relief.

There were other adjustments. Charingate, the Bodwells' home, was larger than the Harringtons' but it felt smaller, more crowded. There was always someone in the same room or just in the next one, ready to do her bidding. And Manfred fussed at her if she tried to do anything for herself.

Still, it was fortunate that Manfred had so many servants because they had not been married a week before it had become necessary to bring Neville to live with them. The Earl of Iversley appeared in a coach that was even more resplendent than the one the major had borrowed, and haughtily whisked Mr. Diakos away. He said that his great aunt needed an attendant. One did not argue with an earl, especially not an earl who looked like

Apollo in his chariot.

Iversley was every bit as handsome as Marianne had said. But Camellia found such physical perfection off-putting. She preferred the major's smile, which was a little bit crooked, and the major's hair, which was always a little bit tangled.

All that aside, she could not possibly think of Major Taverston with any residual fondness. He had abandoned his own child!

It had to be from sheer spite. He'd been angry when he thought she'd orchestrated her own compromise, yet he still had been prepared to ask for her. Men understood entrapment. What had evidently confused and infuriated him was that she had *not* meant to catch him. She refused him. That must have touched his pride.

And she must stop brooding over it. She was not being fair to Manfred.

There had been no time for renovations to Charingate to accommodate Neville. Rather, two footmen had muscled him up the stairs and ensconced him in a guest chamber. He adapted. Still, it seemed to Camellia that her brother's world had grown smaller. He was stuck. But so was she. So were they all.

They supped together in an upstairs parlor, a room that was equipped with a round mahogany card table. It was a very masculine room, with heavy, blocky chairs, and musty brown velvet drapes. Camellia found it oppressive.

"Shall we retire to the drawing room?" she said, noticing that Manfred and Neville had both laid down their forks and waved away the footman who would have refilled their wine glasses— Charles, a young man with a pock-marked face. She had made a point of learning all the servants' names as quickly as she could.

"Yes, my dear," Manfred said.

Charles came forward to push Neville's chair. Camellia stood and waited for Manfred. It was as if he had to summon up the will before he could stand. Yet it annoyed him if she tried to help.

They moved to the drawing room, which clearly reflected the taste of the previous Lady Bodwell. Two Chesterfield sofas upholstered in pale pink chintz sat catty-cornered to each other, pushed up against the dado rail. There was one ugly brocade armchair that Manfred always claimed. Three saber-legged rosewood chairs filled out the room. Delicate side tables were placed near the sofas and large French windows brought in light. Manfred had told her she might change anything she wished, but that felt like stepping on the dead woman's toes. She'd made so little of an impression while alive; it seemed selfish and unnecessary to erase the few traces she'd left.

When they were all seated, Mary, one of the maids, entered with tea. Edward, an older footman, brought in *The Evening Post.* He looked strangely agitated as he laid it beside her. Camellia poured tea and passed cups to Manfred and Neville. Then she picked up the newspaper to read aloud.

"Oh, dear God!"

Neville's head jerked up. Manfred gave her his usual blank stare.

"Napoleon." Her voice shook. "Napoleon escaped!"

"Escaped? From Elba?" Manfred said. "How the devil did he do that?"

She scanned the column. Disbelieving, she said, "It seems he simply got on a boat and sailed back to France."

Manfred said, "What colossal gall. The French are beaten. *He* was beaten. They won't want him back."

Neville snorted. "Who knows what they'll want? King Louis is not a man to inspire loyalty."

Camellia remembered the major saying that the French were resentful of their conquerors. That they'd felt triumphant under their emperor. "If Napoleon does take charge again?" she asked, heart in her throat.

"Then we will defeat him again," Neville said, banging his palm on the arm of his chair.

Her hand went automatically to the swell of her belly.

He'll go back. Mark my words. He is a soldier to the marrow.

CHAPTER TWENTY-ONE

CRISPIN PACED IN the receiving room at 54 Rue Royale, the ornate mansion given over to Wellington for his Brussels headquarters. His summons read that the commander wished to see him at once. Apparently "at once" had more than one meaning. He understood Wellington was a busy man, but it nevertheless irked Crispin to be left cooling his heels. For over an hour.

At last, the door swung open, and an aide stepped inside.

"The commander will see you now, Major. Please come with me."

Crispin nodded and followed.

Wellington's office was just as one might expect. Cramped but organized. There was a substantial desk and padded chair, but the duke was not seated. Heavy-browed, hook-nosed, sun-browned, he radiated energy.

"Ah, Major Taverston," he said, then nodded a dismissal to the aide.

Crispin bowed. "Your Grace."

"You are with the fourth division?"

"Yes."

"What do you make of the men?"

"Raw." Crispin had been in Belgium since late April, and it was now early June. His company consisted primarily of new recruits. They were frighteningly ignorant. "But making progress." Progress that had been interrupted when Crispin was pulled from the field to answer a summons.

"Good." Wellington paused as if looking him over. "Are you still reliable? You didn't come to Paris when I asked."

"I am reliable." Crispin knew the duke did not like it when men made excuses, so he gave none.

Wellington turned and went to his desk. He didn't sit, but bent over it to shift a few papers about. Then he straightened. "I'm reassigning your company to Major Lowell. I'd like you to report to Colonel Grant."

Crispin stiffened. Lieutenant Colonel Colquhoun Grant was the Head of Intelligence. Crispin knew him all too well. "Your Grace, I had hoped to return to the battlefield."

He grunted. "Major, your hopes are not my concern. Napoleon is. I need information. *Reliable* information. I need to know his current location and where he means to go next."

A ridiculously tall order. Yet he nodded. "If that is what you require, Your Grace." Wellington would approve of the confidence he projected, but while Crispin felt a whirl of emotions, not one of them was confidence. Only pride that the duke had faith in him. Excitement over the challenge. And self-disgust—spying was a filthy business. Once again, he would have to ignore his conscience, ignore that inconvenient part of himself that felt things.

"Good." Wellington stepped past Crispin and opened the door. "Grant's office is two offices down. On the left."

Crispin walked down the hall, knocked, and entered.

"Crispin!" Grant rose and came forward, hand outstretched. They were old friends, of a sort. Since arriving in Brussels, Crispin had made sure to avoid him, hoping that out of sight would be out of mind.

"Colquhoun." Crispin shook his hand. He found Grant to be a strangely flat-faced man. One with a knobby nose and a wisp of a curl perennially plastered on his forehead. He always appeared to be smirking. Maybe he was. He enjoyed the sport of espionage far too much. "The duke says I am to report to you."

"Of course." Grant laughed. "Did you imagine you would get away with teaching green lads how to march and form squares?"

"One can always hope."

"Listen. Wellington and I have spent the last few weeks sorting through intelligence from sources that contradict each other. We have no idea whether Boney is still in Paris, or at the border, or even already deep inside Belgium. We need you to lay eyes on the man and report back. His last known location was Paris, but that was over a week ago. He had some sort of celebration there on the first. That much has been confirmed. Take a good horse and sweep toward Paris until you find him."

"I am to cross the border?" He wanted to be sure of his orders. Entering France as a soldier was a provocative move, considering they were not yet officially at war.

The cheer fell from Grant's face. "If need be." He cleared his throat. "You know how this works. You're an officer. In uniform, you will undoubtedly be spotted and taken prisoner. You'll be well-positioned to learn things, but it may be difficult to escape with the information." This was Grant's own *modus operandi*— one that Crispin disdained.

"Particularly since I will be honor-bound not to." Those were the rules of a gentleman's parole. If captured, one agreed to stop taking part. Surrender meant surrender. Unless one was Napoleon.

Grant's smirk turned into a sneer. "You know there is no honor in war."

Crispin's face heated. Grant had assigned him far worse tasks. Moreover, he had no high horse to ride. He'd proved himself dishonorable in peacetime as well.

"I'm not eager to sit out the war in French custody."

"Your other option is to masquerade as a civilian. And be shot if you are caught."

"So I mustn't be caught."

Grant shrugged. "Tricky. Your French is better than passable, but you don't look French. You might do for an American, but your accent is terrible. And you are not inconspicuous."

"All true. I don't know why you want me for this job."

"Because *I* have to be *here*. And there is no better second best than you."

FOURTEEN HOURS LATER, Crispin had to remind himself that there were many kinds of filth in the world, and this was by no means the worst. He was somewhere near Beaumont, a town at the southwestern border with France. Wearing tattered clothes hurriedly purchased in a second-hand shop in the Brussels stews, he was lying on dirty straw in a cowshed that had never seen a shovel. The stench of manure made his eyes stream. It brought back a long-ago memory best forgotten.

He closed his eyes to run again through the maps Colquhoun had shown him. The prevailing intelligence indicated Napoleon intended to enter Belgium through Mons. Wellington suspected he would then try to flank the British to the right, cutting off their supply lines and their retreat route to the north. Colquhoun thought the opposite. That Napoleon would head to the south, into the gap that remained between the British forces and the Prussians under General Blücher. Boney would drive a wedge between the two armies and defeat them one after another. No one was foolish enough to imagine he could not do it. He was a master of the tactic.

Wellington was wedded to the idea of protecting the northern border as long as doubt remained. Colquhoun wanted proof that Napoleon would head for the gap, so that the British corps could be shifted south to narrow it. Therefore, Crispin was sneaking—there was no better word for it—along the River Sambre, creeping closer to Blücher.

Before dawn that morning, Crispin had seen a Prussian patrol, six men. They either didn't see him or took no notice of him, either of which was concerning. What if he were French reconnaissance? Boney certainly had scouts floating about. Would the Prussians ignore them too?

He resisted the urge to roll over and find a more comfortable position in the straw. If he moved, he was sure to coat himself in crap. But he needed to sleep. He was fatigued and had hours to kill. It was midday, and he was waiting out the sun. When darkness fell, he would make his way on foot to Beaumont, where a tavern keeper in Colquhoun's pay would, hopefully, have something useful to say.

Crispin groaned at the prospect. He was already footsore. He'd left his horse behind when he got close to the border. He was supposed to be a tramp and tramps did not ride. Colquhoun had better be right about Napoleon. Or he was just wandering in the dark to no purpose.

Closing his eyes again, he tried clearing his mind so he might sleep. But the problem with banishing thoughts of war was that it made room for Camellia. Her uncanny beauty. The outline of her shape in the dark. Her easy smile and deep-throated laughter. The way she waltzed. The way she'd felt in his arms. Her generosity and cleverness. Her false innocence. Drifting, he heard her voice. *No better proof of devotion could there be, than loving you till you loved me.*

He started awake. He'd heard something. Scuffing. Breathing. The door to the shed creaked open. A wiry, grizzled man in peasant clothing stood in the doorway, outlined by sunshine. The man stared at him. He squinted back.

"Merde! Qui êtes-vous?" The man's hand slipped inside his shirt.

"Nul. Personne." Crispin sat up slowly, shaking his head, pretending drunkenness while straining his ears for the sound of the Frenchman's companions. He let his hand rest on his pistol under the straw.

The man pulled a gun. Crispin put a bullet in his forehead and the poor devil dropped to the ground.

Crispin swore. He grabbed his second pistol and waited. After several minutes, he relaxed. He laid down his loaded gun and reloaded the other. Then he crept to the corpse. He rifled through the man's clothing, looking for missives. Nothing. There was nothing.

He'd just killed a man for speaking French.

Crispin's hands started to shake. Sweat broke on his brow. He rubbed his face. Counted to twenty. Then to one hundred. His heart finally stopped racing. He made himself look back at the body.

The gun lay beside it. The gun was real.

Still, the frog-eater could be anyone. He could be the owner of the cowshed for all Crispin knew. He had to go. But he couldn't leave the dead man in the doorway for someone to stumble over. A wife. A daughter. *Damn, damn, damn.*

He crawled to the door and peered outside. The surroundings remained deserted. So he rose and hooked the corpse's feet under his arms to drag him into the back corner of the shed. In doing so, Crispin noted the feet. He was slipping—he hadn't checked the boots. Expecting little, he pulled off first the left boot, then the right. Mashed into the right boot was a bit of paper. Crispin's miserable cloud of guilt lifted. A French spy after all.

A few lines of nonsense were scribbled across the slip. Something encoded. Too much for his tired brain. He had to get it to headquarters. He flipped the page over. There was a map. Crudely drawn. Surely the map was for the spy's sake, not Boney's. It showed the River Sambre and a trail or road from French Avesnes to Belgian Charleroi that cut right through Beaumont, with a few landmarks and villages marked along the way. Villages that were likely to welcome the French invaders? Or something else?

He closed his eyes to see again Colquhoun's maps. Charleroi was a long day's march nearly due south of Brussels. The road to Charleroi indicated on the spy's map threaded the needle *between* the British and Prussian armies. Divide and conquer. And

Napoleon was coming into Belgium through Beaumont, not Mons.

Crispin smiled. He had Colquhoun's proof.

Now he only needed to find out where the devil was.

He left the cowshed and followed the river another two hours toward Thuin, thinking himself now roughly halfway between Beaumont and Charleroi. Just outside the town, exhausted, he bought himself a bed in a brothel, always a good place to hide, and paid the girl extra to leave him alone. He woke just before dawn to the rumbling sound of a very large army on the march. He didn't see it, but he heard it well enough. He now knew where Napoleon was. Unfortunately, the general was *here*.

CAMELLIA WAS NOT prepared for the rain of troubles.

Neville had had a chronic cough. They were all used to that. But sometime in early June, it intensified. She didn't pay much attention at first. She had been more worried about Manfred. His tremors were worsening. He had trouble swallowing. And he'd fallen twice. Twice that she'd witnessed. She suspected he'd fallen more.

And then, Manfred's man of business, who had untaken the task of unraveling the Harringtons' finances, had announced that they were in even worse disarray than she'd thought. Neville had debts that outstripped those of their father. Apologetically, Manfred said there was no choice but to sell Neville's farm. She told herself it didn't matter. Neville would never return to it.

Moreover, she had her own concerns. She was now quite obviously with child. The baby would be born in another two months, but she was trying to pretend it would be four. She suspected the servants were whispering behind her back, but she didn't care, so long as they assumed her indiscretion had been with Manfred.

There was also Brussels to worry about. It was assumed Napoleon would march on Belgium, but no one knew when. And in the meantime, the news from Brussels read like the gossip pages at the height of the London Season. It was all parties and balls, and which lovely lady the Duke of Wellington was paying too much attention to. She couldn't help wondering how Major Taverston was faring, if he had found a lovely young Belgian girl to pay attention to. Of course, she shouldn't care. She *didn't* care.

But Neville? One week earlier, she had been with her brother in the sitting room when he had a coughing fit that seemed to go on forever. It left him exhausted. That was when she finally took note. Manfred sent for a doctor, who diagnosed an inflammation of the lungs.

They'd put him to bed. She sat with him throughout the next few days, exchanging herbal tisanes for tea and giving him more laudanum than usual on the doctor's instructions. She would have stayed with him through the night also, but Manfred insisted she sleep for the baby's sake.

Two days ago, Neville had had a burst of lucidity that made her think he was mending. She had just adjusted the drapes to keep the sunshine from falling across his bed and waking him, when he came out with, "Camellia, I hope to see your baby born."

Startled, she'd replied, "Of course, you will. It won't be long now."

"A son would be best."

She laughed lightly, returning to her chair by his side. "I'm afraid I can't guarantee a boy." She expected him to laugh too, but he looked pensive. So she said, "If this one is not, the next may be."

"I suppose." He flushed and looked toward the wall. Obviously, he was aware of Manfred's infirmities, yet he couldn't possibly know that they had never lain together. He was still looking away from her when he asked, "Has he told you anything about his cousin?"

Camellia hesitated. Manfred was very closed mouthed about

him, but she was curious. "He says the man is evil. He does not want the estate to go to him."

Her brother was quiet for long enough that Camellia thought he might have drifted back to sleep. Then he said, "They were always rivals, from what I recall. But the rivalry did not become hatred until they both began courting Elizabeth."

"Elizabeth?"

"The first Lady Bodwell."

"Oh! You knew her?" Camellia's curiosity flared.

"Not well. I was rarely ever home. But I do know she was very pretty. Vivacious. She had a number of suitors but Manfred won her."

It was difficult for her to picture Manfred courting. "The cousin did not take it well?"

"He lured her into his carriage and assaulted her. The week before the wedding."

Camellia gasped.

"Of course, he denied that it was an assault. Never mind that. His intention was not to force her to wed him instead of Manfred. It was only to deprive them of their happiness."

"But Manfred did marry her."

"Yes. But I think his cousin succeeded nevertheless. I don't think Elizabeth was ever truly happy afterward." Neville began coughing again and could not catch his breath for a frightening few minutes. He took the cup Camellia offered him. Another tisane. After clearing his throat several times, he said, "She became a recluse. Manfred told me she could not get past the fear that people were talking about her." He shook his head. "And here I am, talking about her."

"It wasn't her fault. What he did was not her fault." She cringed to think of her own situation which *was* her fault. And Manfred was sheltering her, too.

Neville drew a rattling breath. "Let us hope this baby is a son. Manfred deserves some peace of mind."

That was the last true conversation Camellia had with her

brother. Over the next two days he began wheezing as well as coughing. His breathing grew labored. He woke only to groan and gasp, then stopped waking at all.

And that morning, Thursday, June 15, he died in the early hours while she was sleeping. Neville was gone. And Camilla was mourning another person she'd loved.

CHAPTER TWENTY-TWO

THE DUCHESS OF Richmond was hosting a ball at her husband's capacious Brussels home in the Rue de la Blanchisserie. Wellington had ordered his officers to attend. A *ball*. Crispin thought the man was either a genius or insane. While a few days earlier, he would have staked his life upon genius, he was now leaning more toward insane.

He understood that the duke, legendary for his sangfroid, wished to project calm. Normality. The civilians were not to be panicked. War was not imminent. There was nothing afoot. *But to command his officers to go dancing?*

It had taken Crispin ten hours and three forcibly requisitioned horses to bring his intelligence back to Brussels, only to have it disregarded. Wellington had already received a similar report from Blücher, who was undermanned and falling back. Nevertheless, the duke was convinced the French push toward Charleroi was a feint. The real danger would come from the west, from Mons.

Crispin had had to swallow his fury. Why send him out spying if his findings would not be believed? Colquhoun softened the blow later by confiding that Wellington did, at least, put his commanders on alert, to be ready to march at a moment's notice. Wellington believed a false move would be worse than no move, so he was awaiting a report from his general in Mons.

So here Crispin was. No food. No sleep. But cleaned up and wearing his dress uniform and flimsy shoes, dancing a quadrille with an overly perfumed girl half his age. Ruminating on the absurdity of the world.

How was he to leap the chasm between the cowshed of the previous night and this Brussels ballroom? Midnight had come and gone, but without checking his fob watch, he wouldn't have known. The chandeliers burned so brightly, one could not distinguish night from day. The room was lavishly decorated, with rose-trellised wallpaper and pillars wrapped in ribbons and garlands of flowers. A far cry from manure and straw.

When the music ended, he escorted the blushing girl back to her mother. The lady was speaking with their hostess, the Duchess of Richmond, who was still a beautiful woman though she was in her middle years and had borne at least a dozen children. This could be Georgiana in another two decades.

"Major Taverston," the duchess cooed. "How delightful to see you. Tell me, how fares your exquisite brother?"

No. Georgiana would have more sense. Crispin decided to entertain himself. "He is well. His wife was just delivered of their second son. And he has become quite sought after as a speaker after the publication of his translations of…that Greek philosopher—I can never remember his name."

The duchess stared, befuddled, then understanding dawned and she tapped Crispin's arm with her fan. "Silly man. I meant the earl."

"Oh." Crispin shrugged. "He is also well."

The duchess launched into some inane story about Jasper. Plastering an interested look on his face, Crispin surreptitiously took note of the thinned crowd. It appeared a good number of his compatriots had slipped away. He should too. He needed to rest. He didn't like to think that he was still recuperating, but he was. The last time he'd eaten a fully satisfying meal had been with Camellia. She'd seduced him first with her understanding. Then with her body—she was also the last woman he'd lain with. *And he needed to stop thinking about her. She was Lady Bodwell now.*

While the duchess was talking, Colquhoun sidled up to their group.

"Your Grace," Colquhoun interrupted with a bow. "Please excuse me, but may I borrow the major for a moment?"

"Yes, of course, Colonel." She tapped Crispin with her fan again. "Please give my regards to the earl."

"I will." He turned to follow Colquhoun. When they were several steps away, he said, "What is it?"

"Hurry." Colquhoun picked up his pace. "Word came from Mons over an hour ago. There are no French there. And now Slender Billy has come."

Prince William of Orange. Commander of Wellington's first corps. "And?"

"I don't know yet. He's with the duke. There." Colquhoun pointed. Crispin saw the two men. Slender Billy looked excited and Wellington grim.

They approached Wellington's circle in time to hear him tell the prince, rather loudly, to go get some sleep. "I shall retire as well." He turned and said something to the Duke of Richmond, who nodded. They broke away from the group.

Colquhoun walked faster, Crispin in tow. They joined Wellington and Richmond as they were exiting the ballroom. Richmond scowled at them, but Wellington gave Colquhoun a nod. "Richmond has a map," was all he said.

Richmond took them to an upstairs room, a dressing room that was littered with clothing. Evidence of an indecisive man, too concerned with his appearance. More absurdity.

Wellington shut the door. His jaw was tight. Crispin's heart sank. He'd rather *he* had been wrong than his commander.

The duke stepped to the desk where Richmond was rolling out a map. They all moved closer. Wellington studied it for a moment, then said, "Napoleon has humbugged me, by God. He has gained twenty-four hours march on me."

"How so?" asked Colquhoun.

"Prince William reports a large French force at Quatre Bras."

Quatre Bras. A crossroads just twenty miles or so south of Brussels, along the communication route between Wellington and Blücher. The French must be winged to have come so far so fast.

And damn it. Where were the Prussians? If they'd been defeated…and the French were this close to Brussels…and the British and Belgian-Dutch troops were still splayed across Northwest Belgium…

"What will you do?" Richmond asked.

"I'll concentrate more men around Quatre Bras, but we won't stop Napoleon there." He drew a small circle on the map with his finger. Closer to Brussels. Too close. "We must fight him here. Waterloo."

THE DUKE TOOK Crispin on as another aide-de-camp. Jasper would say he was one of the duke's errand boys, but he was in good company: Somerset, Freemantle, Gordon, Lennox, Percy. A few more. Good men all.

It was to be a day of hard riding. He had a fine horse, Bolt, a gift from Jasper. Bolt was swift, but for stamina, only Mercury could have outridden Wellington's Copenhagen—and Crispin had left Mercury at Chaumbers, safe from the folly of men.

They rode first to Quatre Bras, where the duke assessed the situation. Crispin did too. *Bleak.* By all accounts, the tiny force assembled there was vastly outnumbered by a wing of Napoleon's army led by Marshal Ney. Yet Wellington pronounced himself satisfied. "We will be well-fortified within the hour. We can hold the position."

An hour? Given how far afield the various regiments had been cantoned, that seemed doubtful to Crispin. But then, Wellington had beaten Ney before, in Spain, so one must grant he knew whereof he spoke.

Next, they rode to Brye, where Wellington met Blücher for a quick conference. It was now clear that Blücher's Prussians would soon be attacked by Napoleon's main force. Wellington promised support, on the condition that he was not attacked himself.

But Crispin knew he *would* be attacked. Napoleon had succeeded in driving a wedge between the two allies' armies. How had Wellington let this happen?

By the time they arrived back in Quatre Bras, a battle was underway. If Crispin's confidence in his commander had been wavering, it was soon restored. The man was everywhere. Firing off orders, rallying the troops, seeming somehow to see the whole of the battlefield at once. Crispin dashed about following commands and sometimes giving them. Poor flagging Bolt was shot from beneath him and he had to scramble to find another mount. In the ensuing muddle, he lost his fob watch. For the remainder of the day, time had no meaning. Ney launched one assault after another: calvary, artillery, infantry, then repeat. And each time, Wellington's men fought them off.

Miraculously, Wellington had not misjudged his own strength. Reinforcements arrived in waves. Like the tide coming in. It gave the men confidence to feel their power waxing throughout the day rather than waning. At some point, Crispin sensed that the advantage had shifted to the British. And when night fell, and the firing finally ceased, Wellington still held Quatre Bras.

They held the position but at a cost. That night, the duke brought his staff to the Roi d'Espagne Hotel in Genappe, two miles to the north, to await word from Blücher. Supper and beds were afforded to them, but Crispin doubted anyone slept more than an hour or two. When word finally arrived, it was catastrophic. Blücher had fought long and hard at Ligny. But without reinforcements from the British, he had lost. The Prussians were in full retreat. Which meant Napoleon could now bring the entire force of his army against Wellington.

Stone-faced, the duke sent Lieutenant Colonel Gordon off to Ligny to see if the report was true. Then he said, "If Blücher has retreated, we must do so too."

EARLY THE NEXT morning, the retreat began. Retreat was not surrender. Wellington meant to bring his army to fields near Waterloo and stop Napoleon there. Crispin could not imagine any other commander pulling off so massive a fallback without chaos. Without alerting the enemy to hound British heels and turn a retreat into a rout. In a torrential downpour, no less. There had not been such a rain since Noah floated his ark.

Crispin was given the task, along with several of his fellows, to stake out the positions Wellington was assigning to the various regiments along the ridge of Mont-Saint-Jean. Rain continued to fall in sheets, and the ground was sodden. If boots sank so deeply, it would be impossible to maneuver the cannons. The only consolation was that Napoleon would be equally mired.

Rain doesn't bother me. Crispin remembered saying those words to Camellia. What else might he have said that had been a lie? Had they said anything to each other that had been true? Would he die tomorrow without having the chance to say he was sorry?

"Major Taverston?" A lieutenant whom Crispin did not know well slogged through the mud to draw closer. "The commander wishes to see you. Special orders."

Damn. Special orders could mean many things. On the eve of battle, it was likely one of three: scouting the enemy's position, carrying messages, or interrogating a fresh-caught prisoner. Crispin hoped for the first and prayed it would not be the last. Courier, of course, would be a waste of his talents.

YET IT WAS to be courier. Blücher had not turned tail for Prussia, but had regrouped at Wavre. The two armies were still just a little too far apart for comfort. Communication was critical if they were to be able to coordinate their attack.

So here Crispin was. Pounding along a muddy track through the woods on a strong bay gelding, Wellington's missive hidden in the lining of his jacket, and Wellington's words ringing in his ears. "Don't get distracted, don't get caught, and don't get shot. You have one job to do today. One. To be our link."

The battle had been slow to start because of the rain, but once the artillery began its fire, the farmland quickly became a hellscape. Crispin was attempting to skirt the periphery of the fighting without stumbling into the midst of it, a task made difficult by the ragged lines of the companies engaged. What had seemed clear enough in the scribbled map Wellington had shown him was now obscured by smoke and reverberating noise that made the air seem to shimmer. The big guns crescendoed and decrescendoed in waves, but the earthshaking clamor of armies clashing was unceasing, a constant chorus of men and horses screaming—

A distinctive loud crack sounded, and Crispin lost control of the bay. The horse stumbled, its sides heaving. A terrifying vision of the colonel in his wheelchair flashed before Crispin's eyes before he scrambled free of his dying horse. The next moment, three frogs emerged from the woods, one on horseback and two on foot. They were exuberant, boasting of their prize. The emperor would reward them. They were heroes. *God.* They were fuzz-on-their-chins *boys.*

But boys with muskets pointed at him. He should have made a wider circle around the field. *Damn it.* He raised his hands in a signal of surrender—and cursed himself for what he was about to do.

At a clipped order from the one who was mounted, one of the others approached to disarm him. The moment he was close enough, Crispin grabbed him, wrenched his arm behind his back and spun him to use as a shield. He caught the frog around the neck, tight. Since he hadn't three hands, he let go of the twisted arm, slipped his knife from its sheath, and stuck it in the struggling boy's back. He yanked him hard against his own body, ignoring the scream in his ear. Left hand now free, Crispin pulled his pistol and shot the stunned Frenchy on the horse.

The next instant, there was an explosion, and the boy in the chokehold slammed against Crispin so hard he stumbled backward. His human shield became deadweight. Crispin dropped him, steadied his feet, and faced his remaining captor. They had both spent their bullets. The fellow stared at Crispin, eyes wild, knees shaking. Then he cast a desperate glance sideways.

They both needed that horse.

The boy made a dash for it. Crispin pulled his second pistol and dropped him neatly. Then he went to the horse, who'd remained remarkably calm throughout. A nag. Likely deaf rather than battle-hardened. Or maybe both. He hoped Blücher had a horse to spare. This one would not last.

He reloaded his pistols. Quickly. Then tucked them away. He put his foot in the stirrup, but before he mounted, he heard mewling.

"Maman. Maman."

Christ! He looked about. It was the shield. Knife in his back, gutshot by his jumpy friend, the boy was still alive. Alive with two mortal wounds. It might take all day and night for him to die, but die he would. Alone in the mud, in pain, crying for his mother.

Crispin walked over, flipped the boy onto his stomach, and pulled the knife from his back. Shutting his ears to the sound of whimpering, he slit the frog's throat.

He wiped the knife, put it back in its sheath, and returned to the horse.

Nothing. He felt nothing. He had one job to do. One. He mounted and spurred the nag on.

MY DEAR JASPER, No doubt you've heard rumors that a great and terrible battle took place near Waterloo. By the Grace of God, I am alive and unharmed. One might say I missed most of the fight. Someone had to carry dispatches between ourselves and the Prussians, and I imagine you are glad to hear it was me.

Crispin lowered his quill, disgusted with his own tone. The bloodbath was nothing to be made light of. If Blücher had not been so determined to bring his army to Wellington's aid, the outcome would have been different. Standing by the fireplace in the dining room of the Roi d'Espagne Hotel, using the mantle for a desk, he tried again.

One day perhaps I will speak of the unspeakable. I have never seen, and hope never again to see, such horrors. Suffice to say, whatever you may hear, it was a thousand times worse. At times I thought it could only end with our mutual annihilation.

Major Percy came up from behind and tapped his shoulder. "If you want your letter going with me, give it here." Wellington had awarded Percy the task of carrying his report on the battle, as well as the two captured Napoleonic Eagles, home to Bathurst, Liverpool, and the Prince Regent. The honor might have gone to Crispin. Of all Wellington's aides-de-camp, they were the only two still alive and standing. Crispin was glad Percy had gotten the assignment. He wanted nothing more than a bed.

"One moment." How to convey the unconveyable? He finished with: *Death be not proud, though some have called thee mighty and dreadful, for, thou are not so. Jasper, Donne was wrong. Death IS mighty and dreadful. And too many brave men have discovered that this day. —Major Crispin Taverston*

FOR TWO DAYS, Crispin helped bury the dead and succor the wounded. It was necessary to ignore the inconvenient part of himself that felt things, or he would never have stopped weeping. So many of his fellows were gone. And the list continued to grow.

There were still corpses littering the battlefield, some in piles two or three deep, as well as dying men who had not yet been tended to—men who would never be tended to—but Wellington gathered the tattered remnant of his army to move on to Paris. Blücher and the Prussians had given chase immediately upon Napoleon's defeat, but as far as anyone knew, the emperor had not yet been captured.

Crispin was not the only one who hoped it would be Blücher's men who found Boney. Blücher, furious and merciless, would see him summarily executed. Wellington would not. The only honorable soldier left in this polluted world, Wellington would follow the rules. Once Napoleon surrendered, he would be treated with the respect accorded to any worthy foe. Never mind that the man could not be trusted to keep his word. They could be back at this again in another year.

It was a foregone conclusion that the duke would be given command of the occupying army once they entered Paris. After they crossed the French border, the officers sat down in an *auberge* to sup with their commander. Crispin pushed food around on his plate, pretending to eat. Later, he intended to retire to his chamber and eat the onions and carrots he had bought from one of the peasants Wellington had given his men strict orders not to harass.

"Taverston," Wellington barked, "Colonel Grant has asked that I relinquish you again to his command."

Crispin laid down his knife. *God, it never ended.* "To do what, Your Grace?"

Wellington waved dismissively. "You will have to ask him."

CHAPTER TWENTY-THREE

CAMELLIA UNBOXED HER mourning clothes. She was familiar with grief. After all, she had buried both of her parents. Yet her brother's death hit her harder. It hurt more. She was losing *everyone*.

After letting out the seams of all her black gowns, she discovered that only one silk dress could be remade full enough to fit. It was threadbare at the elbows and frayed at the cuffs, which embarrassed Manfred. He was always turned out well, even if it took hours for his valet to ready him. He told her she must have new dresses made. Although she was loathe to put her overlarge body into the hands of a dressmaker who would guess her secret, she had no choice. If people were going to talk, they would talk.

Manfred managed to attend Neville's funeral, but it was so difficult an outing, she suspected it would be the last time he left the house. His condition was worsening. It was not only that his physical infirmity hampered him, but his frustration made him moody. Little things angered him. Often, he grew annoyed that she had not anticipated one of his needs. Other times, he scolded her for fussing over him. He didn't like to let her out of his sight. He asked her daily, if not twice daily, how long it would be before the baby would be born.

Camellia walked about in a cloud of despair. The hours crawled by. She thought at times that Manfred's immobility must be contagious because she had no motivation to do anything. She felt cursed.

Then, a week after Neville's funeral, she and Manfred were in the parlor downstairs, waiting for tea to be served. It seemed they spent most of their days waiting for time to pass. She heard Tonbridge's church bells. In the middle of the afternoon. Ringing and ringing.

"What can it be?" she asked, moving to the window.

Of course, she could see nothing interesting from the window. And Manfred's only reply was a grunt. But the bells did not cease, so she finally sent Edward into Tonbridge to ask what was happening. He returned winded and flushed, with the scent of ale clinging to him.

"Milord, Milady, the war is won!" His eyes shone. "There was a tremendous battle. Boney is done for. Wellington destroyed him!"

"I knew he would. God bless Britain!" Manfred said, his voice thick with emotion.

"Yes, thank God!" Camellia murmured. She feigned gladness, but in fact, she was almost blinded by fear. There had been a battle? Did Major Taverston take part? Had he survived?

If only she could see him once more. Even from a distance. Just to assure herself he was alive. Because she was losing everyone.

As the weeks passed, Manfred grew more irascible. He insisted he would not be confined upstairs as Neville had been. So Camellia assigned Edward the task of escorting him up and down the staircase. Manfred protested, but she would not budge.

He forgot conversations. Or else he wasn't listening when she spoke. She felt burdened and hated herself for her impatience with him. But she had spent a quarter of her life caring for others and she was tired. It felt strange to think that the one person who had made *her* feel cared for, in little ways, was Major Taverston. Or he did, until he did not.

Camellia entered Manfred's library, bored enough to seek out a book of his to read. But she paused, seeing him slouched in his desk chair. Stepping closer, she saw he held something clutched to his chest. Closer still, she discovered it was a lady's glove. Her heart stuttered. It was not her glove. It must be Elizabeth's. Poor dear Manfred. She *must* be kinder.

She tried to tiptoe out, but he called to her. "Camellia? Come. It isn't your fault."

"My fault? What isn't?" She returned to his side, seeing he'd crumpled the glove and was attempting to stuff it into the top drawer of his desk. He looked groggy. He blinked slowly, then his gaze focused.

"Nothing. I thought…I suppose I dreamed you…the baby. It was a girl."

She sighed. Of course, a girl would not be her *fault*. But before she could respond, Manfred started weeping. She laid her hand on his shoulder. "Oh, Manfred."

"My dear, what will become of you?" Tears continued to spill. "Promise me that you won't make any bargain with Alexander."

"Your cousin?"

"He isn't to be trusted. If he invites you to stay here—"

"I won't, Manfred." She shuddered. Whatever he'd been dreaming must have been a nightmare. "I promise I won't."

He raised his hand slowly to wipe his eyes. "My dear, you will have to go to the earl. To Iversley. He is known to be an honorable man. Explain to him. He will ensure the major takes responsibility."

"Good God, Manfred!" Her throat closed. "I don't want his brother forcing him. What kind of marriage would that be?" A marriage like that of Mr. Cooper's unfortunate sister.

"If I die—"

"This is not something we need worry about. We have years

before we need worry." Yet she knew this wasn't true. Her husband's eyes filled with tears once more. She tried to speak reassuringly. "I can go to Marianne. To Lady Stirling. She has said I'm always welcome." Marianne's latest letter announced she had been delivered of her fourth healthy child. A baby girl. How wonderful it would be to be able to *welcome* the birth of a girl. "And there is no reason to worry now. Another month and we may well be rejoicing over our son."

CRISPIN STOOD ASHORE in Tor Bay with a spyglass. He watched the HMS Northumberland sail away until it was a speck on the horizon, and then gone. The ship was finally *en route* to St. Helena with Napoleon, his entourage, and his guards aboard.

Good. There could be no escape from St. Helena.

Whistling tunelessly, Crispin walked the half mile to the sparse, tiny chamber in the sailors' inn that had been his home for the last month, finished packing his valise, and wrote a quick dispatch to Wellington. His last. The operation had been smooth. The wily old general had not slipped from their grasp. His exile was assured. And Crispin was done. He thanked Wellington for the confidence placed in him. Then he resigned.

Next, he used his knife to pick out a few stitches at the edge of the mattress on his bed. He reached in to retrieve the code book Colquhoun had given him, and sat down to construct an encoded dispatch, this one to the spymaster, which said essentially the same thing—except for the thank you. Although in theory, Colquhoun reported to Wellington, the duke's supervision was a myth. Colquhoun had given Crispin additional instructions which had come from higher up. Most likely from Sidmouth, the Home Secretary. Liverpool, the Prime Minister, was far too decent a man to assign anyone this sort of task.

Napoleon's prison ship was a source of infinite curiosity.

While it sat in the harbor, sightseers and well-wishers ventured near in boats of all sizes, everyone straining for a glimpse of the one-time emperor. Most were annoying rather than dangerous, but the general had a following, even in England. "Steps were to be taken" to prevent anyone from helping Napoleon to escape. If he nevertheless managed the feat, he must be killed. And, of course, the assassin would have to disappear. Perhaps to Canada, Colquhoun had suggested. Though India could also be arranged.

Killing Napoleon would not have weighed very heavily upon Crispin's conscience. Not after witnessing the devastation the man's ambition had caused. Nevertheless, he was relieved it hadn't been necessary.

He put the code book into the stove and watched it burn, stirring the pages until nothing remained but ash. After scrubbing his hands thoroughly, perhaps more thoroughly than need be, he tucked the letters into his bag. As soon as he reached Exmouth, he could pass them off to a courier who would see that they reached the intended recipients in Paris.

Feeling unburdened, Crispin trotted downstairs, bypassed the dining room, said goodbye to his host, and stepped outside where a post-chaise-and-four awaited him. His intention was to travel by easy stages to London. Three days. Perhaps four. He hoped to sleep through most of it. Preferably without the plaguing nightmares.

It was early August. He would arrive, he hoped, after the end of the London Season. He didn't want to get swept up in the Marriage Mart, especially not at the very end of it when the unchosen misses grew desperate. Unfortunately, Parliament was no longer in session, so Jasper and Vanessa might have left the city. Probably Hazard and Alice also. He supposed Reg and Georgiana would be in Cambridge. And Olivia and Benjamin would be at their cottage at Chaumbers. *Homecoming was different when his siblings were dispersed into three different homes.*

If no one was in London, he would head for Chaumbers as soon as he sold his commission. Never again. Never again would he lend his arm to such slaughter.

He tossed his valise into the carriage, then climbed inside. He rapped on the roof to signal the driver to go.

He hadn't told anyone he was coming. Or where he had been. They all thought he was in Paris with Wellington. They'd be very glad to see him, whenever he found them, but not half so happy as he would be to see them.

Crispin leaned back and closed his eyes. Thank God he hadn't had to disappear.

⊰⟫⟫⟫✕⟪⟪⟪⊱

THERE WAS NO one at 8 Grosvenor Square except the servants who maintained the place when everyone else was gone. Crispin had known there was a strong possibility no one would be there. Nevertheless, he felt unreasonably miffed. He assured the housekeeper she needn't air his rooms. He would be returning to his set at Albany.

He walked to Picadilly, avoiding carriages, men on horseback, pedestrians, pickpockets, and hawkers of flowers and hatpins. He inhaled the scent of London's summertime squalor, and told himself he enjoyed the smell of home. Still, an unanticipated prickle of unease came over him as he crossed the courtyard of Albany and put his key into the lock of his set of rooms.

There it was. Empty as Christ's tomb. The furnishings were all draped in white linen dustcovers, giving the room the eerie appearance of a graveyard. This was not something he had done before leaving. He suspected Vanessa would have seen to it. He stepped inside and started to uncover a chair in his parlor, but shuddered and stopped.

He could not bear the thought of spending his first night back in London alone. Especially in this place where he had been closer to death than he'd been at Waterloo.

But where might he go?

Hazard. Hazard and Alice could still be in the city.

He left his apartment and walked to Hazard's townhome. The street was much quieter here, its residents more refined. He knocked. The door was opened by a narrow-faced porter who informed him the viscount and viscountess were not at home. The pronouncement was definitive and quick—the man did not bother to take Crispin's card and see if Hazard was at home *to him*—so Crispin believed the pair were truly gone.

Which left what?

He had other friends in London, but the thought of walking around knocking on doors, begging for company, did not appeal to him. Unfortunately, he'd left England before Jasper had had the chance to submit his name for membership at White's. He supposed he should return to 8 Grosvenor Square, have one of the kitchen maids cook something for him, then stay the night in his old rooms.

Or, he might go to George Street and see if the Hindoostanee Coffee House was still there. He could get a good curried rice. Decide from there.

He stood on the side of the street outside Hazard's house tapping his fingers on his hip, ignoring the occasional passers-by.

How ridiculous. How could he be so indecisive over something that mattered so little? He'd go to 8 Grosvenor Square. At least there, the servants knew him.

CRISPIN SPENT A week in London, trying to reacclimate himself to his old life, but he was having a difficult time remembering what that life was. He knew his old self didn't wake thrashing and crying out in the middle of the night, dreaming of the battlefield—the piled-up bodies of men and horses, some still twitching in their death throes—the circling crows and scrawny dogs—the scavenging peasantry, who would hurry a soldier along to his Maker if it helped them to snatch a brass button. His old fearless self would have returned to Albany, not quailed at the thought of so much solitude.

He had tasks, so he performed them. He spoke with an army agent and filled out the papers to sell his commission. He bought a pianoforte and arranged to have it shipped to his cottage in Binnings. He visited an employment agency to advertise for a valet and a cook. And he went to Jasper's tailor to order three new jackets and a half dozen shirts and trousers. For fun, he put them on Jasper's account.

He felt industrious, but very much alone. The aloneness was his own fault, so, finally, he wrote to his siblings, telling them he was in London, then waited for a response. Three days later, he had a letter from Jasper.

We are coming to London. DON'T GO ANYWHERE.

For the first time in a long time, Crispin felt himself smile.

CHAPTER TWENTY-FOUR

CAMELLIA WAS IN her bed, unable to sleep. She was huge, and the air was unbearably hot. The linens were damp with sweat. Any day now, she told herself. Any day.

She had been praying for a son, but now she prayed only for the baby to hurry up. She could not bear the uncertainty any longer. The nursery was ready. She'd hired a wet nurse. The midwife from Tonbridge was on alert, though she pretended to believe she would not be needed for another two months. If only the baby would come!

The house was silent. Silent enough to hear the twittering and cooing of early morning birds outside.

The quiet was shattered by a horrible, prolonged thudding noise and a muffled shout. She peeled herself from bed and pulled her wrap around her body. She heard more shouting. A panicked clamor. She hurried, waddling, from her bedchamber, then stopped dead at the top of the staircase. Manfred lay at the bottom. Servants clustered all around. The blood rushed from her face to her feet, and she had to lean against the wall lest she faint.

"Is Sir Bodwell all right?" she called.

Mrs. Clay shouted back. "Lady Bodwell, stay there. We'll send for the doctor."

"Manfred?" Her voice rose shrilly. "Manfred, are you hurt?"

Then she heard him moaning and swearing. *Thank God.* She

started carefully down the stairs.

⟫⟫⟫✦⟪⟪⟪

MANFRED WAS BRUISED all over and had broken his hip. His hip. Like Neville. He was in terrible pain and confined to his bed. She could do nothing but sit with him and dole out laudanum.

The next night, her water broke. Mrs. Clay put her to bed while Edward ran for the midwife. She labored all through the night. She prayed first for a boy. Then she prayed for God's will. A boy or a girl. Any end to the agony.

The midwife told her to push. She gripped Mrs. Clay's hand hard and pushed, again and again, until at last, she heard Mrs. Clay's cry of delight. The midwife put a bloodied hand on her shoulder.

"Relax, Lady Bodwell." A moment later, she said, "You have a son. A beautiful boy."

Camellia wept with relief. "Neville," she murmured. "His name will be Neville."

She slept. When she awoke, hours later, she saw the wet nurse seated in the corner of the room, cradling the baby. Mrs. Clay was bustling about. The midwife was gone.

"Has anyone told Manfred?" Camellia asked.

"Oh! You're awake. I went to tell him earlier, but he was sleeping," Mrs. Clay said. "The laudanum. I don't think he heard."

Camellia pushed back her blanket. Her linens smelled rank. She sat up. "Please have someone come change the bed." As she swung her feet to the floor, Mrs. Clay hurried to her, horrified. "Lie down, Milady. What can you be thinking!"

"I'm going to Sir Bodwell."

"Lady, you must—oh!"

Camellia stood, straightening her nightdress. "Give me my wrap." Mrs. Clay did, still frowning. Camellia took short, painful steps to the nurse. "Let me hold him."

The nurse stood and placed little Neville into her arms. Camellia peered down at him and her eyes moistened. He was healthy, hefty, and bald. With bright, bright blue eyes. But all babies were blue-eyed, weren't they?

She limped toward the door.

"Lady, let me carry him," Mrs. Clay said, coming up behind her. "You shouldn't be walking."

"No. Wait here." Camellia wasn't sure what words might emerge from Manfred's mouth if she woke him.

She left the bedchamber and walked carefully down the hallway to Manfred's room. She entered without knocking and approached her husband's bed.

"Manfred?" she whispered. "Manfred?" She touched his shoulder. "Please wake." She shook him gently until his eyes opened. It took a moment for him to get his bearings.

Then he started. "Camellia? Is that…?"

"Your son."

"Praise God!"

"I want to name him Neville."

"Of course. Anything." He smiled and wept at the same time. "Thank you, Camellia. Thank you."

He was thanking her for giving him a son that was not his own. She was not cursed. She was blessed.

THE SERVANTS SEEMED willing to believe that Lady Bodwell delivered her baby at seven months because of the shock of her husband's fall. Never mind that Neville weighed nearly eight pounds and had a lusty cry. Even if they didn't believe it, that was the story they spread.

Camellia had never loved anyone so much as little Neville. It bothered her even to surrender him to the wet nurse. If she could hold him all day long, she would.

But she had another responsibility. Manfred faded quickly after Neville's birth. It was as if he was now content to let go of life.

She tried to coax him to hang on. Reading to him. Feeding him. Singing to him. Bringing Neville in and laying him down on the bed. But Manfred was in such pain it seemed cruel to beg him to keep suffering. He was immobile. He complained of exhaustion. Exhaustion with life.

He had a son. Alexander would not get the estate. That was all that seemed to matter.

A fortnight after Neville's birth, Manfred passed quietly in his sleep. Camellia was now a widow with a son. Everything had changed. Except that she was still wearing black.

AFTER MANFRED PASSED, Neville could not keep down his feeds. The wet nurse first downplayed the problem as fussiness. Or colic. But then she, too, became concerned. Neville was clearly hungry. He cried constantly. Wet tears at first, and then dry. When the nurse put him to her breast, he suckled voraciously. But moments later, he would cast up the milk.

"Milady, I've never seen the like," the nurse said, wide-eyed. She pointed out the spatter. "He doesn't spit. He vomits clear across the room."

Neville bawled piteously until he crashed back to sleep.

Camellia called back the midwife, who suggested a different wet nurse. Camellia brought in another woman, but the result was the same.

She sent for Mr. Bartholomew, the local physician, a man she knew well and trusted. By then, four-week-old Neville no longer had the strength to cry. He weighed less than he had at birth. He suckled poorly, but still vomited with force.

Mr. Bartholomew shook his head. He gave Neville a pat on the head, then turned to Camellia. He frowned, full of sympathy.

"My lady, I have never seen this, but I've heard tell of it. I believe your son's stomach is blocked. Milk will not pass out of it."

"I don't understand."

"Ah. Well, you see," the doctor scratched his chin, "milk should flow freely from the stomach into the bowels." He repeated, "But your baby's stomach is blocked."

"How do we unblock it?"

"I'm afraid we can't."

Camellia stifled her panicked cry, but her voice rose and cracked. "Then what do we do? How can I feed him?"

Mr. Bartholomew was quiet for a moment. Then he said, "You might try smaller feeds. Use a dropper. Small amounts may slip through."

"And if that doesn't work?"

"I think you had best pray that it does."

⫸⫷

SEPTEMBER WAS SLIPPING away. A little over a month had passed since Crispin had received Jasper's letter and he was growing impatient. Of course, Jasper hadn't said *when* he was coming. A taste of his own medicine. Crispin was getting an inkling of how annoying it was.

Even more annoying, in the past month, Crispin had received two urgent invitations from Lord Sidmouth, the Home Secretary, an unscrupulous politician if ever there was one. Yesterday's invitation had the wording of a summons. *The Home Office requires a man of your caliber.* For rooting out "domestic troublemakers." He'd sent back an emphatic no.

He was tired of being two or three or four different people, depending on the circumstance or the company he was in. He recalled his desire for consistency of self. He wanted to *be* himself. He was not a spy. He was a civilian, a gentleman, a *Taverston*, and he was going to live as one.

For a start, he'd hired himself a valet. The man was middle-aged and stodgy, which would not have been Crispin's preference, but the applicant's previous employer had died, and his only reference was the widow. He was unlikely to be hired elsewhere, and Crispin could not turn the poor fellow away. Gerald. To his pleased surprise, Gerald was proving enormously competent. Crispin's boots had never sported so high a shine.

Early that morning, he went riding in Hyde Park on one of Jasper's London mounts. A sleek gelding. He really did need more than one horse of his own. Perhaps in the afternoon, he would go to Tattersall's and look over the stock.

As he returned to 8 Grosvenor Square, he saw a train of four carriages coming up the road, with Jasper and Reg riding alongside the first in line. Heart swelling with gladness, he trotted the gelding up to greet them.

In the drive, they all dismounted and embraced. It was impossible to miss the relief intermixed with his brothers' joy.

In another moment, a horde of Taverstons spilled from the carriages. The first to reach him was little Hannah, who must be four now; or could she be five?

"Major! Major! I have a pony!" she exclaimed, dancing about his knees.

He swooped her up and spun her, her braids whipping around. "Where? What is his name?"

"Duke!"

Benjamin and Olivia followed on her heels. Benjamin said, "Have you anything else to tell the major?"

Crispin set her down and grinned. In Olivia's arms, wrapped in a light blanket, was the newest Taverston.

"I have a brother!" Hannah shouted.

"Oh, fine, fine," Crispin said. "I'm glad to see you have your priorities straight." He shook Benjamin's hand, and gave his sister a sideways hug so as not to crush the baby. "Who have we here?"

Olivia grinned at him and said, "This is Christopher."

His heart gave a hitch. "May I?" He held out his arms.

"Just don't spin him the way you did Hannah. His head will fall off."

He laughed and took the bundle. The baby yawned without waking. Gazing at the perfect round head and pink mouth, his heart softened. He'd been nine years old when his mother had placed baby Olivia in his arms. Now, he felt the same drowning surge of love he'd felt then.

"He's tiny."

"He's not even four weeks old."

Ah. That was what took them so long. A very forgivable delay.

However, the little creature started squirming and his eyes popped open. Crispin handed his near-namesake quickly back to Olivia. Then he turned to Reg and Georgiana, who had two babies to present. Reg had taken Arthur from a nursemaid. The fellow was gigantic compared to how he had been when Crispin had first met him. Georgiana held Randolph. Crispin smoothed his hand over one nephew's head, then the other.

"Good show, Georgiana," he said, wondering if Jasper would now hound him to have that embarrassing talk with Reg about French letters.

Then he embraced Vanessa. As he was doing so, she whispered to him, "I am here if you need to…to talk."

Alone among the other Taverstons, Vanessa truly understood war. She had followed the drum on the peninsula and had fled the French army while retreating pell-mell to Corunna. She'd lost her first husband there. She would read the published accounts and understand. But even she could not *know*. Not Waterloo.

"I might," Crispin whispered back. "Thank you." But he didn't want to burden her. She was surrounded by baby Taverstons. None of them were hers and Jasper's. He added, "I can *listen*, too."

She nodded and stepped back, so that Crispin's mother could approach.

Mother put her hands on his shoulders and studied him. "Will we go through this again, Crispin?"

He shook his head. "I've resigned my commission."

Tears sprang to her eyes. "Thank God."

He hugged her tight, then released her. He glanced around, feeling empty armed, as he scanned his burgeoning family. Someone was missing. He tried to tell himself it was Hazard and Alice, but it was not. Surrounded by his loved ones, he was nevertheless alone.

≫≫≻≺≪≪

AFTER A LONG visit in the parlor, during which babies were carried off, then brought back, then carried off again, and eventually tea was served and then cleared, Jasper rose and asked Crispin to accompany him to White's. He pointed out that the parents in the group were used to country hours and were beginning to droop.

Crispin changed into evening clothes and followed Jasper. His brother evidently wished to speak with him alone.

As they strolled along the darkening London streets, Jasper said, "I'm impressed with that knot in your cravat."

"I have a new valet. Gerald."

"I saw him in the hall. He seems rather conventional."

Crispin laughed. "Yes, well, that is what I am striving toward now."

"Good luck." Jasper flashed him a grin, then said, "I'd like to put your name up for membership. Hazard is going to ask you to join Brooks's. You may join both. But you absolutely must be a member of White's."

Crispin tensed. "And why is that? Will it look bad if your brother joins a different club?"

"No, idiot. Because I've missed you. And I'd rather not have to join Brooks's to spend time with you."

Crispin laughed. He wanted to comment ironically, but could think of no comment to make. Instead, he said, "I'd hoped you would bring Mercury to London."

"Mercury is my lure to bring you back to Chaumbers when we go."

"Ha! You're getting good at this."

As they walked, Crispin asked about Vanessa's health. Jasper confided that they had been abstinent for a few months, but would soon try again. Crispin did not confess that he had been abstaining as well, for no explicable reason.

"What about French letters?" he asked.

Jasper shook his head. "The doctor recommended complete abstinence." Then he grinned. "Fortunately, there are ways around that."

"And Reg? Did you talk to him?"

"I did."

"Was it awkward?"

"Not so very. I didn't go to him. He asked me." Jasper snickered. "He was very grateful when I explained."

Crispin laughed. It was not actually funny, but he laughed. It relieved him of a burden. He had purchased one such French letter, at a very dear price, from a fellow officer, just in case the duty of telling Reg fell to him.

They talked about Chaumbers, and how well Benjamin and Olivia were doing, until they reached White's and went in. The décor was all dark wood and bold patterned wallpaper, with gold-and-blue trim. Windows were shuttered against any nighttime disruptions from outside. Lamps burned along the walls. Bookshelves and racks holding broadsheets beckoned. As they walked through the dining hall, Crispin was obligated to take a glass of sherry and accept the congratulatory comments of several of Jasper's friends, before he and Jasper were able to find two empty armchairs near a window. They hadn't been seated more than three minutes before Lord Kelley came up and asked Jasper for a word. He stiffened, nodded, then rose to walk off with him. A political disagreement, no doubt. Crispin sipped from his glass, aware he should rise and find some fellows to talk to, but he was afraid to be asked about Waterloo.

He watched a short, jovial-looking, dark-haired fellow cross the room and head in his direction. He didn't know the man, so was relieved when a group of three men seated in a cluster behind him rose in greeting.

"Lord Stirling! Good evening."

There was much back slapping and hand shaking before the four men sat down. The name Stirling scratched at Crispin's memory. He had no business eavesdropping—he was no longer a spy. But it irked him that he could not place the name.

"We didn't think you'd make it tonight. Don't you have a guest?"

"My wife's guest. Lady Stirling practically threw me out of the house so they could continue to gossip unmolested." Lord Stirling laughed. Then stopped abruptly. "It's a sad case, actually. Lady Bodwell is an old friend. She deserves better than so much misfortune."

Crispin's grip tightened on his glass. He remembered now. The Stirlings were Camellia's London friends. *What misfortune?*

"Lady Bodwell?" Another of the men mused. "Is she not Colonel Harrington's sister?"

"Yes. She married Sir Bodwell from Tonbridge."

"The colonel passed recently, as I recall, didn't he?"

"Yes, poor soul."

Damn. It was no surprise, Crispin thought, but sad, neverthe-less. He was tempted to turn around and insert himself into the conversation, but then his eavesdropping would be evident, and what he was doing was rude. If he got himself blackballed, Jasper would be furious.

"Bodwell has always been sickly, hasn't he?" asked the same man.

"I never knew him," Lord Stirling said. "But I suppose he must have been. From what I understand, it was a marriage of convenience. Bodwell's property was entailed."

"Ah." The stranger's tone grew solemn. "Past tense?"

Harrington and Bodwell both? Crispin's chest grew heavy.

Another voice piped up. "Couldn't do the trick before he died?"

"Well, that's the worst of it." Lord Stirling cleared his throat. "There *was* a babe. A boy. But he came much too early and didn't survive."

Oh, God, poor Camellia. That first thought was followed immediately by a flash of unease. He counted back the months—a fog of illness and laudanum, but, surely... *came much too early.* Too early to survive. Relief overwhelmed his pity. His conscience was clear of this at least.

"Bodwell's cousin is apparently a rogue. So Lady Bodwell fled to us."

Crispin drained his glass and set it down. He felt sick. Camellia had far more than her share of misfortune.

"The blazes!" said one of the men. "That's too bad. How long will you have her?"

"I don't know," Lord Stirling said. "She has nothing." Crispin could imagine him shrugging, pretending a lack of concern, though he could not be pleased with being saddled with his wife's friend.

"Didn't Harrington leave her anything?"

"There was a house, but Bodwell sold it to pay the old fellow's debts." Stirling paused. "I don't mind having her, of course. My wife says she is as close as a sister. So, there we are."

"Is she pretty, at least? Decorative?"

"Now, now, none of that." Then Stirling laughed. "She's quite a beauty, actually. But bad luck follows her so closely, I'm almost afraid to have her in the house."

Jasper returned. Stone-faced. "Kelley is an idiot." He sat down, then stood back up. He nodded at Crispin's empty glass.

"Let's go to a tavern. Or a coffee house if you'd rather." He stopped. "Is something wrong?"

Crispin stood up and glanced at the men behind him to burn their faces in his memory. He was going to have to pay a call on Camellia to offer his condolences. He could do nothing less. *Good God!*

"Crispin?" Jasper said. "Is there something wrong?"

"Nothing. A coffee house would be better."

CHAPTER TWENTY-FIVE

CAMELLIA WAS GRIEVING her son, her husband, and her brother. She'd lost her childhood home and her married one. She'd had to leave Tonbridge. And she was destitute. Marianne said she might stay with her forever, and she was grateful for that, but she dreaded the thought of being a burden upon her friend. *Forever.*

Once, she had been the cherished daughter of a respectable country gentleman. How had she ended up here?

It went without saying she should never have forced herself upon Major Taverston. But even if she had not, her brother would have died. She would still be impoverished. Of course, she would not have married Manfred. So she would not be a widow, and she would not have suffered the loss of her baby. But then, she would never have had a child to love. And she had desperately loved little Neville.

What ifs were useless. She must simply endure her grief, and try to make herself useful to the Stirlings. Her only other option was to apply for a nurse's position at Chelsea Hospital for room, board, and a measly eight pounds a year. The pity was, she *would* rather be a burden on Marianne than spend the rest of her days nursing the dying. She'd done enough of that for a lifetime.

A new widow was not supposed go about in public until a year had passed. Not even swathed in black. She didn't *want* to go out. But Marianne insisted the rule did not apply to a small charity event, held in the mid-afternoon, to raise funds for an orphanage. Marianne was one of the sponsors and was nervous that not enough ladies would attend. A few musicians had volunteered their time, and some of the older children, all girls, would be singing. It would be soothing, Marianne promised.

So, Camellia ventured out. She wore a new dress of black crepe that she'd had made in Tonbridge after Neville's death. Thank God Manfred's cousin had not confiscated her clothing. He'd claimed everything else in the house.

There were two dozen or so ladies gathered in Mrs. Galway's receiving room. Marianne introduced her to several, including Mrs. Galway, an imposing triple-chinned matron whose social rank was not impressive but whose bank account was. The room had three brick-red walls and a wall of windows. There were scattered couches and chairs, but rather than sit, the ladies milled about, sipping lemonade or ratafia.

In one corner of the room, a plump young lady, or possibly one with child, was holding court. Camellia could not help stealing glances at her. The lady had a very determined way of gesturing. She was brown-haired with an unremarkable face, but her Pomona-Green dress was extraordinarily fine. Although it was not fussy, the fabric was top quality and her modiste knew how to style a dress to flatter.

"Who is that?" she finally whispered to Marianne.

Marianne followed the direction of her gaze. "Oh, that is Lady Haslet. The viscountess. She is a great benefactress of the orphanage. Apparently, she arrived back in London just this morning, because she wanted to be here for this."

Lady Haslet? Camellia had heard the name before. From Marianne? "Are you acquainted with her?"

"Not yet," Marianne said, smiling like a cat in cream. "But I expect to be introduced."

Mrs. Galway suddenly announced, in a booming voice, "We should make our way into the music room. The performers are ready to begin."

They filed across the hallway into a room where chairs had been arranged in curving rows to face a small makeshift stage. Large vases on pedestals in three of the corners held fragrant bouquets. Candles were lit in tall stands all along the walls. It was quite lovely.

Once the guests were seated, the musicians took the stage, four of them with stringed instruments and one with a flute. Then came a dozen girls. Camellia guessed them to be ten to fourteen years in age, in matching brown dresses, with scrubbed faces and excited smiles.

Camellia found the various performances moving. And when the young orphans sang *Amazing Grace*, they brought tears to her eyes. Of course, everything did anymore. She dabbed her eyes with her handkerchief. It would not do to start sobbing.

When the concert ended, many of the ladies crowded about the girls.

Marianne said quietly, "The goal was to find positions for these girls in service. I imagine we've succeeded."

"Oh. Oh, yes, how clever."

"Are you all right? You look a bit peaked."

"I'm fine. It's a little warm in here, but I'm fine."

"We can leave. Some of the others are."

Camellia knew she should say they might stay as long as Marianne was needed. After all, she was one of the organizers. Still, she said, "Yes, I would like to go home."

Marianne picked up her reticule, took Camellia's arm, and led her to the exit. She gave a little wave to Mrs. Galway across the room before stepping into the hallway. There were several other departing guests buzzing about, among them Lady Haslet, who was giving directions to a footman, indicating a box for him to carry.

Camellia stopped abruptly. That footman! He was the brawny young butler who had turned her away at Major Taverston's door. The man raised his head at that same moment and caught her eye. His jaw dropped, and he reddened. Camellia looked quickly away, her face growing warm.

Marianne mistook the reason for her pause and murmured, "Oh, bother. We haven't been introduced. And we can't very well introduce ourselves to a viscountess." Marianne nudged Camellia's elbow to guide her to the door.

Outside in the drive, Marianne asked one of Mrs. Galway's footmen to summon the Stirlings' coach, which was somewhere in a long line of carriages trailing up the road. As they waited, the viscountess emerged from the house, waving. She hurried toward them while her footman walked staidly behind.

"Please excuse me," the viscountess said, reaching them. "I know this is terribly gauche, but I am Lady Haslet. And you are Lady Stirling? And Miss Harrington?"

Marianne and Camellia both curtsied. Of course, the viscountess was permitted to approach them. It seemed odd though, to Camellia, that she was known to her as Miss Harrington.

"We are. It is a pleasure to make your acquaintance," Marianne said. Camellia only nodded agreement.

"And I, yours," the viscountess said. She frowned and focused on Camellia. "I do hope you'll forgive me my intrusion, but my footman has asked to speak with you. He says it is important, or I would never presume."

"Important?" she echoed. Her knees weakened. So the footman had named her to the viscountess. But surely he would not spill her secrets here.

"He is not given to impertinence. But if this is too great an imposition, I understand."

Marianne looked horrified, but Camellia said, "I'll speak with him if it is important."

"And private," the lady said. "Lady Stirling, I have some questions about the orphanage."

As the two moved away, the footman came nearer. He bowed to Camellia. "My lady, I apologize for my breach of manners."

"What did you need to say?" He had practically thrown her from the major's doorstep. She could not possibly be more mortified than to stand here and have him address her.

"The letter you gave me to give to the major—he would not take it."

Blood pulsed in her neck. "What do you mean?"

"You said it was crucial that he read it. I tried to give it to him. But he…" The man wrung his hands. "I should not be betraying the major's privacy. And he specifically told me not to say that he was ill."

"He was ill?" Camellia's blood chilled.

"I should be sacked for telling you. But yes, he was deathly ill. And drugged with laudanum. I tried—"

"Did he recover?" She couldn't bear it if he told her that the major, too, had died.

"He did, my lady." He cleared his throat. "But the letter…he didn't read it. He had me put it in the fire."

Camellia caught her breath. If he hadn't read the letter, he couldn't have known. "In the fire?" All this time, in her heart, she had been accusing him of dishonor. Of spitefully abandoning his own baby. But he hadn't known?

Still, he'd burned the letter. Unread. What kind of man would do such a thing?

"Yes, my lady. He wasn't rational." He spoke in a rush as though determined to say his piece. "You said it was crucial, and I promised to deliver it. I'm sorry that I could not. Please believe that I have regretted it ever since." He stared down at his fingers, twisted together. Then he took a step back. His shoulders seemed to relax as though he were free of a burden.

"One moment. You said he recovered. Did he…do you know if he was at Waterloo?"

"He was. I believe he survived. But truly, I should not say more. It is not my place. I merely wanted to confess that I failed to honor my promise to you."

She nodded. Thoughts and emotions crowded her brain, and

she couldn't sort them. She managed, "Thank you for telling me."

He bowed and retreated quickly. *The major hadn't known about their son.* She walked the short distance to Marianne and Lady Haslet in a haze.

"Thank you, my lady," Camellia said.

A smile of relief crossed the viscountess's face. "Oh, is it settled then?"

"Yes."

The lady reached out and pressed her hand. "Then I am glad. Marianne has asked me to tea next week. I know what a painful time this is for you, but I hope you will join us. And that you will call me Alice." A tiny grin slipped onto her face as she let go. "My husband is fortunate to be called everywhere 'Hazard.' When I complained that I was saddled with an unwieldy title he suggested I go by 'Hazardess.'"

Marianne laughed. Camellia managed a smile. "Tea at Marianne's house would be lovely. And please, call me Camellia."

"Good. Very good." She brushed her hands together, as if to say *that is that.*

Marianne said, "This is my carriage. We must go. Until next week?"

They exchanged goodbyes and were helped by grooms into the Stirlings' coach. As they rode away, Marianne gave Camellia a questioning frown.

"That was certainly unusual."

Camellia sighed. "Yes, it was. But there is no cause for concern."

"There isn't? Whatever he said has made you pale."

"I'm all right. I just…I'd met him before. He was apologizing for a trifle."

"A *trifle?* Footmen do not address ladies over trifles. And trifles would not make you pale."

"I cannot betray his confidence."

"A *footman's* confidence? For Heaven's sake, Camellia."

"I know. It is odd. But please. I just need to think about this for a while."

MARIANNE KEPT HER busy throughout the day. At supper, Philip was full of questions about the concert. There was no room for Major Taverston to intrude on her thoughts, though he stood firm at the edge of them. That night, Camellia tossed and turned, mulling over what this might mean.

The major deserved to know the truth. Or did he? Would he want to know? It would be difficult enough to decide whether to tell him that he had a living son. But one who had passed? What purpose would it serve to tell him?

She had sworn to Manfred she would tell no one. But the inheritance was no longer at issue so that promise was moot. Moreover, Manfred believed that the major *had* been told.

Feeling overly warm and uncomfortable, she threw off her blanket and rose. The window drew her. She pulled back the curtain and regarded the stars a moment, trying to picture her loved ones among them in the Heavens. Then she pressed her forehead against the cool glass.

Clearly, she should tell him. Baby Neville had only lived for a few weeks, but he *had* lived! *Neville* deserved to have his existence made known to his father.

Or maybe, Camellia thought, she was merely trying to preserve Neville's memory by telling the truth of his birth to the only other person to whom the truth might matter. But what if it did not matter to him? What if he scorned her for telling him and said he did not care? His contempt, contempt for their son, would destroy her.

But shouldn't he be given the choice to care or not care? Did he deserve that choice?

He could well disbelieve her and accuse her of hidden motives. Which was absurd. What could she possibly hope to gain by lying about this?

Maybe her motives *were* questionable. Did she wish to hurt

the major the way she'd been hurt? Or did she imagine sharing her suffering might lessen it?

Or, worse, did she simply wish to see him once more?

And that raised the definitive question. How on earth was she to see him to tell him? She could hardly pay him a social call. And if she did do something so outrageous, who was to say he would not, once again, simply have a porter turn her away from his door?

Chapter Twenty-Six

T HE TAVERSTONS NEVER stopped moving—in several different directions all at once. It amused Crispin to witness the bustle. To take part in the bustle. Over the next four days, he never found himself alone for long. He and Jasper started out each morning with a brisk ride in Hyde Park. He had a long conversation with Benjamin about his investments and the renovations at the Binnings cottage. Reg and Georgiana took him to a scientific lecture that he pretended not to understand, just for the pleasure of hearing Georgiana explain it. Olivia asked him to come with her and Hannah to feed the ducks in Green Park. He escorted his mother shopping. He was growing quite competent at holding babies, even crying ones, when the whole family gathered for tea.

It soothed his soul.

It was also his excuse. He had not yet paid a call on Camellia. *Camellia*—she was no longer Miss Harrington, and he could not bring himself to think of her as Lady Bodwell. He knew he should go to offer his condolences, out of respect for the colonel, at least. But what could he say to her? What could he say that would sound sincere? He pitied her, but when he searched his heart, he was still angry. She had used him for some purpose he could not begin to fathom. She'd believed him to be so dishonorable that he could deflower her and not care. She mocked his bedsport. She spurned his offer of marriage.

She'd hurt him. It angered and embarrassed him to admit it, but he'd been hurt.

That morning, because of poor weather, Jasper had cut short their ride. Crispin taunted him over it. London's misty excuse for rain was nothing. This was the closest he'd come to referring to events at Waterloo. The weather. He was starting small.

Jasper had gone to change his clothes, but Crispin went straight to the kitchen to ask Cook to prepare a half-dozen boiled eggs and a bowl of oat porridge. Then he went to the morning room. This room had always seemed to him too formal for its intended use. The floor was nearly black, and the walls were papered in dark blue with small golden-yellow curlicues. It took the sunny presence of his family to brighten the place. Nevertheless, Crispin was not going to wait for someone to join him. He was hungry and didn't want to watch Jasper, or anyone else, eating the tempting things he could not.

He had just sat down with his newspaper and tea when Vanessa marched into the room, boots clicking on the wood floor. She had a strange look on her face. Concern and annoyance. He hoped she wasn't going to ask him again if he wanted to "talk." She came up beside him and hovered. Without so much as a *good morning*, she launched into what was bothering her.

"Your mother is trying to convince Jasper to hold a ball."

"A ball?" He watched her tuck an errant lock of dark hair behind her ear. "Why would he do that? The Season is over."

"Think, Crispin." She huffed. "Why would your mother want to throw a welcome home ball for you?"

A ball for him? "Lud." He groaned. "She wants to marry me off."

With a short laugh, she said, "Now you know how debutantes feel."

The thought of being swarmed by silly, young, unmarried misses gave him the shudders. "Tell Jasper no."

"I have been, but he is folding under pressure. Your mother is very persuasive. I see now where you get it from."

He tried to grin at her but couldn't. "All right. Thank you for the warning. I'll talk to her."

Vanessa wasn't finished. She studied him a few moments. "She isn't entirely wrong, you know. You might start thinking about—"

"About saddling some poor chit with my sickly self?" He scowled. "Vanessa, if you are going to share breakfast with me, change the subject."

She pursed her lips, then sat down beside him. "All right. Did you know Alice is with child?" She waved a hand at him. "Don't give me that I'm-so-sorry look. I am thrilled for her and even more so for Hazard. Now tell me your plans for the day so I know when I should serve tea."

She obviously didn't want to talk about her misfortune any more than he wanted to talk about the war.

"This morning, I'm strolling over to Albany to pull the dustcovers off the furniture. I need to decide if I should keep the set or just let the lease go. It's more convenient to stay here when I'm in London. Unless Jasper objects."

Little inconsequential decisions. He hoped his life from now on would consist of such.

"You know he won't object. He'd be delighted."

"Ah, but since I haven't ruled out the set, I've scheduled interviews with a couple of cooks. The agency is sending them over this afternoon." He pinched his lip. "I know what I need, someone who will put up with my persnickety requirements and not mix flour and cream into my food, thinking I won't be able to tell. But I've only ever hired a valet. If you are available, I could use your input."

She squeezed his arm and smiled. "I would be delighted. Do you have their names? References to go over?"

He looked at her blankly. "Should I?"

Vanessa laughed. "My word. You do need help."

To Crispin's surprise, the first decision came easily. He found he felt rather attached to his apartment. Surveying the nearly empty shelves of his library, he had an urge to fill them. His own books. His own space. He wouldn't mind a little privacy. His siblings had detached themselves from Jasper's coattails. He should as well. And it was likely true that when none of his family were in London, he would feel less lonely here than wandering the empty rooms of 8 Grosvenor Square.

Crispin cast another look around his library. He might change some of the furnishings. The previous owner had been elderly and must have been short. If this was going to be his London home, he should at least have a desk chair better suited to his height.

He moved to his parlor and examined the walls, which were covered with a large expanse of green-and-yellow floral paper. A few paintings would be nice to break that up. He sat down in his most comfortable chair to take a mental inventory. There were heavy brass trimmings on the mahogany side tables. Very staid. If he removed two of the four tables, could he fit a pianoforte? But he'd already bought one for Binnings.

Binnings. Autumn was a good time to be at the lake. He could stable Mercury there. Perhaps add another horse or two. Maybe a broodmare—that was something to consider, wasn't it? A few broodmares. Ah! He was waking up to the possibilities of civilian life. And his family could come visit *him*.

As Crispin rested back in his chair, letting his mind wander far afield, he grew aware of someone knocking on his door. Who would come calling? He should have brought Gerald. An earl's brother shouldn't be serving as his own porter. He couldn't very well announce to an unwanted visitor that he wasn't at home.

He roused himself, went to the entry hall, and pulled open the door.

Unbelievably, there, on his doorstep, bathed in sunshine, stood Camellia. His pulse quickened. She was draped in black, like a medieval nun, just as she'd been the first time he'd seen her, with that uncanny tuft of white hair slipping out from under her bonnet. Still beguiling.

And still mad. She must be mad. To come here alone? Why in God's name…was she going to attempt to seduce him again? He felt a surge of desire. An unwanted response to the unlikely possibility.

"You shouldn't be here." His voice rasped as though he'd stuffed his mouth with gravel.

She stared at him, but said nothing. That was how she had played it the first time, slipping soundlessly into his bedchamber.

"How did you know I was here?" he demanded. Was she following him about? Spying?

"I-I took a chance. You were not at home yesterday, so I thought perhaps you would be today."

She didn't know he had been staying at his brother's. How unfortunate she had come to Albany at a time when he happened to be there.

"Well, don't stand on my doorstep. I don't want it spread about I have widows calling on me. They will line up around the block."

After she stepped inside, he closed the door, turned his back on her, and walked to the parlor, chased by a faint scent of lilacs. He heard hesitant footsteps, as though she were peering about to ascertain if they were alone. For a minute, he considered leading her to his bedchamber. Just to make her uncomfortable. *What was wrong with him?* She was not the enemy; there was no reason to be cruel.

Except that she had caught him off-guard. An unpardonable offense. She always caught him off-guard. *He* had intended to call upon *her*. That was the acceptable way of doing things. Why must she always choose the unacceptable?

In the parlor, he gestured to the couch, a comfortable couch with deep cushions and rolled arms. It looked designed for trysting. At least, it did now. He'd never thought that before. "Have a seat, Camellia."

She scowled at him. "Thank you, *Crispin*." She said it sourly. Not as though they were friends, but rather acknowledging that they were purposefully disrespecting one another. She stepped to the couch and sat. Black crepe billowed around her. She looked very small. Small and sad. Small and sad and determined.

"I should offer my condolences," he said, forcing the words from his mouth. "You've suffered loss, and I am sorry for you. You know how much I admired the colonel."

She nodded and murmured, "Thank you."

After that perfunctory exchange, they were silent. She appeared horribly uncomfortable. Still, he waited for her to speak. There was no reason to make this easier for her—whatever *this* was.

When the silence had gone on too long for *his* comfort, he said, "The condolences are also for your husband and your baby. Imagine my surprise when I heard."

"I—I must...but did you..." Rather than complete her thought, she shook her head. Her eyes looked shiny, and her chin quivered. He hoped she would not resort to tears.

"I meant to call on you," he said, deciding to stop towering over her. He sat across from her on a too-short, gray-and-white-striped chair. "It didn't occur to me that you might hunt me down." He laughed meanly. "I don't know why it didn't. Propriety has never guided you before."

"Please don't."

He felt a pang. Of guilt? Of anger? "Don't what?" Now he was being snide and disingenuous. The woman brought out the worst in him. The very worst. She couldn't have come to extract his condolences. So what the devil did she want?

She gave him a narrow look, but didn't answer. Ah, she wielded silence as a weapon. It took great effort not to drum his fingers against his knees. He refused to be nervous. To act nervous. Hadn't he always said uncomfortable conversations were his strength? He attacked them head-on.

"So," he drew out the word. "I can only assume that you've realized you made a mistake, *my lady*. You should not have chosen Sir Bodwell."

She blinked rapidly and twisted her hands in her skirt. "It was not a choice. I had no choice."

He snorted. "Oh, come now. No one forced you into my bed. *That* was your choice." He leaned forward, elbows on thighs. "And you told me you chose not to marry. Not to marry at all." He cocked his head to one side. "Or was that supposed to be a gentle rejection of my suit?" *A gentle rejection after harshly informing him he was a terrible lover.*

"No. No, I meant it."

She was trembling. *Damn it.* He steeled himself against pity. There were facts he needed to know. His voice flattened as he slid too effortlessly into his interrogator's role.

"Yet within a few weeks, you married Sir Bodwell. You tell me what I am supposed to think. That you suddenly found yourself madly in love with a dull fellow twice your age who talked of nothing but farming? That you were swept off your feet by an old man with one foot in the grave? Or did he coerce you?"

Her face went ashen. "Don't speak ill of Manfred."

He laughed. "So it was love?" He felt a mounting rage—and he was not given to rages. "Or was *he* a passionate kisser? Could *he* satisfy you in bed?"

She jumped up, blushing furiously. He stood also and moved toward her, sneering. "If you've come to give me a second chance—"

"Stay back!" She held up her hand, palm toward him.

He halted. Her expression was both fierce and alarmed. *The devil.* Aware of how threatening he must appear, he took a step backward. *Words* were his weapon. Silence was hers; words were his. He would not have touched her. Not in anger. Surely she knew that.

She lowered her hand. Then she breathed in raggedly and exhaled slowly. "This was a mistake." Her voice shook. She gestured for him to step aside. "I will leave you in peace."

"Another mistake? I thought, perhaps, that you recognized your error, *Lady Bodwell*, and hoped to rectify it. I understand that titles are appealing, and that Manfred had property—"

"Is *that* what you think?" She gaped, wide-eyed as though stunned. "That I rejected your...your mean-spirited, resentful offer of marriage for the material benefits Manfred could provide?"

Mean-spirited and resentful?

"Why else?" He tried to be flippant, but he felt cold inside. Could she give any answer that would not cut him to the quick? "I also have property, you know. Property that is not entailed. And I might not be titled, but I am heir to an earl. Admit it, Lady Bodwell, you backed the wrong horse."

She remained silent, but wrung her hands. Was that confirmation or denial?

He raised one eyebrow in a mocking fashion. "Why *did* you come here?" He pitied her situation. The unfairness of it. Women's lot. But what did she expect of him? Another rescue? Another proposal? "Your circumstances are unfortunate, but not my concern. I owe you nothing."

She turned her face away. "I never thought you owed me anything. Never. I thought I owed you."

"Oh, come now. What could you owe me?"

With a groan, she said, "Nothing. I was wrong. I should not have come."

"But you are here. Tell me."

She rubbed her eyes, but she did not appear tearful, merely tired. "There is no point. You have the answers that suit you. Believe what you will. It no longer matters."

"No longer? I think it safe to say it never did."

She caught her breath sharply, the surprised sound made by a soldier suddenly on the wrong end of a bayonet.

Why? What should have mattered to him?

She locked her eyes on his. Searching. He had to break the gaze first, fearing what she might find.

Pain. Not anger. Pain. Oh, God—he had *cared* for her. Fool, fool! She'd filled the empty place in his life. And now that empty place was a chasm.

"No, you don't know," she whispered. Then she shivered. "I'm so sorry."

Without waiting for his reaction, she started toward the parlor door. He stood rooted to the spot, replaying the entire exchange swiftly through his mind, trying to resee everything differently, stripped of his anger, trying to understand why her apology sounded so full of compassion when he had done his best to be cruel. *Mean-spirited and resentful.* Sickly, weak, spiteful, mean-spirited, and resentful. She knew him well.

He heard the swish of her skirts moving down the hall. He turned, opening his mouth to call her back, but the cry stuck in his throat. The front door opened, then closed.

"What don't I know?" he whispered.

CRISPIN WAS IN no mood to interview servants. He thanked God for Vanessa, who took charge. They brought the women into Jasper's office, one after another. Vanessa sat at the earl's desk and asked questions, while Crispin stood brooding behind.

The first woman was too young. Too flirtatious. She tried ingratiating herself with them both, until he informed her that whomever he hired would be expected to spend several months in Binnings. That was not acceptable. Apparently, she had a young man in London.

The second woman smelled of gin.

The third woman…was Mrs. Clay. Had he not been battered enough?

"Mrs. Clay," he said, forcing a smile. "What are you doing in

London?"

"You are acquainted?" Vanessa asked, shooting him a look of surprise.

He could see now the benefit of asking the agency for names and references upfront.

"Lady Iversley, may I present to you Mrs. Clay. She was cook and housekeeper for Colonel Harrington. Mrs. Clay, this is my sister-in-law, Lady Iversley."

Mrs. Clay curtsied awkwardly. She looked awed.

"Well, then," Vanessa said, pleasantly. "Never mind references. I suppose the major knows your work."

"You've left Tonbridge for London?" Crispin asked. Was she still in contact with Camellia? That would not do. He was feeling hunted.

"Aye, well, I have a brother here. And no work in Tonbridge. The old gentleman passed, you see. And then Sir Bodwell did, too." She flushed. "You knew, I hope? I'd hate to be the bearer."

"No. I am aware."

"And, of course, poor Lady Bodwell has gone to live with Lord and Lady Stirling."

"Do you see her often?"

Mrs. Clay's eyes flew wide. "Lord, no. I wouldn't presume."

"Mrs. Clay," Vanessa interrupted, bringing them back to the business at hand. "Major Taverston expects to spend half his time in the lake district. His cottage is small and rather sparsely staffed. Are you able to travel?"

"To the lake district? That would be lovely. I've never been. And the major will tell you, I'm used to small staffs. It don't bother me to do some housekeeping."

"Very good." Vanessa looked down at the paper in front of her, then back at Mrs. Clay. "The major is particular about what is served at his table. Can you pay strict attention to instructions?"

"Oh, aye." She beamed at Vanessa. "Don't I know he likes his rice and peas. No gravy. No bread. No cream. Lady Bodwell gave me a list."

It was unfortunate, but Mrs. Clay suited his needs perfectly.

"I'm sorry," Vanessa said, her brow furrowed. "Who is Lady Bodwell?"

"Colonel Harrington's sister," Crispin said. "She married a local gentleman."

"Oh!" Sympathy washed across Vanessa's face. "And they both passed?"

"And the babe, too." Mrs. Clay's head bobbed up and down. "It was a real shame. Then the cousin swooped in and took everything."

Vanessa gasped. "She lost a baby?"

"A boy. Made Sir Bodwell so happy, don't you know? He went peacefully. But the babe was a struggle."

"Born too soon?" Crispin asked. That was what the fellow at White's had said.

Mrs. Clay flushed and nodded. "Yes." She lowered her voice and added in a confidential tone, "They were seven months married, you see. But we still thought the babe would make it. He was robust when he was born. Eight pounds at least, we thought. But he wouldn't eat, and the doctor said there weren't nothing Lady Bodwell could do."

Vanessa's eyes welled with tears, alarming Crispin.

"Mrs. Clay," he said, hurriedly coming around the desk to usher her out. "Of course, the job is yours. Come to Albany in three days. I will have a key made for you. There are servants' quarters in the attic. My valet will show you."

He escorted her to the door, where Gerald was waiting to see her out of 8 Grosvenor Square.

Crispin turned to Vanessa. "I'm sorry. I never would have asked for your help if I'd known it might be upsetting."

"I'm fine," she said, though she sounded unsettled. "It is only that babies' lives are so precarious. So much can go wrong. Even for full-grown—"

"But Lady Bodwell's baby was not full grown. Seven months—"

Vanessa made a noise like a snort. "Crispin, you can't be that naïve. The Bodwells were married seven months when the baby was born. That doesn't mean the baby came early. It means they married too late."

Crispin stared. "No." He shook his head. "No, I don't think so."

She gave a laughing huff of disbelief. "She said he weighed more than eight pounds! I suppose that means nothing to you, but seven-month babies don't weigh eight pounds."

He counted months again, ticking them off on his fingers, but now he could not recall when Camellia had married Bodwell. After he'd been sick. But no. That was when he'd heard. They had been married *while* he was sick. Six…seven…eight…

Oh, God, no.

CHAPTER TWENTY-SEVEN

MARIANNE HAD BEEN out to a Society friend's breakfast when Camellia slipped from the house to see Major Taverston, and was still gone when she returned. Camellia was thus able to hide in her bedchamber until her swollen red eyes were merely pink.

Why had she believed the major should be told? The rationale she'd used to convince herself now seemed absurd. Knowing that he'd fathered Neville could only cause him pain, and she had no wish to hurt him. Obviously, she *had*, more than she'd known. There was something sad, even pathetic, in the way he had tried to rub salt in her wounds by comparing his aristocratic birth and his property to Manfred's.

Like a wounded animal, Major Taverston was dangerous.

The clock on her wall showed it was now a little after four. It was rude to be late for tea, so she hurried to the parlor. The floorboards in the dimly lit hallway creaked beneath her feet. Drawing close, she heard voices.

Bother. This was the day the viscountess was coming. How had she forgotten? Camellia picked up her pace.

The parlor was a cluttered, formally decorated room, that always struck Camellia as a bit *much*. There were vases, candlesticks, and figurines in every niche. The chairs were of rosewood and a fine chintz that was yellow with dark-red cherries. The drapes, open to allow a view of the garden, were the same shade of red. Marianne and Alice were seated on a Chesterfield sofa, upholstered with yellow-and-red stripes. Marianne's jonquil gown clashed with the sofa, but Alice was dressed in an exquisite deep-blue moire that complemented everything in the room.

"Ah, here she is," Philip said. He rose and swept a hand toward Camellia, letting his quizzing glass fall to dangle by its chain. Philip was not a tall man, but he had an aristocratic presence. However, he wasn't as imposing as the man rising to his feet from an adjacent chair. "Lady Bodwell, this is Lord Haslet."

"Hazard," the man corrected him. He smiled and bowed. A viscount! Camellia hurriedly curtsied. He was significantly older than Alice—gray at the temples with deep laugh lines by his eyes. Perhaps she shouldn't be surprised. Peers generally found themselves young brides. Still, one could not deny that he was handsome. Handsome, distinguished, and meticulously dressed in a gray jacket and fawn trousers. His cravat was elaborately tied, and his boots were so highly polished they seemed to give off light.

"Lady Bodwell and I have already decided that she is *Camellia*," Alice said with a light laugh. "Come, sit with us." She patted the sofa to show there was room. Camellia crossed the floor to reach them.

"I've never seen such a perfect dress," Camellia said. Surely Alice was increasing, but the drape of the fabric made it impossible to tell.

Alice grinned. "Did you hear that, Haz?"

"Indeed, I did. And may I say I told you so?"

Face alight with laughter, she said, "Hazard dresses me now. Apparently, left to my own devices, I am a frump."

Camellia smiled at the comfortable way they teased one another. When Alice patted the sofa again, Camellia sat. Marianne and Alice were talking about another event to raise funds for the orphanage. She listened with half an ear. With the other half, she tried to catch what Hazard and Philip were discussing. They sounded serious. Something political. She heard "the Irish" a few times and once "Liverpool."

Alice turned to her. "You must have been to Tunbridge Wells. You're from Tonbridge, aren't you?"

Camellia started. "Yes, I am." She wasn't sure how the topic had changed, but she tried to jump in. "From what I understand, it isn't as fashionable as Bath, but I thought Tunbridge Wells was lovely." More than lovely. She'd waltzed there with the major.

"And the waters?"

"Oh." She frowned. "I couldn't say. I didn't take the waters." Seeing Alice's disappointment, she added, "But my brother did. And his valet said that it helped."

"And what was your brother suffering from?"

"Alice is asking for her father, who has the gout," Hazard called across the room. "Alice, my dear, please do not give everyone the impression that I am decrepit."

"Your hearing is remarkably intact," Alice called back.

At that moment, the butler entered the doorway with a silver tray in hand and announced, "Lord Stirling, you have a caller."

Philip raised his hand, and the butler brought him the tray. He lifted a calling card from it, perused it, and frowned. "Well, yes. Yes, bring him up." The butler turned to go. Philip said, "A fellow up for membership at White's. I can't imagine why he's come."

Conversation returned to Alice's intention to visit Tunbridge Wells. Then the major stepped into the room. Camellia stifled a gasp.

Alice cried, "Crispin! Oh, how wonderful."

He cut an impressive figure in finely tailored civilian clothes: pale-blue superfine trousers and a dark-blue cutaway jacket, paired with a crimson waistcoat. It did not help Camellia's state of mind. Why must he be so attractive?

Hazard rose and went to shake his hand. "White's? Ah, poor fellow. You are playing right into Jasper's hands." He glanced around. "Who do you know? You must know everyone. Lord

Philip Stirling." He gestured with a nod. Then, "Lady Marianne Stirling. And Lady Camellia Bodwell. Everyone, this is Major Crispin Taverston, one of Wellington's finest."

The major gave them each a stiff bow. He looked pained. "I didn't know you and Alice would be here. I would not have interrupted a gathering—"

"Don't be silly!" Marianne said, rising. She went forward to welcome him. "Philip and I are delighted to make your acquaintance. I was just about to ring for tea. Please join us."

He pursed his mouth. "Thank you. But I came to speak with Miss Harr—with Lady Bodwell. If it is not too great an inconvenience." The words would have been polite, but it sounded more like a command than a request.

Philip frowned. "Lady Bodwell is in mourning and not receiving callers."

"Philip, really," Marianne said, then tittered. "How stuffy you sound when Camellia is here having tea with our guests. And if Major Taverston is a respectable gentleman, he may certainly join us."

"I'll vouch for Crispin," said Hazard. "I've known him for years."

"That might not be to his credit," Alice said, smirking.

Philip thrust out his chin. "Very well, but it is up to Camellia."

She didn't want to be browbeaten again. She'd said she was sorry. What more had they to say to one another? What else would he accuse her of? Nevertheless, refusing would be suspect, so she said, "I'll speak with him." Her voice was so weary Marianne looked startled.

"In private," the major said, brooking no argument.

For a moment, the whole room fell into an uncomfortable silence. Then Marianne said, "Why don't you go for a turn in the garden?" She pointed to the window. "Right out there." The implication was clear. Camellia's friends would be watching.

He turned to her. "Will you?"

"Yes, of course."

She mumbled her *excuse me*'s and beckoned for the major to follow. They went down the staircase, then out a side door. He walked stiffly and his face was strangely tight. She led him into the garden, which was flush with towers of blue delphiniums, white puffs of hydrangeas, and fragrant roses that were pale pink to bright red. They went down one path, then another. When she knew they were no longer visible from the parlor window, she stopped and faced him.

"Major Taverston, I suppose it is my turn to ask. Why have you come?"

He stared at her, then blurted, "The baby was mine."

"Oh!" Her throat closed so tight she could not breathe. She became lightheaded; her vision swam. As she began to sink, he put an arm around her waist, catching her.

"Sit. Sit down." He lowered her gently until she was sitting on the ground, then knelt in the dirt beside her. "Breathe slowly."

She did. In a minute or two, the garden stopped spinning.

"Are you all right?" he asked. She nodded. He took a few shaky breaths of his own. "What…what was his name?"

"Neville," she murmured. "For my brother."

"Ah. Good." He sat back on his haunches, staring at the ground. "Did Manfred know?"

She nodded again. "I told him. Before we were married. I had to be honest—"

"Of course. Of course, you were." His face twisted, agonized. He spoke so quietly she had to strain to hear. "You came to me first."

"Yes," she whispered.

"I—" His voice cracked. "I never knew my own son." His shoulders convulsed and he buried his face in his hands. She stared, helpless. She hadn't known what to expect from him, but it was not this.

"Crispin." She put a hand on his shoulder. James had spoken to her in confidence. She didn't want to betray that. But she owed more to Crispin than to James. And she couldn't bear to witness such hurt. "You were ill. It isn't your fault."

"You wrote me a letter, I think." He caught his breath and swiped tears from his face. "I never read it. I don't know what became of it." He ground his fist into the dirt. "God, I hate myself."

"You were ill." She choked back her own tears. *Deathly ill. Irrational with laudanum.*

"He was my son. And I turned my back on him. And on you! That isn't who I am. You must despise me. If I had known, believe me, if I had known—"

"I had to go to Manfred. I couldn't wait any longer. There was no time."

"I'm not blaming you. You did the right thing. The only thing. And God bless Manfred. He must have loved you very much."

This, here now, was the man she had thought him to be.

"No. No, he wanted a son that much." She hitched her shoulders. "I think he married me *because* I was with child."

Crispin regarded her a long moment. Then he pulled a handkerchief from his jacket and wiped his face and hands. He stood and gave her his hand to help her stand. Gesturing to his knees, the pale-blue superfine now filthy, he said, sounding more like himself, "A little hard to explain. The black of your dress hides the dirt, fortunately."

"I doubt anyone will be crass enough to say anything."

"You don't know Hazard."

He toed the dirt from around one of the paving stones and wiggled it loose. "You'll see," he muttered. Then he used his handkerchief to brush his trouser legs as best he could before offering his arm to her. They took a few steps along the path, then he groaned. "What was he like? It is unfair of me, but I have so many questions."

"I don't mind speaking of him." It kept his memory alive. "He was beautiful. He had your eyes. The brightest blue you ever saw."

"Blond hair? Taverston blond?"

"No. He was bald." Her voice caught. He would have been blond. She and Manfred were both dark. "He was so sweet. So precious. Looking into his eyes you could see an old soul."

"How did he die? If it isn't too painful…if you can say."

"He couldn't eat. Rather, he could not keep anything down." His arm went limp, so her hand fell away from the crook of his elbow. Seeing his appalled expression, she said, "It was not that food bothered him. You mustn't think that." It was not a curse inherited from Crispin. "The doctor said that the outlet from his stomach was blocked. He said there was nothing I could have done. Babies with this always die. They don't grow up to pass it down."

The blood seemed to drain from his face. "How long did he live?"

"Four weeks. He died in my arms."

He winced. "I'm sorry you had to bear that alone. You've borne so much. And this." He gestured about, seeming to encompass the Stirlings' home, her mourning dress, everything. "If I can do anything…"

She shook her head. "You can't. I don't want to court scandal. I skirted so close to ruin. I just want to live quietly."

"I understand." He puffed out a breath. "But I cannot simply walk away from the consequences of our folly."

"Not *our* folly. The fault lies with me. You would never have—"

"No, Camellia. Trust me. I would not have lain with you if it was not something I wanted to do."

Her neck and face warmed. It mortified her still, what she had done. "I truly thought," her voice dropped, "that I had taken the right precautions. But I don't regret—"

He dismissed that with a flick of his hand. "Where is he buried?"

"The churchyard in Tonbridge," she whispered. "Next to

Manfred."

Crispin nodded, jaw clenched. They continued in silence to the side door of the house. They carried such a cloud of gloom, it seemed to dim the riotous colors of the garden.

"Would you mind if I went to see him?" he asked.

"Why would I mind?"

"I feel I have no right to claim…to claim grief."

She halted. The poor man. Guilt radiated from him. "You have every right."

"Would you like to come with me? I'll borrow Jasper's carriage again. We can go and come back in a day."

Was that an offer or an entreaty? "Of course I would like to." How like a man to think it a simple thing. "But people talk. I don't dare."

⇶⫷

FROM THE MOMENT they reentered the parlor, Camellia could tell Crispin was himself again. Or his other self. He stood with a relaxed formality and addressed Philip directly.

"Lord Stirling, you might want to have your gardener look at the paving stones by the roses." He indicated his knees. "One of them felled me."

Philip looked startled. "Major, I apologize. I hope you weren't hurt."

"It's nothing. But if it had been one of the ladies…"

Flushing, Philip stammered another apology. It was unfair of Crispin, so Camellia laughed. Then she slapped her hand over her mouth and continued laughing behind it. When all eyes turned to her, she said, "But you should have seen him. He toppled over like a tree in a strong wind."

Hazard joined her, laughing at Crispin. Then Alice did too.

"I'm sorry." Camellia looked to Crispin with a very slight attempt at looking regretful. "I shouldn't have laughed, but I haven't felt like laughing in so long."

There was a glint in his eyes before he turned back to Philip. "It was only my pride injured. And Lady Bod—excuse me, Camellia—is not helping." Then he laughed too, dispelling any tension. "And I should apologize for bursting in as I did, and insisting to speak with her. I didn't want to embarrass her, but I fear my attempt at discretion made it worse."

Camellia could not guess where he was going, so she merely put on a disturbed expression and waited.

"I had a very fine pair of dueling pistols that I accidentally left in Tonbridge with the colonel. I wrote to the cousin—"

"Alexander Pritchard," Camellia put in. "A dreadful man."

"Who denied possessing 'anything that was not his own.' He intimated that Camellia might have sold them." Reddening, he appeared sincerely abashed. It was disconcerting how easily he lied. "I didn't come to accuse her. Only to ask if she might know what happened to them. I would not have blamed her if she had sold them. I left them behind, after all, and they could well have been Neville's."

"Had I opportunity, I might well have sold them," Camellia said. It wasn't hard to feign anger. "Alexander claimed everything in the house, whether it be Manfred's or Neville's."

A chorus of support arose. Crispin interjected, "Haz, if you are not going to Tunbridge Wells with Alice and her father, would you object to me playing escort?"

Hazard tapped his quizzing glass. Camellia had no time to wonder why Crispin thought Hazard would not escort his own wife, before the man said, "I have no objection if Alice does not. So long as you are not planning to put those dueling pistols to use, should you find them."

"In truth, I don't care much about the pistols. I was only going to give them to Jasper as a jest."

Hazard and Alice laughed at what was evidently a private joke.

"But I may pay a call on this Mr. Pritchard."

Something in his tone caused a chill to run down Camellia's spine. Everyone went silent.

Crispin smiled. "Alice, if you would like a companion, may I suggest Camellia? She knows the area well."

"What are you plotting, Crispin?" Hazard said, narrowing his eyes. "My wife is not one of your pawns."

Camellia tensed. One of his *pawns*?

"I'm not *plotting* anything," he answered with a touch of offense. "And even if I were, you can't think I would involve Alice. Especially not—" he halted. "I would not involve Alice. I just thought Camellia might like the opportunity to visit her loved ones' graves."

Hazard was still giving Crispin a studying look. Then he let out a long sigh. "I trust you know what you are doing?"

Crispin turned to Alice. "Have you any objection, Alice?"

"Of course not. It will be a great deal more enjoyable with you there. And Camellia, please say you will come, too. I would love to have your company."

"Well, yes, of course. Thank you." She tilted her head. "And thank you for thinking of me. You're very considerate."

She saw what he had done. He'd raised everyone's suspicions. But no one knew what they were suspicious of. And no one bothered to question her inclusion at all.

CHAPTER TWENTY-EIGHT

CRISPIN SHOULD HAVE anticipated that visiting Tunbridge Wells with Hazard's viscountess would be entirely different from taking Old Harry there. Hazard had sent a man ahead to make the arrangements and cover all the costs, leasing a townhouse for an entire month. There was nothing for Crispin to plan. Nothing to execute. He could exert no control, and that *itched*.

They were to travel in two coaches. One for Alice, her father, and Camellia. The other for Haz's servants. Crispin borrowed Caliban, one of Jasper's geldings, to ride alongside. Haz would have lent him a mount, but that would have left him feeling even more beholden. More like a hanger-on. He should have more than one horse so he could keep one in London.

Just before they set off, Hazard pulled him aside. "I don't know what you are doing, but as I once told your brother, I fear one day one of your blunderbusses will blow up in your face. This had better not be that day."

The man was dead serious.

"Very nice, Haz. But if you want a threat to be effective, it should be more specific. And I suggest putting a tad more menace into your voice." Before Hazard could reply, Crispin added, "I would never do anything to endanger the ladies." He sniffed. "If it will set your mind at ease, I won't go looking for the pistols."

"Then why are you going?"

Crispin hesitated. Then "confessed." "My mother is plotting to throw me a welcome home ball. I need to leave London for a while."

Hazard studied him a moment, then chuckled. "You're wasting your time. You can't outrun your mother. You'll be wived before you know what happened."

He grinned. "Now *that* is a terrifying threat."

CRISPIN STARED DOWN at the small sandstone grave marker. *Neville Bodwell. Beloved son.* Had he been a better man, the stone would read Taverston. *No.* Had he been a better man, this baby would never have been conceived. All his reasons for foreswearing marriage and fatherhood still pertained.

There was a touch of autumn chill in the air and the sky was overcast. Nevertheless, after just two days in Tunbridge Wells, Crispin had hired a gig—an open carriage for propriety's sake—to bring Camellia to the churchyard in Tonbridge. Thankfully, no one else was about. He would have been particularly peeved to run into the rector or his unpleasant wife. It pained him to think that Camellia had been subjected to Mr. Castor performing the funerals. One after another.

To his left, she stood weeping freely, yet he felt only emptiness. Disconnection. How was it possible that he could have had a son and not known? He'd thought seeing the grave would make the babe feel more real to him. In coming here, he'd expected to feel the same surge of love he felt when he held Christopher, Arthur, or Randolph, or when watching Hannah frolic about. Instead he felt bitter. Ashamed. Mean-spirited and resentful. But he would not unleash any of that upon Camellia. Not again.

In her time of crisis, she had come to London to find him. Even after the ghastly way he had treated her, the reprehensible things he had said to her, she'd trusted him to do the right thing. She'd *trusted* him. And he'd failed her. She had to have believed he ignored her letter. Why didn't she despise him?

Camellia was still crying. He didn't know what to say to comfort her. He had envisioned sorrowing together, but he was failing her again. Finally, he thought to give her his handkerchief. Hers was an insufficient lacey thing. But he performed the gesture mutely. After several more minutes, trying to grieve while his gut churned with self-loathing, he walked away. Wandered away. Through grounds peopled with corpses.

Amongst the tombstones, he found Colonel Harrington's grave. He bowed his head, thinking to pray, but a rush of memory came upon him. A maddening scene of smoke and noise and confusion. He'd ached to jump into the heart of it, to fight alongside the infantry, but Wellington had given him explicit orders not to. The commander believed there were men, touched by the finger of God, who could ride through cannon fire and emerge unscathed. Wellington was such a man. He thought Crispin was too. And, critically, communication with Blücher had to be maintained. *At all costs.*

In the aftermath, there had been men on the field, both allies and enemies, begging for death. Shattered limbs, missing faces, eviscerated innards. It was death as far as he could see. What blasphemy to call such carnage a victory. They said even Wellington had wept.

Camellia slipped up beside him and put a hand on his arm. He realized he was speaking aloud. Muttering to Old Harry's ghost. Apologizing for surviving.

"Crispin?" she whispered.

"My God. What did we do?"

She linked her arm through his and peered into his face. "At Waterloo? Napoleon had to be stopped. You did what you had to do."

He groaned. "I have nightmares."

"Of course you do. You'd be inhuman not to. You know

Neville did, after Vitoria. They'll fade with time."

After a moment, he pulled himself together, taking note that her eyes and nose were pink, and her voice was hoarse. Perhaps they should not have come. "I thought the baby's grave would unman me. Not your brother's."

"You aren't unmanned. If you think so, you have the wrong definition of a man." She looked up, and he was drawn to do so also. The sky was darkening. Clouds were rolling in. "Thank you for bringing me here, but we'd better get back to Tunbridge Wells before the rain."

She was blessedly matter-of-fact. And blessedly generous. She didn't chastise him for walking away, embittered, from Neville Bodwell's grave, without having shed a single tear.

TUNBRIDGE WELLS HAD entertainments. Nothing like London, Crispin thought, but enough to occupy its visitors. Yet Alice and her father went only to the medicinal baths each day, and Camellia did not even do that. Unlike their first trip to the town when she wanted to see and do everything, now, except for the brief visit to the graveyard, she would not leave the house. To Crispin, Society's rules for widows seemed punitive.

One morning, after they had been there a week, he wandered into the bookstore. Its selection was poor, but he did find a copy of *Pride and Prejudice* by their favorite anonymous lady. That afternoon, they began the book together, reading aloud. Camellia began.

It is a truth universally acknowledged, that a single man in possession of a good fortune, must be in want of a wife.

Crispin yelped, and Camellia laughed. That same throaty laugh he remembered. It was good to hear.

They were sitting in the conservatory, a well-maintained

indoor garden filled with greenery, but at that time, no flowers. No blooms to drown out the light scent of lilacs. Sunlight streamed through the windows. *This strange feeling must be contentment.* They passed the novel back and forth, taking turns as their voices tired.

"She seems to have modeled Darcy after Jasper," he mused, after finishing one of the chapters. Seeing her surprise, he laughed and said, "You'll have to meet him. You'll see what I mean."

"I have."

"You have what?"

"I've met the earl. And your comparison seems apt. He came to take Mr. Diakos away to care for your great aunt. I'll admit I was quite angry. I do think Neville's final decline began when Mr. Diakos left."

Their great aunt? She was as robust as a draft horse. Crispin didn't know whether to appreciate Jasper's discretion or to be angry he'd lied. And now, he must confess. "He did not fetch Adam for our aunt. He brought him to London to care for me. I didn't ask it. He took it upon himself."

"Oh!" Camellia flushed. Then grew pensive. "I suppose I should have put two and two together. Well, then, I can't be angry with the earl anymore. Of course he came for Mr. Diakos."

"I'm sorry."

"No, don't be." She sighed. "In truth, Neville was dying since Vitoria."

They sat in silence for several minutes. Crispin tapped his fingers against the arm of his chair. A question was working its way through his brain. If Jasper hadn't claimed Adam by saying *Crispin* needed him, how had Camellia known he'd been ill?

"Camellia, who told you I was sick?" He tried to make the question sound casual, but her eyes widened with alarm, leading him to demand, "Was it Hazard?"

"No." She shook her head. "Don't be angry. It shouldn't matter."

Of course it mattered. "Who?"

"Your porter. He isn't working for you anymore. Please don't make trouble for him."

"James?" He wouldn't have thought the man would be loose-lipped. But then… "He was never my servant. He was Hazard's spy." He paused, glancing around at the potted bushes as if he expected to see the footman lurking behind them. "When Adam came to London, James went back to Hazard and Alice." Which explained nothing. "Why, *how*, did he tell you?"

"I came upon him by accident. At a charity event that Alice attended. He saw me and guilt prompted him to tell me you didn't read my letter. Please don't fault him."

"Lud." A damning memory returned to him. He ran a hand over his brow. "I told him to burn it, didn't I?"

"Apparently."

"What a blackguard I am."

"You aren't. James said you were deathly ill and…"

"And?"

After a moment's hesitation, she said, "Drugged with lauda-num."

All his worst secrets, spilled. He couldn't sit still, so he got to his feet and began pacing between flowerpots. She was watching him with a curious, concerned expression. "I hate the drug. I hate taking it." He coughed. Choking on his words. If he owed anyone the truth, it was Camellia, but he would almost rather she believed him to be a blackguard. Now she would know he was *weak*. "Ever since I was a child, a schoolboy, I've been sickly. Scrawny. My parents brought in physician after physician. They never could figure out what was wrong."

"Sickly? How?"

"Dyspepsia. Poor appetite. Aches in my bones. Flux." He grimaced. What an inappropriate conversation to have with a lady. "There have always been things I wouldn't eat, instinctually, from childhood, but even with avoiding things that I knew made me feel awful, my health fluctuated. And from time to time, it got very bad. It *gets* very bad, and I never know why." Then he sniffed. "That isn't true. Sometimes I do know why."

He tried to distance himself from his narrative, explaining as if he was speaking of someone else. A sorry creature who had come close to dying while studying at Oxford, then decided he should perish on a battlefield so that his death might mean something. He discovered he did better in the army where no one pressed food upon him, or cared what he ate, or even whether he ate. Then he met Adam. And since then, he'd been trying, systematically, to find out what he could eat and what he could not.

What he couldn't confess was how Adam's theorizing and battle plan had given him hope. He'd never had control over his own body, but Adam made him believe it might be possible. Except it was so damned *hard*.

She said, "I would not have guessed that you were 'sickly' when we met. Of course, you were particular about food, but you never seemed ill."

"I was doing very well for a while. Better than I ever have been. But I gave into temptation after leaving Tonbridge. It was stupid of me. Self-destructive."

Adam had warned him his next bout could be worse. His gut was "primed to become inflamed," whatever that meant.

She frowned. Her eyes did not leave his face. "Why did you?"

"I think you know."

She stood and came toward him, her hands clasped before her. "I suppose it was because I made you do something you were ashamed of. And when you tried to make it right, I would not let you."

"That is an interesting way to put it. It's true, and yet, not entirely true. You didn't *make* me do anything. I told you before, I wouldn't have lain with you if I hadn't wanted to. Desperately." His voice rasped. "I desperately wanted to."

"But you would not have come to my bedchamber. To my bed."

He half-laughed. "No. I would not have." He had *some* self-control. "I still don't understand why you came to me."

She turned her gaze downward. "Please don't judge me harshly."

"I won't. By God, Camellia, at this point, I couldn't possibly."

"I wanted to know what it was like. That's all." She crossed her arms, hugging them to herself. "I thought I was...not just thought, I *knew* I was never going to marry. The years when I might have met someone, someone besides Manfred or Mr. Castor, I was taking care of my parents. And then Neville came home and needed so much. I loved my mother and father. I wanted to be there for Neville. But looking ahead, I saw I would never have a...a life of my own. I had no dowry to tempt a suitor. And my looks are strange, I know—"

"Strange?" He wanted to rattle the brains of whoever had told her this. "Camellia, you are beautiful!"

She tossed her head. "I'm not. But Crispin, listen. I wanted to know what it was like to lie with a man. The big mystery. I thought it was my last chance to find out."

"Curiosity." He felt a drag on his heart. "And I was conveniently there."

"No. Not only that." Pink stole into her cheeks. "You were perfect. I didn't want to have to marry to satisfy my curiosity. To be trapped for life. And I didn't expect you to offer for me."

"But how could you not have?" He was a gentleman. More than that, he was a Taverston. "Did I seem so blackhearted?"

"No. No, of course not." She bit her lip. She looked so hesitant that he knew her explanation would rip him apart.

Even so, he pressed. "Did you think I was without honor?"

"Neville said you would return to the army," she said, soft voiced. Apologetic.

"Which would be inconvenient, but would not preclude marriage."

"He said you were a rake." Her words were barely audible.

"A rake? *Me?*" His first thought was that was preposterous. But then...yes, he could believe Harrington found his morals questionable. Jasper certainly did. And Reg probably did too.

"I'm certain now that he only said it to protect me. He was afraid I would fall for you. He thought to warn me off."

"Instead it made me appealing. For your experiment." It was almost humorous. Or it would have been had it happened to someone else.

"It was terrible of me. Thoughtless and selfish."

"But understandable."

"Was it?" She glanced up, a little hopeful, then away. Then she murmured, "But I would not have done it if it hadn't been you."

"No?"

"No. I suppose I was a bit infatuated with you."

His heart warmed. That was kind of her to say. To admit. She was braver than he was. He'd been more than "a bit" infatuated. He still was. Was she? He couldn't see how. Still, he took hold of her hand, wondering if she could feel the heat of his palm through their gloves. She had been curious about that elemental act, and what had he shown her? That it was painful and unpleasant?

"I hope that Manfred...acquitted himself better. You deserve—" He stopped. She was shaking her head.

"He was not well," she said. "We were never together."

"Oh." One might think that would please him, but it did not. "Oh, Camellia. I'm sorry."

"Yes." She snuffled and tried to smile. "I have uncommonly bad luck."

"I should have kissed you."

"Oh," she groaned. "Please let us not talk about that fight. We said such awful things to one another."

"I said awful things. You spoke the truth." He lifted her hand and kissed the back of it. "I was wrong not to kiss you." She was blushing furiously now, turning his heart to pudding. "It is my worst regret." It was not only kisses that had been lacking. He'd read Aretino's *Amours*. It *had* been instructive. While much of it seemed incredible and not particularly enviable, he did learn that there were things he should have done. Things he would have liked to have done. To do. But would not. He edged half a step closer. "May I? Just a kiss, Camellia?" Nothing more. He was not *that* amoral.

She made a small squeaking sound of assent, tilting her face up to him. Letting desire overcome his anxiousness, he touched his lips to hers. Desire took over completely. Kissing was not difficult. Not a puzzle to solve. Not when her lips were so soft. Yielding. Sweet. And responsive.

It was more than one kiss. Rather it was several minutes of kissing. His hands ached to explore her. He wanted to lay her down amongst the greenery. But he drew back. Stepped away.

"Camellia, I care for you a great deal." *Care for?* That was weak. He was in love with her. Of course, he was. If he hadn't been, he would not have been so furious with her. He would have been relieved by her rejection, not cut to the quick. How could he recognize love so easily in others yet not in himself? How smug he'd been, barreling in to straighten out his brothers' relationships, when he was incapable of managing his own. "If I were able to court a wife—"

"It was just a kiss." She laughed awkwardly. "I don't expect a proposal. Let's not have *that* fight again."

"You are young and beautiful, Camellia. And generous. Clever. You deserve better than to be tied to another wreck of a man."

"You are hardly a wreck."

"But I will be. My disease will return. It always does. And one of these days, it will kill me." He had to eat, after all. He had to eat in this world, with all its hidden poisons. "I love you too much to put you through that."

There. He'd managed to say the words. And in response, her eyes softened. Glistened.

"Oh, Crispin." She breathed. Then she said in a singsong voice, "If you knew how devotedly I've loved you, and how long…"

"Camellia, I can't—"

"Don't torture yourself making excuses. If you *were* to ask for me again, I would still say no." Her eyes welled, and tears leaked from the sides. "I can't do this anymore. I can't be the uncomplaining nurse. The selfless wife. The grieving widow." She turned away and plucked at the leaves of a stunted orange tree as if the plant had offended her. "This is the most selfish thing I have ever said, but *I* cannot put *myself* through that."

"That is not selfish. It is self-preserving." He was not hurt, but he was devastated. This conversation had all the elements of two fools throwing away a chance for happiness. But it was a false chance. And they must not be taken in. "I should leave. We can part friends now. If we continue to spend so much time in each other's company, people will make assumptions."

"That I have set my cap for you."

"Or that I am taking advantage of you. Or that a wedding is imminent." He'd leave before nightfall. Slink out. "But Camellia, if you should ever need anything, please get word to me. I won't fail you again."

CHAPTER TWENTY-NINE

ALICE APPEARED UNDISTURBED by Crispin's disappearance, even though he'd left without taking leave.

"That is what he always does." She raised her hand to summon the footman to the table, which was as elaborately set for three as if at a formal dinner party for twenty. "Would you take that plate away and bring Mr. Fogbotham one without the beef and gravy?"

Mr. Fogbotham sighed theatrically, set down his fork, and pushed his plate away. "So close."

Camellia liked the old gentleman. He was heavyset with kind hazel eyes, and he seemed fondly amused when his daughter coddled him. He walked with an odd limp, favoring his right big toe, but if he was otherwise bothered by gout, he hid it well.

"I think he believes it preserves his air of mystery," Alice continued.

"Does he have an air of mystery?"

"He thinks he does." She laughed, her green eyes twinkling.

"Have you known him long?" Crispin had only been gone a few hours, but Camellia missed him dreadfully. As more evidence of her *infatuation*, she was curious what his friends thought of him. She knew there was a short window where she might get away with probing. By his abrupt disappearance, he'd made himself fodder for gossip.

Alice tilted her head, considering. "Almost three years. We met when Jasper was courting Georgiana."

"Georgiana?" She thought the countess's name was Vanessa.

"Yes. Well, Reg won her. It all worked out for the best. Crispin was with Wellington on the peninsula then, so he was only ever home briefly. But whenever he appears, everyone adores him like a demigod." She paused. "That sounded more negative than I meant it to. It's only natural that they worried about him at war, and clung to him when he was home." Then she laughed. "Georgiana is my cousin, did you know? So I've spent a lot of time with the Taverstons. They are all exactly what they appear to be, except for Crispin. I suppose he is as mysterious as he pretends to be." She cut the meat on her plate into tiny pieces. "But you must know him better than I do. Wasn't he visiting your brother for quite a while?"

"A few weeks."

"*Hmmm.* Oh, thank you." She nodded to the footman who set a new dish in front of Mr. Fogbotham, then went on as if she had not been interrupted. "A few weeks is barely enough to scratch the surface." She took a bite of her own beef and gravy, then frowned as she chewed and swallowed. "Did he do anything about those pistols?"

"Those…? Oh, the pistols. No. We only went to the churchyard."

"Now, see, that is strange. Haz says he's like a terrier. Once he gets ahold of something, he doesn't let go."

Did he not?

Alice shrugged, unconcerned. "Perhaps he'll be back. He arrives as mysteriously as he leaves."

AN UNEXPECTED BENEFIT of having accompanied the viscountess to Tunbridge Wells was that Camellia was making a fascinating friend. Alice had appropriated the study in the townhouse for her own use. When she returned from taking her father to the baths, she spent at least two hours each evening reading several newspapers. She also combed through every political pamphlet her father was handed in the street. She wrote long letters to her husband, and received equally thick letters in return. Once, Alice invited Camellia to attend a meeting of local suffragists. By the time the speakers were finished, Camellia was completely persuaded. Women deserved the vote.

"Haz is committed to this," Alice said, as they walked back to the townhouse. "But frankly, we are a long way off. We haven't even swayed Jasper." Her brow furrowed. "It's hard to press Vanessa to push him. Wounded veterans are her cause. And she has a lot else on her mind."

"Wounded veterans?" *Oh, Neville.* She had never thought of him as part of a cause, but she was glad someone did. "That's a worthy focus."

"Yes, but don't you see? If women had the vote, they would push for more programs to help the downtrodden. Women have more empathy. Men count their shillings. And the men who have the most shillings count them most carefully."

That was painting with a broad brush, but Camellia understood what Alice meant. And yet, it seemed helping wounded soldiers was a more direct route than gaining women the vote. More achievable. Even if it helped in a limited way, it was something.

"What does Vanessa—I mean Lady Iversley—what does she do?"

"She supports a boot factory. The workers are all veterans. They make high-priced boots for ladies." Alice paused and lifted her hem to display Hessians tooled with flitting butterflies. She laughed. "It is now *de rigueur* for ladies of fashion to own at least three pairs."

Camellia could not support a factory. She couldn't even buy a pair of boots.

"What we need," Alice said, "are more men in Parliament like

Hazard. Men who know the meaning of compassion."

"Are they so rare?" She could list a few: her father, Manfred, Mr. Diakos…she wasn't sure she could include Crispin.

"Rare?" Alice smiled. "Compassionate men? No, I suppose not. But they are not the type of men who stand for office. That's what makes Haz so useful."

"Useful?"

Alice laughed. "Oh, I didn't mean useful. I meant unique."

THEY STAYED IN Tunbridge Wells for the entire month of October. Mr. Fogbotham said his gout was improved and, as much as he enjoyed being with his daughter, he was anxious to return to his home in the country before the weather turned.

Camellia was also ready to leave. Crispin hadn't come back, and it was a daily struggle not to bring up his name. Alice was a perceptive woman. Camellia didn't want to give herself away.

To her surprise, on the carriage ride back to London, Alice asked her if she would be interested in a position as a companion.

"I know I'd be stealing you away from Marianne, but Hazard worries about me venturing about so much when he isn't available to accompany me." She added with a smile, "He thinks I am out troublemaking."

Mr. Fogbotham snorted but made no comment.

Camellia would be paid, a lowering prospect for a gentlewoman, but companion was an acceptable position for a wellborn but destitute widow. Rather than being dependent on the Stirlings, she could earn her own way. She didn't think Marianne would be miffed. Rather, she would have a vicarious thrill, thinking of Camellia living with a viscountess. She accepted on the spot, and refused to consider the possibility that her decision had been influenced by the friendship between the viscount and Crispin.

LORD HASLET'S LONDON townhome was the most subtly extraordinary residence Camellia had ever seen. Everything in it spoke quietly of wealth. The entrance hall was paneled in dark wood, but was nevertheless bright because of the abundance of candles. Alice pointed out Hazard's private library, a small room set off from a balconied walkway overlooking the high-ceilinged ground floor, a unique architectural feature.

"I don't bother him there," Alice said, taking Camellia upstairs. "I swear he goes in there to nap. There is a better library on the ground floor. We strategize there."

"Strategize?"

Alice laughed. "This is a not-very-closely-guarded secret but please don't repeat it: I write his speeches. I don't tell him what to say. Not usually. I just tell him how best to say it."

"Do you!" Even though *she* had discovered how smart Alice was, she had assumed Hazard had married her because she was so young and pretty.

Alice gestured to a wing that belonged to Hazard's mother. "She doesn't emerge often, but she entertains all the time. Haz adores her, and I do too. And she loves me because 'someone' finally snared her son." In response to Camellia's bemusement, Alice said. "You'll get used to us."

"Where is Hazard?" He hadn't seen his pregnant wife for a month, yet he was not there to greet her upon her return. To Camellia's mind, that was a mark against him.

"He's out in the country. He'll be home next week, I expect." She took Camellia down a long, carpeted hallway. "Those are Hazard's rooms." They walked a bit further. "These are mine." And further still, "And these are yours." She opened the door to a fair-sized bedchamber. The bed was encircled by gauzy, yellow bed curtains. A nightstand held a pretty porcelain washbowl. Cerulean-blue drapes were pulled back to reveal a view of the back gardens. Alice indicated a door in the side wall. "Your dressing room. I hope you'll be comfortable."

"Good Heavens. How could I not be?"

Alice grinned. "I know. Believe me, I know. We could fit my father's house in just one wing of this place." The grin fell away. "And if I don't give Haz an heir, it will all go to his cousin, a drunken, gambling, wastrel."

"The property is entailed?" So she and Alice had something in common.

"This house is. And one of Haz's country estates. I told Haz he should introduce a bill to outlaw entailments, but he said he cannot. It's too self-serving. He said he'd consider it when we have a son."

When. She had to admire their confidence. Pray God it would be rewarded.

AS A PAID companion, Camellia was much less constrained than she'd been as a simple new widow. Over the next week, she accompanied Alice to two teas, a musicale, a lecture, and a suffragists' meeting. They also made a trip to the lending library and to a shop that sold ladies' shoes. Alice insisted on ordering a pair of Vanessa's friends' boots for her. "It is practically a uniform in our circle," Alice said, giving Camellia a twinge of discomfort. She hoped Crispin wouldn't be annoyed that she had wheedled her way into the Taverstons' circle. He'd wanted to part friends, not be thrown into her company again and again.

Upon their return from the shop, Alice retired to her chamber to rest. Camellia went to the music room to play the pianoforte. When she wearied of that, she headed to the library to find something to read. The door was open. She stepped into the doorway and stopped in her tracks.

Hazard was home. He and Alice were in the library, beside

one of the large windows that let in the afternoon sun. They were standing very close together. Hazard had his hand on Alice's belly, and she had her two hands on his. She was giggling. Hazard's expression was one of wonder. Of awe. It was a beautiful moment. And a very private one. Then without removing his hand, Hazard bent down and gave Alice a glancing kiss on the forehead. Camellia backed quickly into the hall.

Alice had said she'd get used to them. She supposed she would. But what an odd pair. They clearly adored one another; yet if not for the obvious evidence, one might imagine them to be chaste.

⫸⫷

IT WAS LATE November, and London was becoming a sodden mess. It was cold, foggy throughout the morning, and dark by early afternoon. The streets were icy and slick, and Hazard forbade Alice from going to a meeting of the orphanage trustees because it was actively sleeting. Nevertheless, he struck out for his club.

Camellia sat in the parlor with Alice, who was sewing a dress for her baby. Alice made neat, tiny stitches effortlessly. She hardly even seemed to be paying attention to her work. Camellia was sewing also, turning a hem on one of her chemises, while her heart ached for little Neville.

"Nobody is in London," Alice complained. "I don't mind missing our meeting since half the ladies have escaped to the country, but if Haz can go out—"

"He doesn't want you to slip and fall."

"Yes, well, I don't want him to slip and fall either." Alice made a face, then set down her sewing. "I hope you don't think Haz and I are quarreling."

"If you were, it would be none of my business."

Alice scowled. "Well, we are," she confessed. "Jasper has

invited us all to Chaumbers, but Haz doesn't think we should go."

"Your confinement will be in early January?"

"Yes. Which is why I think we should go now, while I can still comfortably travel. Everyone will be there for Christmas, and I want my...my family around when the time comes."

"And what does Hazard want?"

"He wants to wrap me in cotton wool and prevent me from moving for the next two months."

"My dear," Hazard said from the doorway. They both jumped. "You are exaggerating. Moreover, I think you will change your mind about Chaumbers."

"What are you doing here?" Alice demanded.

"This is my home."

She snorted. "You were going to Brooks's."

"*I* changed *my* mind. See how easy it is?" He leaned against the doorjamb.

"Well, I won't change mine about going to Chaumbers. Everyone will be there!"

"Ah, no." Hazard waved a piece of paper at them. "I just received the post. No one will be at Chaumbers this Christmas."

Alice stared. Then in a small, frightened voice, she asked, "Why not? Is something wrong?"

"It appears Crispin has finally put his Binnings cottage in order and is summoning us all there."

Camellia was glad Alice whooped, because it drew attention away from her own gasp.

Alice asked, "Oh, Haz, please! Will you allow us to go?"

"Are you certain you feel up to it? Binnings is a three-day journey."

"Yes. Absolutely."

Camellia held her breath.

"That decides it." He let go of the doorjamb and brushed imaginary dirt from the front of his jacket. "Crispin's first family reunion at Binnings? I wouldn't miss it. And I would feel a true villain if I left you behind."

Alice hopped up and ran over to her husband. He wrapped his arms around her, and she stood on tiptoe to kiss his cheek. Then she looked over her shoulder at Camellia. "You must come with us. Please say you will."

Camellia's heart raced with a mix of excitement and dread, but she managed to say calmly, "Of course. If you'd like me to, I will."

CHAPTER THIRTY

CRISPIN EXPECTED HIS brothers to arrive separately since they were coming from two different places. But Reg and Georgiana must have gone first to Chaumbers because the whole family appeared *en masse*. Nervous and irritated to be so, he threw on his greatcoat then stepped into the muddy drive to welcome them to his refurbished home.

He directed the coachmen to take the vehicles around back to the carriage house as soon as the footmen finished unloading the baggage. Jasper's footmen. Two of his own stood watching, unsure what to do. Crispin had hired extra servants to round out his household for the next three weeks, through Christmas and into the New Year. He'd asked Gerald to serve as butler until after the holidays when he would find a replacement for old Badge. He had enough people, good people, but Jasper would, naturally, assume otherwise.

"No, Crispin," Jasper said, turning up his nose. "I'll send them into the town and stable the horses at the inn. The carriage house is falling down."

"It was." Crispin tempered his annoyance by reminding himself that his neglect of the property had been unconscionable. And since each of his siblings had honeymooned here, they all were aware of its flaws. But Jasper should *look* first. "I had it torn down and rebuilt." Now was not the time to explain why he'd significantly expanded the stables. Not while Jasper was frowning as if doubting the veracity of his words. "I'm keeping Mercury here, so it should be fine enough for your nags."

Vanessa came up beside him and took his arm. "Crispin, the façade is lovely! The new door. The steps. And Jasper, look at the windows!" Her smile lit her whole face. "Did you have them all reglazed?"

"No, just washed." Vanessa had seen the house at its worst. That was all she had to compare it to. But his mother and siblings would be remembering how it was back in their younger days. He hoped the changes would not disappoint. "Come along." He circled his arms to beckon them all. "I'll give you the tour."

Georgiana and Reg each carried a babe, while their cheery young nursemaid followed, an overstuffed traveling bag in her hands. Benjamin carried Christopher. Olivia walked alongside them chattering and gesturing. Their nursemaid was a grand-motherly woman named Miss Jamison, who held Hannah's hand until the energetic chit broke away and darted for Crispin.

"Uncle Major! Is this your house?"

"It is." He wondered if Olivia had been coaching her to call him uncle. A sweet gesture.

She took hold of his hand. "Mama says be careful inside. Hold hands." *Less sweet.*

Straight-faced, he said, "Child, your mother is a hypocrite. She was never careful in her life."

"Crispin!" Olivia cried out, laughing. "Watch what you say. She is a parrot."

"Wipe the trepidation from your faces, Taverstons. I've had the whole house stripped, sanded, cleaned, aired out, repaint-ed...and much of the furniture is new."

He led them inside, with Hannah still clinging to his hand. The entryway was little changed except that it was dust-free, and the floor had been redone.

"Have a peek into the dining room," he said, throwing open the double doors. The walls were covered with a peacock-themed paper that Mrs. Peele had recommended. He'd worried it would be gaudy, but with the mahogany table and chairs in place, he thought it looked fine. He glanced at his mother to see her reaction. She would have chosen the décor he'd had to discard. Thankfully, she was smiling.

He took them through the downstairs sitting room, his study, the music room with his new Broadwood pianoforte, and the morning room. He was gratified by the approving *ah*'s.

They went up the main staircase to the first floor. Here was the library. He'd had to throw away a large number of moldy books, which he regretted, but they'd had uninteresting titles, and he was looking forward to filling the shelves with ones he would actually read. Poetry and novels. Perhaps he'd slip in a few French political philosophers to alarm Jasper.

"The library is a work in progress," he said, and steered them toward the bedrooms. "Mother, if you don't mind, I've put you in Olivia's old bedchamber. Olivia and Benjamin will be in mine, upstairs, to be nearer the nursery."

"Of course, I don't mind. Are you usually in your old chamber or your father's?"

"Father's." He cleared his throat. The adjoining bedchamber belonged to the wife he could never have. Every time he looked at the door between the rooms, he felt Camellia's absence. *No, not just then.* She was absent from every room in the house. The shakiest wall here was the one he'd attempted to put up around his heart. "But I'm down the hall in one of the guest chambers for now. I thought I would let Haz and Alice have the connecting rooms." He had no idea what their sleeping arrangements might be. This way, they could work it out between themselves, privately.

"Yes, that makes sense," Mother said. "Alice is in her last month, and I'm sure she prefers her own bed."

"Hazard must, too," Reg said. Georgiana made a face at him, and he smiled at her. A private joke.

Crispin swung Hannah's hand. "Shall we go see the nursery?"

Hannah nodded solemnly. They all climbed another flight of stairs. He gestured to the right. "Jasp, you and Reg still have your old rooms. If your snoring rattles the windows, Vanessa and Georgiana can have guestrooms on the first floor." He was fairly certain his siblings, unlike most aristocratic couples, shared bedrooms with their spouses.

"We'll make do," Vanessa said.

"And here is the nursery." He flung open the door. "The nursemaids' room is adjacent." They all crowded in. There were four cribs and two small beds, everything bright and new. For the finishing touch, Crispin had found several delightfully silly drawings that must have been made by Olivia when she was little. He'd had them framed and hung on the freshly painted walls.

"Charming," Olivia said, grinning. "Where did you find them?"

"Stuffed inside Father's desk drawer." For a moment, his sister's smile dimmed. She had been their father's pet. This moment, the family all together without him, deserved a pause for reflection. Father had not had the chance to know his grandchildren. Then again, they didn't have to worry about how he would have taken his daughter's marriage to a steward.

"Are you hungry?" he asked Hannah. When she nodded vehemently, he grinned and said, "Mrs. Clay is eager to show off her peach cake." He hoped the meal was up to standards. His need to impress his family was somewhat pathetic, and yet, there it was. There it always had been.

WHILE EVERYONE ELSE had their white soup, followed by rabbit stew, bread, asparagus wrapped in ham, and a variety of other food Crispin wouldn't touch, he stuck to his beef broth, filberts, lettuce, and beans. There was cake for dessert. He abstained, eating only sweetened preserved peaches.

Gerald entered the dining room. He always looked so serious that it was difficult to tell if something was amiss. Crispin waved him closer. "What is it, Gerald?"

"Another carriage, Milord."

"It must be Haz and Alice," he said, getting to his feet, grinning. "Stay. Finish. I'll bring them in."

He left the dining room and hurried outside to welcome the last of his guests. Because they were coming from London, he wasn't expecting them until tomorrow, but he was glad they'd made quick work of the journey. Hazard helped Alice from the coach, while more footmen and maids emerged from a second carriage. Crispin exhaled his annoyance. It was not only Jasper who mistrusted his ability to provide adequately for his guests. The servants' accommodations in the attic would be brimful. They would be tripping over each other.

Never mind. Gerald would sort them out. There was something to be said for stodgy.

"Haz! Alice!" he called out, approaching them. Hazard had visited the cottage before, many years ago, but Alice had never been. Hazard waved a quick greeting before turning his attention back to the coach, hands outstretched. A moment later, another woman alighted.

Crispin sucked in a breath. *Camellia.* They'd brought Camellia. *Why?* Hell, it didn't matter why. His heart thudded so hard he thought he could hear the flimsy walls around it crumble.

He gathered his wits with a reminder that he was the host. "Gerald, have the viscount and viscountess's things taken to the suites. And put the other lady's things in the blue guest chamber." Then he strode forward, bowed to them all, and said, "Welcome to my cottage. Now everyone is here." *Everyone.*

AFTER A CLAMOROUS round of salutations, they settled down to finish their cake. Crispin volunteered to give the new arrivals the tour they'd missed.

"If you don't mind," Alice said, "might I see the rest of the house tomorrow? Right now, the only thing I want to see is a bed."

"Oh. Oh, yes, of course." Crispin felt a twinge of embarrassment. Despite the artful draping of her dress, Alice was obviously heavy with child. Her fatigue showed in her face. He wasn't generally so imperceptive, but his attention wasn't focused upon Alice.

"I'll show her to her room," Mother said, rising. "Then I must retire as well."

"Yes, all right," Crispin said, a little dejected at the thought of everyone going their separate ways so soon. He wanted a reason to remain in Camellia's company.

Vanessa said, "I propose the men go have their brandy and let us ladies go to bed."

Jasper grinned agreement. "I hope you have a good bottle, Crispin."

He snorted. "Several. I knew you and Haz were coming."

"I will have to bow out," Reg said. "Georgiana and I are worn to the bone. We haven't stopped moving since we left Cambridge."

"Then I'll bid half of you a goodnight." Crispin's gaze slipped to Camellia, then away. He took a chance. "Rather than watch Haz, Jasper, and Benjamin try to outdrink one another, I'm going to take a walk down to the lake."

"It's dark out," Mother said, in a warning tone.

Crispin laughed. "Yes, Mother. I know how the sun works. But we have the moon and stars, and I can find my way to and from the lake with my eyes closed." He made a show of surveying his guests, and let his attention rest upon Camellia. "You've not been to this part of England before, have you? Would you like to see the lake district's most beautiful lake?"

She started. Then quickly said, "I would."

"Excellent." Smiling too broadly, he stood and spoke to the nearest footman. "Have Gerald bring a couple bottles of brandy and a few glasses into the sitting room. Camellia?" He went to her and crooked his arm. "Shall we?"

When she put her hand on his arm, warmth spread through his body. He prayed no one else would express interest in a jaunt to the lake. And prayed, too, that they would ascribe his bordering-on-inappropriate-invitation-to-a-widow to exuberant delight in showing off his property.

He had a housemaid to fetch his coat and Camellia's pelisse, then he swept her out the front door, down a path past a dormant garden, and into the woods. The sky was clear, and the moon was nearly full.

"I hope you don't mind that I've come," Camellia said.

"Mind?" He chuckled roughly. "What is the opposite of mind?"

"I'm Alice's companion, you see, so they asked me—"

"They *hired* you?" He felt a flicker of irritation.

"I like to think of it as a stroke of good fortune. I don't want to be a continual burden on the Stirlings."

He grunted. She needed to work. And he wasn't usually such a snob. "I feel responsible for your situation."

"You shouldn't. Nor should you pity me. Alice and Hazard treat me wonderfully. And watching Alice is an education."

"I'm sure." It was true that her circumstances could be worse. But she was a *guest* here, and would be treated as such. They entered the woods, and he tucked her arm more firmly against his side. "Watch for roots and sticks. The path is mostly cleared, but I keep finding surprises."

"Haz said this was a summer escape for your family when you were young?"

"Yes. It was deeded to me. My father wanted us all to have something. Reg has a house in Bath that he lets out. Olivia has an eye-watering dowry. And I got this. Careful!" The descent to the lake was mostly gradual, but there were a few step-offs along the path, less of a risk for his long legs than they would be for hers.

She took an awkward step down, and they kept walking. "It's lovely, from what I've seen. Does this mean you are forsaking London?" He caught a hint of concern in her tone.

"No. I'm keeping my set at Albany. For now, at any rate."

She smiled at him, drawing his eyes to her lips. Which meant he stumbled over a root. She laughed. "Watch out. You don't want to muddy your knees again. You'll get a reputation for clumsiness."

They proceeded more carefully until they emerged into a clearing at the edge of a large lake, its surface rippling lightly. Moonlight played across it like fire.

"Oh, Crispin." She sounded awed.

A large rock protruded from the water at the shoreline. When they were younger, they used to dive from it into the ice-cold lake. Even Olivia. Nothing fazed her. But more recently, he came out here just to sit and think.

"Come up with me?" he asked, extending his hand. "It's a bit of a climb, but there are toeholds."

She squinted skeptically. He remembered her fear of heights. "If you fall, I'll catch you." When she laughed, he said, "You don't have to if you don't wish to."

"No, I will."

He helped her scramble up the back of the rock, then followed. They sat on the surface where it was flat. Unfortunately, there was a strong breeze blowing. Crispin placed himself where he could best serve as a wind block for her. "Tell me what you have been doing since leaving Tonbridge."

"Following Alice about." She gave him an overview of life as Alice's companion. He had to admit, it sounded interesting. And Camellia did have more freedom to venture out with the excuse that she was being paid to accompany the viscountess. "And what have you been doing?" she asked.

"Fixing the house. It was sorely neglected while I was on the peninsula. A series of misunderstandings left it barely occupied. And while I kept saying I wanted to make it whole again—"

"Yes, I remember. You came down to see us in Tonbridge when you said you'd gone to London to buy furniture."

He nodded. "My intentions were good, but I kept procrastinating. I suppose I was worried I couldn't master the task. And if that were the case, I'd rather not know."

"But you did."

"Yes." He listed a few of the things he'd seen to, then laughed. "You'll see the house tomorrow. I don't need to bore you with the details. It's kept me busy."

"And now that the renovations are finished?"

He hesitated, then said, "Ah, well, there is always more work to be done."

"What kind of work?"

He gazed out over the lake. His plan might not even be feasible. Even so, he confided, "I'd like to try breeding horses." He heard her intake of breath and faced her. "I think perhaps the notion might have come from you. You said your father bred horses?"

"Yorkshire Trotters. Carriage horses." She smiled. "Horse breeding would suit you—all the planning and arranging."

"Yes, I've had great success as a matchmaker." When she snorted, he drew in a mock-offended breath. "It's true!"

"Of course, it is. Do you know Hazard and Alice want you to stand for the Commons? They were plotting how to convince you the whole way here."

He laughed hollowly. "Politics is Jasper's realm. I learned very young not to tread in his footsteps. He casts too big a shadow." *God.* He told this woman things he would never tell anyone else. "He is *perfect*, you see. You must agree." If she denied it, he would know her for a liar.

She leaned closer. And kissed his cheek. Then she murmured, "Perfection is boring."

He had hoped they would reach this point, though they had

taken a circuitous route—by way of Jasper's perfection. Moreover, he'd envisioned himself initiating. For once. *Ha!* With Camellia, he was never in control. He turned toward her, put one arm around her to draw her still nearer, then plucked off her bonnet and slowly pulled the pins from her hair. Like silk running through his fingers, it tumbled past her shoulders, soft and lustrous. Then he tilted her chin upward and kissed her. They kissed until they were both breathless.

In the back of his mind, these past several weeks, he'd been pondering his life. What was the point of it? Renovating a home to rattle around in alone? Scrutinizing every morsel he put in his mouth, just to live one more day scrutinizing every morsel? Why? But now, he was embracing the woman he loved in the moonlight. If one could have a moment like this, life was worth living.

"There is a boathouse." His voice hitched. He didn't know how to ask. Coaxing and compliments were beyond him. He pointed down the shoreline. "You can just make it out through the trees."

"I see it."

He cleared his throat. The boathouse had also been renovated. It was patched, painted, and spider-free. "There are cushions. In the boat. But we could take them out and put them on the ground."

Her head turned. She stared at him, wide-eyed, yet did not ask the obvious question: why on earth would they?

He wanted to lie with her. That went without saying. He wanted to redeem himself for his previous failure. He wanted her to experience pleasure. With him. But his mouth was dry, and his palms were sweating, and he couldn't say any of those things.

Instead, he said, "You won't be trapped. There are no obligations."

"If there is a child—"

"Then we marry, of course. But there won't be. I—I have a French letter. It's reliable. Do you trust me?"

She regarded him a long moment. Then she scrambled to her

feet and held out her hand for him to take. "Yes."

THEY WALKED HAND in hand along the shoreline to the boathouse. They didn't speak. Crispin imagined they were both afraid any words might break the spell.

He opened the door to the building, and left it propped open for light as he ushered her in. She stood along the wall next to the door, arms crossed over her chest, hugging herself as if cold. Or afraid.

He pulled the cushions from the rowboat and laid them together on the ground. In his mind's eye, they had been longer and wider. In fact, they were too short to serve for a mattress and too narrow for two people to lay side-by-side. He stripped off his coat and spread it on top, then frowned.

"Maybe we shouldn't." The last thing he wanted was for her to have another miserable experience with him.

Camellia set her jaw, walked forward, and lowered herself to the cushions. He followed and sat beside her.

"If you want to stop, at any time, Camellia, tell me. If I do anything you don't like, tell me to stop."

She gave a shuddering sigh and nodded. "Please be quiet and kiss me."

He did. Running through his brain were the maneuvers performed by the protagonist of the *Amours*, but he shunted those rather fantastical exploits aside, in favor of what seemed right for them. Kissing her, he stroked her silken hair until her shivering calmed. Then he removed her pelisse and loosened the layers beneath to glide his fingertips over her shoulders and breasts, as she had done with him. She *hmmmed* appreciatively. When her breath quickened, he explored further, with his hands and his lips. Slowly. Listening all the while for her response. Sensitive to her movements, closer or away. Trying to ignore his own arousal, even though that became increasingly difficult.

The book had mentioned, over and over, a woman's bud of pleasure. He had his doubts such a thing existed, until he trailed kisses down her body, between her thighs, and she suddenly arched her back and moaned his name. He groaned in concert, wanting to take her right then. But he continued what he'd been doing, in part because she pressed her hand to his head, making her wishes delightfully clear. Her breath came in stuttering gasps. She cried out, and then went still.

He waited a moment, torn between triumph, relief, and desire, before kissing his way back up her body. "Camellia, my love, I want you."

She nodded.

He unbuttoned his jacket and fumbled in his purse for the French letter. He had a moment of terror, thinking he might have taken it out and stored it somewhere, but thankfully found it. In too much of a hurry to undress, he simply dropped his trousers and smalls and pulled on his "armor."

"Don't let me hurt you," he said.

"I won't. You won't."

"Oh, lud." He rolled on top of her. "I love you, Camellia. You can't know how desperately I do."

CHAPTER THIRTY-ONE

MARIANNE WAS RIGHT. The act of love was sublime. Camellia wished she could lie in Crispin's arms forever, but practicalities intruded. First, their "bed" was too small, and they had to sit up or fall off. And second, they had been gone far too long for a simple viewing of the lake.

They rose and helped one another to straighten their clothing, a task they lingered over. Until Crispin halted abruptly and swore.

"What's wrong?" Camellia asked.

"Your hair. I mean, it's down. We left your bonnet and pins on the rock."

She clapped a hand to her head, startled as if shaken from a dream. "We have to go back!"

They moved quickly. Crispin scrabbled up the rock, crawled over the surface, then swore again. He came down with a single hair pin. "The wind must have blown them away." He cast his gaze about. "You don't see them here on the ground, do you?"

"No. We won't find them in the dark."

"Don't panic." He smiled, not very reassuringly. "Everyone has gone to bed except three men who are likely to be ape-drunk by now. We can sneak in and not be seen."

Sneak in. Now it all felt sordid. "All right. Hurry." She would not feel safe from scandal until alone in her bedchamber.

They were to enjoy no leisurely stroll back up the path. She nearly sprinted past the garden, Crispin on her heels. Then he caught her arm. "This way. Back door." He had that set look on his face. That calm I-am-in-control look. "From there, you can go up the servants' stairs. One flight. When you exit the stairwell, go to the first door on your right. That will be your guest chamber. No, wait." He shut his eyes and pursed his mouth, as though he were trying to see something on the back of his eyelids. "The left. First door on your left. The right will be Mother's."

A chill ran down her spine. "Are you *sure*?" If she burst in on the dowager countess, disheveled as she was, her life would effectively be over.

"Yes, I'm sure. The left door."

She was more frightened than ever she could remember. "What will you do?"

"I'll join the men. If they intend to twit me over how long we were gone, better that they get it out of their systems tonight, before everyone gathers again."

She felt sick. "Will they? Twit you?"

"I have no idea. But don't worry. They are easily diverted. And hopefully, they are so bosky they won't notice the time."

His hand slid to the small of her back. He guided her to the rear door, then inside. They tiptoed to the kitchen. And stopped short.

Gerald was at the table, the silver spread before him. The room smelled of polish. Gerald turned. "Milord? What can—" His eyes widened, and he clamped his mouth shut. His expression went blank. Then he put his back to them and returned to his task.

Camellia heard Crispin sigh as he nudged her along to the stairwell. He whispered, "I'm going to raise that man's wages." He kissed her quickly, then indicated the stairs. "First door to the left." He hurried away.

How had sublime become tawdry in the space of a few minutes?

And worse. What was she to do with the fact that she'd given Crispin not just her body, but her whole wounded heart?

⇒⇒⇒❯❮⇐⇐⇐

JASPER AND HAZARD were drunk, all right. They were red-faced and roaring with laughter as Crispin entered the room. Benjamin, unfortunately, was merely smiling and a bit glassy-eyed. His rummer, on a side table, was full. Jasper and Haz had apparently never put theirs down.

"Ah, here he is. Settle our argument," Jasper said, waving him in. "You are good at that."

"All right." He played along. "State your cases. Succinctly, if you can."

"Haz believes you can be persuaded to stand for the Commons. As a Whig."

"Not a Whig," Haz protested. "He's a Taverston. A Tory by blood. But he can be a backbencher, voting his conscience."

"The devil!" Jasper laughed. "You and Alice will have his conscience voting Whig."

"Not necessarily. We haven't persuaded your conscience yet," Hazard said, then drained his glass. Jasper paused his argument to refill it.

Crispin stepped into the breach. "If Jasper's case is that I cannot be persuaded to join Parliament, I must award victory to him. I have no interest in politics."

"So you say," Hazard said. "But the war is definitively over this time. You've sold your commission. Your cottage is beautifully refurbished."

"Haz's case is 'what is there for Crispin to do now?' But I have the answer," Jasper crowed. He was loud, brash, and amused. Crispin rolled his eyes.

Hazard blew a razz of derision. "And I am positive he will refuse."

"Refuse what?" Crispin asked.

"Lord Sidmouth," Jasper said. "He asked me to speak with you about a position in the Home Office. He needs a personal secretary—"

"Oh, good God, Jasper! No." A wave of revulsion swept over him. "I'm not going to spy on my countrymen."

Silence fell. Even Hazard looked shocked, and he had been the one certain Crispin would refuse.

"Not spy," Jasper finally said.

Hazard said, "Sidmouth is an arse. He sees traitors to the Crown behind every bush. He thinks any man with a new idea is a provocateur. But he would not ask a gentleman to *spy*."

"He would. And he has. And I've said no. If he presses you again to enlist me, Jasper, I would appreciate it if you will repeat for him my refusal. Word for word. I will not spy on my countrymen."

Jasper set his rummer down. He looked sobered. "I will. I will tell him. I'm sorry, Crispin."

"For?"

"For my naivete, I suppose. For pushing Sidmouth's case. I envisioned you organizing his correspondence, or something equivalent."

Still appearing shaken, Hazard said, "A filthy business. Spying. During peacetime, I mean." He drew his gaze away from Crispin. "I understand the necessity in war."

Benjamin cleared his throat. "Perhaps now is the time to tell them what you do have planned."

Crispin nodded. The perfect time. It would divert attention from all other considerations. And there was no reason to keep it a secret. "I'm going to breed horses."

Jasper's brow wrinkled. "Where?"

"Here. Walk out to the new stables—"

"Benjamin, you knew this?" Jasper turned to frown at their brother-in-law. "Yet you let Haz and me argue like two bosky fools?"

"Yes. Because it was not my news to tell." He leaned back. "I only knew because Crispin asked to purchase Winner. Olivia refused, of course, but said she would lend her for the purpose. As long as she gets first right of refusal for the foal."

"Mercury and Second Place?" Jasper started to grin. "I will outbid her for that foal. Crispin, that is a superb idea. But beyond that pair, do you know what you are getting into? Horse breeding requires a substantial investment. And…and knowledge of the art."

"Yes, I do know. But I have a ridiculously wealthy brother, who I can tap for a loan. And Olivia has suggested one of the hands in your stable to steal away to be head groom in mine. She says he knows horses." He turned up his palms. "I intend to go slowly. To see how it goes first with Mercury and Winner. Besides, the worst thing that can happen is I am left with too large of a stable and too many horses."

Hazard stepped around a chair to come clasp Crispin's shoulder. "If Jasper balks, talk to my man of business. Or have Benjamin talk to him. If Olivia is involved in this, I can't see any way for it to fail."

"Thank you, Haz." He grinned. "And yes, I intend to consult with Olivia." And Camellia. He hadn't thought of including carriage horses, but why not? "And you, Jasp. I've often wondered why you have not turned breeder yourself. Your stable is one of the finest."

Jasper shrugged. "Too much work. I prefer to buy good horses rather than make them."

Crispin looked around the room, then focused on the empty bottle and half-empty second. "There is no point in having a drink. I will never catch up. I'm going to bed."

Goodnights were offered all around. Crispin escaped the room and made fast for the stairs. When he reached his chamber, he closed the door quietly, then leaned back against it with a sigh of relief. Tomorrow's talk would be nothing but horses.

Yet as he straightened, his relief spiraled into regret. Camellia *belonged* here. With him. *The devil.* He wished they *had* been caught.

But no. If he were to propose under these conditions, she would assume he felt coerced. She would say no. He would be hurt. They would start the whole damn cycle again.

⟫⟫⟫⟪⟪⟪

CAMELLIA BARELY SLEPT, so as soon as she heard enough movement in the hallway, she rose, dressed, and went down to the morning room. She had to face the day. Face the butler who'd seen them. Face Crispin without tumbling into his arms.

Crispin's mother, the dowager, was at the table with Hannah in her lap. They were both sipping tea, though Hannah's was so pale it had to have been watered down. The dowager was a dark-haired, regal-appearing woman, who hardly seemed old enough to be a grandmother.

"Good morning, Lady Bodwell."

"Camellia. If you please, my lady." A risk. The dowager carried herself with the dignity of her rank. Yet it would be awkward if everyone else called her by her given name and the dowager persisted in using a title that reminded Camellia of all her mistakes.

The lady smiled. "And I am Beatrice. My husband disapproved of such informalities, but I have to say, I find it refreshing."

Hannah bounced in her lap. "Meela, I am Hannah."

"Ah, no." Beatrice repressed her smile. "*You* must call her Lady Bodwell."

"Why?"

"Because it is the polite thing for little girls."

Hannah seemed to accept that. She didn't argue. Camellia went to the sideboard, fragrant with warm bread, oranges, tea, and strong coffee. She poured herself a cup of tea, then returned to the table to sit.

"Did you enjoy the view of the lake?" Beatrice asked.

Camellia started. Then she managed a smile. "It's beautiful."

"Crispin has done a marvelous job with the house. He has changed enough to reflect his own taste, but left enough that it still feels like home."

"Were you here often?"

"Several weeks a year. The children loved it. I wish we could have come more often. And I hope everyone makes more time for it now. They are all so busy, but I know Crispin wants company. And time slips away." She stirred her tea, and her thoughts seemed to take her elsewhere. Camellia didn't know whether to respond or not.

Fortunately, Hazard and Alice entered the room, arm in arm. They said their good mornings, then Alice sat, and Hazard went to prepare her a plate. He heaped it full: eggs, kippers, toast, cheese, orange slices. Alice laughed when he set it before her.

"Is that all?"

Hazard smiled. "You must eat for three."

"Three?"

"Or four. I won't be eating this morning. I doubt Jasper will either."

Crispin came into the room. "Your sins will find you out."

Hazard chuckled. "Lord, I hope not."

Olivia and Benjamin arrived next. They were an interesting pair. Olivia smiled readily, and seemed to have inexhaustible energy. Benjamin was quieter. Thoughtful. Olivia sat beside the dowager and murmured to Hannah, while Benjamin fetched tea for her and coffee for himself.

"Did you like the lake?" Olivia asked abruptly, turning from Hannah to Camellia.

"Yes," Camellia said. "It's lovely. Restful."

"Did Crispin take you up on the rock?"

For a moment, she misinterpreted the question and stared, startled. Then she quickly answered, "Yes." She glanced at

Crispin, who hid his face with his teacup and hands. She felt certain he was snickering behind them. It wasn't funny.

"The moon can be spectacular," Olivia mused.

"Yes. It was."

Benjamin sat. "Crispin, I've told Olivia your secret is out."

Camellia choked.

Olivia cried, "And I'm so glad! I wanted to bring Winner with us, but Jasper insisted it would be too cold for me to ride, and I couldn't tell him why it was important."

Camellia let out her breath. His other secret. Crispin said, "There will be time after the holidays." He avoided her eyes by rising and returning to the buffet. While he was there, Reg and Georgiana arrived. They gave their greetings. Camellia felt Georgiana's gaze skitter over her. Reg sidled up beside Crispin. Camellia thought he passed something into his brother's hand.

"It's cold out there this morning," Georgiana said. Her voice was strained, as if she were trying too hard to sound normal. "Reg and I took a quick walk to the lake." She looked everywhere except at Camellia.

Wherever that conversation was going, it was interrupted by Jasper's entrance with Vanessa. He was whey-faced and grabbed only a cup of coffee. But it was Vanessa who looked at the offerings on the buffet, went pale, and said, "No. I cannot." Then sped from the room. Jasper set down the cup and hurried after her.

There was a long, quiet pause. Then Beatrice said, "I suggest we all pretend we didn't notice that." Everyone nodded solemnly. Camellia didn't understand why they looked so disturbed. Vanessa had to be with child. Were they not pleased?

They breakfasted in silence for several minutes. Gradually, conversation resumed along safe lines. Then it turned to Crispin's "secret." He'd evidently confessed to the men last night that he was going to begin breeding horses. And they'd deemed it a worthwhile endeavor.

"But will you be able to let go?" Alice asked. "You'll fall in love, won't you? I mean, with the foals?"

"Ah," Hazard said. "The lady raises a valid point. Beneath that rigid exterior, I believe you do have a soft spot."

"When expedient," Crispin said, voice flat, "I can harden my heart."

Georgiana gasped. Reg put his hand on hers as if to shush her.

"Are we still talking about horses?" Olivia asked, looking around with a grin. "Or should I ask what Reg sneaked into Crispin's jacket."

Crispin stood. He gave Olivia such a black look that her eyes went wide, and she blanched. Then he turned from the table and strode from the room without a word.

"I didn't mean anything," Olivia said, her voice hushed and frightened. She looked as though she might cry.

No one else spoke. Beatrice appeared miserable. Alice and Hazard were subdued. Benjamin was stone-faced. And Reg and Georgiana looked guilty.

This was absurd. Camellia stood. "Was it the bonnet I lost at the lake?"

Reg did not respond, but Georgiana nodded and said, "A silly reason for such a fuss. It's so windy out there, I almost lost my own." Her voice trailed off. Olivia's eyes went even wider.

"I'll go talk to him." Camellia looked to Reg. "Where am I most likely to find him?"

"In a mood? He usually goes for a ride. If he's gone to get Mercury, you won't be able to catch him."

"I'll catch him. He'll have to saddle the horse before he can ride."

She left the morning room, unsure who knew what, but certain they would piece the story together. Or *a* story. She headed for the front door, only to be blocked by Mrs. Clay.

"Have you seen the music room?" the woman asked. "The pianoforte is new."

Camellia frowned. "I'll see it later."

"I think you should go see it now." She spoke like a poor

actress in a coarse comedy, while pointing down the hallway.

"Oh, for Heaven's sake." Had the woman been listening behind doors again? She changed direction. "Thank you, Mrs. Clay."

She found Crispin alone, sitting on the bench before the pianoforte. It was another lovely room. A little dark because no candles or lamps had been lit, but there was some sunlight from the window. The walls were covered with lavender paper dotted with black treble clefs. A cabinet in the corner was open, displaying a pile of sheet music.

Crispin looked up. Chagrin spread over his face.

"I'm sorry, Camellia. I handled that badly. I should have laughed when Reg tried to be surreptitious. He and Georgiana cannot dissemble for the world. For God's sake! He should simply have waited. It must have been burning a hole in his vest pocket."

"Laughed?"

"Laughed and thanked him. It was windy last night. Your bonnet loosened." He rolled his hand as if finishing the story without words.

"Georgiana tried that."

Crispin snorted. "And how did that work?"

"She made it worse."

He was quiet a moment. Then plinked a few keys, stopped, and faced her again. "The thing is, Camellia, they won't say anything. Not outside of this house. I expect to be bullied, but no one will bother you if I tell them not to. They will show you no disrespect. They won't believe whatever story I tell them, not now, but they will pretend to accept it."

"But you will be lying to your family."

"Not for the first time." He sounded rueful. "I'm sorry. Truly. I understand this is awkward for you. If you don't want to stay here...I don't know. I can throw a tantrum. Send everyone home."

"You can't do that."

"I can spin the tale so that they are angry with me. And gentle with you."

"How? By telling them you are merely taking advantage of a poor widow? They won't believe that."

He grimaced. "They might."

"I doubt that. Besides, I have a better idea."

"Anything. Whatever you want me to do—"

"Marry me."

He stared. Then blinked. "You didn't want to be trapped."

"I'm not. I trust that your family won't betray us. It would even surprise me if Alice were to dismiss me. I'm not asking you because of what happened last night or this morning. I'm asking because I want to be your wife."

"You said you can't go through it again. Caring for another dying loved one."

"You don't appear to be dying."

"My health cannot be counted upon."

"Crispin." She exhaled. "I was wrong. I don't regret the privilege of caring for my parents. Or the short time I had with my brother. I don't regret marrying Manfred and easing his passing by presenting him with a son. He was a good, good man. And I certainly do not regret Neville."

"You are too generous."

"No, I am realistic. Life is short. I want to seize it, not avoid it. I love you, Crispin. However much time we might have together, I want it. I want it all."

He turned his head, and stared out the window. He drummed his fingers on his knee. Then he faced her again. "Yes."

"Yes?"

"Yes, I will marry you."

"You will?" She felt a bit breathless. Stunned.

"Of course, I will. I wanted to propose to you last night, but I was afraid you would break my heart." He stood. "Come with me."

"Where?"

"To the morning room. If you would, stare at me dewy-eyed and pretend I asked you."

CRISPIN STEERED CAMELLIA back to the morning room. Jasper had returned. *Good.* Everyone was there. Except Vanessa, but she'd hear soon enough.

"Taverstons," he said, leaning against the buffet. He dropped Camellia's elbow and wrapped his arm around her waist. "May I—"

Olivia jumped up with a squeal. Then everyone applauded. Even his mother. Camellia tensed, then relaxed against him. He tightened his hold. *God.* He loved his ridiculous family.

"When is the wedding?" Jasper asked, when the applause died down.

He wanted to say as soon as possible. But he didn't want to imply urgency was required.

Camellia answered, "My late husband passed in September. So…nine months."

"Nine months!" Crispin protested. "Nine *more* months? Camellia, nine months is too long."

"Now you know how I feel," Alice groaned.

"Amen," Georgiana said, then laughed.

Crispin swallowed his protest and took what little control they left to him. "*Early* next September, at the church in Iversley Village. You all must be there."

EPILOGUE

Nine months later...

CRISPIN WAS ON his way to another family wedding. The last. He galloped Mercury up the beech-lined drive to Chaumbers, first heading to the stable to leave the horse with George. Then, for old time's sake, he sneaked into the house through the back door.

From several steps away, he heard Cook and Mrs. Clay in the kitchen arguing good-naturedly. He'd sent Mrs. Clay to Chaumbers in a post-chaise the week before. She was to be in charge of preparing Crispin's meals, even his plate at the wedding breakfast. That was a potential cause for friction, but Cook had no reason to feel put out. There was more than enough for her to do. In addition to all the Taverstons, Hazard, and Alice, the Stirlings had been invited with their brood.

Crispin had also sent Gerald with Mrs. Clay, which meant he'd been a week without a valet. No real hardship, but he was in great need of a decent shave.

He walked into the kitchen. The two cooks barely looked up.

"Can someone direct me to Lady Bodwell?" he asked pleasantly.

With a one-shouldered shrug to indicate she was unimpressed with his comings and goings, Cook answered, "She was down at the Carrolls' cottage. Maybe she's back."

"Oh." He turned to go find her. He hadn't seen the love of his life since the christening in July, and even then, it had been difficult to steal private moments.

Peters came out of the pantry with a large box. "Major? You're here. The earl asked that I send you to his office the moment you arrived."

"Do you have to tell him you saw me?"

"We all saw you," Cook said. "Get on with you."

Civilian life was absurd. He was reduced to taking orders from the servants.

Brimful of good humor, he went upstairs to see what Jasper wanted. The office door was open, so he didn't bother to knock. Jasper was half-standing, his hip resting on his desk, talking to Vanessa, who was seated on a new two-person couch. It held two persons. Vanessa cradled the babe christened Isabel in her arms. "Belle" appeared to be sleeping, so he tiptoed in, blew his sister-in-law and niece a kiss, and shook Jasper's hand.

Crispin was still heir to the earldom, but no one worried any longer that the status would last. Belle had been born at nine months, hale and whole. Vanessa was still glowing. And Jasper was more contented than Crispin had ever seen him.

Alice had been delivered of her babe at Crispin's Binnings cottage on New Year's Eve. *Lucy.* Haz could not have feigned so genuine a delight. He doted on his girl and headed off any suggestion that a boy would have been preferable with the calm statement that "We are just getting started. Alice has promised three of each. The order does not matter."

It was funny, to Crispin, how, where there was no concern about succession, Georgiana and Olivia had popped out sons with no trouble. Of course, he would never say such a thing aloud.

"You wanted to see me?" he asked Jasper quietly.

"Yes. I have a wedding present for you."

"Another one?"

"Spitfire was not a wedding present. She was an investment."

Spitfire was a gorgeous silvery-gray thoroughbred that Jasper had stumbled upon at Tattersall's. She was fast, but her trainer said she was not fast enough to win, so her owner was selling her as a broodmare. Jasper made her a gift to Crispin's enterprise, insisting only that he be given the first foal. For a while, Crispin had been calling his brother Rumpelstiltskin, but the joke had grown old. Winner was in foal now. Spitfire would be next.

"So what have you?" Crispin asked, resigned to being the recipient of Jasper's boundless generosity.

Vanessa stood and practically plunked Belle into Crispin's arms. "I'll be right back."

She left the room. Jasper said nothing more. Then Camellia entered, smiling madly, still dressed in unrelieved black—that would end tonight. It had been a year and one day since Manfred's death. Crispin would have rushed to embrace her, no matter that Jasper was watching, except that he had a baby in his arms.

"Camellia," he said, giving her a crooked smile. "I intended to find you first."

"Belle's charms outstrip mine." Camellia laughed. "I want to see this."

"See what?"

She tilted her head toward the door. Vanessa returned with Adam in tow.

"Adam! Good God!" He felt a warm rush of affection. "Come for the wedding? Who found you?"

"I did," Vanessa said. "At an apothecary in London."

Adam made a perfunctory bow. "Congratulations, Major. I think the colonel would be very pleased."

"That is debatable. But thank you."

"And there is my present," Jasper said. "Actually, it's probably more of a present for Benjamin."

"What is?" Crispin could not guess what he meant.

"You should have your own steward. Benjamin has too many balls in the air, and frankly, I need his focus on Chaumbers. It was one thing when you just wanted a little advice now and then—"

"Oh, lud." Crispin winced. "Jasp, I'm sorry." He'd encroached increasingly upon Benjamin's time. He was perfectly capable of spending money without help, but not keeping track of it. He hadn't even realized his brother-in-law was doing so until Benjamin had opened an account book and shown him his expenses. "I'll find someone to hire."

"I already have." Jasper swept his hand to indicate Adam. "A man of many talents."

"I need work," Adam said. "Mr. Carroll has shown me your books. I can add and subtract." His lips curled. "Mostly subtract."

Crispin glanced sidelong at Jasper. His brother was shrewd. Adam could no doubt perform the functions of a steward—Crispin's estate was comparatively small—but he would also be keeping an eye on his health. Strangely, he was grateful, not annoyed. Or maybe not strangely. His family's concern had helped keep him alive. And now, life felt more precious than ever.

"Welcome to the fold, Adam," Crispin said. He gave Belle back to Vanessa in order to shake the man's hand. "Now, if you will all excuse us, I have a few details to go over with my bride-to-be." The wedding was not for three days, and he was not going to wait. "Camellia, are you in the guest wing?" She nodded. "Good." No one would hear them even if they were loud.

CAMELLIA WORE RED. She thought it accentuated the strangeness of her looks, but Crispin admired her in red and that was all that mattered.

The little church in Iversley had an ancient appeal, with pew benches smoothed by long use and stained glass windows that looked medieval. When the organist struck up a march, Marianne proceeded down the aisle. Then Philip escorted Camellia, after having practically insisted he would give her away. She might rather have asked Hazard, who had grown on her.

Crispin waited at the end of a long red carpet. His smile lit the room. Jasper stood beside him. Camellia didn't care how many people swore the earl was the handsomer—they were all wrong.

Philip deposited her beside Crispin, then stepped away.

As the rector began to speak, Camellia sent quick thoughts heavenward. A thank you to Manfred for the kindness that had shielded her. A hope that he was happily reunited with Elizabeth. And a prayer for the souls of both of her Nevilles.

Crispin touched her hand. When she slid a glance at him, he slipped her a rolled bit of paper. He was better at stealth than his brother. The rector droned on, so she unrolled it, her eyes cast modestly downward.

Methinks I lied all winter, when I swore, my love was infinite, if spring makes it more.

It was John Donne, not Crispin Taverston. But he'd admitted he could not write his own.

"…is commended of Saint Paul to be honorable among all men: and therefore is not by any to be enterprised, nor taken in hand, unadvisedly, lightly, or wantonly, to satisfy men's carnal lusts and appetites, like brute beasts that have no understanding—"

Crispin tapped her wrist and sneaked her another tiny scroll.

Come live with me, and be my love, and we will some new pleasures prove

"First," the rector intoned, "it was ordained for the procreation of children, to be brought up in the fear and nurture of the Lord, and to the praise of his holy name."

A third bit of paper tickled her palm, and she closed her fingers around it. He must have them stuffed up his sleeve, but she had no such convenient place to hide them.

"Secondly, it was ordained for a remedy against sin, and to avoid fornication; that such persons as have not the gift of continency might marry, and keep themselves undefiled members of Christ's body."

She felt a smile playing about her lips and an inappropriate heat crawling up her neck.

I am two fools, I know, for loving, and for saying so in whining poetry.

She snorted. Still Donne. Though that one sounded like it could have been Crispin. The rector halted, scowling. Crispin's eyes widened. Then he flushed and bowed his head, a picture of contrition. After an uncomfortable moment, Jasper said in an authoritative tone, "Proceed."

It was good to have an earl in the family.

The ceremony was lengthy, but before she'd worried the paper in her palm into powder, she was pronounced Major Crispin Taverston's wife.

They left the church into a blizzard of rice and seeds thrown by the locals in Iversley Village. Ducking and laughing, they climbed into their carriage to return to Chaumbers for the wedding breakfast.

"Have you any more poetry hidden on your person?" she asked, settling onto the bench.

Crispin grinned. "You are welcome to look."

"I can't make a thorough search," she said with a regretful pout. "It won't take more than a few minutes to get back to Chaumbers by coach."

His grin broadened. He called through the window, "Dan! Take the long route home. By way of Crofton." Then he drew the curtain closed.

About the Aut

Carol Coventry is a born-and-bred Je Kentucky. A quarter of a century worki taught her that, after any tough day, i like a guaranteed happily-ever-after. Esc is like a mini-vacation. After spending so like a native and began spinning her romance.